ISLAND OF

LOST SHADOWS

ISLAND OF

LOST SHADOWS

E. SANTHOSH KUMAR

TRANSLATED BY
P.N. VENUGOPAL

NIYOGI
BOOKS

Published by
NIYOGI BOOKS
D-78, Okhla Industrial Area, Phase-I
New Delhi-110 020, INDIA
Tel: 91-11-26816301, 49327000
Fax: 91-11-26810483, 26813830
email: niyogibooks@gmail.com
website: www.niyogibooksindia.com

Editor: Gita Rajan
Design: Shashi Bhushan Prasad

ISBN: 978-93-83098-87-3
Publication: 2015

This is a work of fiction. The names, characters and incidents portrayed in it are the work of the authors' imagination. Any resemblance to actual persons, living or dead, events or localities, is entirely coincidental.

Printed at: Niyogi Offset Pvt. Ltd., New Delhi, India

In what language does rain fall over tormented cities?

Pablo Neruda: (*Book of Questions*)

IN SEARCH OF MISSING SOULS

By noon the bus arrived at Irutti, a town on the Kolli hills. Although known as a town it was nothing more than a modest junction with a few shops, a couple of makeshift restaurants, a roadside market where vegetables, fruits, tapioca and dry fish were heaped on the ground and an old deserted bus stand. The place was cool despite it being summer. It was lunchtime by then. The bus stopped there for half an hour. Coming down south, Irutti was the most prominent station on the way to Pullani.

From Irutti it was a steep descent. It would take at least three hours to reach Pullani. The road cut through evenly cropped tea plantations. It was a vast sea of green. Huge trees lined up the boundary and their branches danced in the cool breeze. Sivan fell asleep.

By the time he woke up the bus had reached the plains after cruising the hairpin bends. There were telltale signs of summer all around. Dry grass, trees with drying leaves, dusty wind, the hoary sunlight of the evening and people in sweat-stained clothes. A waiting room at the bus stop, almost dilapidated. An old cow lay there ruminating. A metal signpost on the roadside read: PULLANI- 6 Km.

So it is not very far. Maybe one or two stops.

Sivan was thinking of the two student comrades who had come to Avalam bus stand to see him off. The tall and slender one had said, 'Comrade, Pullani is our area. There are a few very dedicated buddies at Pullani. Once you reach Pullani, it is only a short distance to Karadi-Papa's island.'

'Yes, just a little,' the other endorsed.

The first one handed over a piece of paper to Sivan. Must be the directions and the code word, he guessed. 'Be careful,' the student said.

Sivan did not relish the extra caution in the tone.

'The island is your next shelter, comrade. You don't have to worry about anything once you reach there,' the first one continued. 'Old timers call it, *pathalam*! The place lives up to its name! Real netherworld. It used to be the land of the paniya since ages. But now it is known as the island of Karadi-Papa. So safe. Not even a fly can access the place. Even if someone happens to enter, he will not return for sure. That's Papa!'

'Yes! That's Papa!' the other seconded. A cynical look, which seemed genetical, was apparent on his face.

'You know what? He is a man of the Calcutta Thesis times,' there was a sense of pride in his words. 'You know, two companies of police ransacked the entire state, but without any success. You can stay there for as long as you please, comrade. You can read, think and write a lot. You can resume the work on the magazine. The island of Karadi-Papa is the fit place for everything.'

He looked around to see if anyone was noticing them and continued.

'It is so safe there. But reaching there is a job! You arrive there and Papa will take care of you. Maybe he is old now. But he is still the iron-man he always was.'

'Solid steel!' the second one added.

It was twilight by the time the bus stopped at Pullani junction. It was a task to get out of the crowded bus. The smell of sweat from the bodies of labourers returning home and the stench of arrack pervaded inside the bus. Sivan somehow made his way through the jostling crowd. He stood still for a moment breathing in the fresh air outside. But looking around, he felt unsure, whether he had really reached *the* Pullani junction which the student comrades were referring to. There was hardly anybody there, other than those who had got down from the bus.

The light was fading. There were no electric lamps. Even though it was summer the atmosphere was gloomy with an overcast sky.

It had been a day of travelling for him. He had started very early from Avalam bus stand. The road from Avalam to Pullani passing through the winding ghat roads was expected to take a long time, though the distance was only forty kilometres. But it had taken even more time than he had anticipated. Buses were infrequent. And he had to change buses at several points en route. He was exhausted travelling the whole day.

Sivan was quite upset when he was told about the new shelter. What does it mean? Hiding away in some forest when the world was boiling over? But in a calmer mood, he felt there was sense in what they were suggesting. The comrades were indeed having a tough time shifting him from shelter to shelter. Work was suffering, what with bringing out even pamphlets becoming impossible. As for the magazine, it had not been published for months. After the Kangazha action, most of the frontliners were in the wanted list. The police had succeeded in rounding up many comrades. Going into hiding was the only way out, it seemed. But this again was turning out to be too risky in the town with each passing day, as the police were able to penetrate even the most secure hideouts. If their suspicious eyes fell on a safe house there would be at least two policemen in mufti observing it. Even permanent residents were being questioned and beaten up. The situation was volatile; anything could happen anytime. Hiding in remote villages or forests seemed to be the only way left. This shelter was the result of a wide search and detailed analysis.

Sivan chewed the piece of paper after learning by rote the routes and the code words. Code words have a nauseating taste, he thought. He spat out the chewed pulp into the drain without drawing anyone's attention. Though there was a direct bus from Avalam to Pullani, he had chosen to break journey at several places for obvious reasons. That he came late to Pullani was, therefore, natural. The comrade who was supposed to meet him there; had he gone away? Sivan waited by the roadside.

He saw a tall, lean man approaching him. Yes, it must be him. There was no one else in the vicinity anyway. When he came closer, Sivan blurted out the code words with some trepidation.

'Achu.' He did not say a word more, no code words, nothing. He then walked ahead. Sivan began to nurse doubts. Is he the one? He had mentioned his name, but not responded to the code. Sivan stood still, debating what to do. Achu turned and signalled to follow him. It was almost an order. Though he did not like it, he followed Achu like an obedient animal.

'We've to cross the river. Please hurry, comrade,' Achu urged. Is the shelter across the river? Could be, the students had mentioned an 'island.' How is it going to be after crossing the river, he wanted to find out. How far from the river bank? And how long a stay there? He was also curious about the red-hot comrades of Pullani and about the activities of the organisation in the surrounding areas. But Achu was just hurrying along without any show of friendliness. Since there was a standing order about not being too curious, Sivan did not ask him anything. Perhaps Achu's responsibility was only from Pullani junction to the next stop, wherever it was. Maybe he too had only that much information. And maybe he was walking far ahead of Sivan in order to avoid conversation or discussion.

The path to the river landing was narrow. It lay there long, amidst fallow farmlands, like the skin of a snake moulted in summer. Sometimes the road vanished at a turning and reappeared. On both sides were short bushes with coarse, sharp leaves which brushed against their bodies. Perhaps because he was so exhausted, he felt that the fields were never-ending. At last, at the point where the path disappeared from sight, there appeared two coconut trees whose heads had been singed by lightning. In the dim evening light, they appeared to be poles propping up the skies. He listened; yes, there was the sound of water flowing. He heard the birds chirping. Must be very near the river now.

As they approached the landing, the comrade stopped and turned to face Sivan. What was the name he had mentioned? Was it not Achu?

It was most likely a false name. How could he be confined to such a small name? Though he walked with a slight stoop, he was indeed quite tall. His eyes had a bright sparkle. It was not possible to evade his gaze. On his forehead the scar of an old wound, red-coloured, stretched above his left eye. Sivan was noticing it only now, despite their being together for quite some time. On closer scrutiny, it looked like a tiny reptile. Achu tried to cover up the scar, perhaps conscious that Sivan was staring at it.

'The ferry has already left for the other shore. Now it has to be called back,' Achu said looking at the boat landing space. The landing and the surroundings were deserted. It was getting darker. The current was not very strong in the river, maybe because it was very wide there. A flock of birds flew past in a formation through the crimson sky.

'He is not to be seen,' said Achu. 'Has he gone?' he was scanning the other bank.

'What can be done if the ferry is not available? Can one swim across?' Sivan was fidgety.

Achu laughed. 'It will be difficult. The river is quite wide.'

'Where is all this water from, even in this drought?' Sivan asked remembering those slim rivers, which one could walk across, in the summer.

'The paniyas have built a check dam with stones and wood in the upper river area. It is kept filled during the rains. It may have been opened now for agricultural purposes.'

Achu stepped into the river and washed his hands and feet. The water was very cold, his expression said.

'It is risky to get down here even in normal times. Unpredictable currents.'

'Have you tried swimming across, comrade?' Sivan asked.

'Me? Oh no. I don't swim, comrade.' Achu lowered his voice.

Achu held his hands close to his mouth and hooted loudly. Nothing happened. He repeated it three or four times. After a while, an answering hoot was heard from the opposite shore.

'Oh, the ferry is coming,' Achu said with apparent relief. Sivan too was worried as to how he was going to spend time with Achu if there was further delay. He had been observing Achu without his knowledge. Must be above fifty, his hair showing signs of greying. He had wrapped around a *mundu* with a red border. It was soiled. There were stains on the short sleeved shirt. Achu seemed unmindful of such things. He behaved like a man in a great hurry.

Sivan felt that Achu had not talked about anything till now. They heard one more hoot from somewhere in the river, as they stood there listening to the flow. Now it seemed to be closer. On peering harder, one could see dark figures from the middle of the river. A country craft was approaching.

'The ferry has come. Didn't you hear the hoot?'

The ferryman changed the bargepole for a paddle and brought the craft closer to the shore. He flashed a torch at Achu. He was alone in the country craft.

'Fed up waiting, Achu?' He asked without raising his voice. Achu remained silent.

'Had to fetch a cot to the island. I had gone for that,' the ferryman said, stepping on to the land.

'Tell me, did you hand over that letter to Papa?' Achu asked.

'Who can see Karadi-Papa in person these days? He is always busy. You know that his accountant died recently. I handed over the letter to that dwarf.'

'Then? Did you get any reply?'

'Reply? He made some sort of signs with his hands,' the ferryman said scornfully.

'What did he mean by that?'

'I don't know. A paniya with no sense! You don't bother, Achu. Will Papa ever say no to your requests?'

Achu stared into the darkness, brooding.

'Where is the cot from? A new one?'

'No, it was the one used by the accountant. When he died, his sons took the body home on that cot. Now it has been sent back.'

'Why was it taken back? What use is an old cot there?'

'What do you mean! How can it be given away like that? It is mature *kanhiram*! Sleep on that and your lifespan increases. Wasn't that accountant active and vigorous even at ninety?'

Maybe inspired by the discussion on longevity, the ferryman broke into a song.

Sivan felt that it was only then that the ferryman noticed him. He could see even in the spreading gloom, the flash of suspicion in the ferryman's eyes.

'He is our man,' Achu said. 'You have to ferry him across and take him to the Mansion. Don't collect any fare.'

'Are you not coming, Achu?' the ferryman asked. Sivan too had the same thought.

'I've a watch to deliver. A Rado. It is an antique. I got the spare parts only today. He must be fed up waiting. Already very late, no?'

'Oh, you and your business! Always, "no time". You are the one who repairs time, no Achu?' the ferryman laughed.

'What of it? Only repairs no? Can I stop the needle of time? It will go on ticking, at its will! Convey my regards to Papa.'

'Okay,' grunted the ferryman and added under his breath, 'Who is going to meet him?'

As Sivan was stepping into the country craft, Achu walked up to him. Sivan had one foot in the craft and the other on the shore. Achu took his hand for the first time since they met in the evening. Sivan felt those hands to be very cold, a strange kind of coldness. Like that of a corpse, an unwarranted simile flashed across his mind. Achu bent down and lowered his face as close as to kiss and then whispered into his ears, 'March ahead comrade! He is one of our old timers. History says that he has been with the movement ever since its birth. You can trust him. What he undertakes will always be done. Definite.'

Sivan was still doubtful. Is not Achu responsible till I was entrusted to the next safe house? Is it proper for him to delegate it to the ferryman and vanish?

As if he guessed Sivan's dilemma, Achu brought his face still closer and said in a firm voice, 'Victory to revolution!'

Sivan felt the chill of his saliva on his ear.

As if to reassure himself, Sivan said, 'Lal salaam!'

Darkness had spread over the river. Only the pale light of the moon as thin as a mere sliver, emerging from behind the clouds, remained. The sound of the current was stifled when the ferryman struck the river bottom with his barge pole. Sivan looked back. Comrade Achu was still standing there watching the ferry. Didn't he say he was in a hurry?

The ferryman was manoeuvring his pole standing straight. They did not speak to each other. The river flowing in the very dim light, the ferry crossing its stream gently, two silent men in the boat and one keeping vigil on the shore; all together, it was a dark visual frame.

'What's your name?' the ferryman asked.

Sivan was in a dilemma. Which name should I tell him? He had not anticipated the ferryman asking his name.

'What boss, don't you have a name?' the ferryman laughed.

He mentioned the alias. Pavithran. Or was it the real name? Was Sivan just another alias during one of his earlier lives in hiding? Which of them was true? The shirt of poet Sreenivasan, somebody else's name, a life in hiding; whose role am I enacting now?

'How are you related to Achachan?'

'A friend,' Sivan's voice was jittery.

'You are here to take care of the accounts?'

Sivan nodded to stall further questions.

He dug the pole in and looked at Sivan. As he couldn't see clearly in the light allowed by the sky, he flashed the torch at Sivan's face.

'Cot made of *kanhiram* is the best for sleeping,' he said as if giving out a piece of advice. 'Even *Kalan*, the god of death, wouldn't dare touch the one on a *kanhira* cot, goes the saying.'

Sivan did not respond. Who in reality is this Karadi-Papa? What is the business he runs, if it requires a full-fledged accountant? And he is the one who was with the party right from its inception? And they say the police could never trace him. Must be an old timer involved in some revolutionary action. Maybe living peacefully now, fed up with everything. What could be his age? Very old, most probably. If not, would everyone call him grandpa?

'What's your name?' Sivan asked, to prevent further questions.

'Moosa. Pullani Moosa to be precise,' he smiled pausing in the midst of rowing. 'Friends call me Pullani Cobra.'

'Moosa, how long since you became a ferryman?'

'This job? This was started by my father. He was a friend of Karadi-Papa. It was he who brought Papa to the island long ago. On a raft. Pullani Ibrayi, that was my father's name. You may have heard.' Moosa then sat cross-legged. That part of the river was almost still, with very little current.

'How many hours do you work?'

'There are no specific hours.'

'Is the day's work over?'

'My work is not that kind, boss. I've to be there when I'm wanted. Take the goods that are needed there. Fetch banana, areca nut and pepper from there. These are not routine work. When there is work, Papa's workers will call me. Three of them!—Either Ayyakkuru or Thechappan or his wife. Once in a while someone like you come visiting. They would also pay me something.' He stopped speaking, to work the pole.

'People like Achu will not bother to cross the river. Instead they will ask me to carry the message. He is busy, no? I go and convey. This is a difficult job, boss. Can never be free. But, there'll be times when I don't have to lift this pole for days together.'

The ferryman pushed in the pole and hoisted himself above the ferry for a few moments. It seemed the current was strengthening.

'Where do you live?'

'Me? I'm on this side. Not in Papa's territory.'

'Why?'

He laughed loudly instead of answering. Then he glanced at himself and said in all seriousness.

'I didn't go. That's all. You know, I was not like this. I was a handsome young man.'

A heavy breeze blew. The ferry swayed wildly. Was there an unusual smell in the air? It was a putrid smell indeed. Moosa did not seem to notice it. Is it something only I feel? Moosa struck the pole on the opposite side to which the barge was tilting. Sivan could now see a floating object touching and floating alongside the boat. Something heavy and dark. Not clearly discernible in the very dim light.

'Something is up,' Sivan's voice was jittery.

Moosa pulled out the pole, balanced himself and looked. Then he bent down and tried to gather the scent. All the while the craft seemed to be staying still in the water.

'It's decayed,' said Moosa.

'What's it?' Sivan was nervous.

'The hunters may have decided to discard it.'

'What *is* it?' This time Sivan's voice was trembling.

'A pig,' Moosa said very casually. 'Not because it's *haram*, but because no one wants it these days. So they must have thrown it into the river.'

'Are there hunters up there?' Sivan was incredulous.

'What a question? Won't there be hunting in a mountain,? Deer and rabbit are always around. And there's a double barrelled gun at the Mansion.'

Sivan did not comment.

'This seems to be two days old. Must have got blocked amidst the rocks.'

Moosa rowed the barge backwards a little, changed direction slightly and then rowed forward. The pig's body swirled as if caught in a whirlpool and then drifted away. It was then that Sivan noticed with a shock it was headless; its head had been chopped off!

Suddenly another chopped off head sprang into Sivan's mind. A cry from the innards of the big house in Kangazha had been stifled halfway. The head from which blood was dripping was lifted up by strands of the long grey hair. Slumber was weighing down its eyelids. Two raindrops fell deep into the half open mouth. Time lay frozen.

Sivan watched the cadaver of the pig till it vanished from sight. It was huge. The sky was now overcast with clouds. It was completely dark. Moosa was peering into the darkness ahead and rowing.

Where is this barge going to? Everything is as mysterious as darkness. Where is this '*pathalam*' the island where paniyas lived? Why did a revolutionary movement maintain contacts with one who had isolated himself from the mainstream and lived a luxurious life besides hunting animals? Who named him Karadi-Papa? Why was he known by that name? This Moosa would be aware of everything. But how could he ask Moosa for details after introducing himself as a friend of Papa? Even if asked, the possibility was that he would evade the issue altogether.

The river darkened, a sign that the shore was nearing. Bushes and short trees appeared like ghosts. The landing and its surroundings were as silent as a huge animal waiting for its prey. Not a bit of light anywhere. The strange hoot of an unknown bird broke the silence.

'Sss … ss ... slow ... careful ...' Moosa cautioned Sivan as he stepped onto the land. Moosa extended his hand as a support, tilting the pole to one side.

As soon as his feet touched ground he understood that it was marshy land. His feet were sinking and he stood straight with great difficulty.

Moosa flashed the torch and said, 'See, that is the way. It's a single-file path. Don't worry, keep going straight. Very soon you will see the lights of the Mansion. It is easy from there.'

'So you are not coming?' Sivan was apprehensive.

Moosa's laughter rang out. 'Buck up! There is no need for that. No one in the Mansion would have slept. They know that you are arriving.'

'How do they know? Has anyone told them?'

'Achu must have informed. Sure. Perhaps that letter was for that purpose. For that matter, they will be aware even if they are not told.'

Sivan stood there with his feet in the mud. Waiting for the barge to leave.

Is the opposite shore visible from here? Is not someone standing there? Achu? Has he not left as yet? Is he waiting for Moosa to return? Why? Had he not said that he was in a hurry? If not, couldn't he have accompanied me?

Is he waving from the other shore? Not sure. Could be Achu. Victory to revolution, Sivan chanted in his mind.

Standing there all alone in the island without a spark of light and without a sliver of sound, yet another panic seized him. Had he been turned over to the wrong hands? Was he walking into a trap? Achu, is he an enemy agent?

Sivan stood there stunned for a minute. Achu—who is this Achu? He had not replied to the code word. The codes were written on the paper given to him by the student comrades. When asked '*are you the head guard*?' the reply had to be '*only for the typhoon.*' Instead, Achu had merely nodded his head. It was my fault, Sivan admitted to himself.

But even the student comrades had mentioned the name Karadi-Papa. However, I had only one day's acquaintance with those student comrades. What if it was a grand trap laid by all of them together! What if he had just rowed down into the open mouth of a class enemy indulging in sensuous pleasures with sex, liquor and hunted meat, in a lonely island?

What should be the next step? While trying to free his sandals from the swamp, the feeling that he had fallen into deeper mire oppressed him.

Sivan smelled his body. He was apprehensive that the putrid stench of the decaying pig, entangled on the barge was emanating from his own body.

Grime and filth covered body, untrimmed beard, overgrown hair, bloodstained scars of beating all over, clad only in an undergarment; this was Sreenivasan's image Sakunthala carried in her mind in later years. A dog chain was around his leg, his hands crossed over each other and handcuffed. Sunken eyes that had lost all sparkle. She could look at him for only a fleeting moment. She then felt that the surroundings were darkening and that she was losing her eyesight. That was Sreenivasan for her now, both in the conscious and the subconscious. That momentary glimpse had wiped out all the other images of a lifetime lived together.

That was the day she had last seen him. He had looked at her and their son with those paralysed eyes. Feebly moved the handcuffed hands. That's all. Sakunthala's mind was vacant beyond that. Thereafter, she would remember that last meeting if she came across his photograph. And then she would feel that all his other images were unreal.

While shifting from the rented house, Sakunthala removed all the framed photographs from the wall carefully. There were so many of them in the small house they were living in. Sreenivasan had managed to get that old house at a very low rent. That was one year before his disappearance. When they started living there, they had brought with them all the old photos. Snaps taken at various occasions. Relatives and friends during their wedding, parents, rare pictures taken during the school anniversary celebrations, photos taken on their son's birthdays ... all of them were black and white. One among them was the wedding photograph of Sakunthala and Sreenivasan. They had got themselves photographed in a studio in the town after their wedding; ten years ago. She looked slightly scared in that photo. It was obvious on a closer look. Sreenivasan, however, was smiling. A smile with lips slightly curved and with light sparkling from his eyes. Sakunthala would invariably remember that day when she saw that smile in the photograph. It was their first day out in the company of each other. That was the day she had seen a lion for the first time in her life—it ignored her, of course—in the zoo they visited, a film with Prem Nazir and Jayaabharati in the lead roles, lunch at a Udupi hotel and the time spent in the park till the return bus, watching children play … they were all there, shadow-like, in her memory even now.

But what had vanished from her memory was that smile. The smile that only he possessed, both in the photo and in real life, the unique imprint of that smile was no longer there. Or some other colours had spread over it. The one who is with me in the framed photo on the wall is someone else. Or a Sreenivasan from another birth.

Another birth? If so, what happened to him in this birth?

It had been two months since Sakunthala had been struggling with this question. The image of his, chained like a dog, had been haunting her all these days.

Theirs was a measly life. Sreenivasan was a proofreader in an evening daily. The salary he received was not sufficient to meet even their bare needs. To supplement his meagre income he'd go to the town on his weekly holidays to take English classes for college students. Sreenivasan loved to teach, especially poetry. And he wanted to be known as a poet. But in those days his poems were never published in leading magazines. He was incessantly trying for that. He would become sad when the poems came back with regret slips. He would spend that whole day in a sort of gloomy meditation. On the other hand, he needed only small things to make him happy. If he was able to write four lines, if he got a listener and if the listener commented that the poem was good, poet Sreenivasan's day was made. He would go around the house humming a song. Sit still and meditate for the next four lines. He would recite to her his poems that were published in the evening daily he was working for, or in similar small time publications. Sakunthala was no connoisseur of poetry, but she would listen to it because it was something which he enjoyed doing. Sreenivasan was considered a poet in his friends' circle. They used to call him poet Sreenivasan, half in jest. 'Here comes our poet!' 'Did the poet have tea?' they would ask. Occasionally he'd go for poets' meets. Famous writers attending the meet recognising him was 'breaking news' for him and he would make it a point to mention it to Sakunthala.

It was this fascination for the well known and famous that led him to problems, in a way.

In course of time his literary circle enlarged. Those who came to attend functions in the locality would contact Sreenivasan. They would stay overnight as the guests of Sreenivasan and Sakunthala in that little house. Their discussions would go on till late in the night and then Sakunthala would remember her father. He was also like this. But his guests were politicians, not poets. When the communist party was banned, it was for shelter that many leaders would arrive there. Her father was never a party member. But so many of the top leaders had stayed in their small house and had shared their meals. He took all these as big occasions and events. Yet, her father lived in penury and died in penury. Sreenivasan too was going down the same path, she would feel at times. Losing their privacy, their household expenditure going up: the losses were always theirs. Perhaps Sreenivasan may have been deriving some sort of pleasure out of it. Those who stayed, dined and discussed also used to take with them his poems; for publishing. But she had never seen any such poems published. She had the feeling that all of them forgot him the moment they walked out of their house.

Sakunthala last saw Sreenivasan at a temporary camp set up by the police at Chaloorkunnu, four miles from Avalam town. It was a hilly area. One could see parts of the town from there. She also saw the blue tint of the sea, vehicles moving in a row on the winding roads and the shadow of the mist-covered Kolli Mountains. It was her first-and-last-visit to that place.

The police camp had been set up in what was once a factory. It was an old and dilapidated building. It had been many years since the loss-making factory had closed down. A huge machine lay still and rusted in the middle of the building like a weighty reminiscence of the old factory. The police had made some modifications by erecting a couple of iron poles. The gaps on the top of the walls were closed with bricks. They had also hired a few houses in the area for the top officials when they came on inspection. Many police vehicles could be seen day and night in the open space in front of the building.

It was there that Sakunthala had the vision of the weak, lost and emaciated Sreenivasan, a vision that was to stamp itself in her memory forever. She had not known then that it would be their last meeting. Had she had even an inkling of what was waiting for her, she would not have gone there in the first place.

Sakunthala learnt quite late that Sreenivasan was there at the Chaloorkunnu camp. It was four or five days since he had gone missing. In fact, she had not met him even before that. Sakunthala along with their son had gone to her parents' home as per his instructions. It pained Sakunthala even now that he had lied to her. She would not have objected to it had he told her the truth. How many similar incidents were there in her early life! Her father had given shelter to so many leaders. Though she was a little girl at that time she had never spoken about it to anyone.

A friend will be there for a few days; he is coming to complete the writing of a play; that was what Sreenivasan had told her. In addition, he had been entrusted with the task of writing a few songs for the play. Writing of a play demands concentration and that play was to be staged immediately. Sakunthala could take their son and go to her home for a week. It was anyway vacation time and it would be a change for him. These were his directions.

'Oh, so you are chasing me out, eh?' Sakunthala feigned annoyance. 'Okay, when do you want me to go?'

'Immediately. Tomorrow morning itself.'

'Tomorrow? What will my people think if I land up suddenly?'

'Why would they mind? It is your home. They will be only too happy to see you there with Sasi.'

The next day he accompanied them to the bus stop carrying their essentials in a bag. He did not remain there till the bus arrived as it was time for him to get to work.

'One week, that will be enough. I'll come there on the eighth day. By that time the play and songs will be ready,' he had said.

'Will you bring me a top?' asked Sasi.

'Yes, I will,' he had winked at Sasi.

When the child insisted on going to him and started crying, she had pinched him. And the child started bawling more loudly. Sreenivasan had turned around and looked at her with resentment for hurting the boy.

When a week passed by she thought that maybe the playwriting was not over.

'Doesn't Sreeni have to go for work, my dear? Will they pay him salary if he spends all his time with drama and songs?' Her mother would ask.

Sakunthala just laughed in reply. Sreenivasan did not like others knowing about his financial difficulties.

Two more days passed. Sakunthala was really worried. Why was Sreenivasan not coming? Relatives and neighbours had started enquiring about him. She confined herself to a casual, 'He'll be here tomorrow.' But by then a feeling of doom was gripping her. He could've sent a letter, she thought. Come a play and forget your wife and child! Yet, she did not feel like going back on her own. Sreenivasan was not an ordinary man. Was he not a poet? How could she disturb a writer? What if he did not like it?

Ten days had passed by. The next day she decided to go. Rest of the playwriting can be done in my presence, she said to herself. She started off in the morning bus with Sasi. She was seized by a seemingly inexplicable anxiety throughout the journey. But that was a characteristic trait. She had no peace of mind till anyone near and dear to her, who had embarked on a journey, returned safe. Where would they be now? Is he careful crossing the road ....

The house was locked from the outside. Which meant that Sreenivasan had gone to work, she concluded. But that also meant that the work on the play was over. Then why hadn't he come to fetch them? She was a bit upset. Suddenly she noticed that the lock on the door was another, an older lock; not the one they had been using. What happened to it? A plethora of doubts assailed her. She could not open the lock with the key she had with her. Perhaps he has given the key to one of her neighbours, she thought.

Old Anthony Appappan, their nearest neighbour, walked up to her, just then.

'Oh dear, where is Sreenivasan?' the old man asked. She was baffled. So he has not seen Sreenivasan.

'Must have gone for work, Appappa,' she said, more to console herself.

'We thought he had gone to fetch you. It is three or four days since Sreeni left.'

She was baffled. Where has he gone now?

'He is so careless,' the neighbour smiled. 'He had left the house open. It was the worker who came to water the coconut trees who told us that the door was open. Our son went in and looked for Sreeni. But he was not there. He waited till evening. Then he locked the door with this padlock. Here's the key.' He extended the key to her.

She accepted the key. So sad, he left without even locking the door! What if someone were to take away the valuables? But then she reasoned what great valuables were there in this house?

'Maybe someone asked Sreeni to accompany him,' Sakunthala tried to justify Sreenivasan's actions. 'There was another man with him, no?'

'Along with him? Someone did come here one day. They came to my house by mistake,' the old man said. 'I don't know if Sreeni went along with them.'

'Yes. It was the one who writes dramas. When did he leave?' Sakunthala asked.

'Yes, could be the same. They came asking for poet Sreenivasan.'

'They? There was only one person, no?'

'No, there were two! Of course, I don't know if they were the drama people. I directed them here. But those fellows, they did not give me small change for even a packet of beedi.' Anthony Appappan continued. 'Tell me daughter, does he get any money from writing dramas like this?'

'I don't know Appappa,' said Sakunthala. She knew very well that he never got any money.

'Maybe he gets it once in a while. Lottery!' there was the sparkle of greed in his eyes as he was speaking. 'That's why he left the house without locking. I had thought that he had gone to your place.'

Sakunthala entered the house. The unfamiliar smell of a house locked up for a few days greeted her. There were a couple of unwashed vessels and dishes. So he must have had to leave in a hurry. But where to? Even if it was so, he could have informed her by merely mailing a postcard.

A lizard was coming down the wall. There were black lines on its body. Sniped tail. It was a bad omen, she thought. She was frightened.

It was evening and still there was no sign of Sreenivasan. Her attention was on the pathway throughout the time she was engaged in household chores. Usually Sreenivasan would reach home by evening. His newspaper would be out in the stands by three. Once in a while he would meet friends and spend some time. Otherwise he would be there by twilight. But it was late today. Darkness had spread. She was restless. It had never been like this. She felt insecure, sleeping in that house without him. She thought of asking someone from the neighbourhood to give her company. Yet she spent the night alone, hoping that Sreenivasan would be there by the morning. Why create a fuss?

It was an unending night. She got up from her bed frequently and looked out. Was he approaching their house from afar? Was she hearing knocks on the door? Was he calling out to her? She had no inkling then, that these doubts would not leave her till the end of her life. She shifted and shuffled through the night unable to close her eyes. She sobbed silently without disturbing her son's sleep.

Sakunthala set out for the town early in the morning along with her son. The newspaper office where Sreenivasan worked was her destination. An inner voice was telling her that he'd be there. She had been to that office once. It was during the wedding of a friend of hers. One had to walk some distance from the bus stand to reach the office. She reached the office cajoling her son to walk and also carrying him intermittently. As soon she entered the office, she was again upset seeing his chair vacant.

'That's what I'm also asking,' the editor countered her query. 'Where is he? It is more than a week since he has been here. No information. And we've been very busy. I was thinking of sending a man to your home. But this is really surprising. You too don't know his whereabouts?'

The editor was an old man, but not too old. Glasses with a thick frame. A blue hat to conceal baldness.

Losing control, Sakunthala burst into tears. The editor was worried.

'Please be seated. We'll find out,' he said. He was thinking hard as to how he could pacify her.

He ordered sweets for Sasi. Sakunthala did not touch the tea offered by him.

The editor made many phone calls. He also sent a man to the police station.

Time passed. The one who went to the station had not returned. All the while Sakunthala was sitting on a chair placed just outside the room of the editor glancing through periodicals. Even when her eyes were fixed on the magazines, her mind was elsewhere. Sasi was taken care of by the other staff. He was given a seat behind an old typewriter. Tak, tak, tak ... he went on typing the letters he did not know. Each letter talked to him through meaningless sounds.

The man who had been sent on the enquiry mission returned around four. Sakunthala too entered the cabin when he started reporting to the editor.

'Everything is guesswork,' he told the editor. 'They had been to Sreeni's house in search of a big fish. They couldn't get him. Sreeni was taken away instead of him. He is ok. When things clear up, he is likely to be released with a warning.'

'Did you see him?' the editor asked.

'No. a friend of mine is there in the police. This information is from him, based on some guesswork. But it is for certain that the police had been to his house for the big fish. My contact has admitted that much. It seems the big guy too has been nabbed from somewhere else. That too is not for sure. All in all, it is most likely that Sreeni too has been taken away by them.'

'Where to?' the editor asked.

'The local police are not sure about it. All this was undertaken by the crime branch. Anyway, he suggested that we make enquiries at the Chaloorkunnu camp.'

Chaloorkunnu camp! The editor's forehead creased as he heard the name. The kind of news that was coming out from there was not all that hearty. He took care to keep his face composed and expressionless. However, Sakunthala was able to make out that the editor was agitated.

'Don't be afraid, Sakunthala,' he tried to console her. 'We will follow it up tomorrow morning. You stay at my house tonight. I'll talk to my wife. You will have company that way.'

Sakunthala watched him slowly dialling the number with his index finger.

She stayed at the editor's house that night. She couldn't sleep that night too. The anxiety to know what had happened was consuming her. Sasi was taken care of by the grownup daughters of the editor. He was a new plaything for them.

Thus Sakunthala was alone that night. Sleeping alone in the room, she experienced the most unbearable loneliness; an orphaned feeling. Why have the police taken Sreenivasan? Who was the one staying with him? So he was lying about writing the play. She felt like crying when she thought about it. The knowledge that even after ten years of marriage he had not taken her into confidence pricked her like a thorn.

The next morning, she saw the editor ready to go out quite early. He had a brown hat on. Sakunthala thought that he was going out in search of Sreenivasan.

'I'll also come with you sir.'

'I forgot to tell you, Sakunthala,' he said, deliberately avoiding her gaze. 'I've a meeting of editors today. There is also a possibility of the Home Minister Kumaran Nair attending it. So I've to reach there early. He is a stickler for punctuality.'

She looked at him with disbelief. He was trying to wriggle out of her gaze.

'Ours is a small newspaper, child. If I don't reach there in time, it will be noticed. It is the time of heavy censoring. One has to survive, no?'

He gulped down the cup of tea his wife brought, standing there.

'In my opinion, Sakunthala, you should go home today. We can decide the rest of the things after serious thought, no? Most probably, they will release Sreeni once they get the full picture. Now if we newsmen start enquiring at Chaloorkunnu ...'

'I shall go alone sir.'

'Alone?' the editor was taken aback.

He handed over the tea cup to her and said in a low tone, 'I'd advise you not to go to Chaloorkunnu now. I understand that visitors are not allowed there. Let me see. If I get an opportunity during the meeting, I can directly take up the matter with the minister.'

He was lying, Sakunthala was certain. Being evasive.

His daughters came out with Sasi. There were signs of disturbed sleep on his face.

'Uncle is going out, son. You should not leave without having lunch,' the editor patted his cheek. 'Malu dear, get a nice chocolate for him, okay?'

Sivan tried to free his leg from the mire, but in the process the sandal on his left leg got struck in the mud. He felt a putrid smell spreading from the gluey swamp. Maybe the remains of an animal, whose taste Karadi Papa dislikes. How many such cadavers have floated down this river?

It was pitch dark. Sivan was unable to find out the lane indicated by the boatman. He remained still for a while. As his eyes got used to the darkness, he found that he had reached a strange place with weird flora and fauna. When the wind blew, the giant trees and plants swayed ghost-like. Their leaves rustled together making moaning sounds. Not a soul to be seen anywhere around. Had the boatman reached the other bank? Was Achu still waiting for him there? The river seemed to divide the place. The other side is another world. Humans, their culture and their civilisation, all cease at the riverbank. On this side there was only the music of the sedately flowing river. The treachery of the enemy in packing him off to a desolate swamp where neither revolution nor any peoples' movement had ever peeped in burnt his heart. He could see, as if in a nightmare, a ferryman rowing away to the outer rings of darkness and the figure of a tall man waiting for him.

The sandal pulled out of the swamp had thick layers of mud sticking on to it. Washing it in the river, Sivan tried to see across the river. Silence and desolation all around. Return seemed impossible. Was it feasible to swim across? How deep was the river? He wondered.

An icy wind was blowing. Loneliness, as sharp and biting as severe frost. He longed for the presence of human beings. Something, a guerilla fighter was never supposed to wish for. He was tempted by the thought that the company of humans even from the enemy's camp was better than being stranded alone on a riverbank. Sivan looked in the direction pointed out by the ferryman. Two fireflies appeared from nowhere. In the pale light shed by them he could see the semblance of a path and trodden grass. He followed the fireflies. Broken banana stems strewn on the path obstructed their light occasionally.

Sivan suddenly felt that there was someone hiding in the dark. Are the leaves shaking? He remained still for a while. The fireflies again appeared like the eyes of darkness.

Suddenly, a fierce bolt of lightning splitting the sky struck across the earth. The two fireflies were lost in its abundant glow. But in that fraction of a moment Sivan saw in the distance what looked like an abandoned two storey mansion. The ageing walls of the mansion were built with rough hewn laterite. Moss covered the tiled roof. A stunted neem tree in the front yard, like an aged ghost, keeping watch. Further down, at some distance, humble earthen huts cluttered together.

The light ceased as suddenly as it came. Thunder shook the darkness. Its reverberations seemed to float on the ground for quite a while. Pitch dark all round. No fireflies. Dry leaves floating away in the wind with a crackle. Followed by a drizzle. Come what may, he thought and walked where his feet led him. It was a clear path for a few minutes, when he heard the feeble sound of flowing water. Damn it! Back to the riverbank! Must have taken a wrong turn. Now he had to retrace his steps. He cursed himself. Where to but? Into the den of a class enemy leading a fetid life immersed in indulgent desire and lust? No, will sleep at the landing. Can somehow cross the river once the day breaks. There is something soothing in sabotaging the calculations of the opponent. There is *a revolution* in it. But how?

Within no time, the opposite view became active. What if the feeling of having arrived at the enemy camp was wrong? Why couldn't

Achu really be a comrade or a fellow traveller? What was the proof to the contrary? He had to be a sturdy link in the inevitable revolution. If not, how could he have known of his arrival at the junction? Was it not to avoid formalities that he did not respond to the secret code words? Didn't he whisper 'victory to revolution' when bidding goodbye? Will a spy or an enemy do that? Moreover, if he indeed was an enemy would he have left without leading me right up to the camp? Would he trust a prey to a third person or abandon him to the solitude of a river landing?

On reaching this point in thought, Sivan felt ashamed. Ashamed that he suspected the sincerity of his comrades. The diffidence of the body leads the mind astray.

There was no time to lose. One had to reach the hideout at the earliest. Karadi Papa would be fed up waiting. There was every chance that he was an old revolutionary. Most probably the comrade had been thrown out from the phony organisation that had abandoned the path of armed revolution. Counter revolution kills its children at the embryonic stage itself. Only a few, very few, escape from being stillborn. Karadi Papa was a genuine revolutionary of that genre. Not a fraud. The venerable revolutionary was waiting for another revolutionary of another generation. There should not be any further delay; must reach him now. He felt that keeping awake an elderly person was reactionary in itself.

But was there not another hurdle? Yes, the headless cadaver of the pig … bloated up and blocking the barge. A carcass thrown away by the hunter. But there was a possibility that it was just an allegation made by the ferryman. There was no guarantee that he had even met Karadi Papa. In any case, the class enemies had been employing every kind of allegation through the times. He was one who had been there with the party even when it had taken the most extreme stand. He may have abandoned everything later on, losing heart at the revisionist character of the organisation. Now the mushrooms of revolution that sprout following the Spring thunderstorm may have attracted him. Perhaps that's why, despite his advanced age, he had agreed to take under his wing, a new comrade.

Yes that must be the truth. That brought him cheer. The rain stopped right at that moment and the moon showed its anaemic face from behind the rain clouds. Now there was just enough light for walking. At least the shadows were visible. A narrow path with trodden grass. It started from the river landing. Young banana plants on the sides. He carried on forward, breathing in the air cooled by the drizzle. The dark shape of the mansion was visible from the crests. Not a single lamp was burning in the building. Tired of waiting, had the comrade gone to bed? Then he would have to be woken up. That was a pity. But there was no other go.

After one more descent, the two-storey building could be seen very clearly in the moonlight. It was not very far now. The narrow path was giving way to a broader pathway. The swampy nature of the soil had disappeared now and the ground was firmer. At every step he was feeling more secure. Perhaps this was the way to the front of the house. Thinking so, he had hardly taken four steps ahead, when he heard a sharp,

'Hoy!'

Sivan was stunned and turned around swiftly. He had heard a sound. Who was it?

Silence prevailed for some time. Then there was the sound of footsteps hurrying.

'Hey, stop. Stop there,' someone shouted piercing the calmness.

It was a bizarre sound. Like emanating from the throat of a dead man. Stunned momentarily, his legs came to a halt. Blood seemed to freeze.

The small penknife tucked into the mundu fell down in the confusion. Sivan tried to retrieve it. He could not find it. He straightened and tried with his legs. Has it gone down into the soil? It had been with him for quite some time. It had two folds and had sharp edges like the tiger's nail. Just press its handle and it would spring into action like a wild animal. Sivan again stooped down and examined the area, but to no avail.

The thought of Chitrabhanu, the writer, came to his mind. Lasar, the owner of the printing press, too cropped up. Lasar was sleeping in a drunken stupor. Chitran had taken the knife from his side and had given it to Sivan. Sivan had then indicated that Chitran could keep the knife himself. But he had retorted with a smile that he did not want such weapons; the pen was the writer's weapon.

Where would Chitrabhanu, be now?

Sivan looked behind. A boy was coming towards him, lantern in hand. The shadows of the trees staggered in the shaking light of the lantern. As he came closer Sivan understood that it was not a boy, but a very short man. Sivan did not want to search for the fallen knife in front of him. So he just stood there.

Raising the wick of the lamp and extending the lantern to Sivan's face, the dwarf asked, 'Are you the one who were supposed to come today?'

Sivan hesitated for a while. He was a very short man. Limbs like those of small children. But they were plump and round. There was a wart above his upper lip. However, the face revealed that he was middle-aged. Closely cropped curly hair. He was not wearing a shirt. Instead, he had wrapped a long frayed towel around his upper body. The gleam of the lantern was reflected in his eyes.

'There's a well there,' the sound was quite near now and its boom had lessened. 'It's very deep.' So that was why he had shouted with urgency.

Sivan looked at the spot he had pointed. All he could see was an assortment of plants of low height.

'Are you that person?' he asked again.

Sivan nodded. Sivan was not sure whether the dwarf had seen it in the dim light.

Silence reigned for a while. What was to be said? What was the code word to be used here? Sivan tried to remember. However, he could not recall either the student comrades or comrade Achu making any mention of it.

Gathering courage, Sivan finally asked, 'Are you Karadi Papa?'

The dwarf laughed trying to suppress the sound by cupping his mouth with his hands.

Sivan found it quite strange. The dwarf instead of answering his question was laughing nonstop. Why was he laughing like this? Is he not Karadi Papa? Yes, he did not have the physical attributes of the person Sivan was expecting to meet. But should that make this guy laugh in this manner?

'There's no Karadi-Papa!' said the dwarf.

'No?' Sivan felt the ground beneath him caving in.

'He is there. But he is god. Almighty!'

'Me, man of Pappayi. I call him Grandpa. Karadi is his nickname,' the dwarf explained. 'He knows that he is called Karadi. If he happens to hear it, he will take up his gun! Double barrelled! And bullets will be sprayed, dhe, dhe ...' he imitated the action of shooting.

His shape was weird. He hardly came up to Sivan's waist. Plump, rotund body. His gait was like the rolling of a ball.

'Ayya, what is your name?' he asked Sivan.

'Pavithran,' this time he did not have any hesitation in mentioning his name of the underground.

'Pavitharan...?' he repeated that name with an outlandish action. 'Very good name.'

What good was he seeing in a name?

'And you?' Sivan asked. But next moment he felt that that was not necessary. There was no need to get too friendly. Who knew what kind of a person he was?

'Ayyakkuru.' He must be the dwarf the ferryman was referring to. Ayyakkuru! What a name! Perhaps the 'kuru' has been added to compliment his height or the lack of it.

'I'm the servant of Papa. His slave.' He shifted the lantern to his left hand. The light too shifted and along with that, the shadows.

'You have taken the wrong path,' said Ayyakkuru and Sivan was shocked. He lowered his head and stared hard at the short form standing in front of him. Terror enveloped him like darkness.

Wrong path? Are my apprehensions coming true, Sivan mused.

Trunks of huge trees were blocking their path. Heaped one over the other. The smell of old timber. Trees bereft of roots or leaves lying on the ground like destitute human beings.

All of a sudden, Ayyakkuru bent down and kept the lantern on the ground. He then picked up something from the pathway and flung it away over his head.

'What is it?' Sivan asked.

'A Snake. Ayya, there are plenty of snakes in this area. That was a king cobra. Highly poisonous.' Ayyakkuru was quite cool about it. He lifted the lantern and started walking. He stepped on the logs like an acrobat jumping up and down. The tiny light of the lantern danced in tune with his deft movements.

'This is the back side of the house. We've to go to the other side. Hold my hand, sir.' He extended his undersized hand to Sivan. That was the hand that had just now touched the snake. Sivan did not take the proffered hand. They changed the route and were now walking through a sand-paved path.

The front side of the mansion had wooden balustrades, some of them withering with age. Ayyakkuru climbed the steps and gently pushed the double door. It was not closed from inside and opened with a groan.

'Please be seated,' said Ayyakkuru. But the corridor where they entered on climbing the steps did not have any chairs. Ayyakkuru took out a palm mattress from the beam and spread it on the floor. It was very old, with frayed edges. Sivan did not sit on the mat, instead he sat cross-legged on the floor. The floor was paved with tiles. It had become smooth and soft over the passage of time.

'Where are you from, sir?' Ayyakkuru sat on the steps and asked. Should I tell him from where I am? A growling sound was heard from outside, just then.

'Who is there?' Sivan asked.

'A monkey,' Ayyakkuru's tone was matter of fact.

When he heard the sound again, it seemed so like that of a man. Do monkeys cry making the same noises like men?

'The monkey belongs to Thechappan. Crying because he is hungry,' explained Ayyakkuru looking about. 'Sinners! Thechappan and his woman. Won't feed the monkey. But will kill and eat anything if they get the chance. Thieves!'

'Keep the lamp here,' said Sivan, for lighting a beedi.

'Yes sir!' Ayyakkuru pushed the lantern closer to Sivan with great respect as if he was executing an order.

'Can I get something to eat?' Sivan asked lighting a beedi. He was terribly hungry.

'Yes sir. Dinner is ready sir.' Ayyakkuru was pointing to the next room.

Sivan drew in a couple of puffs. He felt his body going light. Did he hear that cry again? He listened blowing the smoke away.

'The bed has been got ready for you to sleep,' Ayyakkuru said in soft tones. Sivan grunted.

'I've kept a blanket too,' he continued. Sivan found Ayyakkuru's fawning distasteful. He again dragged at his beedi.

'I want to have a bath,' Sivan gave him a hard stare.

'Okay, ayya,' he was subdued.

Where is Karadi Papa? Should I go, meet him? Is it not the norm? Suppose one of the comrades was to ask him won't he be forced to say that he had not met Karadi Papa the day he landed there?

However, he did not make any enquiries about Karadi Papa with Ayyakkuru.

Must take a bath. The grime of a long span of life had glued to the body like a thin membrane. Ayyakkuru went out to the back of the house on hearing Sivan's desire to have a bath. Sitting in the light of the lantern Sivan felt that the big house was a ship and he the lone sailor in it. It is the calm sea outside. Friendly waters. Waves of darkness rise up occasionally on the wings of the wind. There are no sounds.

Ayyakkuru had returned.

'I have filled water in the bucket. Let's go,' he said taking the lantern. Sivan walked through the heaped logs once again. The lantern in Ayyakkuru's hand seemed to have the same characteristics as Ayyakkuru; suddenly dipping and disappearing. Its light was staggering behind the darkness.

It was a wooden bucket. A towel was hanging on the clothesline behind it. Sivan hung his shirt on the clothesline and poured water on his body. He did not undo his mundu. That too had to be washed. The water was icy cold. There was a freezing sensation as he went on pouring water on his face and limbs.

Sivan dried his hair with the towel and then wrapped it around his waist. Would've to find out if fresh clothes are available. As he turned, he saw Ayyakkuru averting his face. So he had been watching me have a bath all this while, Sivan thought.

He remembered Sreenivasan as he squeezed water out of the mundu and shirt he had washed. Those clothes belonged to Sreenivasan. The shirt did not fit him. They were given to him by Sreenivasan to change the soiled ones.

It was not only clothes that Sreenivasan had given him.

He had had no information about Sreenivasan, just as that of Chitrabhanu. Both of them were writers. Two dreamers! Literature was not his cup of tea, he knew. A revolution was impossible to happen on the might of such fragile minds. Sivan had tried his utmost to keep away from romanticism. Still, many men of letters befriended him, gave him shelter. Who was dependent on whom?

The clothes wouldn't dry if it rained. So Sivan was reluctant to hang them on the clothesline in the backyard.

'Will it rain?' Sivan asked.

'Rain? Rain where, ayya ? It has been long since it rained here,' he started walking with the lantern.

But didn't it rain when he was coming from the riverbank? Didn't the soil become all gluey? He could not digest Ayyakkuru's comment.

They came to the front veranda once again. Ayyakkuru handed him a striped *lungi*. He wrapped it discarding the bath towel. The *lungi* smelt of naphtha balls.

'Ayyayyo … you hungry? Shall I serve you dinner?' Ayyakkuru asked. His stomach was growling with hunger. Sivan nodded.

'We'll have food. It's all ready.' There was affection in Ayyakkuru's voice. Sivan went along with Ayyakkuru. They were passing one room after the other in the mansion. Sivan had to lift his legs to unusual heights to cross the threshold. The scent of oldness pervaded. Finally, they reached a long hall after crossing several small rooms and corridors. That must be the kitchen. It did not have doors. One side was raised and was serving as the hearth. There were couple of vessels and plates. A cool breeze wafted in through the smoke-stained wooden grills.

Sivan was trying to catch a scent. The scent of food. He felt aromas tenderly touching his tired nostrils.

'Please sit here sir,' Ayyakkuru said spreading a grass mattress on the floor. There were no tables or chairs in the kitchen. But to one side there was a large wooden chest and on top of it there was an *uri*, a rope potholder, hung from a rafter.

Ayyakkuru kept the lantern on the chest. Sivan thought: he had stayed in attics which were the abodes of rats and bats and in tiny rooms without any ventilation or light. Does this midget know of it? Being a comrade of the early days, Karadi Papa may be aware of such a kind of life, perhaps. Thousands of people without a roof to sleep under, live on the road like dogs. Life in the underground is a similar phase. Sacrifices come naturally.

Ayyakkuru, standing on his toes, was trying to reach the pot on the *uri*. Sivan sat back and watched the muscles of his raised arm bulging. Though the potholder was not at a great height, Ayyakkuru was struggling to reach it.

'It is not warm anymore. But the rice is excellent,' he said transferring rice into a plate. Sivan said it did not matter. It had been ages since he had had food that was warm or fresh. But there was the warmth of the burning hunger.

He had not had rice for meals for days together. He made balls of the rice and swallowed them as if a most sumptuous dinner had been served to him. There was only some gravy without any pieces, to go along with the rice. Perhaps because of the frantic nature of his eating, a big ball of rice stuck at his throat choking him. His eyes bulged.

Ayyakkuru laughed seeing him struggle for breath. The same laughter, hands cupping his mouth.

Then he fetched a pitcher of cool water for Sivan. He could now feel water trickling down his throat. He got back his breath. But he was gasping and his glance shifted between the rice and Ayyakkuru.

Just as the urgency of his hunger had subsided, he realised that what he was stuffing in was stale food. Its putrid taste was making him nauseous giving him a puking sensation. But how could he afford to show revulsion after the frantic greed he had displayed? What would Ayyakkuru think? Moreover, millions of human beings on the face of this earth are struggling because they cannot access even this kind of food or even worse? Despite such thoughts, Sivan found that the evil taste was persisting. He stopped eating.

'Ayya, why did you stop eating?' Ayyakkuru asked.

'Enough.'

'You are not hungry anymore?'

Sivan nodded.

'Maybe the curries are not good. That Mary doesn't know cooking. Do you know Mary? She is the wife of Thechappan. Sometimes, Papa becomes furious and flings the pot away.'

'Do you like curries?' Ayyakkuru asked as if probing about a matter of ut most secrecy. 'Meat?'

'Not particularly.'

'It's jungle meat. A pig was shot two days ago. A double barrelled gun. Bang, bang! But the pig escaped.'

Sivan did not tell him that the bullets had struck the animal and that the wounds putrefied later on and the headless body of the pig floated down the river.

Ayyakkuru gathered the leftover rice and curry. He kept all those along with Sivan's plate in one corner of the room.

'I'll wash them.'

'No need sir. I'll do it tomorrow morning.'

Sivan once again followed Ayyakkuru and the lantern. Now they were going upstairs. The steps were wooden and were quivering and shuddering as one climbed. But still Ayyakkuru was very fast! He was rolling up like a ball defying the gravitational forces. Sivan struggled to keep pace.

Walking through the corridor Ayyakkuru entered a room, throwing its doors wide open. 'You will get a good breeze if you leave a window open,' he said.

Sivan surveyed the room. It was quite spacious. There was a cot with grills right at the centre of the room.

'New cot!' Ayyakkuru said. 'Specially arranged for you.'

The old bedspread had large square designs on it.

Ayyakkuru remained there for some more time. Sivan looked out through the window into the pitch dark night, in order to get rid of him. The mammoth shadows of huge trees stood there silently like ancient statues.

Ayyakkuru coughed. Sivan turned to see him lowering the wick of the lamp.

'There's water,' he pointed to the pitcher below the window.

The top of the trees were almost on the same level as the room. They were swaying in the light breeze. Has it started drizzling? But Ayyakkuru had said that it has not rained in the island since long.

Sivan suddenly had the feeling that someone was staring at him. He turned to find Ayyakkuru peering at him. He looked away when caught in the act.

Sivan was quite annoyed. He was like a spy watching every movement.

Ayyakkuru smiled awkwardly. He lowered his eyes.

'I'll be late. You go and sleep,' Sivan was harsh.

Ayyakkuru walked out of the room with heavy steps. He closed the door. Sivan felt the building heaving when he climbed down the staircase.

The light too vanished with Ayyakkuru.

Sivan lowered himself on to the bed. Exhaustion would have caressed him to sleep. And everything would be alright if one had a good sleep. All the doubts, fears and apprehensions were due to lack of sleep.

The smell of cockroaches from the old bed sheet pierced his nostrils. To which age did it belong? Hadn't Ayyakkuru told that the cot was specially made for him? He touched the grills of the cot. Time has whetted its edges like that of a sword. Hadn't the boatman mentioned about a cot? Is it the one on which he is sleeping now? Had he not said that it was a cot made of *kanhiram* and also that it was a century old?

His apprehensions were unending. He again recalled the words of the ferryman. That it was the dead man's cot. One who had slept on it till the other day was no more. But is not his presence felt? Was he touching that bony body when leaning to the sides? Was he hearing the dying man's groans? The bitter scent. Death that crouches even on to the cot of *kanhiram* ... Those primal instincts seemed to ridicule his logical reasoning.

He gradually fell asleep. Into a slumber, like a boat floating in an endless stream. The boatman is singing an old song. The lyrics are not clear.

Is it *the boatman* singing? No it is not his voice. Then who is it? As he was trying to recollect, he felt something striking the side of the boat. A cadaver. He woke up with a shudder. The resonance of the song was still there, wafting from unknown distances.

He stood there cocking up his ears. Yes, it seemed that someone was taking quick steps. Or was it running away? The railing of the staircase was rattling, wasn't it?

Sivan sat on the bed doing nothing. Must be mere hallucination. A cool breeze was flowing in through the window. The trees were swaying. Only the sound of their leaves rustling. Nothing else. He lay down again.

Footsteps in the corridor again as he was slipping into sleep.

Sivan got up. His eyes had got used to the darkness by then. He tiptoed towards the door noiselessly. And tried to open it.

He was chilled to the bone; like a corpse. The door, he found, was locked from the outside.

'What's your name, dear?'

'Sakunthala.'

'And Where are you from?'

'Near Muttuthara.'

'Oh, near Muttuthara ... where exactly? I am familiar with Muttuthara.

'At Palakkara. Near Devi temple.'

'That is … our KP was there, no? Is your home near KP's house?'

'… I'm KP's daughter.'

'Daughter! Are you KP's daughter? Really! Why didn't you say so in the beginning, dear?'

Sakunthala was surprised that the politicians still remembered her father.

'Oh, you Kurup! It is about this girl you talked to me yesterday over phone? I thought it was someone else. Who do you think she is? She is our child. Daughter, of the one and only KP. And who is KP? You may know him in a different context, Kurup. He was the clerk of advocate Raman Menon. Even that description will not do. He was more familiar with the law points than Menon. But the real thing is something else altogether. KP was a party man. Not a member, but a party man! How can I ever forget him even if all others do? Once upon a time it was in their family house that we people used to take shelter while in the underground. Do you have any memories of it, child?' Sankaran Adiyodi asked her with a loud guffaw. Sakunthala nodded. The gloom on her face may have made him realise that his loud laughter was not appropriate for the occasion. He picked up a pen from the table and began scribbling on a pad.

Sankaran Adiyodi was the member of parliament from Thavalam constituency. Sakunthala had concluded from the words of the editor that he could be of help. However, she had not disclosed to the editor that she knew Adiyodi through her father. She had her reasons. It was at least a quarter of a century since Adiyodi had established contact with her father and sought shelter at their house. She was a small child at that time, studying maybe in the first standard. There were only shadows of people in her memory. Enormous changes had taken place in all of them in course of time. They had all scattered in different directions. The party itself split into two. Her father was not with either faction after the split. He was only a silent party worker even earlier. His last years were spent in isolation without any contact with anyone. It was already six or seven years since he had died. Not many people of the earlier period had come visiting all these years. None of her family members too showed any keenness to re-establish contact with the old timers. In such circumstances, it was too much to think or hope that a prominent personality like Sankaran Adiyodi would honour old bonds.

'I have lived there, in forty nine,' Adiyodi recalled. 'KP and I would play cards throughout the night. KP's mother was there during those days. She would chide us for keeping late nights. They were old timers, no? And then we would hide somewhere for playing cards!'

Since the editor had insisted, the local committee secretary of the party KG Kurup had accompanied her. He was taken by surprise at Adiyodi's narration.

'Okay, tell me, what happened to your husband?' Adiyodi asked, leaning forward.

'Missing,' the party secretary said very lightly.

'Yes, you told me that over the phone. But you had mentioned that he was taken away by the police.'

'Yes, that's exactly the problem, Sankaran *Etta*. Now they say that he is not with them.'

'Then where is he?'

'They have him, sir,' Sakunthala said, 'I had seen him.'

'Seen him? Where?'

'In the camp at Chaloorkunnu. I had a glimpse of him.'

'Chaloorkunnu? But why should the police take him into custody at all?'

'That could be on the basis of a suspicion,' explained the secretary. 'Sreenivasan may have been mistaken for some other person. But they now claim that they have not arrested him. I have made enquiries.'

'Why should the police come out with a lie in this matter?' Adiyodi asked Sakunthala.

'I don't know, sir. But the person I saw was him,' she was on the verge of a breakdown.

'Sakunthala, are you certain that the person you saw was Sreenivasan?' It was the secretary's turn to be sceptical. 'You see, I had enquired at the Home Minister's office. Is there any information about Sreenivasan, that was what they asked me in turn. Moreover, it seems he had applied for leave for a few days from his office.'

'I see. Why did he take leave?' Sankaran Adiyodi asked.

'For writing a play, he had said,' replied Sakunthala.

'Ok. So, he is a writer, eh? That's good. Then, did he write the play?'

'I do not know sir. I was at my home for a few days.'

'Please don't misunderstand me if I ask you something. You are like my daughter.' Adiyodi was all courtesy. 'There were no issues between you for living separate, no?'

What is it that they are leading up to? This is a new twist. Was Sreenivasan running away from me? She remembered how Sreenivasan had lied to her. Sakunthala could not control herself any longer.

'I did not want to upset you. But when one enters into a problem, one should know all the aspects, no?' Adiyodi consoled her.

'I too had come to know that Sreenivasan was taken away for interrogation. This information was from the local police. But now even they say that they are not certain,' the secretary said.

'May be true, may not be true. There are many reports of this kind floating around. Anyway let me make some enquiries. I'll call Kumaran Nair. Not of much use. He may play hard to get. But he has to be asked. After all it is our party's government. Any other steps, only after this.' Sankaran Adiyodi collected Sreenivasan's address and the details of the newspaper he was working for. Adiyodi knew the editor in person.

'Don't be afraid, Sakunthala. Now let's assume that the police has taken him into custody, the chances for that are slim, but those are things we can find out. After a few days they themselves will come and hand him over to you. This I can guarantee. If we cannot find out what happened to someone dear to us what is the point in my sitting here saying that I am a member of the parliament, especially when our party is in power? You go home without any anxieties. I'll keep you informed.'

There were very few households with telephone in her neighbourhood.

Giving the phone number of the newspaper office, Sakunthala made a request. 'Please tell them sir, not to harm him in the camp. He is innocent.'

'No need to stress that. Sakunthala's husband has to be a good man. And KP's son in law! No one would do him any harm. I'll see to that.'

Adiyodi got up from his chair and saw her out. She thanked him with folded palms as she left.

It was evening. The sun was setting. Adiyodi's words had brought some relief. He will talk to the police and also call the Minister. Adiyodi seemed to be a person who kept his word. The police cannot ignore an instruction from the Home Minister, the secretary was confident. He had some business at the party office and so Sakunthala had to return alone. He had offered to put her in a bus, but she had declined the offer. It was not dark as yet.

But she was sort of scared to go home these days. She had not clearly explained the situation to her mother. Sakunthala was afraid that her mother may get a shock. Her mother had a tendency for that after the death of her father. The doctor too had advised that she should not be told anything that would upset her. But what posed trouble for her were the queries of her son.

'*Amma*, did you see *Achan*?' he would ask each time she got back home.

'Eh ... *yes*,' she would be non committal.

'When will *Achan* come?'

'Next week.'

'Will he bring the top?'

'Yes.'

'What colour?'

'Red.'

'No, not that colour.'

'Then what colour do you want darling?'

'Blue.'

'I'll tell him.' And she would burst into tears pulling him on to her lap. He would be baffled. Why was she crying?

'It's okay *Amma*, a red top will do.'

It was past seven when she reached home that day. Sasi was not there at the front veranda. Usually, he would be waiting there for her. She would buy at least a toffee for him. But she could not do even that. A bus was ready to depart when she had reached the bus stand and so she did not get an opportunity to buy even a chocolate.

'Where is Sasi?' Sakunthala enquired as she stepped in.

'He is feverish. Because of the cold I think,' said her mother. 'I have given him a *panikkoorkka*, to bring down the fever. Did you see Sreeni?'

'I met Sankaran Adiyodi.'

'Who? Comrade Adiyodi? And then?'

'He said there is nothing to worry about.'

'But where has this boy gone to, O God!' her mother exclaimed. 'You had said that you would meet him today?'

'Yes, I'll see him without much delay,' Sakunthala said going into the room where Sasi was.

Sasi had fever. He was sleeping. He was talking in his sleep. He had become debilitated with just a day's fever. She covered his forehead with a piece of wet linen.

'His body is burning, Amma,' she said.

'He will be alright. This is because he was running around and playing. The fever will reduce by morning,' her mother too felt his forehead.

But the fever did not come down in the morning. Sakunthala took him to a *vaidyar* along with her mother. He prescribed a tablet and a *kashaya*. Wet pieces of linen were alternated on his forehead. Still the fever did not come down. The boy's body was trembling and he was groaning and talking in his sleep. Neighbours and relatives persuaded her to take him to an allopath at Muttuthara. Walking with Sasi on her shoulders to the doctor in the evening, she longed for Sreenivasan. Sreenivasan would not go to office on the days when Sasi was unwell. He would be more worried than her. He would take the kid to the doctor and would remain with him at home.

Suddenly, the image flooded in. A figure smeared with dirt and grime, unkempt beard, unruly hair, bruises and welts all over the body, wearing only an undergarment. Wasn't it him? The local party secretary had argued with her that that could not have been him. She saw that image again in her mind. Not just once, but repeatedly. There was no doubt. It was Sreenivasan. She would recognise even his shadow. When she visualised him chained like an animal, she could not withstand it. The small body of Sasi sleeping on her shoulders seemed to weigh her down and it seemed to be burning with heat.

'The temperature is quite high,' said the doctor after examining him. 'When did the fever commence?'

'Two days now.'

'I can give you the medicines. But he requires more attention. It is better to take the child to the hospital.'

Sakunthala was scared. Her eyes brimmed. Is there anything seriously wrong with him? She found that she was tongue-tied.

'No point in getting alarmed. The temperature is certainly on the higher side. That has to be taken care of. Is there no one else with you?'

'I'll take him to the hospital, doctor.'

The evening sky was overcast as she left the doctor.

The skies opened up just as she reached the hospital in town by the last bus. It was raining throughout his stay in the hospital. Sometimes whispering, sometimes thundering. Sakunthala did not go home at all. Sasi's fever took several forms. Sometimes it reached the peak, sometimes it came down and entered the zone of peace and calmness. Sakunthala remained at his side, praying and making offerings to gods. Looking at his weak face, she remembered Sreenivasan. Sasi was in hospital for seven days.

'You must take care. Don't let him out for playing for a month. He needs rest,' the doctor said while Sasi was getting discharged. 'The fever was quite serious. It had induced fits. Could recur.'

Sakunthala was upset. The doctor's prediction was proven right. The shadow of that fever was with Sasi throughout his life. He had several attacks. He would fall down, his limbs would thrash and his mouth would froth. He was never the same child again. Some unknown fear always pulled him back like an invisible tether.

There wasn't any news of Sreenivasan even a week after they returned from the hospital.

Hadn't Sankaran Adiyodi promised to inform the editor if he were to get any information? Has he forgotten the whole thing? That was not possible. The warmth with which Sankaran Adiyodi had spoken about her father precludes that. But still, grief was brimming over.

Sasi was up from the sick bed and had started drinking *kanji*. Sakunthala started for the town the day she felt that Sasi had recovered to some extent.

'*Amma*, you going to meet *Acha*?' Sasi asked in a feeble voice. He had become very weak, she noticed. She was baffled not knowing the answer to that question. The child did not ask that day to remind his father to bring the blue coloured top. Perhaps he did not want to upset her. How fast children learn, Sakunthala thought. They study each situation minutely. They also acclimatise very fast to the surroundings, like vegetation. She prayed to be given at least that much of strength and courage as shown by children.

On reaching the town Sakunthala's first visit was to Sreenivasan's office. The editor was not there when she arrived. Sakunthala noticed that most of them were being very sympathetic. That made her restless.

'When will he come?' she asked the peon.

'I cannot say. A political leader has died. He has gone to offer condolence,' the peon said.

She sat on a chair placed in front of his cabin and waited. It was a room redolent of newspaper rolls and ink. Busy employees. At least some of them did not know who she was. It was as if they all had forgotten that Sreenivasan had worked there till recently.

The editor arrived by noon. It was quite obvious that he was taken aback seeing Sakunthala.

He asked her into his cabin and told her, 'Sakunthala, you may have known Cherukunnam Varkey, a socialist leader. He was more well known as Varkey *Asan*. He had been with Gandhiji in the olden days. And was also there with the prohibition movement. *Asan* passed away this morning. I had been to his place.'

He took his seat and doffed his hat. It was out and out white khadi. Then he took a towel and wiped his face. Sankaran Adiyodi must have called Kumaran Nair and Adiyodi would have passed on some information to the editor. Sakunthala thought he was about to convey that to her. She was looking at him expectantly.

'Things are getting more and more complicated in Sreeni's case.' She felt that the muscles on the editor's face were tautening. 'Different views are floating around. Couple of policemen admit that he was taken for questioning. But others, especially those of the local police, who were on duty say that he was never taken into custody.'

He stopped for a moment. Then he continued with hesitation. 'However, they are all in agreement on one thing. That no one knows where he is now. If at all he was taken into custody, it would have been only for questioning. But he jumped from their jeep and ran away. Is it not a shame for them to admit that someone simply escaped from their hands? Maybe that's why they are denying the news about custody. Anyway Sreenivasan has not reached the Chaloorkunnu camp.'

'That is a lie, sir. I saw him there, no?'

'What if the person you saw was not Sreeni?'

'I saw him sir. Many others could make a mistake. But not me, not in his case.'

'Sakunthala, you were quite agitated that day. I had noticed it, but I did not mention it. That was why I had advised you not to go to the camp. But you went there and you were in an unsteady condition. Whichever person you see, you feel that it is the person you are looking for. Now let's assume that the person you saw was indeed Sreeni. But he could even then have escaped from their clutches while being taken to some other place. The police may have slightly altered their version. But the overall conclusion that can be reached is that Sreenivasan escaped.'

'Do you think that he is daring enough to do that, sir?'

'I know he is not. But is it not circumstances that motivate one to do things otherwise unthinkable? Many wicked things are taking place at Chaloorkunnu. Everyone knows that. Maybe Sreeni too was beaten up. He could have thought of escaping, to avoid that happening again.'

'Sir, did you see the Minister?'

'Who? Kumaran Nair? Why? Was there any information…?'

'Sir, you had told me that there was a meeting in which the Minister was to participate. And then comrade Adiyodi had promised to talk to him. I had given him your number.'

'Kumaran Nair did not come for the meeting. Instead he had sent his private secretary. But today I ran into him at the house of Varkey *Asan*. But I could not talk to him. He was very busy. Oh, yeah, Adiyodi also was there. However my guess is that he also might not have come across any new information. Otherwise it would have been discussed then and there. He knows me very well.'

'If so, what do we do now?' Sakunthala was dejected.

'Wait … and wait; what else can I say? But you can meet Kumaran Nair. At his convenience. Sankaran Adiyodi is there in the TB today. It will be easier to meet Kumaran Nair if Adiyodi comes along. But I am not in a position to accompany you today. I've some urgent work to finish. I have to write an obit of Varkey *Asan*. Can we forget a person like him? So you will have to go alone, Sakunthala. But you can always contact me over phone for any help.'

She understood that the editor was again avoiding her.

Sakunthala got out of the office where Sreenivasan had worked. It was to be her last visit there. She found out the directions and hurried to the TB.

The moment she saw Adiyodi, she sensed a change of attitude in him. He did not offer her a seat. It took him a while even to raise his face and acknowledge her presence.

'I forgot your name.' He stared at her with cold eyes.

'Sakunthala.'

'Eh, eh. I would have had more freedom had KP been there.' She waited not knowing what he was coming to.

'I'm not talking as a politician, but as a family man. You women have certain responsibilities. If you forget them, it is risky not only for the family, but also for the society.' He took off his glasses, kept them on the table and took out a small vial. He went on to take a bit of snuff from it and snorted it following it up with couple of sneezes.

'We too have been active in party work; we have lived in the underground. Didn't I tell you, in forty-nine, the party was banned? It was then I had come and taken shelter at your house. You may not be remembering all that. But we never forsook our responsibility to the society. Either wife or mother, there would be a woman to take care of that. In my case it was the mother. She used to beat me if she thought I was on the wrong path even after I had grown up.'

Sankaran Adiyodi was about to smile, lost in reverie. But soon he regained the serious air and continued.

'Here, just see, what happened. Your husband deliberately keeps you away from your home. Then he arranges for someone else to come and live there. Why? If the intentions are above board, is it not along with the rest of the family that one entertains a guest? I don't have to mention it, you know it. In those times we came and lived in your house when women and children were very much present, isn't it? You did not question him why you were being sent home. That was the first mistake.'

'He said it was for writing a play,' stammered Sakunthala.

'It was not for writing a play, but for enacting one.' Anger was welling up.

'And then? Whom does he have with him? A first rate ... criminal. What else can one call a person who goes around beheading people. If you were not aware of all this, whose fault is it?

'Not only this. Your husband also is not all that innocent. It seems he used to write using the name Buddha!'

Was it not at Chaloorkunnu she had heard of Sreenivasan writing poems in another name? Sakunthala tried to recall. She got through to a detached face and an apparently dispassionate voice.

'Buddha! What a name to be given to those who chop off heads! I read some of his poems. Even if he had not sheltered that killer, the police would have interrogated him. Does Sakunthala have any idea of these things?'

'He used to write poems.'

'Poems! And what poems! Is it stuff people like us are unaware of? These poems assume that people will take up arms and march ahead, on just hearing it once!'

There was not much point in remaining there any more, Sakunthala felt.

'Another thing. I made a thorough enquiry. This guy ... what's his name ... eh, Sreenivasan. It is true that he was taken by the police for interrogation. The police have admitted that much. But the truth is that he escaped. He is capable of that. You are not aware of his potential, that's all. Anyway he is not there in their custody now. Things being like that how can they provide any clue to his whereabouts? But as I told you, his path is wrong. When I called Kumaran Nair, he literally jumped at me. After he cooled down, he cautioned me, "*Sankara Etta*, don't interfere in this. Your image will get tarnished." Look, there now? At this age I have to accept advice from the likes of Kumaran Nair! All this for your sake!'

There was a phone call and Sankaran Adiyodi talked over the phone with astonishing gentleness. He reverted to his emotionless approach as soon as the phone was placed back on the cradle.

'Now, listen to this too. The police is certainly looking for him. but don't nourish the hope that they will release him immediately if at all they get hold of him. His activities and involvement are beyond your imagination.'

Just as Sakunthala was stepping out of the room, Sankaran Adiyodi advised her, 'If he happens to come home, the police will be watching. So don't try to hide him. It will only multiply the problems. You should inform me immediately. We will try to save him by seeking clemency. I'm ready to fall at the feet of Kumaran Nair for that. It doesn't matter to me. After all, you are the daughter of KP, no?'

Just then a strange kind of courage overtook Sakunthala. She felt all her grief and fears fading away. Why am I talking to all these people as if I am the vanquished? Sreenivasan has not done that serious a crime. Her father too had not seen anything wrong in providing shelter to people like Adiyodi at that period of time. And Sreenivasan would never commit a crime that would cause misery to others.

No I will not accept defeat, Sakunthala decided. If I do so, Sreenivasan will hold me guilty. She started walking towards the door.

'Ok, let a week pass. I'll call Kumaran Nair again.' Sankaran Adiyodi said gently.

She turned around. 'No need for that sir. You needn't take the trouble to call the Minister,' Sakunthala was calm and steady as she said this.

'In politics we are honour bound to shoulder troubles,' he was obviously abashed by her words.

'No. Even if he comes out, he will not seek clemency as you suggest.'

'Eh? Why?'

'He wouldn't have done anything wrong. Those who haven't done anything wrong will not have to seek any mercy.'

Sankaran Adiyodi took off his glasses and put them on again. He then opened the vial of sniff, tipped a bit of it on to his palm and pretended to be totally engrossed in it.

Sivan's mind was preoccupied while trying to open the wooden double door. All sounds from outside had ceased. It must be him. Ayyakkuru, the dwarf. On the very first sight itself there was an ominous aura about him. Though he was reluctant to look at you straight, eye to eye, he was stealing sly glances all the while. He would avert his eyes when confronted. Was there anything wrong with him? Or was he revelling in the absence of Karadi-Papa? Making him eat stale food, sleep on the dead man's cot … was it all his handiwork? Ayyakkuru was having fun at his expense, Sivan concluded.

Once again the pendulum of suspicion began to swing. The incidents from that morning made a beeline for his mind. The students who had come to see me off, was there a hint of ridicule in their conversation? Karadi-Papa, whom even two companies of police could not nab at the time of the Calcutta Thesis! Karadi-Papa! What a name! There is derision in that name itself. And that fellow Achu, who waited for me at Pullani. Who is he? Is he really a party comrade? Did the students include him too, when they said that there are firebrand comrades at Pullani? Yet Achu did not respond to the code word which they had passed on. He was always in a hurry. Was he not running the entire distance to the riverbank like a machine? Perhaps he was afraid he would have to face questions. And then he left in haste citing feeble excuses. Abandoning me to the blackness of an unknown territory. Throwing me into a river through which the carcasses of animals float. Where did the links break? Or rather, new links coupled together?

Nothing was clear. Other than that he has been trapped in solitary confinement inside these old walls.

After pushing and hammering the door and shouting at the top of his voice, Sivan tried to reconcile to his real situation. Who was there to listen to his shouting or cries? Karadi-Papa will have to come. Whenever that was to be—and whether he turns out to be friend or foe, my future is in his hands. Wait till he comes. There was no other way.

It had suddenly become very cold. A strong wind was blowing. The window which was open, slammed shut. Sivan opened it and looked out. The top of the trees were swaying wildly. There was not a spark of light anywhere. Even the fireflies had disappeared. Sivan lay down on the bed looking into the darkness and the moving forms in it. Slumber stumbled back in search of him.

It was broad daylight when he woke up. The windows were open. They looked like the wings of the mansion. The morning sun sketched pictures of the tree tops on the wall of the room. He then saw the closed front door. A huge cockroach slowly crawling through the double panel. Sivan focused his attention on it. It was much bigger than the ones usually seen. Must be aged. Its movements were very sluggish. Sivan tried to imagine it as an ancient battleship. The very thought suddenly transformed the meaning and significance of its journey to a different plane. Its paths and destinations become important. Its route was obstructed once in a while by the crevices of the old door. Then it got out and tried to climb up the door through another path. It kept on shifting its trail. But its destination was always the same. The cockroach disappeared into the other side of a panel after wandering and stumbling for a while. Sivan stood up and looked through the window. The trees were thick and huddled together. There was no one in the compound. Two cows were grazing in the distance. Beyond that it was barren land. Bright sky. The burnish of sunlight on the edges of the grey clouds. Where was the river which he had crossed to get there?

The river was on the opposite side, Sivan found out. Looking through the pigeon hole on the other side, the courtyard of the mansion was visible. There was a drying neem tree in the courtyard. It was a gnarled old tree and there were leaves only on some of the branches. Was it drying up or was it on the way to blossom? Beyond that, there was the path with steep ups and downs leading to the river. Overgrown bushes on both sides of the path. It ended at the river. The desolate boat landing and the surroundings were clearly visible. Was it through this path I reached here the previous night? He could not be sure. The whole place was strange terrain. The huts which had remained in the mind as slivers of lightning were not to be seen at all.

The thought of how to escape obsessed him. Where is that dwarf? Where did he vanish to after putting me in here? He listened with his ears close to the door. Not even the whisper of a footstep. He called out Ayyakkuru's name. With a shock Sivan recognised his own voice reverberating in the room. That doesn't matter, he thought. Did he have any other option to get out? However, was there any point in shouting for Ayyakkuru? He was the one who had locked the door from outside.

'Oooy …' Sivan called.

'Anybody there?' he tried again. Not a sound; no response.

'Please open the door.' He banged the door. The cockroach came out from its hideout. And scrambled up the wall.

'Please open the door,' he was louder this time.

Who knows whether Papa could hear him? His ears may not be all that keen. Must be pretty old, no? Even then, he might appear if he happens to hear. Sivan called out again and this time he thought he heard a faint sound. Was it not the sound of the staircase trembling? Yes it was. The sound was growing. Footsteps. They were quite near.

Suddenly the door opened with a groan. Oh, was it so simple!

Was it not locked? He was ashamed at the thought that all this while he had been shouting and clamouring, standing behind a door that was shut, not locked. But it was certainly locked the previous night and in the pre-dawn hours. He had tried the door. Did Ayyakkuru come there and open the lock quietly? Bizarre.

Much more bizarre was the gigantic figure blocking the door!

Very tall, slightly bald, big eyes and a somewhat stooped posture. There were creases on the broad forehead. The massive body was covered with grey hair. Hair even on the folds of the ears. He was wearing a blue striped lungi and was bare-bodied. Short, plump hands, but long legs. There were scars of old wounds on the strong shoulders. Sivan looked straight at him, but an unreasonable fear made him withdraw his gaze quickly.

'Achu had told me. You were a bit late yesterday?' His voice was gruff.

'The door ...' Sivan could not complete.

'Door?' he clutched the door panels and looked at Sivan.

'Yes, the door. It was locked from outside.'

'It was closed, not locked,' he said with a strange laugh. The neat row of teeth was visible. Surprising, that he was able to maintain his teeth so well even at that age.

'I'm Pappachan. I'm also called Pappayi.' He smiled. 'Did you sleep well?'

Sivan nodded.

'You are a lawyer, no? Achu had written. That's good. Papa would love it,' he said.

I did go to the law college for two years. But how did Achu come to know of this?

'Who is this Papa you mentioned...?' Sivan asked. So the one who is standing in front of him is not Karadi-Papa?

'What? You don't know that? Haven't you come here for Papa?' he winked.

'Where is he then?'

'Oh, Papa doesn't come here too often. He is now quite old, no? We've to take care of everything.'

What is this man talking about? To take care of what?

'I was late yesterday. Went to bed straight. Woke up only now, hearing your call.'

So I had woken him up from his sleep. That too, to open a door which was not locked. Sivan was at a loss of words.

'There was a timber auction in the Karappuzha range. It is somewhat far. But still I went there,' explained Pappayi. 'The tussle is with youngsters. So the competition is very stiff.'

He was talking about forests and timber.

'The bid went up slightly. But that doesn't matter. Papa is not in a hurry. Just cut and leave it on the ground. Let it become mature. The price will go up like that of gold.'

He entered the room and made an inspection of the cot on which Sivan had slept. He scratched the sides of the cot which had become dark with age. Sivan noticed his long nails which were like caps for the fingers.

'Listen sir, you can use this room. But I'll take this cot. I need a cot that is sufficiently long. Look at my body. Yesterday it was put here by mistake. Stupid fellows!' Pappayi smelled the cot. He caressed its legs. ' 'It's the core of the tree indeed! The saw will snap if one attempts to cut it. And a chisel will break if carving is tried.'

That was providential. Sivan had not wanted a dead man's cot. It must have been a deliberate ploy on Ayyakkuru's part to frighten the guest.

Sivan accompanied him through the corridor. The corridor was brightly lit now. Nothing was clear the previous night, in the dim light of Ayyakkuru's lantern. Smooth floor tiles. Cobwebs on the tiles overhead. Must be ages since the walls were whitewashed. The coat of lime and cement had worn off the red bricks. An old picture was hanging on the wall. It seemed to be that of men with raised fists. Pictures of gods were most unlikely in the den of revolution. But the forms were not clear.

They walked ahead.

'Are you familiar with timber and its measurements?' Pappayi asked. Sivan felt like asking why one should be, but resisted the temptation.

'The one who died was brilliant. He dealt with all the intricacies of the timber business till the very last day. Don't forget that he was ninety! But he was very dear to Papa. All the calculations were on his fingertips. The moment you think of something he would come out with a plan. However, he could not hold a pen. He wanted a scribe for everything.'

'That cot in the room, it was the accountant's, no?'

'How do you know?' Pappayi was surprised. 'The old man had been asking for a change since long. So your arrival was timely.'

Timber accounts! Sivan felt insulted.

So that was what Achu wrote about him? Was he brought to that island as a substitute for the old man who kept the timber accounts? Or is it that Achu just used it as a pretext to find a place? Maybe the comrades thought this as a good temporary shelter.

So then, who is the comrade of the Calcutta Thesis time? Is it comrade Karadi-Papa?

'Achu is an old hand. It was Achu who brought all the clocks here. You see, the time here is older than him. That is the fun. So, how can Papa refuse if he requests? We then came to know that you have studied law. You know the thing with law and court cases. Didn't I tell you about a few lads who are becoming stumbling blocks in our business? Now they will be very cautious knowing that there is a lawyer to deal with.'

As they were coming down the staircase, Sivan saw Ayyakkuru standing there looking perplexed. Crooked dwarf! He was surreptitiously glancing upwards. His Adam's apple was bobbing, the warts on his face throbbing. He averted his glance when one noticed him. After three or four steps Sivan stared fixedly at him. He felt that Ayyakkuru was writhing like a fish on the hook.

'Stand aside, you ass,' Pappayi said feigning a slap. There was affection in his words. Ayyakkuru shifted himself slightly, with a peeved look.

'A dwarf is a good omen.' Pappayi turned to Sivan and commented. 'But he lacks commonsense. Always blocks your way.'

Ayyakkuru was looking at Pappayi with a grief-stricken face, a sentiment that did not suit him. Tears were welling up in his eyes. The laughter and frolic of the previous night had vanished.

'Yesterday night he locked the door from outside,' said Sivan. 'I called out in the morning thinking that it had not been opened.'

'You dwarf! You locked up *Vakil* sir?' Pappayi slapped Ayyakkuru hard. Sivan was stunned. He had not expected his complaint to be taken that seriously. Pappayi's fingers were found stamped on Ayyakkuru's cheeks as angry red marks. Pappayi raised his hand again.

'Leave it comrade!' Sivan intervened. 'It was probably a prank.' Was it a blunder to call him comrade? He did not seem to have noticed.

'What a prank to play when someone just arrives!' Pappayi was trembling with rage. Sivan could see the hair on his ears standing stiff. Ayyakkuru was rooted to the spot, head bent. Why doesn't he move? Why stay there to get beaten?

'Out of my sight! This sir is Papa's man. Remember that. If I hear anything like this again, I'll cut you into pieces and throw them in the well.'

A stream began to flow from Ayyakkuru's eyes. He wiped the tears like children do and blew his nose.

Pappayi seemed to have thawed. He consoled Ayyakkuru holding him close and patting him on the back.

'Don't just stand there and sob. Go, ask Mary to hard boil two eggs. I am starving!' he said.

Ayyakkuru promptly ran to the back of the mansion. His running was like the rolling of a big block of stone. He made bestial noises while running.

'He requires a couple of blows once in a while. He is always jumpy. But one can only feel pity for him. He cannot answer back. After all a dumb fellow, no?'

'Dumb?' Sivan was bewildered, what is this man building up now?

'Yes. He is a paniya boy. There are his kinsmen on the riverbank. You can see their huts on the way. The whole lot is crooked. They will steal if they get a chance. Not the type you can rely on. But this guy, he cannot talk back, no? That's why Papa let him be here.'

Being a mute is also a quality? Sivan pondered.

However, he had seen with his eyes Ayyakkuru mouthing words. He had heard with his ears Ayyakkuru talking in mixed Tamil. And this man here says that he is a mute. What was happening? Or was it that whatever he saw and heard the previous night were mere fantasies of a tired brain?

Continuously on the move for a very long time, different people, various hideouts—what is happening to me?

'So, *Vakil* sir, have a bath, have breakfast and get ready. We will go to the hills. Work is going on there.' Pappayi told him.

Thechappan came in with the breakfast.

Thechappan was a tall lean man. In one hand he carried a pot of coffee and in the other, dosas in a plantain leaf. There was a chutney with green chillies and small onions to go along with dosa. So spicy was the chutney that Sivan's eyes began watering when he commenced eating. He took a sip of coffee. It was very hot. His tongue was scalded as if being sliced.

'How is it, is it not spicy enough, sir?' Thechappan asked standing at the door. 'I would always ask her to make it more spicy and sour, but Mary invariably bungles.'

Thechappan did not seem to be making fun of Sivan. So do they normally have even spicier food?

'However, this is sufficient for dosa and *kanji*,' Thechappan continued sneaking a look around. 'But this won't suffice if one is to pour a drink. Oh, I forgot to ask, you have no problem in joining me for a drink once in a while?' Thechappan glanced at him with a smile.

'Of course, lawyers are generally good company. I used to know a few during the time of my case.' He suddenly stopped as if his tongue was on fire.

'I'm bored drinking alone, sir.' He continued after a pause. 'There should be someone to talk to while sipping. But how is it possible here? Who is available here? The workers from the hills come occasionally. Shameless fellows. They want everything for free. How does it benefit us? Will anyone offer eats and drinks without return? That leaves the jungle men living in those huts. Who? The paniyas! But they are unreliable. Not the type we can mingle with. And then there is that dwarf. Do you understand who I'm talking about, sir?'

'Ayyakkuru, no?'

'Yes. A good-for-nothing! He is also a paniya. Achayan brought him up. He is always begging to be thrashed. That is his character. In any case, what is the point in offering a cosy bed to a leech? One who survives on wild tubers and birds in the jungle; how can he be content here?'

'Can he talk?' Sivan asked.

'Will the Lord give horns to the horse, sir? Nay, He cannot talk. That's fortunate. No one could've lived peacefully here, if he had the gift of talking too.'

Thechappan placed two more dosas on Sivan's plate despite his refusal. And some more chilly chutney. Sivan gasped.

Thechappan did not allow Sivan to wash the plates.

'Mary will take care of all that,' he said.

'Who is Mary?' Sivan asked. The name was familiar. Yes, the ferryman Moosa had mentioned it. Ayyakkuru too.

'My woman. Please come to our place once you get free time, sir. You can meet everyone around.' He once again cast a careful glance around and continued, 'Sir, if you agree, I'll keep aside an original brew. We will have a get-together. A rabbit has been trapped. To tell you the truth, Mary is an expert in rabbit dishes. The meat is slightly sweet.'

When Thechappan left with the plates Sivan concluded: either he had reached the wrong place or those traitors had sent him to the enemy camp. In any case, this was a place no revolutionary would want to be seen at, even in his most depraved dreams. Every moment spent here is a waste. Deviation from the destination. Got to escape. But how? Pappayi, Thechappan, Ayyakkuru, Moosa ... all live on the leftovers of Karadi-Papa. It is also possible that Karadi-Papa is keeping a tab on me through these people. All my moves are under surveillance by the innumerable eyes of Karadi-Papa. Challenging it could culminate in my death without seeing the outside world ever again.

Sivan heard the sound of a vehicle disrupting his thoughts. It was a jeep.

A jeep in this island?

The drone of the jeep ceased and Pappayi got out of it.

'Are you ready sir? Let's leave before the sun becomes too hot,' he said in his booming voice.

Sivan got inside the jeep.

The vehicle was passing through an area thick with tall grass. There were no trees there like the surroundings of the mansion or the riverbank. The grass was drying up. The yellowing grass lay exhausted on the jeep track too. There were rising clusters of boulders beyond the grass. They were shining in the sunlight. Sivan was sweating in the roofless jeep as the day became progressively warmer. Pappayi did not seem to notice it.

Then Sivan saw two short men walking ahead tending a flock of sheep. They had dirty reddish rags wrapped around their waists. It was as if a white wave of sheep was leading them. The speed of the jeep decreased considerably as it came close to the herd. The flock was blocking the road. Pappayi sounded the horn.

The dark men turned around and saw the jeep. They tried to manoeuvre the sheep to the sides of the road. In the ensuing chaos, the sheep scattered in different directions. They started bleating loudly. Pappayi was furious and went on blowing the horn continuously. The dark men, with a guilty look on their faces, stood motionless on the flanks and lowered their heads.

'Stupid paniya donkeys!' Pappayi shouted reversing the jeep. After reversing a few metres, he accelerated and shot forward. The sheep dispersed quickly as the jeep came at them menacingly, crushing the dry grass. A couple of them fell down as the side of the jeep brushed past. The sound of the combined bleating of the sheep followed the jeep for a while.

'People who should be burnt alive! It's all because Papa gives them leeway.' Pappayi continued to fume.

Pappayi! Sivan had a sudden feeling that he had met someone like him at one time or the other.

Yes. In the past, prior to arriving on the island, there was a feudal lord, Chathara Menon of Meledathu family at Kangazha. The picture of comrade Sekharan going up the shaky stairs with a lantern in hand in the pitch dark night came to his mind. The light from the lantern struck the eyes of the stuffed animal heads adorning the walls of Meledathu house. Those eyes sucked away the light as if they were black holes, and they left behind darkness. Is the same darkness visible in Pappayi's eyes?

'How was this jeep brought to the island? By boat?' Sivan asked as if to change the topic.

'A jeep cannot be loaded on to the wooden boat, sir. There used to be a bridge across the river in the upper region. It's mountains once you cross the bridge. A road goes through the mountains. Not tarred. We have to drive through boulders. But the bridge is not there anymore. It was lost in the last floods. So the jeep got trapped here. Moosa brings diesel for it in cans.'

'Not building a new bridge?' Sivan looked at him with hope.

'We should get the correct type of wood. That is the issue. But not having a bridge is not much of a problem. The trees from the hills can be towed across the river. As for people, they cross over by ferry.'

Pappayi was slowing down the jeep. 'It is said that there is a tunnel from the upper reaches of the river to the mountain. Some of the elderly paniyas know its location. But those dogs will not reveal it. That is a pity!

Sivan was relieved. So this was not a closed island after all. There were at least secret routes from here to the outside world.

When the schools reopened after the vacation, Sakunthala shifted Sasi to a school near her family home. She had already vacated the rented house they were living in, finding it difficult to stay there alone. There were only a few household articles and furniture to be transported, just enough to fill a small van. The photos which were hung on the walls were the last items to be loaded. They were kept on top of all other things. Their wedding photo too was there among them. Sakunthala felt even that photo had undergone a transformation in the last two months. An indifference, as if she were watching someone else's photograph, enveloped her.

Sasi had not fully recovered. The symptoms continued to occur intermittently. He had lost weight in that short span of time. He could not attend school regularly and when he did, Sasi remained aloof. He did not participate in games. The teacher no more punished him when he made mistakes. He was being given the consideration of being an ailing student. But he was indifferent to that too.

Days passed by, but Sakunthala was not getting any information about Sreenivasan. She had not slackened her search. She had met all those with whom she or he had the least bit of acquaintance. Police stations, offices, houses of political and social workers; no one had any inkling. Yes, we had taken him into custody, the police later on agreed. But he had escaped. Before reaching the camp. This was the version of the police when questions were put to the police through peoples' representatives. There was no reason to disbelieve the police, was the stand taken by the 'leaders.'

'There is logic in what they say. Or why should they admit that he was taken into custody? Are there any eye witnesses? So he has escaped for sure. What for and why he did so is not known. The police are also silent on that aspect. Maybe he was beaten up, tortured. He was after all new to such treatment. Perhaps he was terrified. Or maybe he was feeling sort of ashamed that he was taken away by the police and that is why he is not showing up. It is also possible that the one who was in his house has hidden Sreenivasan somewhere. He will come, that is my guess. Will they dare lie to me especially when I belong to the ruling party? This was the logic behind their approach.

Then who was lying? Sakunthala asked herself. Was it that the person she saw at Chaloorkunnu camp was not her husband? If Sreenivasan had escaped from the clutches of the police why was he not writing to her? Maybe because the police was still after him? If it was risky to send a letter to their address he could write to any of their friends, who would in turn inform her.

At times she was furious with Sreenivasan. Why did he leave her alone? None of this might have occurred had he taken her into confidence. The hide and seek game started from the time she and Sasi were kept out, on the pretext of the playwright. Or had it commenced still earlier? If what comrade Sankaran Adiyodi and Kumaran Nair and the police officer said was correct, he used to write poems in another name. Buddha it seems. Then why did he not tell me? He was the kind of person who became overjoyed over even a line of poetry. He would bring home the copy of his poems published and show it to her even if it was an obscure periodical. He would show a kind of boyish elation over it. But in the end ... Sakunthala could not at all understand why she was kept out. That thought was as inconsolable as his disappearance and was potent enough to push her into a deep anguish.

Yet Sakunthala would go investigating after small leads. The frequent journeys she undertook on this count had made her bolder.

Her present was so different from the days of the past. A vacation had transformed an entire life. Earlier she needed the help of Sreenivasan even for boarding a bus. So she would somehow avoid travelling when he was busy. They had even quarrelled over it. I was a little bird living under a wing, she mused. I was rescued from the kites by the elders. Now I've been pecked out into the big world outside. I became a grownup girl not at the age of thirteen. It is now, after the disappearance of Sreenivasan.

Sakunthala was arranging the furniture and other paraphernalia in her family house when she came across the small notebook in which Sreenivasan used to scribble his poems. He used to carry it along with him almost all the time. On certain mornings he would be jotting down in it as soon as he was up. Though he knew that she would make fun of him, he would say, 'My inner eyes opened Sakunthala, I got four stanzas in the sleep.'

'Oh, is it so? Then let's not cook anything for lunch today.'

'Is poetry a comparison? Is it not more important than cooking rice?'

'No.' Sakunthala would be emphatic. 'Hunger will not subside by reading poetry.'

'It's not like that my dear, you will not feel hungry if you listen to four good stanzas of a poem.' Sreenivasan would try to establish his point by reciting his own poems. 'Now suppose one became hungry. There is enough stuff in poetry to satisfy the hunger of the entire human race.'

'Eh? But this is your poem, no? There is not even a loaf of bread in it, let alone satiating the entire human race!'

He would burst out laughing despite the serious posture he had adopted.

'A time will come Sakunthala, when the words of the poet will be enjoyed as music,' Sreenivasan would continue like chanting a mantra. 'A time when even a buffoon like you will enjoy poetry.'

'Buy me some poison before that.' Sakunthala did not like being called a buffoon. Hearing him call her a buffoon, Sasi too repeated it once. She did not want to be abused like that in front of the child.

'He too will understand the truth at one time or another,' Sreenivasan would laugh again.

This was how they quarrelled. It was not so big an issue that they took twenty four hours to resolve it. Sreenivasan would have written another poem in those twenty four hours. She was in demand as the one-woman audience to hear it being recited. So poetry was also a mediator resolving the quarrels between them.

Sakunthala recalled all this when she stumbled upon the notebook. Most of the poems in it, she had heard him recite. There were many fragments, left for completion later. A few without any title. Or there would be a title and then a blank page. She felt she was hearing the echoes of Sreenivasan's voice. His name was there on most of the pages. His signature that looked like a swan was interspersed on many pages. He would fill the pages with his signature whenever he was unable to write poetry. Though not a famous poet, Sreenivasan was quietly confident of his abilities. Or he would be agitated, in frustration. Sakunthala on the contrary had the feeling that it was somewhere in between that he had to place himself; a poet with moderate skills, even though she did not express it. He would be upset if she said something like that. Moreover, what did she know about poetry? Whatever may have been the objective truth; he believed in the poet in him and was proud of it. He was proud even of his attractive signature, Sakunthala thought.

It was then that she noticed an address scribbled on the last page. It was not in Sreenivasan's handwriting. As if scribbled in haste. He had never mentioned this name, Sakunthala thought. Again gaps in communication, again silences. It is not lies, but silences that rewrite relationships.

It was the address of a person named Chitran—Chitrabhanu Kuroor. The address of the newspaper where he worked and a phone number.

Perhaps this man had something to do with the vanishing of Sreenivasan? Or was it this man who had stayed with him? She decided to find out.

Next day she reached the office of the newspaper Chitran was working for. He was on leave; she was told. Her suspicions snowballed. It is him, it must be him.

'Where does he live?' she asked. 'I have got to meet him.'

'Please be seated,' the girl in the reception told her politely. 'Let me enquire with the desk.'

Sakunthala got into an auto rickshaw to reach the address given to her by the receptionist. Generally she preferred walking. She was not at ease travelling by auto rickshaws when she was alone.

The surroundings of the house where Chitran lived were practically deserted. There were only a few houses around. Two rain trees with thin leaves welcomed her into the compound. The door was closed from inside. It was opened only after repeated knocks and very reluctantly at that, she felt.

A very sallow looking man was at the door. Mistrust and fear reflected in his eyes.

'What is it? What do you want?' he asked like a person who was in a great hurry. Sakunthala could see a swollen wound on his forehead.

'I'm Sreenivasan's wife.' She said. He was apparently startled.

'Which Sreenivasan? I don't know any Sreenivasan,' his voice was wavering. He tried to close the door, but Sakunthala lunged forward and held on to one of the panels. But he persisted with his efforts to close the door and her hand got caught between the frame and the door. It was very painful.

Then he opened the door. There was a red mark on her hand.

'Did it hurt?' he asked in the same quivering voice. 'Come inside, quick ....' He shut the door as soon as she entered. Sakunthala quelled her agitation of being in a closed room with him.

'I came to meet you. Chitran … Chitrabhanu, no?'

'Yes, it is me,' he said, glancing at her with suspicion.

The room was an utter mess. Books and magazines were strewn all over the place. The ashtray was overflowing. Many pairs of sandals and a small bicycle stood in one corner.

'There's no one else here. My daughter and wife have gone home,' Chitran said. His appearance was weird. Unkempt hair, unshaven face, must have been days since he had had a bath. Sakunthala's eyes slowly scanned the room.

'Why have you come here?' he asked.

'I found your address in the notebook. From whom is he running away?'

Chitran seemed to be recollecting. Furrows appeared on his forehead.

'Notebook? I don't know anything,' he said without looking at Sakunthala.

'You can't evade it, so easily.' Sakunthala's voice was firm. She showed him the last page of the notebook she had found, 'Is this not your address?'

He just stood there silently, looking scared.

'Why are you keeping mum? This is my husband's diary, and your address is clearly written. Can you deny it?'

He remained still.

Sakunthala was unkind; he was certainly concealing something.

'Yes, I had written it.'

He brought a chair and placed it near her. He barely had the energy to lift the chair.

'Sreeni wrote in my diary too,' he said in a very low ghost-like voice. 'The police got a clue from that.'

She was quiet. So he must be knowing about the man who had stayed at their house, she thought.

'Look, did anyone see you come here?' Chitran asked. There was fear in that question.

'What if someone had seen me?' She was defiant.

'You shouldn't have come here.'

'You know. Perhaps you are the only one who knows. Where is he? Tell me.' Sakunthala was panting. And he says I shouldn't have come here!

'I don't know. Please believe me. That's all I can tell you now.' Chitran avoided looking at her.

'You are lying …' Sakunthala raised her voice.

'I introduced the comrade to Sreenivasan. And arranged for him to stay there. Beyond that, beyond that … I do not know anything.'

'Whom did you introduce him to?'

'Comrade, the comrade … who was linked to the Kangazha issue …' he hesitated before mentioning the name of the comrade.

Sakunthala had never heard that name. However, there was every chance that he was the one. She could guess certain things from the unfinished sentences and the sudden intervals in conversations of some of those she had met. Many things fitted in. A measure of clarity was emerging. What was the real nature of Sreenivasan's connection with those people?

Sometime ago, she could not have imagined Sreenivasan getting to know a person of this kind. But now it was not so. Sreenivasan could get into relationships with any kind of people. He could intervene in any type of events. He could write poems in false names. Everything was possible. That was a part of his life of which she had no idea. A room in his life where she was denied access. A dark quarter.

'Forgive me. It was only for your good that I said you should not have come here. Please pardon me.' Chitran pleaded. 'But … anyone would come. However, the truth is that I've not seen Sreeni after that day. Please trust me.'

'But I had seen him.' she told him about her visit to the Chaloorkunnu camp and the momentary glimpse she had of him.

It was the day after her coming to Avalam town, in search of Sreenivasan. Sakunthala had gone there from the editor's house. The editor had left early morning with the excuse that he had to attend a meeting of editors.

His wife was ready to accompany her, but Sakunthala declined the offer. Why bother others was her thinking. What certainty was there that Sreenivasan had been there in the camp? Moreover, she guessed that the editor would not like his wife accompanying her on such missions. She took Sasi along with her so that he did not become a burden to them.

Buses did not go all the way and she had to walk two kilometres after getting off the bus.

A long building across an unending open space; that was the camp. It had an asbestos roof. There lay a huge rusty machine resembling the fossil of a prehistoric animal, inside the building. Nothing else. A mysterious and frightening silence enveloped the entire area. She found the building and the surroundings scalding in the April heat. There were many jeeps parked helter-skelter. Sakunthala could feel the eyes of the police guards devouring her body. Each lingering look was like rubbing disgusting filth on her body.

Most of them threw up their hands. We do not know. Who told you that your husband was brought here? What for should we have taken him into custody? Only those who are under strong suspicion are brought here. They are not allowed any visitors. And if indeed your husband is in here, it is your fault too. Because is it not the responsibility of the woman of the house to see that her man does not go astray? The times are different now. No one should be under the impression that they can go about scot-free after committing notorious crimes. And most important of all, you, a woman, why did you come here?

'Look here girl, times have changed. Don't poke your nose into unnecessary issues, that's my advice,' said an elderly policeman. 'Anyway, no one is keeping your husband here.'

'If you are not convinced, go and ask the boss,' said another. He then went to the room of the officer to report the visitor. He might have felt it potentially dangerous for a woman to hang around there.

That was how Sakunthala reached the police officer's room. He was a rather short man. The officer was in civilian dress wearing dark glasses. He signalled with his hand that she take a seat.

She did not sit down.

'I don't like anyone standing in front of me for no reason. Sit down.'

Sakunthala sat down reluctantly.

'Right. What's your name?' the voice was heavy.

'Sakunthala.' She was scared.

'Sakunthala … Oh, it seems all Sakunthalas are fated into searches of one kind or the other, no?' he was smiling.

'It is good that Sakunthala has come here. You can help us. We too are in search of your husband.'

He continued after a pause. 'Not for nothing. It's for asking him details, you know, for interrogation. Do you have any idea as to what all he has done?'

Sakunthala looked at him in bewilderment. He offered a crystal paperweight to Sasi. He did not accept it.

'Accommodating *wanted* criminals in his home. Writing poems for them! Okay, have you read his poems?'

She did not speak. Is it that she had never really understood them, even if she had read them?

'No chance. Because he had used another name while writing such poems.' She could feel the scorn in his words.

Sakunthala was pained. Poems in another name? Why? So, had Sreenivasan been hiding many things from her? What for? She was not aware of her eyes moistening.

The officer waved a couple of magazines at her face and continued. 'We'll certainly have a few questions for him if we succeed in getting him. About these poems and the reasons for writing them …'

The officer again questioned her to find out whether she had any knowledge of such activities. He was quite gentle in his approach. But those dark glasses … What was it that they were hiding from me?

Unusually for him, Sasi was silent while getting out of the office. She kissed him tenderly. Sakunthala noticed that the child did not wipe away the tears from his cheeks.

Where to now? She lost her way and walked in the opposite direction reaching the rear of the long building. It was the junction of several sewages. There was a rotten smell all around.

It was there that Sakunthala saw Sreenivasan most unexpectedly. She had no doubt. It certainly was Sreenivasan. She could see him for only a moment. Body full of dirt and mud, unkempt hair, red blood coated lesions ... He was wearing only a soiled underwear. There was a rusty chain around his legs. His hands were crossed together and handcuffed. Sunken eyes from which all the glow had been drained. She was shocked by the pitiable sight of her husband standing like a trapped animal. She felt blackness descending on her.

When she regained consciousness, Sakunthala found herself sitting on the ground in the midst of four or five policemen. Sasi was crying, 'Amma, Amma.'

But her mind was still with the vision of Sreenivasan she had, just before she had collapsed. She could never put out of her mind the pathetic look ever after.

'That was Sreenivasan.' Sakunthala said returning to the present. 'Who else but me, his wife, can say that, so emphatically?'

'What you saw must have been the truth,' Chitran said softly. Sakunthala was relieved to find one person who trusted her words. At least he was not trashing it. She sat down on the chair he had brought for her.

Sakunthala looked up at him.

'Very often there are policemen in disguise, around this house. Even as it is ...' he hesitated, 'police would know anyone who comes here. That is why I had said that you should not have come here.' He spoke in very low tones. His hands were trembling like the tender branches of trees caught in a breeze, Sakunthala noticed.

He paused for a moment anxious about some commotion outside.

'It's true that the police saw the address Sreeni had written in my diary.'

'But how did they come to know that such an address was there in your diary?' Sakunthala asked.

Chitran bowed his head. He resembled a little sparrow drenched in the rain.

'Were you also taken to the camp?' Sakunthala asked, breaking the silence which had reigned for a while.

'To the camp? I don't know. I was blindfolded. They had put me in a dark room.'

'Did they torture you?'

'Yes, a little.' He softly touched the wound on his forehead. Blood was oozing as if from a pin prick, even now.

After pondering over something for a while, he displayed his knees and thighs to her. He had lost the shame of his body. Sakunthala saw scars and blisters all over his body like in burnt pictures.

'I managed to resist for quite some time. But then I couldn't withstand anymore.' He stopped for breath.

'They did not beat me anymore. Instead they tied me to a table and beat up others in front of me.'

'Sreenivasan too?'

'I don't know. I was taken away much before that.' He again bowed his head. 'They let me go after two days.'

He was silent for a while. His eyes were brimming.

'My last meeting with Sreeni was after that. I called him and he came. I then asked him to accommodate the comrade in your house.'

Sakunthala looked straight at his face. He was unable to meet her eyes. He bowed his head.

'The body was my problem. This damned body of mine!' Chitran continued looking at his wounds as if they were perilous creatures. 'Pain ... the fear of pain. We all become the slaves of the body at some point in life. Now I have a feeling of extreme hatred towards my body.'

The shadow-like image of Sreenivasan projected itself in Sakunthala's mind, then. A slice of a sob blocked her throat.

'I came out admitting everything and praying for clemency in writing. Otherwise they wouldn't have freed me.'

Sakunthala stole a glance at Chitran. He was crying.

'I had a longing for life. My small address as a journalist, an income, a family, little pleasures ...' He stopped in the middle. Sakunthala bowed her head to avoid seeing him cry.

'But beyond all that the trepidations of my body, the dread of pain ... that scorched me. Then the doubts ... Initially I did not believe the policemen. But sitting in solitude and thinking ... and thinking about it, I felt that what they were saying could be true as well.'

She did not quite understand what he was leading up to.

'Me and Sreeni and many others like us; for whom were we taken into custody? Were they really playing us like puppets? Who should have trust in whom? The police say that everyone is their man. What does it mean?'

Even now she was not able to make much out of his ramblings.

'To tell you the truth, I do not know what to believe, what not to believe. I'm even losing the sense of my individuality.'

Where is he leading to, Sakunthala tried to guess. About whom is he speaking?

'You should not feel bad,' Chitran looked at her and said in low tones. 'According to the police, many of those whom you see are their agents.'

'Sreenivasan too?' Sakunthala asked.

'I wanted to believe that. When undergoing the torments of a hideous hell, who can remain exempt from it?'

She shot up from the chair as if seized by the devil and rushed at him. She grabbed the collar of his soiled shirt and shouted, 'Has Sreenivasan become one of them? Is he living somewhere as a collaborator?' Chitran did not respond immediately. She could see the shadow of helplessness in his eyes. Tears had made them turbid.

Still she sensed that her life was hanging on the answer to that question. She did not want anything, but Sreenivasan being a traitor was something she could never live with.

'Perhaps it was not about Sreeni ...' Chitran mumbled. 'Had it been so, he would have come out, no? The truth is that I've not seen him after that day's meeting.'

'Where should I look for him now?' Sakunthala asked, deeply disappointed.

'I don't know. Maybe ...' he did not complete.

'Maybe...?' Sakunthala looked up.

'I don't know ... perhaps you are looking for him in the wrong places.' Chitran bowed his head. 'Please go now. What if someone comes here seeing you?'

'What could happen if someone came here?'

'It is dangerous. I'll have to inform them about you, no?'

'I don't bother.'

'But I do.' He spoke curling up like a reptile. 'I'm scared. My body is choking me.'

THE PATH OF LIBERATION

A *cassia* tree:
Like the Sun
Shattered by
The Spring's arrows

(*Poem written by Sreenivasan in the second issue of the magazine* Liberation Path)

The birth of *Liberation Path* was in the form of a manuscript magazine. The cover picture drawn using charcoal and ink reminded one of Picasso's *Guernica*.

The magazine was pioneered by some students who habitually tried their hand at writing poems. The idea of such a magazine was the result of the few rejections they had. Poems which were well received in poets' meet and friends' circles were being regularly returned with regret slips by mainstream periodicals. Most of the poems were not bound by the rules of meter or rhyme. And they appeared to be the translations from foreign languages in their tone and tenor. However, there were reverberations of certain ideas and ideals in them which could be said to be nascent. And that was reason enough for them to become popular among the youth. They were also constantly reminded that the poems appearing in the mainstream had become hopelessly outdated.

There was a poem titled 'Liberation Path' in the manuscript magazine. After discussions, it was chosen to be the title of the magazine. As on the cover, colours were not splashed in the inner pages too. That was the best way to portray the colourless and bland state of the contemporary times, was the argument of the students who had designed the magazine. Six poems including 'Liberation Path' were displayed on the first pages. All of them were popular in the college campuses through poets' meet and sight and sound shows. Chitrabhanu wrote a story, 'The Corpse' under a pen name, Chitran Kuroor. It was a fairly long story and was the first-and-also-the-last creative effort of Chitran. He had left college by then, having completed his studies. He had just started as a journalist working on the desk of a mainstream newspaper and had a decent income. The student comrades used to approach him for their financial needs. Chitran was living with his family in a small rented house near the campus during those days.

An unidentified dead body was the theme of 'The Corpse.' It was quite evident that the accused in the story was an infamous but powerful political leader with his cohorts in the police force. This story was discussed in later years more for its linguistic and stylistic innovations rather than its political connotations. Broken sentence structures, certain interjections for depicting the conversation of the deaf-mutes … these were also loaded with ridicule and double entendre. Apart from short stories and poems there were also translations of certain famous essays. Because of the complexity of the ideas dealt with and the incomprehensible nature of the language, it was doubtful whether anyone had read them with serious interest. However, the extremist nature of the treatises was quite evident.

One month after the magazine was published Sivan met with Chitran on the request of the local party unit. It was a cool January evening. Chitran was in front of teleprinters collecting news dispatched by agencies. He never imagined it was Sivan when he was informed that there was a visitor for him. In fact, he was a little agitated when he knew it was Sivan. While talking to Sivan, he was also keeping a watchful eye around to see whether any of his colleagues were noticing them.

'Chitran Kuroor, no? I'm Pavithran. I had read your story in the manuscript magazine.' Sivan said introducing himself in the assumed name he was known in the party circles. But that was not really necessary. Chitrabhanu had known Sivan much earlier. He was among the audience in a couple of meetings Sivan had addressed. But Chitran chose not to talk about it.

Seemingly Sivan had reached there at the end of a long journey. His dress was dirty and eyes weary. The crop of hair was overgrown and it must have been days since he had shaved. A bag was hanging from his shoulder.

'I know,' Chitran said in a low voice. He turned around instinctively to see if anyone else had heard him.

'I wanted to meet you in person,' said Sivan looking deep into his eyes.

Had Sivan come to talk about the story? Chitrabhanu could not believe it. His was a name that never cropped up in any literary discussions. None of his stories were ever published before this. He was unsure about even the story published in the manuscript magazine. Moreover, Sivan had never been seen in the company of those who write or read poems or stories.

'Do you have plans to carry on with the manuscript magazine?' Sivan asked after a brief spell of silence.

'I'm not the one behind it.'

'I know. But it is people like you who should be in it. The enthusiasm of students may not last. They might abandon it after it cools off. The comrades have an idea that the magazine should be brought out in the best possible manner.'

He took out few bundles of papers from his shabby bag. The closely written letters in them were like black ants moving in rows.

'These are articles collected when a discussion came up some time ago. But it did not click. It may work out now. More so if people like you cooperate.'

Chitran promised all possible assistance from his side. But the decision would be that of the college students. They were the ones who selected the stories and poems, did the illustrations and the calligraphy.

'The decision is to reduce the quantum of literature,' Sivan said putting the paper bundles back into the bag.

The party had not taken over the magazine, the discussion had just commenced. But the content had already been decided! Chitran was surprised.

'We are thinking of printing it. Initially in a smaller size. A matter of fact publication avoiding pictures and drawings on the cover,' Sivan explained. 'What do you think?'

I'm not the person to answer this question, was the thought in Chitran's mind. But he kept quiet.

'Comrade, please discuss this with the students. I'll get in touch with you to find out the outcome.'

'Will the students be in charge of the magazine?'

'That's not the way it is planned. Please look at it as a joint venture. You can collect whatever materials are available with them. Of course, also what you write. As I told you, literature ... not much. More things, much more serious are waiting to be published. You know, there is no paucity of matter. Printing is the issue. These days it is difficult to get even pamphlets printed. Everyone tries to evade saying they are too busy. Oh, I forgot to ask. You must be having connections with those who run printing presses. Do you know any printer who can take up our work?'

It was this enquiry that took Chitrabhanu to Lasar.

There was this man known as *Kambanam* Lasar at Avalam.

Till a few years ago he was publishing a porn magazine called *Kambanam*, which meant 'porn' in local parlance, and that was how he acquired that name. He had become the last word for the sexual dreams of the youth. This magazine which was clandestinely sold even in small shops had become very popular in the schools and colleges at subterranean levels. A question answer column which was handled directly by Lasar openly challenged the moral pretensions of the society.

There was a distinct pattern for the stories that appeared in *Kambanam*. Different from other similar publications, most of the stories were written based on what appeared to be true incidents. There were many who bought the magazine only for the sake of the semi-nude pictures of women in the centre spread pages. Once upon a time, *Kambanam* was a title that heated young blood. And they eagerly waited for the new issues.

Lasar was the all in all of that publication. In his early days, Lasar was involved with the stage, writing and directing plays. However, he was a total failure in that field. It was then that he came up with *Kambanam* for sheer survival. The experience of working at a printing press for a year came to his aid. Lasar bought an old press. Except for seeking the help of a few writers once in a while, the entire work of the magazine—deciding the matter, writing, setting types, proofreading, why even binding the copies and distributing them—was done by him. The truth was, he enjoyed doing all that. The reason for his defying all the threats that came his way as hazards of the line he had chosen, was the pleasure he derived from it. Of course, it made money. But it was the thrill in the profession that fascinated him. The life of the rich and famous behind closed doors, the promises they made for survival, the leaked news received from those who were supposed to be most loyal and faithful ... Lasar was once the doyen of pornography.

The spy journalists in *Kambanam* scooped up the secret and on-the-sly relationships of those in the top echelons of power. That was the Lasar trademark. There would only be bits and pieces of such stories in the first issue. It was possible that Lasar's agents had only that much of information on the victim. But then the rivals of the targeted hero of the story would provide Lasar access to the rest of the juicy stuff. On the other hand, Lasar would publish only that much of the story even if he had all the details of the episode in his possession. It was a strategy, because then the henchmen of the top man would approach Lasar. Thus the bargaining would begin. Lasar would swear that he was abandoning the rest of the story after extracting maximum possible money from the victim. But he would not return any documents he may be holding. However, it was a gentleman's agreement. The other side had no alternative other than agreeing. And Lasar would not budge whatever carrots were offered. Lasar had absolutely no compunction in such serials coming to an abrupt end. *Kambanam* would simply proceed to unravel another life and that was it.

He was now around sixty. He had married thrice and the nude pictures of all three of his wives were published in the *magazine* during the corresponding periods. There were rumour mongers who held the view that he married precisely for that. Whatever be the truth, all three of them walked out on him. Lasar and his magazine faded in course of time. The new generation hardly knew him.

It was an oversight by Lasar that led to the downfall of *Kambanam.* He published the photograph of a half naked woman sleeping with a powerful politician. The picture was taken at the government guest house in the city, with the connivance of an employee there. The woman turned out to be the politician's wife. Lasar's accomplice lost his job the day the magazine came out on the newsstands. He was nabbed by the police, badly beaten up and kept in custody without granting bail. This guy went to meet Lasar the day after he got bail. He was dead drunk. It ended up in a gruesome quarrel and Lasar stabbed him with a paper knife.

The police had been on Lasar's trail for quite some time. This turned out to be a golden opportunity for them. He was out there only because those in the high echelons of power were scared of his blackmailing prowess. But now he was nabbed for attempted murder. Everyone saw to it that he did not get bail. Police burnt all available copies of the magazine. The printing press was locked up and sealed. An era of longing and lust was reaching an unusual end.

By the time Lasar was out of jail, the generation which had got sexually excited reading the *Kambanam* stories had passed their youth. The charm and seductiveness of the sex bombs who had reigned on the centrespreads of his magazine had faded. No one waited with bated breath for their nude pictures. There was no one left to listen to his *agony-uncle* counselling, challenging the phony morality of society. Rust had taken over the machinery in the press.

However, Lasar was not familiar with any other work. Lasar went about raising small loans from friends and managed to buy a letter press. That was a very old model. Magazines or books of standard size could not be printed in it. He turned into someone printing 'death intimations.' *Kambanam* Lasar thus became *Maranam* Lasar, loosely translated as *Death* Lasar. His life too had changed. He had become an addict of *ganja* while in jail. But it was not easily accessible outside and so he shifted to liquor. He couldn't stop once he started drinking and inevitably landed up in his own urine and vomit.

Liberation Path was redesigned so as to be printed in the letter press of Lasar. Lasar's drink-drained fingers trembled as he picked up and placed the types for the articles of which he did not understand a word and the few poems that were there as part of the content. The work had such an urgency that it had to be finished as soon as possible for him to buy liquor for the day. While thus engaged he would invariably recall the olden days. How nimble his fingers were when fixing the types for the *agony uncle's* question answer column! He would experience the ecstasy of an orgasm while picking up the types for stories which contained the descriptions of the secret parts of the woman's body. Now there was nothing. He was working only for the bootlegged arrack. There were several arrack rivers flowing through his veins.

Most of the contents of the first printed issue of *Liberation Path* comprised articles and essays. Majority of them were procured by Sivan. Chitran even felt that it was all by Sivan writing under different names. The style was so alike. Chitrabhanu too unknowingly acquired that contagious style, when he translated an English essay, a job assigned to him by Sivan. There were six or seven essays in thirty six pages. Two poems and the story by Chitran Kuroor were retained in the printed version. Literature was included due to the pressure exerted by the students. However, the poems were shifted to the back inside cover.

'Has not attained the quality of the manuscript magazine,' the student comrades commented. Sivan smiled. They were assembled in an old house in front of the college. The five hundred copies that were brought from Lasar's press in a push cart were stacked in small bundles in a corner of the room.

'There should be more poems. We'd also suggest that comrade Chitran should write another short story for the next issue,' the students insisted.

'Poems and stories are mere imagination, no?' Sivan argued. 'Dreaming alone will not suffice.'

'Sleeping and dreaming. What else have you been doing here? Some write poems. You fill pages with essays, no one comprehends. Both are one and the same, comrade,' said a comrade who seemed older than the others present there. He turned out to be a comrade named Sekharan who was behind the bars for a few years for his involvement in the Thelakkara police station attack. He held the firm opinion that time should not be wasted on articles and magazines.

'Then let's go and bomb the places,' one of those present made fun of him.

'Why not? That is exactly what is required. Actions of such gravity should be undertaken if anything is to work.'

'Revolutionary attempts without a solid theoretical base, is immature. Your past, comrade, is its greatest proof,' Sivan explained.

'The fruit is ripe. It will rot, if you wait. Theorising without action is mere talk,' Sekharan retorted.

In the next days the discussions became debates. As a result, the point of view that action should be given priority, was recognised as the unanimous decision. The article written by Sivan and published in the next issue of *Liberation Path* in the name of Pavithran was an ill concealed call for action.

It was for the first time he was using that name in print. That was how the second edition of *Liberation Path* found a place in history.

The two poems published in that issue were that of Sreenivasan. They were the first poems—perhaps the last too—written by Sreenivasan in a style altogether different from his usual mode. Sreenivasan, for the first time used a pen name, 'Buddha' for those poems which were untitled.

One of them was a very small poem. Could perhaps be called a single liner.

A cassia tree:
Like the Sun
Shattered by
The Spring's arrows

Chitrabhanu had not liked that poem. But he included it, knowing that Sreenivasan had an attachment to it.

This was only a few weeks before the Kangazha action took place. There was a veil of secrecy around the release of both the issues of *Liberation Path*. But no one seemed to attribute much significance to it. Even Lasar thought of it as nothing more than a long 'death notice.' But an inscription: 'Fifth anniversary of Thelakkara action; brave comrades zindabad!' on the back cover of the second issue, below the poem by Sreenivasan, invited trouble. The insistence of comrade Sekharan was the reason behind its appearance in the magazine, with prominence. The police was suddenly interested and they started scourging for copies of the magazine. People started whispering that there was something dangerous, wrapped in mystery, in the magazine. With that there was a great demand for its copies that had hitherto gone unnoticed.

In college hostels, in town and village libraries, in the godowns of newspaper distributors, the police spread their tentacles. They managed to confiscate almost all the copies within a matter of few days. They had the same set of questions to ask at every joint they raided: who was behind this publication? Who were those who wrote for it? And more important: who printed it?

The police scanned and filtered every nook and corner of Avalam town. The leads they received finally led them to the rustic letter press of *Kambanam* Lasar.

The shutter was down when the police jeep arrived. Since there was no response to knocking and calling out for opening the shutter, they forced open the back door and entered the press. *Kambanam* Lasar was lying on the floor in a drunken stupor. His *mundu* had slipped off his waist, ants were making a beeline for the vomit on the floor. He was ghostly thin and one could count the bones on his skinny body. A cross hung from a black thread was adorning his neck. Newsprint was spread all over the place. And there were copies of *Liberation Path* among the scrap.

Lifting Lasar up, a constable slapped him on his cheek, the police way of waking up a drunk. Lasar was in a tizzy. He spun like a wooden doll. Then his eyes opened and he looked around. He was as weak as the crucifix hanging from his neck.

'What is this?' the policemen asked.

'What is what?' Lasar was genuinely baffled.

'Open your bloody eyes, you wretch! Don't think you can escape like you used to with the porn books.'

'Oh, those books! I had stopped all that long ago, sir. There is no market now for porn. Now 'death-notice' is Lasar's brand. You just wait sir. When any of you die, I promise, I'll print the death notice free.' Lasar spoke with total detachment, without looking at any of them.

No sooner had he finished talking, the policeman slapped him on the other cheek. Lasar spun in the opposite direction.

'What is all this, you have printed?' one of them waved a copy of *Liberation Path* at him.

'Can't you read sir?' he was slipping back into slumber. He had not yet bothered to see which book the policemen were referring to.

'Notice of your mother's wedding, rascal! Who entrusted this work to you, you pig?' one more slap.

Lasar fell down. Blood was trickling from his face. Twilight had crept into the room. He fumbled, but got up and said in a firm voice without showing any trace of the pain inflicted on him, 'You assholes, this is my profession. I'll print again if I get money. Tell me what other way to make some money you rascals? You too grew up reading *Kambanam* and drooling, no? You shut it down by force. I print because there is demand. It is them you should nab, if you are so intent on it,' he continued spitting on to the ground. 'I've to drink and eat. Your bitch wives will come and serve me all that?'

He fell down flat on the ground on getting a fierce kick right across his face.

His head had struck an iron piston of the press while he came down. Blood gushed out. Next moment he was hissing menacingly, waving an iron rod at them.

'You sons of a whore, I will kill you and tear you up. I'm not afraid of death. There's not a single unbroken bone in my body because of your pounding.'

The policemen withdrew a little. But they were able to overpower him sooner than later. Drunkenness and the draining blood had weakened him. He spent the whole night in the lockup with the blood oozing from the gash on the head. He was in a stupor till about midnight. Awake, he started moaning like a bitch. Two policemen whose sleep was disturbed, entered the lockup and beat him up. Lasar regained consciousness late next morning. His head had cleared by then. But he did not seem to remember anything about the previous night.

The police let him out in the afternoon. His forehead was bandaged. Couple of aged policemen who had come for duty in the morning recognised him. They bought him lunch before he left the station, which he ate with consummate satisfaction.

The police were apprehensive that detaining him at the station could prove risky. Moreover, Lasar could be used now. He gave them his word that he'd inform them if anyone connected to the *Liberation Path* contacted him. He was sincere in his promise. He was furious at them for getting printed something that was potentially dangerous concealing the risk involved from him.

The police commenced investigation on the basis of the information furnished by Lasar about the *Liberation Path* and the young man who had brought the matter for it to him. Lasar did not know Chitran Kuroor by that name. The police transmitted messages containing the available details to all the stations. It took them a few weeks to reach Chitran who was working in a prominent daily of the town. It was a big surprise for all. That newspaper was one which often extolled the present government and its leaders.

Liberation Path lapsed after the two issues. Many of those who were involved with it destroyed the poems and articles they had collected for future issues. It seemed that the small ripples it had created for a while had subsided.

But exactly twenty days after the second issue of *Liberation Path* had come out, an earthquake like event shattered that notion. Later on, it came to be known as the Kangazha episode.

adjusting his mask. They started climbing up the stairs with Sekharan leading and a youth with a lantern making up the rear. After a few steps, the young man stumbled and the lantern came tumbling down the steps. The flame flared up and rose. In the flared light, the stuffed heads of dead wild animals fixed on the wall could be seen. Tiger, fox, wolf and bear stared at them with lifeless eyes. The horns of a bison jutted out of the wall like the teeth of darkness. The faces of the henchmen of Chathara Menon had become pale. Drained of blood. The tip of the knife in the hands of Sekharan, now standing on the top of the stairs, shone like a bolt of lightning.

One of them covered the flaring lantern with a soaked gunny bag. The men and the animal heads dissolved into darkness.

Rushing footsteps were heard from the staircase. More men were going up.

Then there was a cry that pierced through the night. It was bizarre and ferocious like the roar of one of the stuffed wild animals adorning the wall of Meledathu *tharavadu*. It lasted for one long moment.

A clap of thunder boomed violently. The old walls and the rough floor trembled in its vibration. All sounds had died down along with light by the time the rumbling of the thunder subsided.

Next morning, the terror-stricken people of the neighbourhood saw a blood-drained human head struck on one of the rusty iron rods of the gate of Meledathu *tharavadu*, the rain soaked grey hair plastered on its forehead. Mouth slightly open, large sized ears with ear rings, eyes from which sleep had been cut off: it was gazing at the villagers with a weird look.

That was the first and last annihilation executed by the comrades of Avalam. The famous Kangazha action. Ten comrades participated in it including those who stood guard.

The killing of the feudal lord was a decision arrived at in a handful of days. Kangazha Meledathu Chathara Menon was identified as the target after many rounds of discussions. Four kilometres from Avalam town, Kangazha was a small village to the north. The feudal lord there

'Keep away you rascals. Bomb, this is a bomb! This is enough to turn you into ashes,' shouted comrade Sekharan displaying a ball made out of cut pieces from a tailoring shop.

Kangazha Meledathu Chathara Menon's minions were shocked for a moment. None of them had seen a bomb in their lifetime. Their advancing legs remained suspended in the air.

The women of the house started wailing. Children woke up and they too joined in.

A comrade who was a porter in the Avalam market, marched the women and children into a room. He shut the door from outside after forcing them to give up whatever ornaments they were wearing. The lamentations became feeble.

They were on a veranda in front of the main building. Walls had not been whitewashed for ages, and the ceiling was thick with dust. Ancient chairs tilting up and down with the souls of the long dead ancestors. The smell of aging was everywhere. It started to rain, with the boom of clouds smashing at the boundaries of the sky.

'Where is your boss? We want him to answer some questions,' one of them growled. No one answered.

'Comrade PKP, why don't we fry them up?' Sekharan once again raised the ball of cloth.

The tough minions of Chathara Menon howled shamelessly.

'Leave it. They are nothing more than scum feeding on his crumbs. We want Chathara in flesh. You go upstairs,' comrade PKP advised, was bestowed with the authority to collect tax from the common people till recently.

Chathara Menon was not actually the landlord, but his younger brother. As per inheritance norms, his brother Komappa Menon was the lord. But Komappa Menon had become insane. Lunacy was a traditional malady in the Meledathu family. One could hear Kathakali songs, even at noontime from the house. The comrades had indeed heard the tunes when they had made a reconnaissance a few days before.

Komappa Menon was singing and dancing to the lyrics.

Pathasam nichayam vaarnnozhinjalavu

Sethubandhnodyogamendado?

It was 'Nalacharitham.' The workers in the compound seemed unconcerned, probably because it was a common feature.

Thus it was the younger brother who was in charge of Kangazha. Chathara Menon had an uninhibited run in a seat of power which was not really his. He would spend the day drinking and playing cards. There would always be five or six tough guys around him as his henchmen. Chathara Menon forced the young women workers to have sex with him. Young girls who had not reached adulthood were his weakness. The number of dark complexioned kids with Chathara Menon's facial features multiplied in Thelakkara.

It was in fact sunset time for the Meledathu family when the Kangazha action took place. They had already forfeited considerable extent of land and farmlands following the land reforms. They were also selling off land because of the insane condition of Komappa Menon and the prodigality of Chathara. To add to all these, the family had to surrender a large tract of land to the temple authorities after losing a law suit. As if all this was not enough, one of the branches of the large family had separated from the main family after securing their share of the assets. Thus, the Kangazha action was organised when the assets, stature and might of the Meledathu family was on the wane.

There were comrades in the party who held the view that there was no point in a rebellion against a power centre whose glory was only a story of yesteryears. 'Meledathu Chathara Menon? He will himself bring ruin to his family. The feudalism in Kangazha will end on its own. Need we take all this trouble for it?' this was the opinion of a few of the comrades of Kangazha. But action was the key to the survival of the organisation. Theory, speeches, discussions; the party could not be kept active and radical only by these. Most of the young men in the party had flocked to it because the revolutionary organisations in which they were, had lacked the desired radicalism. Those extremists were adamant that some drastic steps had to be taken. What and how was immaterial, something had to be done without losing time.

It was the fifth anniversary of the Thelakkara revolt. The event was a police station attack by a group of workers at Thelakkara, near Kangazha. The wireless communication system of the station was destroyed and a policeman's hand was hacked. Comrade Sekharan had participated in that 'action.' Those from Thelakkara had towed a different ideological line from that of the present party. However, the comrades of the new generation were ardent admirers of the revolt and its protagonists like comrade Kuttappu Ezhuthachan, Ayyappakkutty and Chandikkunju. All three of these frontline leaders were no more. Almost all the others who had participated in the police station attack had been released from prison.

Posters and handbills came out in Avalam and surrounding villages commemorating the revolt.

Thelakkara revolt zindabad!

Brave comrades Kuttappu Ezhuthachan, Ayyappakkutty, Chandikkunju zindabad!

Victory to Revolution!

Their path, Our path!

Whose path? Is killing policemen who are mere mercenaries, revolution? Sivan had a tough time convincing them that those slogans were incorrect and that the party line followed by the Thelakkara comrades had become obsolete. As long as the establishment remains a puppet in the hands of the feudal lords, there was no point in attacking the police, which is only a tool in the hands of the establishment. The party could as well plunge into encounters with feudalism directly. Sivan decided to write an article elaborating this stand in the next issue of the magazine.

'Are you suggesting that what the comrades of Thelakkara did was absolute stupidity?' one among the ranks raised a question.

'I'd say that it was their hazy ideology.'

'But they did do something. And what is the point in people like you with absolute clarity, big mouthing lectures and speeches?'

Sivan went into a conference with the frontline leaders. 'Indiscriminate action is not advisable,' they said. 'Care should be taken that the rank and file don't get enticed by wrong policies. However something has to be done urgently.'

Discussions to that end took place in the next few days. There were two class enemies in the line of fire. In fact, Chathara Menon came into the shortlist at a later date. Initially there were only 'Gold Cheeran' the pawn broker and leading usurer in Thelakkara and Chinakkal Narayanan Nair, the former manager of Meledathu family and the present MLA in the shortlist. Both of them were class enemies, exploiters of the people. But they could not be labelled as feudal lords in the full sense of the term. The first phase of revolution had to be the revolt against feudalism. If so who was the feudalist? What were the features of feudalism? It was during the search for the real feudalist that the name of Kangazha Meledathu Chathara Menon cropped up.

The immediate provocation for that was the beating up of Odiyan Thami. It was the story of revenge, which went back in time.

Thami and his ancestors had been traditional workers of Meledathu family. It was said of Thami that he was involved in sacrificial offerings as well as necromancy. He'd do black magic for you if you fetched him toddy and fowl. He was also a devotee of Chathan, a goblins' god. And *Odi*, a clandestine black magic where the practitioner transforms into an animal form in order to kill the enemy was something he inherited. Thami was living in a valley that was under the suzerainty of the

Meledathu *tharavadu*. His job was to rear the bullocks and buffaloes of Meledathu. His wife and daughter too were working for the landlord. Thami would plough the farmland, sow paddy, carry huge bags of rice from the barnyard to the market. It was a sight to see him ploughing the field. The muscles of his arms would dance like antelopes. Mild beads of sweat would be gathering on his forehead. The women planting saplings in the neighbouring farm would be stealing glances at him. But Thami would carry on unmindful of this. He would work from dawn to dusk like yet another buffalo. A boor, who did not have any notion of his own strength.

But he was a transformed being by nightfall, the public knew. The scary nights, when he would be in control of the wandering souls and the blood loving vampires. He punished the souls which strove to liberate themselves from his clutches. He reigned like the emperor of the night, clad in red silk, sketching mystic sacrificial columns in red. Young children would wake up startled by the blood-curdling cries from his nocturnal dances.

However, the rising dawn would distil out his vigour. He transformed back into the same Thami, who knew nothing other than to slog like an animal.

Chathara Menon happened to notice Thami's daughter one of those days. She was about sixteen. He found her quite to his liking. She looked a fulsome woman even at that young age. Tall and comely, hair, thick and long like a string of palm fruits. Heavy, nubile breasts. Anyone would spare her a second glance. Chathara Menon and his henchmen thereafter became regular features on the farmland.

One afternoon, Kochupennu, Thami's daughter, returned alone to her hut. She had stomach ache and lay down huddled on a mat. Chathara Menon's minions followed her to the hut and Menon came to know from them that she was all alone. He rushed there.

'What happened Kochupennu, you here at this time of day? Do you have the habit of a daily siesta?' Chathara Menon asked with feigned intimacy. Kochupennu did not answer him.

'Won't you talk to me?' Menon's amorous chat continued. 'You have become a big girl, you know Kochupennu!'

He continued mouthing inanities. She was scared and got up from the mat. She was trembling and dumbfounded. Her normal practice was to take a diversion and avoid him if the landlord happened to cross her way.

'I'll give you a present,' Chathara Menon chortled. She stood still bowing her head.

Menon came closer and touched her on her shoulder. She stepped back. Scared women always excited him. He closed in on her passionately. When she tried to evade him, he wrapped his arm around her midriff. He loosened her *mundu*.

Blood stained his fingers.

'Oh, periods, Kochupennu?' he stared at the blood on his fingers and was upset. 'So I was correct. You really have become a big girl. We should have a get together when your periods are over,' Chathara Menon said, patting her cheeks.

Thami barged into the hut quite unexpectedly. Thami saw the blood stains on the fingers of the landlord. He stared at Menon, stunned.

Thami who should have shrivelled and bent over with the burden of respect in the presence of the lord was glaring at him! There was a kind of inscrutability in his eyes. The bloodshot eyes of an *odiyan!* The red sacrificial altar in them! A red silk rag was hanging behind him.

Enraged, and perhaps scared, Menon decided to withdraw from the scene.

'Don't you have any work in the field?' he shouted at Thami.

There was the raised sickle in Thami's hand. Bewildered, he had forgotten to take off the headwear as he was supposed to, in front of the lord.

Though Thami had not uttered a word, it was quite obvious that he was not pleased seeing Menon there. Chathara Menon walked out of the hut grunting fiercely. It was a severe setback. Have I been vanquished by a humble low caste worker? He stored it in his memory for wreaking vengeance. Thereafter Menon made it a practice to abuse and even punish Thami, whenever their paths crossed.

Not long after that incident, Thami got his daughter married to a porter in the Manchira market. This porter was the one who participated in trade union activities. The henchmen of Menon whispered among themselves that the marriage was arranged to prevent further intrusions from Chathara Menon. This gossip reached the ears of Menon too. Whatsoever it may have been, Menon did not trouble them for a while. But the lust for revenge remained in him like stagnant water, refusing to flow down the drain.

Thami and his woman were left behind in the hut when Kochupennu left with the porter comrade.

Time passed. Two months before the Kangazha action, a buffalo belonging to Chathara Menon went missing. It was a tiger that caught it; everyone knew. It was not unusual for a tiger to meander into the valley of the Kolli mountains. Thami himself had driven away the tiger more than once, scaring it with flaming torches. What happened now was that the tiger sprang on one of the buffaloes standing in a group, killed it in an instant and dragged the carcass into the forest.

On the third evening, a worker came to Thami's hut seeking him. Thami had just come back from work. When he came out, he saw the goons of Chathara Menon waiting for him.

'Eda, Thami! You come right now to the barn yard. The Elder has some business with you.'

Within a very short while, Thami was slouching in front of Menon with his palm cupping his mouth.

Most of the workers had assembled in the barnyard. Just beyond them were three policemen in khaki shorts, standing with long canes in hand.

A Kathakali song could be heard from inside. It was Komappa Menon.

The rotting head of a buffalo was lying on one side of the yard. The whole place was stinking. Both the horns were intact. Open eyes.

Oozed blood had clotted. Flies were swarming. It was the remnants of the buffalo the tiger had made a meal of.

'We got this from his hut, my lord,' the goons lied.

Chathara Menon's bloodshot eyes enlarged, his nostrils flared.

'What is this, you dog?' Chathara Menon shouted.

'It was caught by the tiger, my lord!' Thami said meekly.

'Chee, how come the head of the buffalo is found in your hut, if it was nabbed by the tiger? You keeping an account with the tiger?'

'Shall we get him, Menon?' the policemen asked. They twirled their moustaches in a menacing manner.

'The likes of him are not for you. I asked you to be here, only because I wanted it to be a lesson for the others.'

'Just look at him, the fat swine, bloated with buffalo meat,' a policeman added fuel.

'It's not that sir. He has a trick with the buffalo head, black magic,' the goons of Menon corrected the policeman. 'Look at his eyes. A thief's look.'

Thami was tied to a pole and one of the henchmen of Chathara Menon started beating him nonstop with a heavy cane.

So amazing, that a muscular one has risen
To kill someone as powerful
As ten thousand burly elephants ...

Komappa Menon's recital of the Kathakali, 'Murder of Keechaka' could still be heard from an inside room.

Thami had a massive body. But that was all. The poor man was crying. Anyone would take pity seeing him cry. He was also pleading—without any sense of shame—not to beat him anymore. After at least a hundred blows, Menon stepped in. He kicked Thami. He beat him on his chest and groins.

Thami fell down.

There were blood red welts all over his body. No one spoke.

Rendering of the Kathakali song had ceased.

Menon brought out a big gun, pointed it at the supine Thami and shouted, 'You pig whore-son, killing my best buffalo for black magic?

I will kill you, bastard.' The onlookers were stunned. He always kept his word. And nothing would happen to him if he kills. Thami lost consciousness seeing the barrel of the gun reaching up to him.

'Leave it Chatharakkammal. This is a lesson for you all. You lying pigs, if any such thing happens again, we'll kill you all, take it from me,' a policeman who was from Kangazha threatened those who had gathered around. The policemen were apprehensive that it would cause problems for them if Menon was to use his gun.

Menon did not shoot only because the police intervened.

'Anyway don't throw away the buffalo head. The two horns should be fixed on the walls of the mansion. It will remind me of this dog occasionally,' Chathara Menon said in a mocking tone.

The crowd dispersed. Komappa Menon's Kathakali songs were not heard anymore.

A couple of workers brought Thami home. His body was as heavy as a corpse that had drowned swallowing a lot of water.

The villagers read this the following morning, on the walls of the Kangazha family house.

'Death to feudalism!

Thami's torture will be avenged!

The very next night the police reached Thami's hut. 'Who are the rascals seeking revenge?' they shouted. They shattered to pieces whatever they saw: pots and pans and the meagre household items. They again beat up the feeble Thami and swivelled his woman around catching her by her hair.

An inspector named Chellappan was in the forefront of all this. He was known as *Idikkula* Chellappan, meaning Chellappan, the wrestler.

'Who is behind you in all this, you scum? You tell them that their machinations will not work when Chellappan is here. If I hear of any such thing again, this hut will not be here anymore. I'll torch it. You and your folks have not reckoned with Chellappan.'

Even after all this happened, Sivan did not accept the arguments of the comrades that action should be initiated against the police.

The police was merely the puppet of the feudal class. He pointed out how history was full of instances wherein many a revolution was lost fighting such trivialities. The comrades should not lose direction when advancing towards the objective of annihilation of the enemy.

'But we've identified the real enemy here,' claimed comrade Sekharan who was involved in the Thelakkara action.

Chathara Menon of Kangazha is the enemy confronting us right now. So there is no need for any more disputes.

He needn't witness the rising sun after the eighth of the next month.

The action on that fateful night was the implementation of that decision.

There were unusual rains on the night of the Kangazha action. The fury of rain had not subsided even when they were retuning in two groups to Avalam before daylight. The blood on the hands was washed away by the rain. It was difficult to get along in the darkness. No one spoke as they trudged through the empty road. There was no definite answer to the question; where are we going to. After about two miles, Sekharan flung the bloody knife into a paddy field by the side of the road and asked loudly, 'Can I have a smoke, comrade?'

Sivan's fingers fumbled in his pocket. The matches and the beedi packet were soaked in the rain. A flicker of light was now visible in the eastern sky.

By about ten the next morning, a few students who had connections with *Liberation Path* came to Chitrabhanu. He was still lying in bed. He asked them to come in, but they refused. They called him outside and revealed the news they had brought for him.

'We don't know how, but that was what really happened.'

'Who told you?' Chitran asked. He just could not believe what they had shared with him.

'It is common knowledge in the hostel by now, comrade. Police had come enquiring about the magazine. And so we are leaving.'

'Where to?'

'Somewhere. You also scoot off if possible. They will start hounding all those who wrote in the magazine. Last time you were spared because they had thought that it was a student.'

Chitrabhanu did not divulge that Sivan was there, inside the house, sleeping.

'Action and rebellion! If you don't have one, yes: we do not have it—that's all. And now, what has been perpetrated! Isn't it really disgraceful, comrade?' a student asked in rage. The muscles on his face tautened. The lines on his forehead turned into deep furrows.

'This is not true, it is my gut feeling,' Chitran consoled himself. 'I think it is a canard circulated by our enemies.'

'There is one such incident in your story, no?' a student asked in scornful rancour.

He was referring to Chitran's story, 'The Corpse' which had appeared in *Liberation Path.*

The news they had brought was more shocking than any number of such stories. He was feeling the intensity of it now. Chitran sat on the steps for a while. Then he entered the room. A bag containing his daughter's clothes was lying there. Sumitra, his wife, had packed them the previous day when they were leaving for a friend's place and had forgotten to take it with her. She had decided to leave rather abruptly in the evening. She was in a bitter mood. They had quarrelled over a few issues in the morning. Chitran was about to leave for his newspaper office. He asked whether she insisted on going that day itself. She did not answer. But she was adamant. And she left, well aware that he wouldn't like it. However, in retrospect, what she did seemed to him the right thing. Or else, how complicated the situation would have turned out into ... It would only have led to more suspicion.

What had really happened? Whose error was it?

Sivan was sleeping in one of the small rooms inside. He had arrived there quite unexpectedly, before sunrise. He was wet out and out, his eyes had sunk deep inwards. The water dripping from his dress formed a puddle as he went in.

'All wet,' he exclaimed. Some crucial event must have taken place; otherwise he wouldn't have come there at that hour. Chitran gave him a towel and a lungi.

He stirred up the hearth, put in a few dry twigs and set water for tea.

Sivan dried his body, changed out of the wet clothes, hung them on the clothesline in the backyard and re-entered the house. He was shivering from the cold. He slowly sipped the hot tea. He was trying to warm his palms by rubbing them vigorously on the warm tea-glass. Silence reigned.

'Anything wrong, comrade?' finally Chitran asked. The fire had died down in the hearth. The embers flickered from beneath the ashes as if gasping for breath.

'Nothing as such,' said Sivan. Everything went according to plan.'

'You mean ...' Chitran had only a bare idea of what was going on. He had never been an insider, the secrets of the party were beyond his reach.

'Yes, exactly. The Kangazha action is over.'

'Then?' Chitran looked at his face.

'Then? Then nothing. Everyone retuned. The news will spread by morning.'

Chitran's fingers trembled. So? He had penned innumerable important news stories for the newspaper. Had copied ever so many from the teleprinter. He was now seized by a panic that he had never experienced in any such situations. Words deserted his lips.

'I want to sleep,' Sivan said in a voice bereft of emotion.

With trembling hands Chitran unrolled the mattress. Sivan lay down without speaking, crossing his hands across his chest. He closed his eyes. Chitran watched him drifting into undisturbed sleep in a short while. However, Chitran himself could not sleep and he tossed and turned on the bed. He saw the day break and the morning sun spreading light. He lay there watching raindrops dripping from the leaves. Sleep eluded Chitran, but he still remained on the mat till the boys came calling.

He felt scalded by the news they had brought. Should I wake up Sivan? He hesitated.

Sivan was sleeping in the same posture. No, he would not have had a wink of sleep the last night. And maybe even the preceding nights.

But he will have to be woken up. Sumitra would return that evening. What would he tell her?

Not only that ... Chitran shivered at the very thought: the police?

But how were they to know? Chitran had the address of a large newspaper. There was no reason for the police to suspect him. Would the enquiries regarding *Liberation Path* lead up to him? The possibilities were very low. If it were to happen, it should have happened already. No one had come for him, even though students had been nabbed for interrogation. As for *Kambanam* Lasar, he knew Chitran only by sight.

Still it was a high risk to provide shelter to the comrade involved in so complex an issue, in this crowded street in the centre of the town. Not just for him, but even for the organisation. His mind actively searched for alternate shelters for the comrade.

'What are you thinking about, comrade?' Sivan asked. Chitran was startled. When had he woken up?

'Nothing in particular,' Chitrabhanu shook his head. But his hands were trembling.

'I'll leave in a short while.'

'Where to?'

'I was coming to that. A place has to be found. Just for a short period.'

'And after that?'

'After that? There won't be anything to worry about after that. The enemy will be frightened even by a hoax. They are shameless cowards. All this show of might is just a mask. Kangazha will be replicated at many places, comrade. Our villages are going to encircle the power centres. This is just the beginning. Our spark has fallen on an ammunition dump,' Sivan was emphatic.

'But ... but …'

'What are these ifs and buts?' Sivan smirked. 'You writers have this disease. Always doubting.'

'No. what the students said … there is a suspicion that something has gone wrong …'

'Like ..?' Sivan insisted.

'Like … you know, a slip up has perhaps occurred …'

Sivan shot up from the bed and sat upright. 'Slip-up? What do you mean? It was a decision arrived at after discussing all the relevant points. There is no question of anything going wrong. Or comrade, are you saying that such feudal lords should be spared? Have you any idea of the atrocities perpetrated by him?'

'But … it seems ... it seems, the one who was finished off in the action was not Chathara Menon …'

'Not CHA-THA-RA- ME-NON?' Sivan repeated very slowly.

'That's what people are saying, comrade. The one, who was done away with, was his elder brother, an insane man.'

Sivan continued to sit tight with absolute detachment. There was not a flicker of emotion on his face, noticed Chitran with surprise and mounting apprehension.

Sivan got up from the bed, tightened the lungi around his waist and went to the window. He stood there staring out. Time trickled by.

'Comrade has not said anything,' Chitran pointed out in a low tone.

'Who is the feudal lord at Kangazha Meledathu *tharavadu*?' Sivan asked in an extraordinarily calm voice.

'Why ask such a question, comrade?' Chitran did not understand the question.

'Who is the feudal lord at Kangazha Meledathu, was my question,' Sivan repeated with impatience.

'The students said that the action was targeted at Chathara Menon ...'

'Leave alone the students comrade, you have not answered my question,' Sivan continued speaking without turning around. 'His elder brother was very much alive, no? According to the norms he was the lord. So in theoretical terms, the organisation has not committed any blunder.'

'But I heard that he was insane ...'

'Naturally! Because insanity is a characteristic of feudalism.'

Chitran's throat went dry. Words failed him.

'There's no point in your being a writer or working in a newspaper. Lack of education is very evident in you, comrade. The party will endeavour to rectify it. You'll get it on your own, if you analyse it a bit. Our action was against a system. That is to be understood. The individual is not important. Your thinking is individual-centric, there lies the whole problem. What does the party have against Chathara Menon, the individual? It is the system which he represents that leads him the way he goes. That is the crucial point. So our action was against that system. We struck right on its head.'

Chitran stood staring at Sivan with disbelief as words poured like a torrential downpour.

'So, there need be no doubts. Kangazha was a resounding success. All the rest is mere speculations of immature students. Okay, now please get dressed, comrade. I had mentioned it no, we will have to find a place somewhere in the interior.'

For whatever reason, Chitran could think only of *Kambanam* Lasar.

'Lasar *Chetta*, Lasar *Chetta*, what happened? No printing today?'

The shutter of the printing press was down. Lasar did not open it despite knocking several times.

'The monster must be in a drunken stupor,' said Chitran angrily. He was afraid someone might notice them.

'Maybe he has gone somewhere. Will he get drunk so early in the morning?' asked Sivan.

'His hands will start shivering if he does not drink.' Chitran again called, 'Lasar *Chetta*, please open the shutter.'

After he made several such calls, the shutter slowly started going up. It was not lubricated for long and so was groaning as if someone was clearing his throat.

It was not Lasar who pulled up the shutter. It was a woman.

The shutter went up. It hit the top making a heavy thud, metal colliding with metal. Can't call her a woman; may be a grown up girl. Maximum twenty. The sari she had draped around was soiled. She was not wearing any ornaments; neither a chain around her neck nor any earrings. There were red dabs on her dry hair.

'Lasar *Chettan* is not there?' Chitran asked.

She looked down without speaking. There was Lasar sleeping on the floor in dirty clothes. Saliva was oozing from his open mouth. There was a yet to be healed big wound on his forehead. Flies swarmed around the open wound. One couldn't guess since when he was in that condition. Or how long he would remain so. Chitran thought of waking him up. He bent down.

'Please don't wake him up. He will get mad.' The young woman warned.

'There was something I wanted to tell him.' Chitran saw a penknife with a shining grip lying on the floor near Lasar's head. He picked it up. Chitran thought of waiting till Lasar woke up. But it was a printing press. Anyone could come in with a piece of work. Those who would come there for getting 'death intimations' printed would usually wait at the press till the work was done. So the comrade had to be accommodated in the living quarters behind the press or in the room where paper was stacked. But how to get this through to a man who was as good as dead?

'Is this girl his daughter?' asked Sivan. The girl was obviously embarrassed.

'I come here to learn the work,' she kept her gaze down.

They felt that they could not take that on face value. Is it that *Kambanam* Lasar is going back to his old magazine? Is this girl here for that?

'What's your name?' Chitran asked.

'Remani.' She raised her face. There were drops of sweat on her forehead.

'He's someone very close to Lasar *Chettan*. He has come here to stay for a few days,' Chitran told her pointing to Sivan. She remained silent not knowing how to respond.

'He is a poet. He has come here to stay here and write poems. So he does not want to be disturbed. You can accommodate him somewhere inside. We can explain all this to Lasar *Chettan* when he wakes up.'

'He will get angry with me,' Remani said with trepidation.

'No, no, we assure you. We are his friends. Everything will become clear once he wakes up. Or shall we wake him up?'

'*Ayyo*, please don't. He hates to be woken up. He will kill me if he is woken up.' Remani seemed to be quite terrified of Lasar.

'Okay. There is a room in the back in which the printed papers are stacked, no? Take him there. Give him a cup of tea once in a while.

Maybe you have the facility for that here. Leave it. It doesn't matter if it is not possible. But don't let anyone else know at any cost. People will come and disturb him.'

She walked reluctantly to the back of the building.

'Please go with her, comrade. When he wakes up just tell him that you are one of the *Liberation Path* crowd. He will understand. I'll come again in the evening. He knows me in person.'

'Will he create problems?'

'No chance. He is a simple guy. He had some raunchy stuff with him, a few years back, that's all. He will not harm anyone nowadays. Moreover he knows most of the big shots here. Just that he has grown old.'

Sivan went inside. There was hardly any sitting space in the midst of the stack of papers. Remani brought a broom and cleaned the available space after rearranging the packets. Now there was ample room for one to lie down. She returned after some time with a glass of black tea. He smiled at her. Sivan thought that now the panic on her face had almost vanished.

Chitran came at four in the evening. Lasar was not up as yet. By then, Kangazha action had become the talk of the town. But Chitran did not make a mention of it to Sivan. Instead, he discussed the story to be told to Lasar.

'What you said will suffice, comrade. That I've come for writing poems in peace ...'

'No, playwriting would be better,' Chitran corrected. 'People will be more at home with it than poetry.'

Kambanam Lasar woke up from his long sleep after a while. He was shivering.

'*Edi* Remani, *Edi*!' he called out. 'Now where the hell has she gone off?' he asked himself. Finally he stumbled on to his feet.

'Where is my knife, you bitch? Nothing will be there, where I leave them.' Lasar's voice was ringing out.

'I didn't see your knife,' Remani answered from somewhere inside the house.

'Who is there to take it if not you? Where have you poked it in, you bitch?'

Sivan came out and smiled at him. He stared at Sivan with the shadow of suspicion playing up on his face.

'Who are you?' he asked.

'It's me, Lasar *Chetta*,' Chitrabhanu showed his face from the inside room. Lasar's face flushed with anger seeing Chitran. Lasar looked intently at him.

'Why are you here at this time? Any damned magazine work?'

'It will take time. We are getting the matter ready.'

'Mmm.' Lasar grunted.

'He is here for just that. He is my friend, Pavithran. He is a playwright. We've come to find out whether he can stay here for a few days and complete a play.' Chitran was pleased with himself for presenting it this way. Lasar also will have some interest as it was related to the printing of the magazine.

'Lasar *Chettan* should not say no. I'll pay whatever you ask for his lodging.'

Lasar did not respond. He was lost in thought. Twilight descended on his body replicating the beams of the roof.

Before leaving, Chitran handed over the penknife he had picked up to Sivan.

'Oh, what use is it for me, comrade? For cracking nuts? You keep it,' Sivan said disdainfully, examining the knife. It was a folding type. Its tip was long and was shining like the tongue of an ancient animal.

'Let it be with you as a friend. Don't show it to Lasar,' Chitran said with a smile. 'And it will not suit me. The pen is the weapon for us journalists, no?'

Sivan tucked the knife at the waistband of the *mundu* he was wearing.

When Chitran left, Lasar asked Remani to boil some water for him to bathe. He applied oil and had a leisurely bath by the side of the well. Then he put on a fresh dress, combed his hair and was ready to go out.

'Where are you off to *Chettayi*, now that it is nightfall?' Remani asked.

'Just somewhere nearby. Look, that drama man here, he is our man. Prepare something for him if he wants to eat.' Remani was relieved. She was afraid that Lasar would punish her for allowing Sivan to stay there without his consent.

Going out to get drunk again, Remani thought. However, she had never seen him dressing up like this when on his way to the toddy shop. But who knows in what dress he is going to return in the night?

Lasar visited Sivan before leaving.

'I'm going to the town. Could be late returning. Don't wait for me, have your food and go to sleep.'

Sivan nodded.

'Have you started the play?'

'Must begin, shortly.'

'It should be a good one. Publishing in the magazine is not enough. It should be staged. Just like the play of Bhasi staged by KPAC, ok? I too have put up several plays. So have you named the play?'

'The Corpse.' This was what came to Sivan's tongue. Maybe the short story by Chitran Kuroor crossed his mind.

'Corpse?' Lasar distorted his face. Then he said recalling something. 'It's a nice title. It'll be a hit if you make it "Corpse Eaters." We had once staged a play with that name.'

'Ok, if you need tea or coffee, ask my wife.' Lasar said. 'It will boost you.'

'Is she living nearby?' Sivan asked.

'She is there in the next room. Didn't you meet her? Ey, Remani, *Edi* Remani!'

'Oh, it is Remani?'

'So you have met her. Yes it is her. She is an orphan. Poor girl. I let her here as a companion. I'm getting old, you see.'

Remani watched Sivan drinking *kanji* sitting cross-legged on the floor. As he dipped the wooden spoon into the gruel in the porcelain plate and raised it to his lips, he saw Remani standing at the door staring intently at him. She had changed into a skirt after her bath. She now looked much younger. Semi-dark in complexion, Remani had long hands and buxom but supple breasts. She was not wearing any ornaments. A faint shadow of distress was discernible in her eyes. Sivan did not keep his gaze on her for long.

'What's your name? She asked. Chitrabhanu had introduced him as Pavithran. Sivan repeated that. He felt he was uttering someone else's name.

'You write plays, isn't it?'

'Mmm,' Sivan grunted gulping another spoonful of the gruel.

'My father too was a dramatist,' said Remani. 'Ramakrishnan. He was popularly known as Kalasadanam Ramakrishnan. He had also written several plays.'

'I've heard of him,' said Sivan from the flicker of a faint memory. He also remembered having seen a play by this man in his adolescent days.

'I had acted in my father's plays,' Remani said.

'Where is your father now?'

'He is bedridden. Very sick,' said Remani. 'Do you want some more *kanji*?'

'Enough.' Sivan got up. He felt that he had had more food than usual.

'What kind of a play are you working on?' Remani asked. This was indeed becoming a nuisance. What should he reply? Neither the name or the plot of any play came to his mind.

'I've given it a name. "The Corpse." But the plot is only being developed as yet.'

She approached him with water in a small pitcher. He extended his hand to take hold of the pitcher. But she did not give it to him. 'I'll pour the water on to your hand. Please step out.'

The odour of woman enveloped him as he bent down to wash his hand. The scent of cheap toilet soap intermingled with it.

'And if you don't get any suitable plot, I've a fitting story which you can convert into an excellent play,' Remani said lowering her voice.

'Which story?' Sivan asked as a matter of formality.

She pointed to herself and said, 'Me, my story. It is very much here. Can you do it?'

Sivan looked at her. Now there was a twinkle in her eyes. In the dim light he was seeing only those sparkling eyes.

'You are a playwright's daughter. So why don't you write yourself?' Sivan asked.

'No, I'm not up to it. Maybe I can act.' She then continued with a pale smile, 'Am I not acting even now as it is?'

Sivan sat in the room allotted to him. A cockroach jumped on to his body from the paper stack. He watched it languidly. It would stop intermittently and observe the surroundings with its whiskers raised.

'Do you really know Lasar *Chettayi*?' Remani who had just come in there asked. Sivan woke up from his thoughts. Why is she asking that question? Who doesn't know of Lasar's past?

'I've heard about his magazine.'

'Not just that. He was involved in theatre too. Are you aware of that?'

He shook his head. He had not heard of the theatre part of *Kambanam* Lasar's life. Lasar had indicated something to that effect when he left. But Sivan had not taken it seriously.

'I guessed that you were not aware of it. You are seeing *Chettayi* for the first time, no? Actually he was a *tabla* player. He was in my father's troupe for a while. Then he was dismissed from the troupe for molesting an actress.'

'Molesting meaning…?'

'How are women molested? He came dead drunk and raped her. That was it.' Remani said as if it was a mere trifle. 'Do you know who that actress was?'

How was he to know, Sivan thought. Or why should one know all this?

Remani continued after a brief pause, 'It was my mother.'

Sivan stared at her not knowing what to say.

'What do you think? Is the story suitable for a play? One husband for both mother and daughter! I used the word *husband* just for the heck of it. Don't read too much into it. What is there in it for a play, you might think. But this is only one part of the story.' Remani grinned.

'In that case, how did you end up here?' Sivan was curious now.

'That's why I said there is a story. To be truthful, it was not a rape.'

'Then?'

'Lasar the *tabla* player deceived my mother. He used to know her since long. In fact even before my father married her. He was after her despite her marriage. The *tabla* was only a ruse. He threatened that he would publicise a letter written by her to someone. She had indeed written such a letter. It was a love letter. Lasar *Chettayi* secured it from some source. My father used to drink a lot in those days. He would have killed her if any such news reached him.'

'What happened?'

'My mother had to submit to him occasionally because of the blackmail. But then they fell in love. People started talking. They even planned to elope when it could no longer be kept a secret from father.'

A factory siren boomed from somewhere nearby. It lasted for almost a minute.

'Are you really a theatre person?' Remani suddenly asked. Sivan could not answer her.

'I don't know why, but I feel you are not. Now even if I'm wrong and you have indeed something to do with the stage, don't stay here for long relying on Lasar *Chettayi*. He is real poison. He is capable of anything. Terrorising, threatening ...'

'If so why did you consent to marry him?'

'Consent! You think all this takes place with consent? What he did to my mother, he is doing to me, that's all.'

Remani described Lasar's visit to her father some time ago.

'Those things just happened, Master. Please forgive me. I've given up everything now. I've committed lots of crimes. I wanted to fall at your feet and plead for forgiveness, Master!' he cried confessing the misdeeds of his past.

Kalasadanam Ramakrishnan did not even recognise Lasar. The past had dropped off from him like leaves in the autumn.

When she brought him black coffee, Lasar looked at Remani and asked, 'Darling girl, you remember me? But how could you? You were only a baby then.'

Remani could not recall seeing him. But she had heard that name. She was also aware of some of the things that had happened long ago.

'I'm a wretch. That you must have heard for sure.' Lasar glanced at her with remorse.

Before leaving he left a few currency notes underneath her father's pillow.

'You are coming? If you come along with me you can learn printing work. You can even take over the press eventually.'

Six months passed by. Remani had forgotten Lasar's promise. She was always running short of money. Food for both of them and medicines for father. She was finding it difficult to manage with the earnings from occasional employment in the farms. Then Lasar put in an appearance once again.

'How is Master, my dear? I'm here regarding the suggestion I'd made last time.' That day also he placed some money under the pillow. This was apparently not the Lasar she had heard of.

He repeated his promise to Remani.

Maybe the past has no relevence now, she ruminated. Who was there to help her now? When that thought took firm root in her mind, she decided to opt for Lasar's press. She had no one to take a formal consent from. Would her father agree had he been aware of what was going on around him?

She found the work in the press quite simple. It was mostly death intimations. A life ends when certain letters and dates are typeset. She too wanted such a kind of life. What is the use of this hellish life of uncertainties bracketed within two dates?

Those were days suffused with the love of Lasar. Every time he returned to her house after his errands, he'd bring her goodies to eat. He would address her only as 'my dear.' Even if there were spelling mistakes and even if the whole work had to be redone, he would not shout at her. All of what she had heard of him was utterly false, she became convinced. Or maybe he always had double faces. Her mother too might have been trapped similarly in the net. Love that would kill.

Lasar wanted to modify his press and needed money. Since he had been jailed and was looked upon as an offender, banks would not finance any of his projects. He was always immersed in ideas of raising funds. Remani too was concerned about him.

This was what led to his showing the back issues of the *Kambanam* to Remani. It was with embarrassment that he did this. However, he emphasised that resuming the publication of the magazine would lift him up from penury. But for that he required a few photographs. Lasar glanced at her meaningfully. Remani was shocked.

'Who is going to know it is you, my dear? People will think it is some actress. Moreover I'd give only such captions.' Remani finally agreed unable to resist his loving pressure. Lasar gave his word that she would never be recognised in the photographs. She had no reason to mistrust him. It was with such tender love and concern that he had behaved with her.

She covered her face with her hands when he clicked the camera. But he slowly removed her fingers winking assurances at her.

'But now the public will say that it is a lie, if I attribute this to any actress,' said Lasar with a sly smirk. Remani could not understand what he meant.

'Who among the stars have such a curvy body, my dear? All that they show off are appendages.'

He took a few more snaps.

'Now turn around. The photos from behind are more stylish.'

She turned around. Silence reigned for a while. Slowly Remani became aware of his breath at the nape of her neck. He kissed her just as she was trying to break free.

She stopped going to the press.

Lasar wept like a child over this several times. He would visit her at her home and plead. It was on the backup of his tears that he finally made her come over to his place.

Lasar started drinking after this. He did not publish the magazine. He would show the pictures to a few and collect money and drink. Coming home he would beckon her and threaten if she did not come near.

'You bitch of a fairy queen! Come closer. Or I'll paste your nude pictures on the market walls. You have no idea of what Lasar is capable of.'

It was more vile than the blackmailing of her mother, citing letters.

'I had to submit to him. Thus came this job of a wife,' Remani said deprecating herself.

'Can't you escape from here?' Sivan asked, livid with anger. So wicked a man like Lasar doesn't deserve to live on the earth, he mused. But who is he from the class perspective? What is it that ceases to be, when he is annihilated? Certainly not feudalism. Lasar is only a third rate criminal. His annihilation is not going to bring about any change in the material conditions.

'Yes, I must escape,' Remani said. 'But …'

'We'll help you.' Sivan stopped suddenly. Shouldn't have said 'we.' Remani needn't know about those things, he felt.

'But ... '

'Why do you hesitate? Is it those photos?'

'Initially they were. But later on I felt those do not really matter. Now … now …'

'What is the hurdle now?'

'Just that I'm carrying his baby now.'

All the courage she had shored up abandoned her as she said this. She started sobbing like an innocent girl.

Sivan placed his hand on her shoulder. It was for the first time he was touching the body of a woman. When he lifted his hand, Remani held it softly. Her eyes were swollen and red from crying.

'Don't cry,' said Sivan. 'Is there any point in crying now?' Remani sat with her head bowed. Neither of them spoke for a while.

'Does he know?'

'Haven't told him,' she replied.

'Maybe, maybe he is lying about the photos,' he tried to console her.

'No. those photos do exist. He had shown them to me. But it doesn't matter.'

'What about the baby? You can choose not to have it. Now the hospitals are well equipped for all that.'

Remani covered her face with both hands and indicated that she didn't want to do it.

Lasar did not appear even late night. Maybe he had fallen off somewhere, drunk. Sivan curled up like a snake in the midst of the paper stacks. His body was paining lying in that awkward position. He thought of going to the central hall and sleeping there. Remani's face came to his mind. Her touch had sent electric waves down his body. He wanted to wipe her tears and hold her close sharing the warmth of her body. He got up.

He stumbled in the darkness while getting out of the room. Sivan sat down on the floor in the more spacious hall. He then heard the steady breathing of someone close by. When his eyes got used to the darkness he could see the outline of Remani sleeping not very far from where he was. She seemed to be in deep sleep. Her breasts were heaving up and down keeping with the rhythm of her breathing. Her hands were crossed. Strands of hair were spread on her forehead. He thought: the sleeping Remani is more beautiful. Then, for no reason, the nude photos of Remani clicked by *Kambanam* Lasar came to mind. He visualised her body without clothes. Someone deep inside him was trying to stop him from such musings. But he could not take his eyes away from her body. Involuntarily his legs moved towards her.

He yearned to kiss her feet which were not covered by her skirt. He raised his hands towards her body. But the extended hands became still. His body was quivering like a bow that had just released an arrow. His body was playing traitor. Stunned, he withdrew.

This is not my destination. There should not be any deviation from the journey I've undertaken.

There was a sound outside. Remani woke up, shocked out of sleep. She was about to cry out in fear, when Sivan capped her mouth with his hands. Her eyes scanned him with suspicion.

'Outside …' Sivan stammered.

'What's there outside?' her voice was wavering.

'A sound,' Sivan said, gathering courage.

'Must be him.' Remani sat up knotting up her loose hair. Some more sounds outside. Someone seemed to be trying the shutter.

'Must be pissed drunk,' Remani said drily.

'Remani, you should go and check,' Sivan said.

'You are trembling,' the look of suspicion again reflected from her eyes. Sivan was overwhelmed by shame.

Remani stood up and slowly approached the shutter. There were three steps going down to the shutter. There was a wooden pillar nearby. She leaned on the pillar and listened. Then she retraced her steps.

'There are some others too.' She lowered her voice and stared at him. Remani was certain that he was hiding something from her.

'Treachery.' Sivan mumbled. 'It must be the police. He is betraying.'

Remani looked at him keenly.

'Who the hell are you?' she stepped back and asked in a hushed voice. 'What have you stolen before you came here? Or whom did you kill?'

'This is not the time to discuss all that.' He closed her mouth with his hands. 'I must hide.'

'And then?' she brushed his hand away and asked him, breathless.

'And then nothing. If they ask, you just say that I left.'

'Whereto?'

'Anywhere. That I'll manage. You say that you do not know anything.'

Remani just stood there staring at him.

'There is no time to stand and stare. Do something and get rid of them.' Sivan pushed her.

She looked at him for a full moment and said as if she had taken a decision. 'Okay. I'll not betray you. Come!'

There was a grass mat beneath the cot Lasar usually slept on. Remani made him lie down on it. Then she rolled up the mat around him and pushed it beneath the cot. She then went to the front. Lasar and those who were with him had already entered the building. They were all well dressed people. There was no one in police uniform. Who has Lasar brought with him?

'You light a lamp,' Lasar ordered.

'You locked the back door from the outside, no?' one of Lasar's guests asked.

'Don't worry, sir, I've taken care of it.'

Remani became aware that Lasar was not drunk as she passed him on her way to fetch a lamp. She had not seen him free of liquor in the recent past. So what was happening? Who is the person hiding inside? She was scared. What would happen if Lasar came to know of it?

Remani glanced at the four strangers in the light of the kerosene lamp. She felt she was witnessing a dimly lit scene from an old play.

'Who is this new *yakshi* of *Kambanam* Lasar?' one of them asked. Lasar laughed soundlessly.

'*Edi* Remani, he is sleeping there, no?' Lasar turned to her.

'He left.' Remani said, as if it was a trifling matter.

'Left?' Lasar bent like a bow and stared at her. 'Where did he go?'

'Who knows? He went away immediately after *Chettayi* went out.'

'And you did not ask him anything?'

'What could I say?' Remani did not look at him. 'He did not come here with my consent.'

Lasar gave her a full blooded slap. So fierce was the blow that he lost his balance and fell down.

One of his guests helped him on to his feet and said, 'What is the point in beating her? In fact, it is you who deserve a couple of blows. Why didn't you lock him up in a room, before coming to us, you ass?'

'Who was the one who went away from here, girl? Did he mention any name?' one of them asked.

'I did not ask his name or birth star,' Remani looked at him rubbing her cheek.

'You fiend! Are you snapping at sir?' Lasar lunged after her.

'What you have here is a smart one, Lasar! You plan to bring out a magazine with her?' One of the guests undressed her with his searing look.

Lasar hissed glaring at her, 'Don't worry sir, I've other plans for her.'

One whole day Sivan was with a young Ayurveda physician, Avalathu Melattoor Narayanan Nambisan. There is an old two storey building in a corner of a vast compound on the side lane going north from the stadium road. It was Nambisan's ancient family house. There was no one living there now. Nambisan used the house to store his herbs and he also made some of his *kwaths*, liquid ayurvedic medicines, and tablets there. Sivan stayed there amidst an array of flowers, leaves and roots in an atmosphere redolent of different types of herbal oils. He could see a woman grinding to paste a host of medicines on a flat mortar. Nambisan would pay a visit once in a while to oversee the activities. Nambisan was the scion of a family that dealt with rare medicines for children. He had started this business on his own only recently.

'Oh, my comrade, no one is going to recognise you if you sit in our shop in the town. I had mentioned this to Soman Master. But he is a man of strict discipline. He said this is the way it should be,' Nambisan said.

'What Soman Master said is right. Master knows the conditions prevailing here. Moreover, you are supposed to stick to it, once you get an instruction, isn't it?'

Nambisan had noticed the hardening of Sivan's tone and became silent.

'Anyway, comrade should not go hungry. Please ask for it, if you feel like having tea. I've asked the women workers here to take care of you.'

In the evening Sivan left the place as decided. He felt he was mitting the scent of herbs. Nambisan wanted to accompany him till the ›us stand, but Sivan discouraged him. The town would be bustling in he evening. It was better to be alone. Even two people moving together vas not advisable given the circumstances.

It was past seven when Sivan turned towards Avalam Bus stand. He elt safer under the dim streetlights. But if a passerby stared at him, he felt hat he was being observed. That was a hangover from the night spent t Lasar's printing press. The spate of threats that came unanticipated ad prompted him to be more cautious. He also felt like looking behind nore frequently. A suspicion that there was someone right behind him. He'd turn his neck involuntarily. A shadow or something moving … t's pursuing me. On one occasion he was convinced that someone was ollowing him. He was also stopping whenever Sivan stopped. If he vent ahead one step, the one who followed would also move one step orward. When Sivan stepped up the pace he did the same, and when e slowed down, he too did that. Exactly like a shadow. To make sure, ivan went in to a small tea shop and ordered tea. He had not guessed vrong. The shadow too entered the tea shop, ordered tea and sat down acing Sivan. Sivan took up a sheet of the newspaper that was lying on he table and pretended to be engrossed in it. His gaze involuntarily noved away from the newspaper to the one sitting opposite. Sivan ound that he was intently looking at him.

Getting out of the tea shop, Sivan walked faster and entered the Avalam bus stand. A town thirty miles away was his destination. There vere very few buses. He got into one that was to leave ahead of others nd got a seat in the rear. But almost immediately the 'shadow' got nto the bus and stood near him leaning on to the steel rod. On closer crutiny, Sivan felt that he had the facial features of a policeman. He was ure that he was trapped. The bus would be redirected to the nearest olice station. He has been nabbed, he was certain.

The bus moved just then. Just as it was gaining speed, Sivan jumped up from his seat and as if prompted by intuition, jumped out of the

'I need something to eat only by noon. Tea is not a mus a packet of beedis.'

Closing the door of the room, Nambisan said, 'You ca house at night.'

'No need. I have to move by evening.'

Sivan spent the day reading the two issues of *Libe* for the second time. It had certainly progressed from the magazine brought out by the students. But much more coul magazine had a very big role to play in an environment in lacked ideological clarity.

It was not tea but ginger coffee that the woman brou Sivan did not say anything even though he did not relish it smiled at him weirdly while taking back the cup.

'Was it too spicy,' she asked.

Sivan grunted.

'You want anything else?'

'I'll let you know,' he said, pretending indifference.

'Don't hesitate to ask if you want anything,' she said away with a smile. She smelled of wild roots and leaves.

'Soman Master had said that a new issue has to be explaining the Kangazha episode,' Nambisan said. Sivan lunch from the packet Nambisan had brought for him.

'What is there to explain about Kangazha?' Sivan felt N taking much more liberties than was warranted from a fell

'There are motivated campaigns from certain quarters

'What campaign?' Sivan questioned Nambisan.

'Er ... that the mission had gone wrong …'

'There was no mistake. The head was the target, not th

'I guessed as much ...' But the voice lacked conviction.

Though he was curt and categorical with Nambisan, S there was some substance in what Nambisan was trying t would be campaigns against Kangazha for sure. A write-u all aspects was called for. He lay down thinking about it.

bus. It was an unexpected move on his part. As the bus raced away he had the relief of a temporary escape. But that was shortlived. The bus suddenly came to a stop a little ahead of him. Sivan guessed that the other person was also getting down.

But that guess turned out to be wrong. Only then did he realise that he was getting paranoid. The bus continued on its way after offloading a passenger.

However these apprehensions did not leave him alone the whole evening. He got into the next bus and purchased a ticket to the last stop and tried to convince himself that everything was alright. After a while he even reached the consolatory conclusion that no one was paying undue attention to him. Sivan started dozing. There was so much of sleep of the previous so many nights to catch up on. He woke up from the nap only after a considerable time. The bus was speeding through a less populated village. Dark figures of the trees and plants were rushing backwards at a furious pace. The bus was no more crowded. All of a sudden a passenger from the seat behind his, touched his shoulder and asked,

'Do you have matches with you?'

Sivan turned around. He was shocked. It was the same man who had followed him to the other bus! How did he get in here? He hadn't got down from the other bus. Sivan felt the stranger's intense glance from his narrowed eyes under bushy eyebrows piercing him like shrapnel.

'No matches.' Sivan mumbled. His fingers instinctively touched the knife he was carrying.

'Oh, you don't smoke?' he probed.

Sivan chose to look into the darkness rather than answer the question.

'Where are you going to?' the stranger seemed intent on striking a friendship. Sivan's instinct was to avoid him. But then he felt that that approach could be counterproductive. He might become suspicious. If he was really following Sivan, he will somehow or the other find out his destination. So he abruptly reversed his decision and told him the name of the town where he was headed to.

‘Where specifically in that town?’ pat came the next question.

‘To meet a relative,’ Sivan could hardly conceal his ire. He then turned to the window and the darkness outside.

The crowd in the bus was thinning out fast. The bus was stopping more frequently now and dropping off people. But there were very few boarding the bus. The town was getting nearer. There were more lights and buildings. The bus would come to a halt in the bus stand in a short while. When was the heavy arm from behind going to entrap him, Sivan was anxious.

However, on reaching the bus stand, Sivan found that the shadow had already left the bus. In fact, Sivan was the only passenger to get down. The bus stand and surroundings were practically deserted. There were a few people anxiously looking at the few buses that were passing through the stand. Sivan did not have a wrist watch. But he surmised it to be past ten.

The instruction given to him was to go to a workshop from the bus stand. The workshop was run by an activist called Paul. But Sivan did not know the exact location. Any auto rickshaw driver would take him there, he was told. It was a fairly well known establishment and being a workshop, auto drivers would certainly know. But would it be open at this hour? What would he do if it was closed? Sivan decided to find out. But there were very few rickshaws.

What were the chances of Paul being there? He knew vaguely that Paul was living near the workshop. It was about four kilometres from the bus stand, on the way to the District Hospital. The chances of getting a vehicle at this time of the night was dim, Sivan concluded. Still he had apprehensions about walking through unfamiliar places late at night.

Luckily, the workshop was still open. The resonance of the hammer striking iron sheets could be heard from a distance. It took him half an hour to reach there.

The workers in the workshop fetched Paul from an inner room. Paul was a middle aged man wearing thick dark glasses. Paul seemed to be surprised seeing Sivan. According to the information he had received, Sivan should have been there the previous day.

On being satisfied with the code word, Paul asked, 'What happened? I thought you were to arrive here yesterday.'

Was there a hint of accusation in his tone?

'No, I was supposed to be here only today,' Sivan was firm.

Paul had come out of the workshop and had taken him aside so as to be out of the earshot of the workers. 'Please ensure that no one else is listening,' he cautioned intermittently.

'I thought you were not coming today, comrade. So I did not arrange a night shelter for you.'

'But I've to spend the night. Even this workshop will be sufficient,' Sivan insisted.

'That will not be proper, comrade. We will be working all night because we have to deliver a bus by morning. You will not be able to sleep with all the noise. Secondly, there is always the risk of one of the workers spreading the news about you.'

'It's night after all. You can tell them that I'm an acquaintance of yours. I'll leave early in the morning.'

'Even that is not safe. Especially because the police were here last month. Not that it was anything serious. Someone had informed them about the first issue of the magazine which they happened to see here.'

Sivan felt that there was some substance in Paul's reasoning.

'Comrade, please wait for a minute. I'll change my dress and then come along with you. There is a possibility nearby. Advocate Bhavadasan. You may have heard of him. He is the son of a former member of the legislature, comrade Narayanapilla. He is also a trade union leader and a member of the Communist Party. He was defeated in the last municipal elections. But you see, he is not a sympathiser of our party. Still I've a gut feeling that he will not reject this plea. Narayanapilla too had spent time underground.'

'Will it cause any trouble?'

'Oh, no. he is a truthful man. Trustworthy. I've been servicing his car since long. In fact, no one else even dare touch that vehicle. It is a problematic Ambassador. Will he say that you cannot stay overnight? No. he'd say so only if there is some other hurdle. If so we will return. But he will not reveal this to anyone.'

Paul was ready within five minutes, in a fresh lungi, cleaning his face and hands off the soot and grime. He had a long cane in his hand.

'Why the stick?' Sivan asked as they started walking.

'To make out the road,' Paul said. 'I cannot see.'

Sivan was shocked. Then how did he run a workshop? And also be associated with an organisation like ours? He wondered.

'I had a fever four years ago. There were boils all over my body. It was then that I lost my eyesight,' Paul explained.

'But how do you manage with the vehicles ...?'

'The boys attend to most of it. I should be there with them, that's all. My experience and familiarity help me understand what's wrong by just feeling the parts.'

Advocate Bhavadasan was preparing the cases slated for the next day. There was light only in his room. There was a white Ambassador car in the vast garage. Bhavadasan opened the door on the second knock. He smiled at Paul.

'Why Paul, this late?' Bhavadasan asked.

'Days and nights have no difference for me, sir.' He seemed to be laughing at himself.

Six cats of various ages and size appeared from inside the house. None of them made any sound. The silent cats glanced at Sivan circling the advocate.

Paul talked to the advocate.

Advocate Bhavadasan did not have any problem with what Paul requested. But Sivan had to leave early morning. His house was the haunt of party workers and clients. Since he kept an open house, someone would see the comrade. However, Sivan assured him that he would leave very early.

'Then there is no problem at all,' Bhavadasan smiled. 'Friend, did you have any dinner?'

It was then that Sivan became aware of hunger. 'I'd like to have a bath first,' he said.

As he was leaving, Paul caressed the car, 'Aren't you keeping smart, my boy?'

He turned to the advocate and asked him, 'He is not all that naughty, no?'

'Oh, no. And if at all he is naughty things will be alright, once he sees your face!' Bhavadasan laughed.

'*Vakil* sir, what happened to your cats?' Paul asked.

'They are all here, man. They should remain silent after nine in the night, that is the rule of the house. No concession even for cats.'

After some time, the sound of the cane knocking the ground could be heard. Paul was returning to his workshop.

By the time Sivan had his bath, the advocate's wife was up. Food was ready on the table.

'Gone cold. Didn't heat it up as it might get spoilt.'

'Does not matter. More often than not I eat cold food.'

The rice had become lumpy. There was *aviyal* prepared with buttermilk and lady's finger fry. Those too had gone cold. Papad had just been fried. Sivan found even the cold food very tasty.

'I'd have given you company, but I don't generally eat after nightfall,' said Bhavadasan with a smile. 'I've a sugar problem. My heart too is not in a very sound shape. I have a cup of rice by seven. That's all I need.'

Till he finished his food, the advocate, his wife and their six cats gave him company. The advocate alone talked. He was talking in general terms. Sivan also understood that the advocate had not mentioned who Sivan was to his wife.

The walls of the advocate's house were adorned with pictures and portraits of various gods and goddesses, so unusual for a party member. Bhavadasan noticed Sivan gazing at them and said,

'It's all her fad. Since we've no children, someone or other has to be looked after and nursed, no? So we have six cats. And then these pictures. I thought it better to let her have her way.'

'Don't make fun of the gods,' his wife said, slightly peeved.

After she went to bed, Bhavadasan discussed politics with Sivan. He argued in low tones that the path chosen by Sivan and his comrades was wrong and that it inevitably led to total disaster. He also advised that the youth should not be led astray.

'On the contrary, we are bringing them back on the right path,' said Sivan with conviction. 'I firmly believe that ultimately everyone, including you, will adopt this path.'

'Provided all those you refer to are still alive,' the advocate laughed. 'Do you know how many die in the lock-ups and the jails? This is apart from those who go missing.'

They did not indulge in discussions for long. The understanding was that Sivan would leave before sunrise. Paul would come around five. He had indicated that it would be best to leave by the first bus. Sivan slept for four to five hours after a long time.

It was still dark when he woke up the next day. He could hear the clang of bells. Perhaps the advocate's wife had started her puja. Just after the chiming of the bells stopped, he heard the knocking of the cane. Paul was announcing his arrival. One of his mechanics too was there on a bicycle.

The advocate and his six cats accompanied Sivan till the gate. The cats continued to maintain their stoic silence.

The mechanic pushed the pedals of the cycle with Paul on the handle bar and Sivan on the carrier.

'Prabhakaran is interested in our kind of activities,' Paul said about the one who was cycling. 'I had him read out the magazine to me.'

Sivan did not make any comment. Prabhakaran's clothes were smelling of lubricants .

The bus stand and its surroundings were just waking up. They had tea from a makeshift shop. Paul waved when Sivan's bus left the stand.

Sivan raised his hand to wave back. But he withdrew it thinking of the futility of the gesture.

'Everything went off well, no Prabhakaran?' Paul asked while returning on Prabhakaran's bicycle. Prabhakaran grunted with relief.

But that was not to be. There were three arrests that day proving that Paul's assumption was wrong.

The police raided the 'Melattoor Vaidyasala' in Avalam town and their two storey building on Stadium Road in the morning. There was a truckload of policemen. They confiscated a few copies of *Liberation Path* from the room where medicines were stored. The employees of the medical centre were questioned, but they hardly had any knowledge of whatever the police were after. Only a woman who was engaged in preparing medicines from herbs told them that a man had been there for a few hours. On the basis of that, Narayanan Nambisan was taken in a van for further questioning.

Nambisan was the member of a temple-oriented family without any political background. He had not been a success in traditional medicine and so had gone off to Mumbai when young. He was in Mumbai for ten years as a stenographer when he came back and started the medical centre.

He had read some revolutionary literature while at Mumbai. A Telegu-speaking roommate was his political guru. It was a great shock to Nambisan's friends and relatives that the police had nabbed him. They could not initially digest this news. His ailing mother was told that he had gone to Mumbai on an urgent matter. Nambisan was presented in the court after intensive interrogation for one week. He had to be helped into the defendant's box. The judge could see the wounds on his forehead and below his eyes. But he ignored them. Such were the times. However, he was released on two personal bonds. He could never concentrate on his business or in his family's affairs anymore. Narayanan Nambisan was one of those acquitted after two years, for lack of evidence. He once again tried his hand at Ayurveda, but failed. He went back to Mumbai and nothing further was heard of him.

Paul was taken away from the workshop around noon. There were only two policemen and one inspector. The workers in the workshop created trouble when he was asked to get into the jeep. They questioned the nabbing of a blind man in that manner. The police ignored their protests. The jeep took a U-turn and sped away raising a lot of dust and sound. They started beating him up in the jeep itself asking for details about Sivan. When the police were there a month ago searching for copies of *Liberation Path*, they had shown some consideration for a blind man. Now they compensated for that.

Paul was produced in court only on the fourth day. He was kept in an unknown camp till then. The police informed the court that he was taken into custody only the previous day. By that time Paul was too weak either to correct it or to deny it. Perhaps it was Paul the mechanic who was tortured most among those who were nabbed by the police.

Paul was born in an impoverished family in the railway colony. He had become the owner of a workshop only by sheer hard work and diligence. His paralysed father was his only living kin. There were some efforts on the part of the workers in the workshop to get him out on bail. However, they withdrew from the scene, maybe scared. He languished in the darkness of the sub jail for more than two years. Paul's father had died during his incarceration. The workshop too had ceased to function. A voluntary organisation which came to know of his sad plight got him admitted to an old age home run by catholic priests. He was assailed by doubts when he sat in the prayer room along with other old men. He felt that a God large hearted enough to take in a blind and tormented man was yet to be created. While chanting the lines of the prayers mechanically, he used to get the feeling that he was standing in front of a dark world that was an endless abyss. And also that he was passing through a marsh where his cane could not get a firm hold.

It was around four in the evening, after he came back from the court, that advocate Bhavadasan was taken away for interrogation. When he got down from his car two policemen in civil dress were standing by the gate. They were mindful of the fact that he was a lawyer. They waited till he had a wash, change of clothes and a cup of tea. The policemen were also carrying the documents legally required for taking a person into custody for questioning.

When he was taken away, the six cats broke their long silence and cried loudly. Their moaning almost sounded like that of human beings.

The police produced him in court charging him with offences that were not easily bailable.

His party showed some concern initially. He used to handle the cases of many of the party members. He did not, however, go up the party ladder nor did he get an opportunity to be a candidate for the legislative elections. Perhaps this sidelining may have become intolerable. He gradually started to keep away from party programmes. In his later years, Bhavadasan moved partly towards the spiritual path. After the death of his wife, he gave up his law practice of fifty years, joined the ashram of a famous sanyasin and took up the responsibility of a school run by the ashram.

At the age of seventy-three, while taking a group of students to Simla, he died of heart attack en route.

His party men came to know of this only after a week. The district committee in which the advocate had worked for a long time merely passed a perfunctory condolence notice and noted it in the minutes book.

Certain stories, ideas, poems, and at times even a few lines may revamp the whole outlook of a writer. He falls spellbound at their magic touch. A strange thought, that whatever he had written till then was worthless and so the life till then had gone wasted, could dominate his mind. It's a dark enlightenment: the epiphanies experienced by famous writers and poets, at one time or the other in their creative life. Sometimes it would merely be a passing notion. Could just be ideas that are based on transitory impulses. In any case, this inner call will overturn the life of the writer. He has no escape from it at least for a while.

This was what happened to Sreenivasan too though he was not a celebrity as a poet. The reading experience of *Liberation Path* was a challenge to his brief poetic life and talent. It actually led him into a difficult crisis. He was haunted by the feeling that whatever he had been writing was not poetry. He read and reread the poems and articles in the magazine. What was it that I had been writing all these years? Poems that celebrate darkness and light and love? Or poetic dramas based on certain episodes from the epics? It was the reading of the magazine that brought him to the conclusion like an overpowering fever that all those writings had absolutely no relevance to the times he was living in. He lost his balance for two days. Many errors cropped up in his work. Those were the worst days for Sreenivasan as a proofreader. Its reflections were felt in the home too. Sreenivasan who would never be angry with his son, caned him for a trifling naughtiness till the rod broke. He quarrelled with Sakunthala accusing her of serving insipid food. Sakunthala ignored all this thinking that the ghost of poetry was haunting him. Sakunthala had not felt anything out of the ordinary till he came one morning and stood next to her with a load of paper, just as she was about to light fire in the hearth.

She poured kerosene for the firewood to catch fire. And then stuffed in a few dry coconut husks. Suddenly Sreenivasan threw in some of the papers he was holding in his hand. She was baffled.

'What are you doing?' she asked.

'Bad poetry,' said Sreenivasan. 'My past was a waste, Sakunthala. That is turning into ash.'

Even though she did not know exactly what those papers contained, she pulled them out of the hearth. The edges of some were smouldering. The words of love poems which he had read out to her several times were already burnt.

'You are mad,' Sakunthala said. 'Staying up all night, night after night, writing these poems! And then burn them! Sheer madness.'

'You cannot understand this,' Sreenivasan said.

'Yes, I can,' retorted Sakunthala. 'Have I not been living with you for so many years? I've the commonsense to recognise your madness.'

Sreenivasan did not argue with her. Let her do what she wants. I've got rid of what I wanted to, mentally. Henceforth Sreenivasan the poet will be a new being. If ever he writes again, it will only be new poems. He sipped the tea she offered and straightaway tried out a new poem. But he could not complete even one line to his satisfaction as he was troubled by a host of tensions. However, whatever he was engaged in, he was full of anxiety about the new way of writing. A new creation was to be attempted. It should have as much reverberation as thunder on dark evenings.

Thus, in the night, the next day, Sreenivasan commenced the beginning of his new poetry:

'A cassia tree,
Like the sun

Shattered by
The arrows of spring'

He felt a jolt as soon as he wrote those lines. The hazy picture of a solitary tree in a vast grassland flashed across his mind. When he recited those lines he was filled with the yellow of those meditating flowers. Yes, this is it. This is the poem I'd been waiting for, all along. He longed to and also made efforts to create the next stanza, but then thought that perhaps he did not have the strength for it that night. The foundation for a poem had been laid. Now it had to be built up from there. Till then the mind had to be kept calm. He was humming that stanza while going to bed. Sakunthala did not make any comment even though she heard his humming. She would not have understood the difference in Sreenivasan's poetry that he was harping on. Spring, trees and flowers had occurred in Sreenivasan's poems earlier also. But Sakunthala did not see the sparks ignited by the clash of words in his new creation.

Sreenivasan was incessantly writing the next two days. Apart from completing this poem he wrote three more. He imagined himself to be a mayfly flying away picking words. He did not go to work those two days.

On the third day he shaved, had a bath and went to his newspaper office. He had four of his new poems with him. The new poems which he reckoned to be quite different from the ones he had written all this time. He had to show them to Chitrabhanu today itself. He was the one who had written that marvellous story. It was also he who had introduced him to *Liberation Path*. His opinion on the poems is important. The possibility of getting them published in *Liberation Path* is also to be probed. His mind was occupied with such thoughts throughout the time he was working. Absent for two days and then quite indifferent on the third day when he puts in an appearance. The editor was quite peeved. However he did not dare take it out on Sreenivasan. It was not easy to get an apt substitute if Sreenivasan chose to walk out.

After office hours, Sreenivasan went to the newspaper office where Chitrabhanu worked. He had to cross the market to reach there. Bicycles, rickshaws and a few auto rickshaws sped past him.

Porters were unloading huge bags containing sugar and rice. A leper whose fingertips had wasted away was begging for alms sitting under a makeshift canopy. Sreenivasan felt that everything in the world was becoming a subject matter for his poems. There has been a definite shift in my perspective, he thought. Now I'm looking at the world in a different light. The articles and the translated poems in that magazine have opened my eyes.

Sreenivasan waited outside Chitran's office. He was at the desk. Couple of important news items had come at the last moment and he had to finish them before leaving. But the moments of waiting did not exasperate Sreenivasan. He was immersed in his poems; reviewing the written ones and contemplating the unborn stanzas.

'Hello, Sreeni, have you been here for long?' Chitrabhanu came out opening the half door of his office.

'It's alright,' Sreenivasan said formally.

They went out through the market to an old restaurant.

'Read *Liberation Path*,' said Sreenivasan sipping tea. 'I'm here to talk about it.'

Chitran scanned the other tables before responding to him. 'What do you think of it?'

'That whatever I read or wrote till now was all wrong. Your story affected me like a typhoon. Please do not think I'm flattering you.'

Chitran smiled. He was quite pleased.

'I feel ashamed when I think of what I was writing all these years. My life too was wrong.' Sreenivasan's words seemed apologetic.

'Don't talk like that.' Chitran stopped him. 'Perhaps we are only beginning to live the right way.'

They were silent as they sipped their tea. It was a joint frequented by fishing folk and the tea glasses had the stench of fish. Sreenivasan had to control his breath to finish off the tea. Though a vegetarian himself, Chitran did not seem to be affected by the smell of fish.

'I've got few of my poems with me. It'll be nice if you could take a look at them,' Sreenivasan said with hesitation.

Chitran went through those poems with curiosity. He read them with concentration, taking his own time. He gave Sreenivasan a hearty smile after reading them.

'What is your opinion?' Sreenivasan enquired with anxiety. My life is hanging on your reply, he thought.

'Look, these three poems are very good.' Chitran pointed out. 'But this one about the cassia tree, that is not up to the mark.'

'It's not about a tree as such,' Sreenivasan stammered. However, he was glad about Chitran's response to the other poems.

'I know, it's only an image. Slightly negative in tone. That's ok. But will an ordinary reader understand the poem?'

Sreenivasan didn't know. He thought about those who read poetry. Do the workers whom he passed by in the market read poems? Are they in a position to understand the other three poems?

'Anyway, you should henceforth write in this style. That is my opinion. These have more life than the earlier poems.'

'I wrote them after reading *Liberation Path*.'

Chitrabhanu only smiled.

'Can you get a few poems published in *Liberation Path*, if it is possible?' Sreenivasan asked.

Chitran had thought of it. But most of those in the editorial were of the view that there's no space for poems or stories in *Liberation Path*. What will be their reaction if I take these poems? There were many who had argued against the six poems that were published in the first issue.

'I'll try. But it's not my decision alone.'

'Chitran, till now, my ambition was to become famous like all other writers. But that is no more my objective. I feel that the readers of *Liberation Path* must read my poems. I wouldn't mind even if my name is not printed alongside.'

Chitran let his gaze linger on Sreenivasan. There was an unusual sparkle in his eyes. 'It's risky to give one's real name. It happened to me unwittingly. Perhaps people may not identify it with me, since the name was given as Chitran Kuroor. We'll find out another name for Sreeni.'

'A pen name?'

'You may call it so. But what I had in mind was a name that is not real. It has been decided not to publish anything with the real name. That is safer.'

'What about not providing any name at all?' Sreenivasan asked.

Chitran didn't seem to have heard. He was thinking of something else.

After being lost in thought for a long time, Chitran wrote below the poem a new name: 'Buddha.' A poet Buddha who attained enlightenment under the Bodhi tree of *Liberation Path*.

Sreenivasan resumed his normal routine soon after. He bought provisions, went to the landlord for paying the rent. He became a concerned family man. Sreenivasan took Sasi to his family house. However, he did not announce to anyone that he had given up his old style of poetry. The passion that had engrossed him after the first few had faded out. Still he was striving for new themes. He was also observing more than what he used to, of everything around him. He did not speak to Sakunthala about either his new style of poetry or about the new name given to him by Chitran. Perhaps it was for the first time in their decade long life together, he had concealed anything from her.

The next issue of *Liberation Path* was getting delayed. Though he had met Chitran in between, Sreenivasan had not enquired about it. What if it was construed as anxiety about his poems? Chitrabhanu too had kept quiet about the poems. On certain occasions, Sreenivasan felt that Chitrabhanu was evading him. Reading the poems, making favourable comments and suggesting a pen name may have been out of mere decency. He also felt that if his poems did not have the standard to be published in *Liberation Path*, then there was no point in writing poems anymore.

Chitran was indeed avoiding him. However, it was not for reasons Sreenivasan had imagined. Chitran had liked those poems. It was with the hope that he would be able to get it published that he had taken those poems from Sreenivasan. But he could not convince the editorial board. Literature was not their forte. They were not interested in anything other than theoretical discussions and translated articles. And hence Chitran had the feeling that the next issue of *Liberation Path* would only have the standard of publicity pamphlets. He disliked such publications. But he faced many practical difficulties in countering the wisdom of full time members of the editorial.

Yet, like a miracle, two poems with the by-line of 'Buddha' were published in the second issue of *Liberation Path*. One was selected by Chitran and the other was the poem of the cassia tree. Chitran was aware that those lines were Sreenivasan's favourites. But the poems were placed on the last page without according them any importance. Chitran knew that they were used only as gap fillers. But he did not mention all this to Sreenivasan.

'Rest of the poems will appear in the coming issues, Sreeni. It is only a beginning.'

'Oh, it's okay. Let's see the readers' response.' Whatever criticisms may come in, the poems were worth the pages of *Liberation Path*, Sreeni thought. That was a relief in itself. How many times he read the stanzas under the name Buddha! He was even able to finish another poem that night. For reasons not quite clear to himself, Sreenivasan concealed from Sakunthala that his poems had been published, albeit in another name. On all earlier occasions, he used to recite to her the published poems. What if all the paranoiac mysteries behind it terrified her? Or suppose she thought he was fooling her by reciting someone else's poems as his own?

The second issue of *Liberation Path* was more dry and drab than the previous one. Apart from serious articles, there were only Sreenivasan's poems to add variety. Even the editorial was a very long treatise. The hammer and sickle on the straw-coloured cover page was quite tiny. So small as to be confined to a little corner. The rest of the space was left blank. This was just a few days before the Kangazha action.

Kangazha action followed. The magazine did not come out after that. Chitran and Sreenivasan rarely met. Sreenivasan continued writing poems, though not meant for *Liberation Path*. He hoped someone would read them. But he did not feel like taking them to Chitran. The newspapers were full of the Kangazha episode. Sreenivasan guessed that Chitran would be busy with activities related to that. Sreenivasan's life passed by in a straight line, of the evening daily and its work pressures. Sreenivasan stopped going to poets' meets. He was apprehensive that he'd have to read his old poems if he showed up there. The new ones had seen the light of the day in another name. If he were to present those poems, the secrecy behind the pseudonym would be out. He would also come under scrutiny. Chitrabhanu would not have decided on a false name without weighty reasons. But the problem was that he was not to be seen at all.

But one day quite unexpectedly, Chitrabhanu contacted him over the phone. Sreenivasan never expected it to be Chitrabhanu when he attended the call in the editor's cabin.

'Sreeni, you are not to be seen these days,' Chitran complained.

'Was busy …' said Sreenivasan, elated.

'I've got the poems with me. You know, the Kangazha incident became quite serious. The magazine is also facing some problems especially with the press. A new press has to be found out.'

'Poems? Forget about it. Let the magazine come out first.'

'When you meet me, bring your new poems. Any new creations?'

'Yes, a few. What else?'

'Nothing special. I'd like to meet you. Today if possible?'

'Today, I've …'

'No, today itself. I'll come to your office.'

'No need. I'll make it.'

'Okay, then. But not in the office. We'll meet in the restaurant. At five.'

'Okay.'

'Bring your new poems.' So Sreenivasan carried a sheaf of papers.

But that was not necessary. Chitran did not refer to the poems at all during their meeting. It was as if he had forgotten about them.

He was in a strange kind of haste, it was clear. There was a kind of perplexity on his face. He had changed considerably since they last met. There was the red scar of a wound on his forehead. He had grown old, Sreenivasan thought.

'What happened? Are you not well?' Sreenivasan asked.

'Oh, nothing. Had a fall,' Chitran answered averting his gaze.

'Sreeni, you have to do me a favour,' Chitran began without any preamble. 'You should accommodate a comrade with you at your home for a few days. It should all be done in utmost secrecy.'

Secrecy? Sreenivasan could not comprehend. Sakunthala and his son were there. How can he let anyone live there without their knowledge?

'Maximum one week. Send your family to some other place. It's vacation time, no?'

Sreenivasan thought for a while. How will he convince Sakunthala?

'He is a very important party functionary. There is no other go. There's police everywhere. We can also think of shifting him in between if we can hoodwink the police. The risk I tell you is only for a week. I can ask only those I can trust, no?'

That Chitrabhanu considered him to be trustworthy gladdened Sreenivasan, despite his mind being in a turmoil.

'And one thing more,' Chitran said, 'this comrade was responsible for your poems appearing in *Liberation Path*. It was because of his insistence that they were published in that issue.'

In the latter days of Chitran Kuroor's life, full of self-loathing, these were the words he hated the most. The hellish guilt of telling a lie to a gentle poet without any qualms haunted him till the end of his life.

Communication became practically impossible when the magazine was shut down. A group of students along with the activists among government employees had been circulating certain leaflets on the sly. A dilapidated house just outside the engineering college was their rendezvous. Students and local comrades used to assemble there and discuss the situation. They were unable to arrive at a consensus on the Kangazha action. Was it theoretically correct? Are such actions to be continued? The pros and cons were discussed and it was decided to bring out a leaflet listing them. However the police got wind of it and they made a surprise raid of the college hostel without the permission of the college authorities. But the students had managed to shift the bundle of leaflets to a government employee's room in a lodge.

That was an interim when even a small note, let alone a magazine could not be published. Those in the censor board were scanning anything and everything that was published. So while going from advocate Bhavadasan's house Sivan was thinking of new devices to communicate with the comrades. He was motivated seeing the old issues of the magazine in the room of Narayanan Nambisan, the young Ayurvedic physician. Even though he had rebuked it when Nambisan made a suggestion, he was aware that there was a growing need for such a magazine. It was not easy to write letters to each one. And going by the structure of the organisation, the comrades may not even know each other. Moreover the police was watching the mail too. It would be like walking into a trap, even after being fully aware of it. What was required was a magazine like *Liberation Path*.

However, Sivan had the feeling that the activities of the students, who were party sympathisers, ultimately turned out to be reactionary. They should have discussed, analysed and arrived at a consensus and then published it as a common decision. But apparently different messages and news with varying content were circulating in that area. It had the character of flawed democracy. There was also a chance of the enemy hand behind it. Whatever it was, such efforts could only lead to confusions among party followers and sympathisers. So a new document had to be presented to the rank and file at the earliest. It seemed impossible to get such a document printed in the present circumstances. More desirable would be to access a cyclostyle machine. The search for that led him to Viswanathan.

Thirty-five year old Viswanathan was a comrade and activist in the union for central government employees. A bachelor, he had been living in an old lodge near the civil station for ages. In fact, the union to which he belonged had no connection whatsoever with Sivan's organisation. The leaders of the mainstream communist movement were at the top of the union. Still a few members had a leaning towards the revolutionary path. There was also the advantage that they were largely left alone by the police as they were known as the workers of the mainstream communist party.

By evening Sivan reached the lodge where Viswanathan was living. He had encountered a few problems in locating the lodge. There were myriad streets and by-lanes in the vicinity of the civil station. Only those who were quite familiar with those alleys could give directions to a newcomer. At the same time, Sivan's style was to find his way on his own, without referring to anyone. It was a precautionary measure to cause least harm, not only to him, but also to whom he might ask for directions. Sivan finally landed at Viswanathan's place after trudging through many a path many a times.

He had to wait. He saw men standing in front of the manager sheepishly and then securing keys for the rooms on the first floor. Sivan understood that the lodge was practically a brothel when he saw women following the men to the rooms. The manager occasionally smirked at Sivan, but Sivan ignored him.

He was told that Viswanathan usually returned to the lodge around nine after his dinner. The manager tried to pick up an acquaintance with Sivan, but he was evasive. It was an old inn with dirty walls. There was a faded photograph of a man with a twirling moustache adorning the wall, perhaps the grandparent of the current owner. The plastic garland on the photo was frayed and old. Beneath the photograph was a shaky table and behind it sat the manager on a wooden bench. He too had a great moustache. Is he the owner of the place? The inmates of the lodge were shuffling in and out and there was the strong smell of cheap liquor everywhere. The manager too seemed drunk.

Viswanathan came in at nine. He seemed rattled finding Sivan there. Viswanathan had not been told that Sivan would be reaching there that day. It was Sivan's own decision. He opened his room without spending much time in the lobby. He was a man of thin frame with glasses and a sparse beard.

'Be seated, comrade.' He pointed to the bed in the room. A small table and the cot were the only furniture in the room. There was no chair and one obviously had to sit on the bed if one wanted to write. The room was like a large box. Books were heaped on the table and the window sill. A clothesline with soiled clothes stretched across the room. As Sivan sat down, his feet touched the edges of a rolled mat under the cot. Viswanathan attempted to open the window, but decided against it and sat at the other end of the cot.

'Comrade, did anyone notice your coming here?' Viswanathan asked.

'I don't think so. The caretaker tried to get friendly with me.'

'Oh, that does not matter. He is not in his senses after dark.' Lowering his voice, he continued, 'There's a policeman in the next room.'

'Is it risky?'

'It's risky only if you go out now. This is a place for a different kind of business. I live here only because the rent is comparatively cheap. Ok, did you have any food?'

He had eaten at noon. Not after that. But that did not matter. Sivan said that he was not hungry.

The cyclostyling machine had been with him, Viswanathan revealed. But it had been taken back by the students of the Engineering college last week.

'There's a very active group there,' said Viswanathan.

'But I must get it. Certain very important things ...'

'You see comrade, I can access them only on Sunday. They have classes rest of the week. My going there is risky. At least a few have suspicions about me.'

'Shall I go and contact them directly?'

'They may give it to you. Some of them know you. But how will you reach there without drawing attention?'

'Who was the one who took it away?'

'I don't know the names. However, they were the students of the Engineering college, I'm sure. They assured me that they will keep it secure.'

'You can't blindly believe the students. Moreover, so many people come and go there!'

'What do we do then?'

'Yes, what do we do?'

Viswanathan thought that he could go and collect the machine early in the morning. Or ask them to reach it here.

Sivan too had the same thing in mind. However, he thought it better to go in person. The college was in the countryside. To be here, in this lodge in the very centre of the town, that too where a policeman lives and many of his ilk come and go is too risky even for Viswanathan. On the other hand he will not be all that known in the countryside.

'Yes, perhaps they could even find out a place for you to stay,' endorsed Viswanathan. 'But you should not stay with the students at any cost. There are ever so many types.'

Viswanathan did not ask where Sivan was coming from. That was part of an understanding. The practice of confining to the essential details. Even the sympathisers, not to speak of the activists, adhered to this code of conduct.

Sivan looked at the titles in the room. Mostly fiction and poetry. He noticed Gorky's *Mother* and Sholokhov's *And Quiet Flows Don*. He turned the pages of a half read novel on the table. It was earlier serialised in a prominent weekly.

'Had seen it in the weekly. Did not read. How do you find it?'

'It's good.' Viswanathan smiled. 'Feel like taking it with you?'

'I don't read fiction,' said Sivan. 'At times I feel that these authors are closing their eyes to the light to make it dark.'

Viswanathan did not seem to have heard what Sivan said. He was lost in thought.

He got up from the bed ready to go out.

'Let's do it this way. There are two plantains in that packet. And there's drinking water in the pitcher. Comrade should not leave this room tonight. You can leave early in the morning. I'll lock the room from the outside and go to the union office for the night. I've some work there, anyway. No one here will suspect anything.'

Before getting out, Viswanathan handed a bottle to Sivan. 'For pissing,' he said.

Viswanathan came back early in the morning. It was obvious that he had not slept at all. His eyelids were heavy. They left the lodge immediately. There was the mild dew of the morning.

The town was deserted but for the milkmen and the newspaper boys. Viswanathan returned to his lodge after directing Sivan to the bus stand.

It was seven by the time he reached the Engineering college hostel. Boys were playing football on the ground in front of the hostel. Viswanathan had mentioned two names; Murali and Riyaz. Their rooms turned out to be in different blocks. It was Murali that Sivan tried first. Sivan was quite surprised that the boy recognised him at first glance. Murali dispatched a friend to fetch Riyaz.

'We had the machine with us. But it developed a fault. It is now with a mechanic,' Murali said.

'We should get it back. Is he somewhere nearby?'

'Not very far. It is a shop on MG Road. The third on the left when you go from here. Perhaps comrade may be knowing him. He is a relative of comrade Chandikkunju of Thelakkara.'

Sivan nodded. Chandikkunju was an accused in the police station attack case. He had died while in prison. All the boys in the hostel seemed to be fans of Chandikkunju.

'But it will be nine by the time the shop opens,' said Riyaz who had just come into the room.

'Will they hand it over to me if I go alone?' Sivan asked.

'Probably no,' Murali was thoughtful. 'We had instructed them not to give it to anyone else.'

'It's already late. We must get it back repaired at the very earliest.' His tone was insistent.

'You be here comrade. I'll go and get it. Wait till it's nine,' Murali said.

'No question of any risk, no? Will anyone be suspicious?'

Neither Riyaz nor Murali replied.

They brought him breakfast from the hostel mess. Idly and sambar. Sivan had not had so sumptuous a breakfast for long. He then lied down and read the day's newspapers. He scanned the books in the room and found all of them to be poetry. That was something that always surprised him. Be it Viswanathan or these student comrades; what they read was poetry and fiction. Is it that they are not interested in books on ideology, economics or history? Is it possible to imbibe the realities of the world by reading stories and poems? The sympathisers of the revolutionary party seemed to be strange islands of imagination. No one seemed to be interested in looking at hard realities.

Murali left before nine. Riyaz had lab in the first two hours. He had gone saying that he'd be back shortly. Sivan heard him locking the room from the outside. Why did he lock the room? He was uncomfortable. Then he went to the window and looked out. The deserted football court and the long grasslands beyond it. A boy was leading his cows through the ground to the grasslands. The day was getting warmer.

He waited.

It was eleven. Murali had still not returned. Sivan was quite suspicious by now. What was happening?

Then the sound of a key turning in the lock and the door opening. It was Riyaz. He too was upset that Murali had not comeback.

'I had thought that he was there in the bus that just came from town,' he said. 'Let me go and find out. It is better that you wait in my room comrade.' They walked unhurriedly through the veranda and reached the next block. There was no one in the hostel, it being a working day. It was good. Saved one from answering questions.

Sivan found collections of love stories and love poems in Riyaz's room. He was frustrated. What revolution these people were going to usher in, he wondered.

It was the engineering books which Sivan went through next. Engineering is better than romance and love. Sivan liked what little he read.

It took two hours for Riyaz to return. He was sweating profusely.

'It is all a mess, comrade!' Riyaz said. 'They have picked up Murali.'

'Who?'

'The police. They took him to the police station.'

'So what happened to the machine?'

'I don't know about that. I think he did not reach the shop. He must have been nabbed on his way there.'

So no question of accessing the cyclostyling machine today, thought Sivan with disappointment.

However, he did not say anything about it as he felt that Riyaz was more concerned about Murali. They will beat him up for sure. And he will spill the beans.

That was a correct guess. After half an hour, a jeep came and halted in front of the hostel. The policemen who came out of it in a rush hurried on to Murali's block. The sound of breaking in the door of Murali's room was audible to them in Riyaz's room. Sivan was relieved that he had shifted rooms.

They saw the angry policemen leave in a huff.

'It will not be safe to remain here anymore,' Sivan said. 'They might come here again.'

Though Riyaz reminded him of lunch, he did not stay back. Sivan got into the next bus. The newspaper office of Chitran with whom he had stayed after the Kangazha action, was his destination. But as there was a chance of his being recognised, he telephoned Chitran.

'Don't come here now,' said Chitrabhanu with some trepidation. His voice was just a whisper.

'I had been asked to contact you,' Sivan reminded him.

'I'm aware of it. I'm getting a safer place. Within two days or maybe tomorrow itself, we will go there. We'll meet after some time.'

Another plan was brewing in Chitran's head. He had Sreenivasan in mind.

Sivan sat on a bench in the bus stand thinking how he should spend the time till the meeting with Chitran.

The police arrested Riyaz and Viswanathan in the next two days.

Riyaz had left behind a half done love poem when he was picked up by the police. He came out within a few days submitting a written apology. Riyaz was an unusual individual unwilling to confess about the inhuman torture he suffered at the hands of the police. He never went back to the Engineering college hostel. He gave up studies. He was haunted by an unwarranted sense of guilt that he had been treacherous in his dealings. He went abroad with the help of a relative in the Gulf countries. Riyaz continued his silent literary activities during his long stay abroad. He was not at all interested in getting them published. He however, published a collection of poems under pressure of his friends. It was titled 'The Betrayer of Life.' He abandoned the work on a novel which had immense possibilities had it been completed. Riyaz returned, at the age of forty, giving up his lucrative job. He bought some land in a remote village and adopted the life of a farmer. A few of his friends came to meet him seeking the manuscript of that unfinished work. It was a hot afternoon.

'Riyaz, heard that you have become a landlord,' one of them said. 'We came here to investigate it. Anyway, this is great. Become a feudal lord, in order to destroy feudalism. No better alternative.'

Riyaz did not argue and just evaded the comments with a smile.

'What is the real motive behind this group visit? How did you come to know that I was here?' Riyaz asked.

'That is not of any importance. Now you get us the novel. Don't fob us off with excuses. We want to read it,' said a friend working in a periodical. Others joined in.

Riyaz plucked a fresh cucumber from his garden and sliced it for them. 'Cucumber is very good during summer,' he said laughing.

No one has any knowledge about his incomplete novel even now.

The police did not keep Murali in custody for long. A close relative of his was a top official in the income tax department in the Centre.

Attending the trunk call from New Delhi, the police officer answered without any interest, 'There is no provision to tell you everything in detail.'

'But we have provisions to tell some details to the public,' the voice from Delhi had an intimidating tone.

Murali was released the very next day.

Murali shifted to Delhi after the completion of his Engineering course. He attended a coaching programme for the Civil Services examination and passed it in the first attempt. He was posted in Bihar.

Murali was never affected by the corruption and the vulgarity of power which had become the bane of the bureaucracy. His was the generous and people friendly face of civil service. He took voluntary retirement after twenty years and joined an organisation active among tribal people. After two years, on a December morning, the jeep he was travelling ran over a mine laid by an extremist organisation as it was negotiating a steep mountain and exploded into the ravines.

Though they tried their level best to search, even using a helicopter, the police were unable to locate the remains of the dead.

Viswanathan was taken away from his office by police dressed in civilian clothes. They got him out of the office by referring to a friend of his from his native place. However, Viswanathan had recognised them to be what they were at first sight. He was kept under custody without noting the arrest and this provoked his union to organise a strike. He was then produced in the court and was granted bail. He was later on removed from service at the instance of the government. Viswanathan took up a job as a teacher in a parallel college and then as a proofreader. He was reinstated in service after the change of government. After years, when the mainstream communist party came into power, Viswanathan became the private secretary of the Home Minister. He was still a bachelor. He was witness to policemen who had tortured him grovelling before him for transfers and promotions. But he did not let loose his authority on them. Viswanathan was one of the rare species that was reaching extinction, men who were able to remain sober despite being endowed with absolute power.

One of the days when Sakunthala was not there, two men walked into their neighbour Anthony Appappan's house enquiring about Sreenivasan. One was fat, but short and dark complexioned while the other was tall and slim. The fat man was slightly old. He was always chewing paan. They had come through the narrow path that bisected the paddy field. It was quite early in the morning and there was the lingering coolness brought on by a light drizzle.

Which is the house of *poet* Sreenivasan was what they asked Anthony Appappan.

Poet Sreenivasan? Who is he? Anthony Appappan asked himself. Is there such a person?

'See, one Sreenivasan lives next door. I don't know if he is a poet or anything like that.' It was after deliberation for some time that he had answered. He was sitting on the cot on the veranda. He took his cane and stuck the floor twice, in memory of journeys he had undertaken in his youth to distant lands with his flock of ducks.

'Even we did not know. But it seems many in our country have been afflicted by the poetry bug,' the older man laughed. Anthony Appappan got up from the cot and hobbled out with the help of the walking stick. He was not that old nor that sick, to use a stick for walking, but it had become a habit. He pointed to the house and said that they could just walk across as there was no fence separating the two houses.

'We'll take a look anyway,' the older one said.

'Can I have money for a packet of beedi?' Anthony Appappan asked.

'This is great! Tips for giving directions! Hey old man, you too have a craze for poetry?'

Anthony Appappan laughed like the quacking of ducks.

In the preceding two days, Sivan had stayed in Sreenivasan's house. He had left for town the previous morning and was supposed to be back in the evening. But he had not returned.

Sivan had written several letters during his stay there. Those letters had to be delivered to prominent comrades. The import of resuming the publication of the monthly was the content of all those letters.

Sivan felt quite secure in that house. The house was in a sparsely populated area. A farmland in front of the house. Anyone coming there had to walk through the path separating the fields and could be easily seen from the house. There were only couple of houses in the vicinity. He slept peacefully after several nights. Those were the rare days when the fear of the enemy stalking him had vanished from his mind. He had stayed confined to a small inside room. Did not step out of that room during daytime. Toilet, ablutions and bathing were shifted to the night. Sreenivasan prepared food for him. He took care of Sivan attending to all his needs and getting him black tea at frequent intervals. Sivan noticed with amazement that Sreenivasan had a worshipful attitude towards him.

There was some truth in what he had told Sakunthala. Sreenivasan was indeed writing a play. A play, which could be staged even on streets with very little paraphernalia. He had commenced the play reinforced by the energy gathered from reading *Liberation Path*. Sreenivasan consoled himself that he was not lying to her at least to that extent. He was delighted when the comrade asked him what he was writing. He talked about the play in detail though he had completed only two scenes. But the comrade's only comment, that the theme was good, had subdued Sreenivasan's enthusiasm. Maybe the comrade's mind was preoccupied, he thought. After all, it was the same person who had insisted on publishing his poems!

Sivan was preoccupied with another thread of thought. All those whom he contacted or all those who supported the party had a bend towards literature. It was the same case whether it was Chitran, Viswanathan or Riyaz. What did it signify? That all of them roosted in romantic poems and stories. Their approach was rather sentimental. Could they be expected to be balanced in their attitude in crucial matters? In the societies where revolutionary changes had taken place, it was the writers and artists who had become the worst revisionists. Astonishing but true. Why are such people more attracted to the party than others?

Sivan had started work on the new edition of the magazine the day he had reached there. Translating some of the articles he had with him was the first task. Couple of others were to be edited. Rereading them, he found the language quite strange. He kept aside the poems that had come by post. Most of them were translations. Maybe Sreenivasan could assess their standard. As it is, availability of space for poems and stories was doubtful. The pages would be over by the time the reporting and analysis of problems and issues were done. Those comrades without any affinity towards literature argued that there was no point in converting the magazine into a literary journal. But most of those who contributed to the magazine asked where else would they publish creative efforts with revolutionary themes.

Sivan planned to pass on the selected matter to the press through Chitrabhanu within two days. First he thought of sending Sreenivasan, but then decided to do it himself. Some instructions regarding the layout and other things had to be given. There were some problems in the last issue. More difficult was finding a suitable press. The treachery of *Kambanam* Lasar was still fresh. And that led his thoughts to Remani. The poor girl was a prisoner there. It was she who had let him out of the press that night. Lasar was sleeping in the inside room, all his fury spent.

'You lied to me about writing drama. Even then I am sad that you are leaving,' she said.

'Why?' Sivan asked her.

'It was a relief for me. To tell everything to ... to someone.'

There was darkness between them too. Outside, there was a slight drizzle.

'I'll comeback one day,' he kissed her abruptly, holding her close, gathering courage.

'Hey, what is this?' She exclaimed but did not make any attempts to free herself.

'It was you who saved me,' Sivan said. 'One day I will save you from here.'

'Sounds like an old dialogue,' Remani laughed. 'You can very well try your hand at playwriting, you will succeed.'

Lasar was snoring loudly. Sivan stepped out into the drizzle.

Which press to try now? Will have to go around and find out. As dusk fell Sivan had a bath at the well. It was getting late. He stuffed the soiled clothes into the bag. He planned to wash them the next day after returning. He put on the fresh clothes Sreenivasan gave him and left for the town by the last bus.

When Sivan left, Sreenivasan thought of going to Sakunthala's place. Sivan was expected only by next evening. He could return by that time. But he was afraid that Sasi may insist on coming back with him. He had demanded a toy, a red top in fact. Or was it blue? If he were to bring them along with him, they would find out about the comrade. But he could be passed on as a playwright. However, Sakunthala may not believe it. Could've told her the truth, he thought. Sreenivasan was abiding by the instruction of Chitrabhanu that everything should be top secret and that the women should not get any inkling at any cost. Weighing the pros and cons, he ruled out going to Sakunthala's house.

He was late getting up next morning. The play was almost complete. The sky was unusually dark. Was there a chance for a summer shower? Then he saw two men walking in the direction of his house from the distance.

They were still very far. Who they were, was not clear. Once they climbed up a slope, he could make out a short and fat man and a lean and tall one. Even though it was too early to decide that they were indeed coming to his house, Sreenivasan was apprehensive. Are they after the comrade? Even if they are, that he is not there right now is a relief. But what line should he adopt to the questions that would invariably follow? What bothered Sreenivasan more was who informed the police?

Sreenivasan was relieved when he saw them enter his neighbour Anthony Appappan's house. That was lucky. May be relatives. How wild his imagination had run!

But that relief was short-lived. As he was making tea, the two walked into his kitchen. Covering up the indecency of walking into a house without even knocking, the fat man smiled at him.

'Sreenivasan, right?' he asked. Sreenivasan nodded.

'Poet Sreenivasan would be more apt, no?'

Sreenivasan just looked at him.

'By mistake we went into the other house. We knew only that you live somewhere in these parts. We had thought that we would be able to come straight to your house. But that we couldn't,' explained the man. He was dark and bald. The front teeth were yellowish. Very small eyes when compared to the bulk of the body. His eyes blinked rapidly while talking. His conversation had the air of intimacy of a close friend.

Who are these two? Why are they here?

'Okay, let me put it straight. Where is our leader?' Sreenivasan trembled.

He couldn't utter a word. So they have come for the comrade. As Sreenivasan remained silent, the fat man repeated.

'Tell us Sreenivasan, we know that he is here.'

'We are from the Crime Branch.' The taller man spoke for the first time. His voice had the stress and weight of authority. 'We have received information that he had come here.'

'Where is he? If we don't get him, we lose our cap. That's the situation.' The first one laughed. 'He goes around chopping heads of people and the police go around trying not to lose their heads. That's the only difference. But there is also a similarity, no?'

Though the question was directed at him the second guy did not show any inclination to enjoy the joke. Instead, his eyes were scanning the house.

'Hey, Sreenivasan, you did not even offer us a cup of tea. Is this the hospitality shown by poets?' the fat one asked spitting out the paan.

Sreenivasan poured the tea into three glasses.

The fat man started sipping the tea even before he was asked to. The taller one avoided it saying that he didn't drink tea.

The taller one inspected all the rooms including the beds. Then he came out into the yard and made a thorough scrutiny. He also walked to the western end of the plot and went into the latrine for inspection. He returned frustrated.

'Not to be seen, sir,' he said. Then he turned towards Sreenivasan and asked sharply, 'Where have you hidden him?'

'I've not hidden him anywhere.'

'Damn it, lying to us, are you?' he raised his hand menacingly and yelled, 'If you try any tricks with me, I will show you my true colours.'

'Hey Pankajakshan, no. don't scare him. Sreenivasan will tell us everything. He did not say he won't cooperate, did you Sreenivasan?' The elderly policeman kept the glass down after finishing his tea.

Sreenivasan just glanced at him and remained mum.

'The tea was fine,' the elder one smiled at him. He then squatted on the hearth. 'Ho! It's quite cool. There was a shower in the morning, wasn't it? My arthritis will flare up at the slightest fall in the temperature.' The embers were still smouldering.

'Oh, we did not get acquainted. This is Pankajakshan, Head Constable. He is just brilliant. I am Sub Inspector Bhaskara Kurup. We came here on getting some information. OK, tell me, that head hunting leader had been here, no?' he asked Sreenivasan with great affection and a warm smile.

Sreenivasan did not deny. Yes he was here. Everyone knows it. Lying will only complicate matters.

'Okay. When did he come here?'

'Two days ago.'

'Where is he now?'

'Gone.'

'Gone! When?'

'Yesterday night.'

"This fellow must have hidden him, sir.' Pankajakshan did not believe what Sreenivasan said.

'It's the truth, sir.'

'Where did he go?' Kurup attempted to light a beedi from the hearth.

Sreenivasan shook his head to indicate that he did not know. But it seemed as if he himself did not believe in what he said.

'So, we were late, eh?' the elder one asked. 'Where did the great man go?'

'He didn't tell,' said Sreenivasan. He realised that what he was saying was indeed the truth. He had said that he'd come back; but he had not said where he was going to. Sreenivasan had not asked either. He was not certain whether such questions were asked at all. Anyway the elder one did not seem to disbelieve his answer. He had lit a beedi from the embers.

'It'll be better for you if you tell us where he went,' Pankajakshan threatened.

'I don't think such matters will be revealed to him. If at all they mention anything, that is bound to be a lie. Okay, how did you get to know him?'

Sreenivasan was in a dilemma. If he revealed the truth, Chitran would be in trouble. He thought for a moment and then said, 'I met him at a poets' meet.'

'Poets' meet? He writes poetry?'

'Poetry … he reads …' Sreenivasan was stammering.

'Smart! But the place where all these smart guys ultimately end up, that is the ugly part. Write poems, write stories and live decently and happily, isn't that enough my dear Sreenivasan? Why should we have any truck with those who pluck the heads of people?' He took a deep puff.

'These fellows are all liars, sir. Couple of blows and they will start singing like a canary,' Pankajakshan said.

'What's the use if he sings like a canary, Pankajakshan? Let him sing like Sreenivasan does,' Bhaskara Kurup laughed.

'When are you supposed to meet again?'

'Nothing was said,' Sreenivasan averted his face.

'It's still cold,' Bhaskara Kurup locked his hands and shifted his bottom.

'Ok. Sreenivasan, why don't you recite a stanza from any of your poems?' Kurup demanded. Sreenivasan recited few lines of one of his abandoned poems.

'It sounds like *manjari*. But the rhythm is broken at many places,' Bhaskara Kurup said thoughtfully. 'And why do you resort to *manjari* and *kakali? Keka* is ideal. There's a swish to it, Sreenivasan.'

Pankajakshan went into the rooms and commenced a scrutiny of the books and magazines. There were a few periodicals which Sivan had brought with him. But there was nothing to link them to him. Pankajakshan scattered the books and magazines on the floor. He found out a diary from the lot and asked,

'Whose is it?'

That was Sreenivasan's diary. Everything from shopping list to notes taken during poets' meet had found a place in it.

'It's mine,' said Sreenivasan.

In order to confirm it, Pankajakshan made Sreenivasan write on a blank page. On comparing the handwriting, he had to concede that the diary indeed was Sreenivasan's. Still he pocketed the diary.

All that time Sreenivasan was apprehensive of something else. In the same room from where Pankajakshan found out that diary there were notebooks with addresses. The articles and notes and pictures the comrade had brought for *Liberation Path* were also there. All these were packed in a paper and kept between books. Somehow it had escaped Pankajakshan's eyes till now. If he saw them …

'You've muddled his books?' Kurup chided Pankajakshan. 'Now arrange them properly as they were. After all, our Sreenivasan is a poet. I respect poets.'

'No need, sir.' As Pankajakshan was about to go into the room again, Sreenivasan stopped him. 'It does not matter sir. I'll do it later.'

Pankajakshan ignored his words and pretended to put everything back. It was quite evident that he did not like the tactics of Bhaskara Kurup.

When he stepped out of the room Pankajakshan had in his hands the bag in which Sivan had stuffed his soiled mundu and shirt.

'Is it yours?' He asked. Sreenivasan was taken aback. It was the dress of the comrade. He had left the previous night wearing Sreenivasan's clothes. Sreenivasan did not know how to respond.

'Do you take dirty clothes to the laundry?' Pankajakshan asked.

'No.'

'Then? Why are these packed in a bag?' There was a gleam of victory in his eyes.

'I asked you, whose is it?'

'That … perhaps he forgot …' Sreenivasan stammered.

'Or has he dumped it here?'

The truth was that Sreenivasan did not really know. Why did the comrade do it this way? He must have planned to wash it today when he returned. Just a word and he, Sreenivasan, would have done the washing.

Pankajakshan was angry. 'Do guests leave dirty clothes in bags when they leave?'

Sreenivasan remained mum.

'Oh, that's a foul, Sreenivasan! Where did you shift him when you saw us? There too you lost your rhythm!' Bhaskara Kurup was laughing when he said this. 'You had said that he had left. But his dirty clothes are here. That too neatly packed. Doesn't it mean that he is ready to leave? No? Just show us where he is hiding. Don't harass that Pankajakshan. Come on, where have you hidden him?'

'I've not hidden him,' Sreenivasan mumbled.

'Then?' Pankajakshan raised his voice.

'The truth is that he has gone from here.' Sreenivasan somehow completed the sentence amidst mounting tension.

'They are all together in this game, sir,' Pankajakshan was agitated. 'Don't give in to their tricks.'

'No. He might have been planning to come back. That's possible.' Kurup was lost in thought for a while and then asked, 'Is it not so, Sreenivasan? He was coming back, wasn't he?'

'That was what he had said …' Sreenivasan agreed.

Kurup was pleased that his assessment was correct. He took one more puff and asked, 'So, when is he expected?'

'He had not said anything specifically.'

'Chhee! Come on, out with it, you …!' Pankajakshan was furious.

'He was supposed to be here yesterday. But he did not turn up. Perhaps ... tonight …' Sreenivasan was trying to conceal the severe trembling of his limbs.

'If that is the case, should we remain here till nightfall, Pankajakshan? Why not make a visit home?' Kurup was seeking permission from Pankajakshan, not the other way round. Sreenivasan thought it strange.

'You leave if you want, sir. But I leave this place only with him. If we are not vigilant, this fellow here will tip him off somehow, for sure.'

Bhaskara Kurup, who was still sitting on the hearth flexed his arms. The fire in the hearth had gone out.

'Ok, but then how do I go back alone? Let him find his way back here after finishing all his work. That will at least spare us some trudging!Okay then Sreenivasan, you can't leave this house till our great friend returns, you understand?' Kurup laughed.

Even though he did not understand, he nodded.

'Pankajakshan, we too are not going anywhere. We will provide him company, what?'

No one spoke.

So the policemen were going to wait. Sreenivasan was restless. What was going to happen? If the comrade comes now, he will be nabbed. What will he think? How come the police lay waiting for him in such a remote village? It will certainly be marked as a folly on Sreenivasan's part. The natural conclusion will be that he was a person incapable of keeping even a small secret. Or will he be seen as a cheat? Sreenivasan was in a turmoil. How will I face Chitrabhanu? He had shown so much faith in me and had entrusted the safety of the comrade to me. Sreenivasan writhed in agony unable to free his mind from self-condemnation. He put his conscience on trial. What went wrong? How can I warn the comrade that the police are lying in waiting here?

Sreenivasan sat near the window gazing out. Even the leaves were still. Silence hung heavy like a lifeless corpse. A pedestrian appearing at the other end of the paddy field was enough to increase his heartbeats. Gradually the face of the man would become visible and a sigh of relief; no it's not him. Perhaps he may have got the information that the police were waiting. Maybe that was why he did not turn up last night. It would be wonderful if that was the case.

The day slipped into evening and still nothing happened.

Sreenivasan had cooked lunch for the policemen. He also made black tea for them at frequent intervals. As night fell, Bhaskara Kurup went out leaving Pankajakshan in charge. He reeked of liquor when he returned. Drinks had freed his tongue and he recited poems and a lot of *slokas.*

Pankajakshan maintained a distance. Bare essential conversation. He had not believed in Sreenivasan's story.

'Sir, the last bus too has gone,' Pankajakshan said.

Kurup's recital came to a halt. He asked as if he had suddenly remembered, 'Pankajakshan, he has not put in an appearance.'

'That's exactly what I meant. What this fellow says need not be the truth.' Pankajakshan stared hard at Sreenivasan. 'What will we report to Dy SP when we get back?'

'What else? We searched for him, couldn't nab him, that's all. Such things are normal in the department.'

'Sir, you are taking this very lightly. These cases do not belong to the normal category. Chandran sir brought me into this case as a special assignment. He will lose confidence in me.'

'I'll be doing the reporting, so you don't have to bother. If he doesn't turn up tonight, we will leave in the morning. How long can we keep waiting?'

'You leave sir, if you are in a hurry. But I had given my word to Chandran sir that I'll only return with him in tow.' Pankajakshan was firm.

Bhaskara Kurup looked at him with tired eyes. 'What is the guarantee that he'll come?'

'He will, sir. He had a very narrow escape from that hostel. He should not be allowed to run free for long.'

Kurup peered at him. Who was the boss here? Who was responsible for the case? This is the flaw of the times. It is as if a constable has been sent to keep an eye on the inspector.

'And if we don't get him, we'll take this guy.' Pankajakshan was emphatic.

'What purpose would it serve?'

'Purpose? Sir, haven't you thought about these things? Providing shelter to such people is also a crime. Chandran sir has made it quite clear.'

Bhaskara Kurup sighed. 'Pankajakshan, I'm getting old. I must not forfeit my pension. And here you have lower ranks imposed on an SI.

I'm not blaming you. But I know it for a fact. You must be having your own instructions. I'm aware of it. My words carry little weight. You are young. Didn't you say just now, sir you may leave? What of it? If I go back without you, they will slit my neck. Such is the times.'

Bhaskara Kurup usually had *kanji* for dinner. He asked Sreenivasan to prepare *kanji*. Kurup relished the curry Sreenivasan prepared with lentils. 'Good. It has punch. Everything to taste.' Kurup said. 'You are a good man. But the company you keep is rotten.'

Bhaskara Kurup lay down on the floor in the inner room after dinner. The same spot where the comrade had slept the previous nights. There were no cots in that house. Head Constable Pankajakshan slept on a mat on the veranda. He did not seem to be sleeping. He was awake throughout the night like a dog that sharpens its ears at every sound.

But Sivan did not turn up that night too. This gave a slim hope to Sreenivasan. Perhaps he will not come at all. Must have guessed the turn of events. Would he have managed some other shelter? If he was to finally come to this very same place, Sreenivasan hoped that the comrade would be vigilant and take adequate precautions.

The next day another policeman came asking for Head Constable Pankajakshan. He was sent by the Dy SP. Jose, that was his name, said, 'Pankajakshan sir has been asked to report urgently. Chandran sir has been summoned by the minister.'

'Did he say it is urgent, Jose?' Pankajakshan asked. However, he then added with pride, 'If not, will he ask me to come back? Something serious must have cropped up.'

'Pankajakshan, when will you return?' Bhaskara Kurup seemed to be relieved that he was leaving.

'That will depend on Chandran sir.'

'You see, I had thought of going home in the evening. How many days am I supposed to be cooped up here ...'

'Don't go home before I come back, sir. We have no idea when the accused might return.'

'We can ask Jose to be here.'

But Jose took Pankajakshan aside and whispered into his ears.

'No, Jose has other things to attend to. I'll tell you in detail after I return,' Pankajakshan said after deliberating for a few minutes.

Pankajakshan was again trying to be authoritarian and Bhaskara Kurup did not relish it at all. However, he did not utter a word. Pankajakshan had direct connections with the higher ups. He was included in special squads. It's better not to provoke him, or I will also end up in the wanted list, Kurup thought. The pension will get delayed, if not anything.

Sreenivasan was somewhat relieved when Pankajakshan left. The extent of his freedom increased, he felt. The whole of yesterday he was under Pankajakshan's watchful eyes. Of course, Bhaskara Kurup also was vigilant, but he seemed to be somewhat softer. He had the nature of a patriarch. Happy if he gets his three meals and tea at the right time. He was not keen to take into custody someone like Sreenivasan. Kurup counselled him, whenever he got an opportunity. That life should be lived in the right manner. Close connection and interaction with criminals is not recommended for gentlemen. Poets were held in esteem even in the olden times. Why? Because their lives were in keeping with the interests of the state. In a way, it can be said that leading the people through the right path is more the responsibility of the poets than the king. One should not devalue such a noble calling. Apart from all that, doesn't Sreenivasan have a wife and a kid? He has to look after them. Who'll be there to support them, if he damns his life getting involved in such situations? Sreenivasan heard him out. And indeed he thought of Sakunthala and Sasi.

It was noon. Sreenivasan served him lunch. There were no vegetables. So he could not make any curry. He roasted papads over the embers and improvised a curry with onions and green chillies.

'You could have fried the papads, Sreenivasan.'

'There is no coconut oil left.'

When he saw only green chillies in the plate, he asked, 'No butter milk?'

'No.'

'Why?'

'No … Usually, we don't buy too much milk.'

'You could have at least prepared dal like yesterday.'

'But ... No sir, green gram was over.'

'Don't keep saying no, no, no … Don't keep singing the song of scarcity my dear Sreenivasan. It will spoil the prosperity of your home.'

'They are really over, sir. I've to restock provisions and vegetables, go out and buy them.'

Kurup weighed the possibility, then dismissed it with frustration.

'No, no. Pankajakshan will chop off my head if he comes to know. Even though a minion, he now has the power of a magistrate.'

While cooking, while eating and while doing the dishes, Sreenivasan was in fact thinking about the comrade. The terrifying thought that he could walk in anytime was refusing to leave him. After lunch Bhaskara Kurup lay down on the bench in the front for a wink.

'Son, I'll lie down for a while. You should tell me if your friend sneaks in. After all our survival depends on him, no? He is bound to be trapped at any cost. Why should I be punished for his vanishing from here too?'

The siesta of Bhaskara Kurup was rather prolonged. He babbled in his sleep and also recited *slokas*.

It was past four. Sreenivasan was surveying the farmland through the window. He saw a familiar face at the extreme end of the fields. He willed it not to be the comrade. But the image was becoming brighter and brighter. It was him. He was clad in Sreenivasan's clothes. A bag on his shoulder. Unshaven face, unkempt hair indicating a long journey. Sreenivasan was upset seeing the approaching comrade. He was coming there expecting Sreenivasan to take care of everything. He did not have any other place to hide. If he was caught from there, Sreenivasan would be held responsible. Those were the moments when the poet in him underwent great suffering.

When he was close enough, Sreenivasan raised his hands and waved at him to keep away. But Sivan was not looking at him. He was looking down and was lost in thought. His movements were that of a free man, completely unaware that he was walking into disaster. Sreenivasan was absolutely distressed. If only he raised his head, he could see the waving hands. And Kurup was still sleeping.

Sivan stepped into the frontyard of the house from the pathway.

'Hey Sreenivasan, let him come. Don't bother waving your hands and legs.' The voice of Bhaskara Kurup rose behind him. Sreenivasan was stunned as if struck by lightning. When did Kurup wake up? He must have seen all the gestures I was making, Sreenivasan thought. Now it will not be possible to act as if it was not the comrade but someone else.

Sivan stood there in the frontyard, hesitating. He must have smelt danger.

'Now, come, come. Have been waiting for you since long,' Bhaskara Kurup said. Sivan entered the room without further ado. Perhaps the reality had dawned on him.

'I want some water,' he said.

'Give it to him,' Kurup ordered Sreenivasan. 'Well, I have heard that you are not an ordinary person. But no more smart games, Okay? If we wait a bit, that Pankajakshan will also be here. We can all go together, what do you say?'

Sreenivasan noticed Sivan stealing a glance at him as he brought a glass of water.

'I want to collect certain documents,' Sivan told Sreenivasan.

Maybe he is referring to the matter obtained for the next issue of *Liberation Path*. But what use is it of in the prevailing circumstances, thought Sreenivasan.

Kurup was listening. He went on chewing paan and stared at them. Neither of them made any comment.

'Documents? Do you really need to take them? Okay, go ahead. Pankajakshan might find them useful,' Kurup agreed.

Sivan went in and returned with a bag of clothes. He took out a soiled shirt and pretended to be busy searching for something in its pocket. Sreenivasan knew that Sivan was making calculations.

Mustering courage, Sreenivasan made a gesture and Sivan replied in the same manner. It escaped Kurup's attention.

Suddenly Sivan's hand struck the glass and it tumbled spilling the water. Sivan thus gained half a moment. He sprang up and lunged forward. Bhaskara Kurup was taken by surprise. Moving his heavy body was not that easy. Still he could get a hand to the bag hanging from Sivan's shoulder, bringing him down. Kurup fell on him like an old lion. Sreenivasan watched them tussling, one trying to get a hold and the other to break free. He did not know what to do.

But he suddenly jumped on the fighting duo. Sivan should be freed from Kurup's grip at any cost. Kurup could not handle two at a time. His hold loosened and in a flash Sivan leapt out and dashed away. Sreenivasan loosened his grip on Bhaskara Kurup only after confirming that Sivan had crossed the paddy field.

Bhaskara Kurup was panting. Blood trickled from a bruise on his forehead. His lips were swollen. He looked helplessly at Sreenivasan. Sreenivasan did not have the guts to face him.

'Tricked! I'm done for. I'll lose my job,' lamented Kurup.

'Sir, you must forgive me. I had no other alternative,' Sreenivasan said.

Bhaskara Kurup sighed. He wiped the blood on his forehead with his finger and licked the finger. He spat out the remnants of the paan. Sreenivasan fetched coffee powder from the kitchen and sprinkled it on Kurup's wound. It was a home remedy practised by Sakunthala. Bhaskara Kurup started crying like a child.

Sreenivasan was sorry for causing pain. But what else could he do? If the comrade was nabbed from his place, that would have caused him greater anguish. What would Chitran think? Didn't he show tremendous faith in him by entrusting him with the comrade?

'Sir you need not reveal what happened here,' Sreenivasan tried to console Kurup. A pale smile appeared on Kurup's lips. The entire despondency of a five decade long life was seen reflected on his face.

Kurup mumbled, 'You have no idea of how things work in the world, Sreenivasan. Those who are supposed to know, get the information as and when anything happens.'

It was dark by now. Sreenivasan saw a jeep coming to a halt where the road ended beyond the paddy field. After some time Pankajakshan and Jose walked into the frontyard of the house. There was one more person, in uniform, with them.

'Kurup sir, any information?'

'No, he has not turned up, Pankajakshan,' Kurup did not stumble.

'It's okay if he has not come, sir. It is guys like this fellow here that we really want. How will this world reform if rascals like him are there?' He looked at Sreenivasan with cold rage.

'What rascal? You trying to terrify us by your staring?' Jose shouted at Sreenivasan. His tone was arrogant.

'Don't bother about anything, just take him, sir has ordered,' Pankajakshan said pointing to Sreenivasan. He stepped on to the veranda.

Kurup did not object. Jose and Pankajakshan handcuffed Sreenivasan. When getting into the jeep Sreenivasan looked around to see if anyone was witnessing the scene.

A kerosene lamp was emitting a pale light in Anthony Appappan's house. A child was crying very loudly. Lucky, no one was paying any attention to the jeep.

The jeep turned into an unfamiliar road after the junction. Pankajakshan was driving. Now they were going through a very dark road. The road was so narrow, the jeep seemed to be brushing the bushes and branches of trees on the sides of the road.

'Hey Pankajakshan, where are we headed to?' Bhaskara Kurup asked in a feeble voice. He seemed to be in pain.

'You don't bother sir. I'm quite familiar with the route,' Pankajakshan laughed. 'This fellow here requires some straightening.'

'Ey, we've left the station behind,' Bhaskara Kurup was all astonishment.

'Is there only one station in this country sir? If one is left behind, another will appear on the way ahead.'

'His custody is to be recorded, no?'

'It is not required is the order.'

'Whose order?' Kurup asked. But no one in the jeep cared to answer him.

It was a narrow untarred road with ditches and potholes all over. Sreenivasan was unfamiliar with the road. He set his eyes on whatever he could see outside. Bhaskara Kurup was sitting in the front. They reached a small junction after four or five miles. Kurup was announcing loudly that he had worked in that area. The other policemen in the jeep did not seem to like Kurup or his words. Perhaps they were not coming out openly against him only because he was their senior. The other three were more serious in their tone and manners. The one who was sitting right in front of Sreenivasan was holding his gun upright. Sreenivasan realised that all of them were happy to have grabbed a quarry. But do they not also fear me a bit, Sreenivasan thought. Perhaps they suspect that I carry some sort of weapon? They had made a body search as soon as he was seated. But they still seemed to be apprehensive and were on their toes.

Just as they passed the junction, the policeman next to him took out a piece of black cloth and tied it across Sreenivasan's eyes thus making it dark inside too.

'Sit tight you rascal. You will be done for if you create a scene,' one of them shouted.

'Why did you blindfold him?' Bhaskara Kurup asked.

'Keep quiet, sir,' another said in scathing tones. 'We have been authorised by the higher ups to do whatever we feel is necessary.'

'So am I not in charge anymore?' Kurup asked. 'I'm the inspector, no?'

'If you are the SI, you should behave accordingly. This is something different. It is not a petty theft or fisticuffs,' the first policeman said.

'It's a special squad for dealing with these people. So the adjustments are different.'

'If you cannot cope up with it, you should have indicated so earlier. This is simply causing trouble,' Pankajakshan growled.

'Careful! don't forget whom you are talking to,' Kurup was obviously hurt.

'Don't be silly, sir,' the policeman with the gun laughed. 'If you create any trouble, the Dy SP will award you with a suspension order. That's it! And you can go around with it for the rest of your service.'

'Considering your present activities, I don't think there will be much delay in your getting it,' Pankajakshan agreed with his colleague.

Bhaskara Kurup did not utter a word for the rest of the journey.

'So, there is no urgency in nabbing the other guy now, sir?' the gunman asked.

'No need for that,' Pankajakshan replied.

'Why so?'

'See, that is the fun of it. Chandran sir called me today to explain this new strategy. Wisdom is in not capturing him.'

'You mean?'

'Yes, exactly. He's sir's own man,' Pankajakshan said changing gear and raising the speed.

'Wherever he goes we get a good bargain. The catch we get is fabulous. See now this guy! So the order is to let him go even if we lay our hands on him.'

'Whose order?' but the question remained stuck at Bhaskara Kurup's throat.

The jeep entered a road that was more uneven.

THE PARABLE OF THE ANTS

The notes written for *Liberation Path* were getting stale. The papers on which policies and strategies were listed started yellowing. Termites passively traversed through the paths of revolution. A terrifying silence reigned. On rereading those notes, Sivan had the feeling that Time was travelling without any sense of direction like a blind cockroach.

Being busy with the loading of wood during the day and writing up accounts during the better part of the night, he never got time to read the old articles and notes. As for the accounts, they are as complex as the jungle paths. They begin at some vague point of time, and keep going on. The market price of timber and the quality, change drastically at the flicker of an eyelid. The methods of measurement change. The passage of time in the island was discernible in the account books. It was difficult to comprehend the records maintained by the previous accountant, the grand old man. His letters baffled Sivan as if they belonged to some dubious script. Intermittently the digits in them maintained silence. Like the paths to the outside world from the island, the paths of the numbers too got blocked. It took him quite some time to get used to them. What was left out untended between all these were the old notes. Reading them in the light of the kerosene lamp, the letters seemed to have verdigris formed on them. The ideas in them too seemed to have gone old.

This is the time for hiding. Or is it the time for confinement? Anyway he had been seeking a way out. Should get back somehow.

The situation must have undergone quite a lot of change by now. Popular movements must be surging ahead. One has to be prepared intellectually to confront the changes. All these thoughts have to be reflected in the fresh notes. But there was no idea of what had really been happening outside. There were no means to access such news. Newspapers or magazines were not available. But that did not matter much as at no point of time has true and authentic news of popular struggles been carried by mainstream media.

The life in the island was monotonous. The island stood aloof like a territory that had been trapped in some other orbit. It had spaces where one could even hide from the sun. The trees, flora and fauna and even the people were different. Ancient and senile trees with their twining trunks stood like sculptures of vicious beauty. Around them lay scattered yellow and decayed leaves. Their roots were thicker than the main trunk. Roots protruded from the soil like old nerves.

Outside the Mansion of Karadi Papa, the paniyas created a settlement of a bereaved tribe who had lost their language. When they trundled away with their sheep, it was as if a breeze of silence was passing by. They never raised the stick in their hand. After the silent procession of the goats, the paniyas were seen to be looking back as if searching for something with their terror-stricken eyes. The light in their eyes which seemed to have emanated from ancient times passed through him as if through glass, Sivan felt. He tried to stay away from them. The walls of the shelter thickened.

However, the life in the island did not seem to be one suited to the revolutionaries. On the contrary, all facilities for a class enemy were found arranged. He had to be up early in the morning and had to report to Pappayi all the details of the wood to be transported that day. So Sivan would keep that ready before Pappayi woke up.

Ayyakkuru would be waiting at the bottom of the staircase in the mornings. The totem of silence was stamped on his face too. The fire of the past flickered in his eyes. Was he preparing himself as the auspicious morning omen for me as instructed by Pappayi? At first Sivan had felt being mocked at and he also carried a sense of belittlement. Good omen! Is it that his search for the elderly revolutionary has led him merely to a cattleshed of superstitions? Where is that comrade who was the great blazing flame of revolution?

Gradually the mentioning of Karadi-Papa dwindled. Pappayi would remind occasionally that the accounts were kept for his sake. Was there really such a man? Was he still there as Pappayi maintained? If at all such an individual was there, who bestowed on him the antecedents of revolution? Or had they been taken for a ride? Perhaps the comrades decided to let him be here in hiding without anyone knowing about it. How could one confirm that their assumptions were wrong? But it was also possible that they had sent someone to summon me. Comrade Achu might have come to the landing on the other side. He might have assigned the mission to Moosa and waited. Moosa might have communicated this to Ayyakkuru. And what is it that Ayyakkuru normally does? Inform Pappayi. It'd have been like the dice in the puzzle falling into the mouth of the snake, and reaching zero.

It was before leaving for the hills that Pappayi usually gave him assignments. He was a man of guesstimates. However, maybe because of experience, most of his guesses were accurate. Not just in accounting, he was well versed in carpentry too. He could correctly guess which tree it was by just touching the wood. This all round knowledge must have been the reason why the toughies, hefty wood cutters and loaders or the bullock cart drivers who drive through precariously perching granite blocks became docile pussy cats in his presence. If he noticed the slightest omission or misdoing he'd explode into expletives as if those in front of him were stray dogs. However, he'd forget it the next minute and display warmth and friendliness.

Sivan made an attempt to evaluate: this is the extension of the age old feudalism. Pappayi is its living leftover. Just like the feudal lord of Kangazha. But here, I too get a share of the veneration he commands. They treat me with the same respect and consideration they have for him. I enjoy that. If any of them fail to extend this reverence, it makes me restless. Because he was with Pappayi most of the time in his topless jeep, the reverential responses came quite naturally. But the jaunts in the jeep were great obstacles too. If the island was indeed a prison, one should somehow manage to get out of it by influencing some of them. But how could he befriend them? Pappayi was with him all the time. Sivan waited for an appropriate opportunity.

But that hardly seemed possible. Spying eyes followed him everywhere, he sensed. It started with the 'good omen' of Ayyakkuru and continued whether he was resting or working. The omnipresence of the formless, shapeless Karadi Papa. It pursued him even in sleep. Sivan was deliberating about it as he walked to the riverside.

There was an estuary of the river at one particular point in the island. It was something like a lagoon, very calm waters. Sivan used to have his bath there. He had thought that it was an uninhabited place. But he could see the huts of paniyas beyond the green curtains of coconut leaves. Huts bowing down to the earth. Crab like human beings inside them.

Sivan had never spoken to any of them. He had hoped to engage them in conversation about the jungle paths or tunnels from the island to the outside world. But will the paniyas ever speak to anyone? Doubtful. When they stumble down your path, or you come across them, they immediately take a diversion. Silence has afflicted their clan like a disease. Even Ayyakkuru lives as a deaf mute. Like a sheep that does not bleat even when separated from the flock.

However, Sivan suspected that they were watching him secretly.

'They dare not look at Achachan in the face. But they are at his call any time of the day and night.' Thechappan one day told Sivan.

'But where's Achachan?' Sivan asked.

Thechappan scanned the surroundings and started to say something, but decided not to, at the last moment.

'The paniyas are not interested in work. They will use birdlime and catch birds, roast them and eat. That's all they want. And if they get a dead animal it is a feast for them,' Thechappan said.

By the time Sivan had his bath and was ready, Thechappan would be there with breakfast. Quite often he'd be drunk by that time and would start babbling about many things, totally unconnected. Sivan hardly listened and only pretended to be listening. Thechappan had a general grudge towards the paniyas and Ayyakkuru was included in it. He displayed it quite often. Most of his idle talk was mocking of Ayyakkuru and scandals about him. According to Thechappan, Ayyakkuru had the master eating out of his palm. That was the main complaint. Pappayi used to visit their house before this pygmy showed up at the Mansion. Pappayi would happily have the spicy food prepared by Thechappan's woman. Thechappan would watch him dine, from a spot outside the house. At times he would drink a little, crack jokes, laugh ... None of this happened anymore. All Ayyakkuru's doing. Animosity simmered in Thechappan's words.

'He is an *odiyan* sir. Look at the way he is standing. He has poisoned everyone with a black magic potion that makes them subservient to him,' Thechappan said.

Sivan would listen attentively, but make no comments.

'Rascal! Does not have an iota of gratitude. What all goodies Achayan used to give us in the former days! Now he sits and stands and sleeps with Ayyakkuru!'

'Sleeps?' Sivan was curious.

Thechappan made retching sounds. Sivan thought he was about to vomit. Instead he just spat.

Sivan had never been to Thechappan's house. He'd invite Sivan almost everyday. Sivan would promise to go another day and thus postpone the visit. Thechappan seemed to be peeved at that. His old monkey was filthier than Thechappan. He was often seen with that animal. It had a long shackle around its waist. Flies swarmed around the many wounds on its body. One could not eat if it was around. The monkey stank. Thechappan may not have been aware of this since he was high on arrack, almost always. One day it was Thechappan's wife Mary who turned up. Mary was heftier than Thechappan and taller than Ayyakkuru. Short and thick legs. Plain face with big ears. Despite all this she had a certain charm. And she was tidy. But she had the peculiar habit of watching him all the time. What was it that she was scrutinising? Sivan, however, was reluctant to look at her. While he ate with bent head, he was aware that Mary was watching him from behind the door.

One day she was leaving with the plates when he heard an 'Ayyo! Help!' Sivan was washing his hands after food. He saw Mary standing there aghast and pale. It was as if she had seen a ghost.

'What's the matter, what happened?' Sivan shouted.

A terrified Mary pointed to the other side, where there was a thick bush of banana plants. He could see someone running away.

'Who is it?' Sivan enquired.

'Snake …'

'Snake? What? Where is it?'

'I saw the snake curled up around his neck.'

'Snake around the neck? Whom are you speaking about Mary?'

'That dwarf. He was hiding here.'

'Why should he be hiding here?'

'He is like that. He will lurk wherever a man and a woman are together. He doesn't like it.'

'But we were not even talking to each other,' Sivan asked. Mary bent her head with resentment.

'Did he misbehave with you?'

'Let him just try! I'll chop off his hand. This now is … the snake. That was what startled me.'

Sivan did not say anything further. He too did not find Ayyakkuru's behaviour acceptable. But it was not advisable to show animosity to anyone on the island. He did not know who would be of what use to him. Moreover, Ayyakkuru did not seem to have taken to heart the unsavoury incidents of Sivan's first day there. Whenever they came face to face, Ayyakkuru would smile at him fully opening his lips. He was the one who changed the bed linen and did the washing for Sivan.

Ayyakkuru was quite meticulous in those duties. But was there not something wrong? What was it that distinguished him from the person he was on the first day? Yes, that mixed lingua. Sivan was certain that Ayyakkuru did speak, on that day. Where has it vanished? For whom was he masquerading as a deaf mute? Absolutely no idea. In course of time, Sivan too accepted that he could not speak. Perhaps Sivan had misunderstood the entire situation because of his peculiar state of mind when he first arrived at the island. But how was it possible for him to have imagined the whole conversation? And he did not know mixed Tamil anyway.

After making a few corrections in some of his earlier notes and after preparing a few new ones, he packed them in an old sheet of paper. So much time had already elapsed and there should not be any further delay. These notes must reach his comrades. This could perhaps be the last hope. He wrote a long letter analysing the situation.

What is happening out there? I don't get any information from the outside world. Where did the link rupture? Did you try to contact me? If you did, I'm not aware of it.

It is also possible that the messages might have reached the wrong hands. In case no attempts were made to contact me, I'd like to make one thing clear. There is no point in hiding in this island any longer. I appreciate your intentions. But this is yet another prison. This is my assessment. The ambience of this place is not suitable for a revolutionary. Coming out is imperative. Does not matter even if the police are still on the lookout. Some other alternative has to be found out. The duty of a revolutionary is to work among the people, organise them and prepare them for struggle. Haven't we learnt that the life of a revolutionary estranged from the people is like that of a fish trapped on land, away from water? In these circumstances, discuss among yourselves and prepare a plan to get me out of this island as soon as you get this message. The next issue of *Liberation Path* should not be delayed any further. The matter for publication is enclosed.

The letter written, Sivan had to tackle another problem. How to get it to the outside world? Entrusting it with the bullock cart drivers who come to fetch the timber? But Pappayi is always there like a shadow. What would happen if he lays his hands on it? How would he react if he becomes aware of Sivan's interests other than the accounting of timber? Will he treat it as a grave issue? So far he had shown interest only in wood and timber. How about handing it over to Thechappan? No, Thechappan is a big mouth. He will brag about anything and make a mountain. He is always under the influence of alcohol. Such a person should not be entrusted with such sensitive documents. They might get lost. Moreover, Sivan had never seen him leave the island.

But there was yet another crucial factor. The letter was smuggled out; but to whom? Who was the one to receive the message? Sivan remembered the comrades of Pullani about whom the students of Avalam had spoken very high of. The courageous comrades of Pullani! But Sivan had never seen any of them. Then? There was Achu. Achu who led him to the island. However the person who dumped him in this prison could only be a counter revolutionary, Sivan felt. Or perhaps only a messenger. But whatever he was, there was no other way. Sivan decided to try Achu. Boatman Moosa knew him. But again, his contacting Moosa could arouse suspicions.

It was then that he thought of Ayyakkuru. Why not depend on Ayyakkuru? It was most likely that he was an illiterate. Moreover being dumb (or was he) there was no fear of his spreading the news. It was Ayyakkuru who went to the riverbank occasionally. He was well acquainted with Moosa. Moosa could locate Achu. But Achu? Doubts and more doubts ... Was it not he who dumped him in this huge prison? Was it not he who insulted a revolutionary by contracting him to keep accounts of the weight and price of teak and timber? Would it be proper to entrust such an important task to him?

Then he dwelt upon the other side. That Achu was an enemy could merely be a conjecture. Not just maybe. It is. All those who participated in the Kangazha action were most probably being hunted down by the police. How many of them would have been nabbed by now? The police would have no mercy on them once they were taken into custody. Many of the comrades who had attacked the Thelakkara station had been finished off before they got out of jail. That has always been the history. The state eliminates all dissenting voices. But people will never knowingly forsake a revolutionary. They will shield him just as the eyelid shields the eyeball. That could be a possible scenario in his case. It was quite possible that hundreds of Kangazhas were happening throughout the country. The oppressed will capture power. All those who had traversed the path of revolution would be set free. They would be lauded. And then Achu will come. Or many Achus … That he should wait till then is the decision of the organisation. Achu is only a messenger, a carrier of commands.

But … trust the carrier. That is the first lesson. The only course of action, therefore, was to make a messenger out of Ayyakkuru.

Whatever happened the publication of the magazine must go on. That was the only way to maintain links and to carry on with discussions. Finally Sivan decided to depute Ayyakkuru.

Next morning too, Ayyakkuru was there at the bottom of the staircase as usual, as a good omen. His sturdy limbs and the visage of a middle-aged man reminded one of a circus clown. The warts above his upper lip were wobbling. Sivan watched him for a while. Shall I do it? Is this dwarf trustworthy? Anyway, Sivan tapped him on the shoulder and said,

'Ayyakkuru, please come upstairs.'

Ayyakkuru's face lighted up. He smiled shyly at Sivan and followed him upstairs. Twice Sivan waited for him to catch up and he noticed the pride with which Ayyakkuru was looking at him.

Sivan closed the door after Ayyakkuru followed him into the room. He was taken aback at this and lowered his face.

'Ayyakkuru, you have to do something for me,' Sivan said.

Ayyakkuru raised his face and listened keenly. Sivan took the packet and the letter and extended them to him.

'You must meet Moosa.' Ayyakkuru stood there staring at him as if he did not understand anything. Sivan mimed the rowing of a boat. And then mimed the words 'Moosa.'

Surprise! Ayyakkuru nodded and smiled gleefully.

'You must give this to Moosa and ask him to pass it on to Achu.' Sivan moved his lips to mime, 'Achu, Achu.'

Ayyakkuru did not seem to follow. Sivan scribbled 'Achu' on a piece of paper and handed it over to him. Ayyakkuru just glanced at it up and down. It was quite obvious that he was illiterate. That is good, thought Sivan and mimed Achu again. Ayyakkuru nodded.

While Ayyakkuru was securing the letter and the matter for the magazine to the tip of his *mundu*, Sivan had opened the door and was asking him to leave.

Ayyakkuru shot a look of mistrust at Sivan. He just hung around for some more time.

'When will you deliver it to Moosa?' Sivan asked him partly with the intention to convey to Ayyakkuru that his job was over.

Ayyakkuru feigned to think. Then left, nodding his head.

There was an unusual incident that day. Pappayi continued to sit in the jeep after reaching the forest range and letting Sivan out. Normally he would get out of the jeep along with Sivan. But today he had not even switched off the ignition.

'What happened? You are not coming?'

'I forgot to tell you sir, I've to go somewhere else. I'm supposed to submit the accounts to Achachan.'

'How do you plan to go?'

'I have to reach the other side. Have to reach Pullani and for that I'll have to cross the river. It's easier that way. I'll take you there one day. But this cannot be postponed further. Perhaps it's already late and he may be waiting.'

'Who?'

'I've asked for Moosa to be there with the boat.'

Sivan shuddered. Moosa was supposed to carry the documents today.

'You asked Moosa to be there? Whom did you send to fetch Moosa?' Sivan was not quite sure of the ground he was treading. However, Pappayi did not seem to notice that.

'O, I asked that Ayyakkuru to go to Moosa. No idea, what he has done.'

So it was now confirmed. Ayyakkuru will meet Moosa. The documents will be handed over. Will Moosa be able to get it away without drawing Pappayi's attention? But is there a whiff of treachery?

Sivan was panicky for no reason watching the jeep going back by the same route it had come. He then took the ultimate decision to get out of the doomed island. Sivan, in his mind's eyes, saw the trunks of huge trees rolling down the hilly slopes. They are retrieved from the river, fastened together like a raft and then towed away to the other shore.

But for me, the river and its possibilities are shut out, he thought. There are spies everywhere observing my actions. The panic of the trapped seized Sivan. He started walking back to the mansion.

It was noon. He wandered through the rooms on the ground floor without any specific purpose. There was nobody around. Sivan stepped into Pappayi's room.

Pappayi usually went to bed quite late and slept till eight in the morning. The dark room in which he slept looked like a bear's den. The shelves were full of small containers and bottles. The paintings on the wall looked like the handiwork of someone with a ghostly imagination. The air was thick with the smell of medicinal oils and herbs. Old account books were stacked in a corner of the room. Different varieties of bottles. A rifle hanging from a nail on the wall. Pappayi's hunting rifle! Sivan thought of the headless trunk of the pig that was floating by the side of the boat on the night of his arrival. The corpse of Kangazha had already slipped out of his memory.

He had never seen anyone going about with that rifle. But on certain nights one could here sporadic gunshots shattering the stillness of the island. Two shots, one after the other. Silence would reign for a while. Then the hooting of paniyas would break that silence. The hooting would continue till the morning. The next day Mary would convert those gunshots into a spicy curry, served in porcelain plates. To kill is to sin, but eat what you killed and the sin ceases to be, Sivan had heard Thechappan comment.

A faded framed picture hung on the wall. The garland around it had withered away. Sivan could not make out which god it was. Or was it Karadi Papa? Where was he? His accounts seemed to extend beyond the borders of *pathalam*. Pappayi's accounts. Who knows whether all of it was really meant for Papa? He had dealings from the island and also from beyond that. Accounting was meticulous and payments were always regular. No one had any complaints and till recently he had no business rivals. But of late certain youngsters had been showing interest. But they had not yet succeeded in spoiling Achayan's party. He had an uncanny instinct which enabled him to outthink and outsmart them.

There was an invisible thread in the accounting also.

Sivan was attending to the details of the trees cut, the wood despatched and the proceeds thereof as also the amounts paid to the forest officials and their superiors. Those details were educating him about the underbelly of the society. A huge Underground! Huge amounts, massive transactions. It was through those accounts that Sivan became familiar with large numbers. Formerly the numbers were mere numbers without any kind of intimacy. Now they assumed a life entirely of their own. In the beginning he used to wonder whether what he was getting involved in, was ethically correct. But the justification was that it was in another name, another guise, a life in the underground.

Sivan resumed his investigation. Walls with calendars. Pillows heaped on the bed, rolled mats on the floor, a long stemmed torch on the wooden table with round legs, two walking sticks ... He pulled out an old trunk, thick with dust, from the far side under the cot. Two cockroaches scrambled away from its top. The box made a creaking sound when Sivan opened it.

The odour of oldness. Sivan suffocated. In which century was it last opened? Even in the dim light he could see a blood stained old rag in it.

On closer scrutiny, it turned out to be a flag. A red flag from which the star had almost faded. Its edges were frayed and it was torn up at the folds. Sivan shuddered.

There was a sheaf of papers beneath the flag. But the papers were blank. Two old pens and a notebook too were there at the bottom of the trunk. Sivan found written pages in the notebook. Ink had spread all over. He held the notebook to the light and tried to read.

'It is absolute starvation in the paniya households. Ailments are not treated. Chanting of mantras in an obscure tribal language is the only treatment proffered. Some quantity of rice has to be delivered to them. Sent a note through the boatman. Not sure whether he will reach it to the right person. If they get the note, they will certainly act. The summer is severe. Even wild tubers are difficult to find. If the rains are further delayed, at least a few will perish.'

On another page:

'... Perhaps the message has not reached the comrades? Went to the landing several times hoping to meet the boatman. But he is not to be seen. Has the note been handed over to someone else by mistake? Or have they been nabbed while arriving with the rice? Lucky that some yam and tubers have been found. Maybe someone will arrive in the coming days.'

Sivan recalled what the comrades of Avalam had told him: Karadi Papa!

He must be the revolutionary who jotted down these notes. If so Pappayi? He has preserved them in this box. Does his past too have a similar colour? Sivan turned the pages with curiosity.

He thought he heard footsteps. He folded the flag, stuffed it into the trunk and pushed it underneath the cot. Sivan concealed the notebook in the folds of his *mundu* and slowly took the stairs. Prompted by an inner urge he turned and looked down to find Ayyakkuru at the bottom of the stairs, his eyes fixed on Sivan. He wanted to ask Ayyakkuru whether he had accomplished the task assigned to him, but he hesitated seeing the expression on Ayyakkuru's face. He should not have trusted the dwarf, Sivan thought.

Had he seen Sivan rummaging through the trunk? But the dwarf was not there when he had entered the room.

Sivan got into his room and hid the book at a spot not easily accessible to others. He visualised the revolutionary who took refuge in the island, intervening in the impoverished lives of the inhabitants and dedicating his life to them. It is possible that he gave up his past life and continued to be in the island. If that was the case, what is his present status? The accounts kept by Pappayi for him, what does it point to? How did he undergo such a transformation?

Pappayi returned by night. Sivan was anxious to know what had happened to his letters and the documents. But he was more perturbed by the mysterious nature of the distant past.

'How was your trip?' Sivan asked quite casually.

'Papa was busy. Could not meet him. I left the accounts there and returned.'

Ayyakkuru was standing just behind him. Had he handed over the documents to Moosa? And what exactly happened?

Sivan was about to get back to his room when Pappayi addressed him.

'Look at this sir. I got this newspaper from Pullani. I don't have a reading habit. But you might like to read. Please take this.' He handed over a newspaper to Sivan.

It was long since he had seen a newspaper. One should know what is happening in the world, however biased the reports maybe. But Sivan did not reveal to Pappayi his eagerness to go through the newspaper.

While climbing the staircase, Sivan knew that Ayyakkuru was following him. But he did not turn around. Did the dwarf hand over the papers directly to Pappayi? Should find out what transpired. Whom to trust and whom not to, was just not clear.

Sivan closed the door. There were footsteps in the corridor. They continued for sometime. Then ceased. The dwarf must have gone back.

Sivan sat on the bed. He leaned on the pillow and stretched his legs. The lamp was conveniently placed on the window sill.

He opened the newspaper. Scent of old paper. The sheets were sticking together. The murmur they produced when separating was disturbing. The sheets had turned yellow. Of which era was it?

He understood exactly how old the newspaper was by just a glance at the main news.

It was a report on the killing of the landlord of Kangazha.

1

'Are you the wife of Sreenivasan, as mentioned in the petition?'

'Yes.'

'You claim that this Sreenivasan is missing?'

'Yes.'

'So you mean it is quite some time since you saw him.'

'Yes.'

'Since when is he missing?'

'Three years.'

'Will it not be correct if I state that you were living separately when he went missing?'

'Not living separately. A few days …'

'Please answer my question. Say yes or no. You were at your parental home when your husband went missing.'

'Yes.'

'Your honour, she was not living with him at that time.'

'And your son too was with you.'

'Yes.'

'Which class was your son studying in?'

'First standard.'

'So, he is now in the fourth standard?'

'No, the third ...'

'Why, did he fail any year?'

'He could not go to the school for an year, you know … he was ill.'

'When the school reopened after vacation, you got him shifted to a school near your house. Is it not right?'

'That was after my husband went missing.'

'My question is whether you shifted him to a new school. Answer yes or no.'

'Yes.'

'Your honour, please note that the child was shifted …'

'Now … Sreenivasan used to write poems, am I right?'

'Yes.'

'Have you read his poems?'

'Some of them …'

'So that means you've not read some of the poems he wrote. Correct?'

'Yes …'

'Do you know anything about the notorious Kangazha murder case?'

'I have read in newspapers …'

'So you were in the know. You may also have known that this Sreenivasan used to write poems in the magazine published by the main accused in the Kangazha case?'

'No.'

'No? Maybe they were poems you had not read. Are you aware that he was using a different name when writing in such magazines?'

'I've heard of it.'

'So you were aware of it. Okay, what was that name?'

'Something like Buddha or so ...'

'Exactly. So it turns out that you were aware of it.'

'Objection, your honour. This information does not have any relevance to this case.'

'No your honour. In fact it is the most relevant information. Allow me to proceed.'

2

'Actually he used to write poems justifying happenings like Kangazha. So it is clear that he was associated with similar activities. Can you deny if I aver that Sreenivasan tried to link himself with such activities?'

'I don't know.'

'Only that you were not in the know. That is all. That means you cannot deny that Sreenivasan was active or at least tried to be active in that line.'

'Objection your honour. Does it have such a meaning? This is merely a conjecture.'

'Allow me your honour. My argument is that there could be such a meaning to it.'

'You allege that Sreenivasan was taken away by the police. How can you claim that?'

'I had seen him in the camp.'

'The contention is that the police took him away from your home. Did you see him being taken away?'

'No.'

'Such an event is not noted in any police records. Has anyone else seen it?'

'...'

'You of course, had neighbours?'

'Yes.'

'Okay, you had neighbours. So, when someone is taken away like this at least the close neighbours would see it, no? The allegation is that it was the police that took him away. Did you witness it?'

'At the camp ...'

'That is not the answer to my question. What I'm saying is, you cannot categorically state that it was the police who took him away from home.'

Silence.

'Is it possible for a police van to come into a village without anybody noticing it? It's unbelievable.'

'That is …'

'Why do you think that the person you saw in the camp was Sreenivasan?'

'Because I know him by sight.'

'Can you say that for certain?'

'Yes, I'm certain.'

'Okay. Here are two photographs. Can you say which photo is your husband's?'

'This …'

'Take a good look. Look at them once more.'

'The first one you showed …'

'Exactly. The photo I first showed you is of Sreenivasan. But the truth is that the second photo I showed you is also of Sreenivasan! There is evidence to the effect that both the photographs are his, taken at different times. What if I say that you cannot trust your own sight?'

'No, it is not like that …'

'Come on, it is not proper to say that this alone is not true.'

'Objection …'

'Allow me. What I'm saying is that the police has not taken into custody Sreenivasan, the husband of this lady from their home. And if at all he was arrested, he has not reached the camp.

'If so, then where did he go? Who was the person Sakunthala saw at the Chaloorkunnu camp?'

3

'What's your name? Tell the honourable court.'

'Anthony. People know me as Chalackante Anthony.'

'What do you do?'

'I don't do anything now sir, simply idling …'

'What was your occupation?'

'Rearing ducks, sir.'

'Up to how many ducks have you reared at a time?'

'Now … how do I quantify them … hundred odd. May be even more.'

'Okay. Suppose one duck from this hundred odd went missing …'

'It'll not happen, sir. There are methods for that.'

'But what if one really goes missing?'

'No, such a situation has never occurred.'

'Have you read the Bible?'

'I cannot read, sir.'

'Is there not a story in the Bible about a missing sheep?'

'Maybe …'

'Okay, so these days you don't tend the flock?'

'No, I mean yes, I don't do that at all.'

'Why? Is it because your health doesn't permit?'

'I just can't. And also because my children asked me not to. They are all quite well off now. They are now ashamed of my ducks.'

'That means you are quite comfortable now! You can live at their expense.'

'That's true. I get to eat three times a day. But there are other needs too …'

'Oh, what are those needs?'

'There are many. Beedis for example. And what do I do when I feel like wetting my throat …?

'Yes, that's true. So how do you spend your time now?'

'Nothing specific. I just sit on the veranda and watch people going about their ways. Just sit there doing nothing.'

'Okay, how clearly can you see things in the distance?'

'I can see very well.'

'Can you see that pillar out there?'

'Yes.'

'What's the colour of the paper pasted on it?'

'Red.'

'Correct! Any problem with hearing?'

'There are no such problems, sir. I've arthritis. It aggravates in winter. I've mutton soup and it gets better.'

'Okay, okay. This lady here, she used to live in a rented house near you, right?'

'Yes.'

'Was she prompt in payment of rent?'

'Yes, even though delayed at times.'

'It is said that her husband, Sreenivasan is missing. Did you know that?'

'Yes, I had heard about it.' '

'Only heard about it, eh? Have you seen any police people going into her house?'

'Not policemen, but some others had come.'

'How can you say for sure that the police had not come to the house? What if they had during the night?'

'I'm always there, no ? Right in front of their house. I'm almost like a dog … sir, the dog that keeps a watch on the flock of ducks. No sleep.'

'Okay. Similarly, will I be correct, if I say that you could hear raised voices from their house at times?'

'Yes, you are.'

'And what if I say that there used to be squabbles between the husband and wife?'

The duck man Anthony nodded his head as if to say it could be so, but not very sure. He certainly did not look at Sakunthala while doing so.

'Did you see some people leaving her house one night?'

'Yes. One night the dog started barking. When I looked, I saw two or three men leaving.'

'Was Sreenivasan among them?'

'No chance, sir.'

'How can you be so sure?'

'The dog would not have barked had Sreenivasan been there. He was quite familiar to the dog.'

'Okay.'

'Your honour, it is quite clear that all was not well between this couple. Writing poems in a false name, sending away the wife and son, quarrelling in the nights, all these indicate nothing else. This old man too testifies the same. We do not know the reasons and there is no point in knowing too. Maybe some family problems. Anyway, the police has not taken him away, says this old man. Then who has done it? That has to be found out. I think that Sreenivasan has gone into hiding. At least his past associations point to that. There is also the chance of his involvement in some terrorist activity or the other. So it becomes all the more important for the police, perhaps more than this woman, to locate him. It is this point I want to emphasise.'

4

'You are Mr Bhaskara Kurup, police inspector, retired from service two years ago, correct?'

'Yes.'

'Many of your batchmates retired as circle inspectors?'

'Yes sir.'

'Are you upset about it?'

'If you ask me, yes. But it is all part of service, sir. Some get good remarks.'

'Instead there were a few not so good remarks in your service book. You were negligent in the performance of your duties, it is mentioned here. Look, this is concerning you, no?'

Bhaskara Kurup set his spectacles right and read the contents of the paper the lawyer extended to him and nodded.

'So it was not for the first time that prisoners got away from your custody.'

'... it was not what happened in this case. It was not an escape.'

'Maybe not in this case, but it has happened earlier.'

'Yes.'

'And it has led to actions against you.'

'Yes.'

'After retirement and of course after getting your pension cleared, you along with some politicians or persuaded by them, came out with a statement, no?'

'Well, a statement was issued. That's true. Please don't say that it was under pressure.'

'Ok let it be. But the petition says that Sreenivasan was captured and taken away in a police jeep by a police squad which included you, correct?'

'Yes.'

'And you waited till the pension was cleared before issuing the statement?'

'No, it is not so ...'

'But documents prove otherwise. Similarly, you also stated that you were asked to leave the squad which was in charge of Sreenivasan. Will it not be correct if I say that it was a ploy on your part to abdicate your responsibility?'

'I was not evading my responsibility. That was what really happened.'

'But then why did you not make a complaint about it?'

'There was no support for that.'

'At that time you were an officer in the police force. It is difficult to believe that men who were your subordinates behaved like that. You were the superior officer. In a force like the police, they were bound to obey you. What other support did you expect?'

Bhaskara Kurup started to speak, but then decided not to.

'Similarly, it was for capturing the first accused in the Kangazha murder case that you went to Sreenivasan's house?'

'Yes.'

'He used to stay there.'

'At that time ...'

'Did he stay there, or no?'

'Yes.'

'Your Honour, Please note this. It's clear that the first accused in the Kangazha murder case was staying in that house.'

'... but he was not there when we reached there.'

'Answer only to the questions, don't elaborate. Okay, so you say that you tried capturing him when he returned.'

'Yes.'

'So as usual with you, the accused managed to give you the slip?'

'We couldn't get him.'

'Is it that you took away someone else as a proxy?'

'Not as a proxy. For committing the crime of sheltering the accused ...'

'If not the one who stole, get the one you saw, is a saying. Your statement ratifies it.'

'That was the order from the top.'

'Can you show any document which contains such an order?'

'It was an oral order.'

'Written orders are normally issued subsequently for all such oral orders, no? Do you have any such documents with you?'

'No.'

'A prisoner who is your responsibility, is allowed to escape and you maintain silence till you complete your service. Then you ensure that all the superannuation benefits are duly received in full. Then, as an afterthought and as a revenge for not being given promotion, you issue a statement accusing your superior officers and colleagues, with the help of politicians with vested interests: will you deny it if I say that this is what has really happened?'

'Yes.'

'By "yes" do you mean that you agree with what I said?'

'No, what I mean is that I deny it ...'

5

'That I'll speak the truth and nothing but the truth ...

'... that I'll speak the truth in the name of god ...'

'Okay, sub inspector Pankajakshan, you were a Head Constable when this incident is reported to have happened?'

'Yes sir.'

'You were working under retired SI Bhaskara Kurup?'

'Yes sir.'

'You had been to Sreenivasan's house in pursuit of the main accused in the Kangazha murder case?'

'Yes sir.'

'Was he there at that time?'

'Yes sir.'

'Are you sure? Your former boss Bhaskara Kurup says that he was not there.'

'Yes, he was very much there. He was living there. We had confiscated his soiled clothes as evidence.'

'Ok. What about the head of that household, Sreenivasan?'

'He was not there. I think that he had vacated the house for this main accused.'

'Who else was there in the squad other than you and Bhaskara Kurup?'

'Constable Jose too was there, sir.'

'The three of you together captured the accused?'

'Yes sir.'

'Did he try to run away?'

'Not then. We were three, no? He came along with us without creating any problems.'

'What happened after that?'

'Jose and the accused were sitting at the back. I was driving the jeep. Kurup sir was sitting beside me in the front seat. It was night. When we reached an isolated turning, the accused said he wanted to pee. We stopped the vehicle. Sir asked me to undo his handcuffs. I had my apprehensions about it. But I had no alternative. Don't worry, he is a gentleman, sir said and so I too relaxed and started to relieve myself standing not very far. Kurup sir started to chew a paan and Jose was smoking. Suddenly the accused jumped over the fence in front and started running.'

'Didn't you chase him?'

'Jose and I ran after him. But there were no lights. It was an areca-nut plantation. There were bushes, fences ... and you know many such obstacles and we had .... no torches. After running around for sometime, we gave up and returned.

'Why did you not report this at the station?'

'There was a reason. When we came back, we saw Kurup sir weeping. Pankajakshan, my pension is gone, he was lamenting. If this is reported to the higher ups, suicide is the only course left to him, he was moaning. Twice before, culprits had escaped from his custody. He had been punished for those lapses. But this was retirement time, no? His daughters' marriages were being arranged. It was certain that those proposals would not materialise if this news came out. When such an elderly person and that too a superior officer, pleaded with you weeping; we had no alternative other than obeying him, sir.'

'So you have never taken into custody this Sreenivasan?'

'No, sir.'

'There were some statements made in this court that it was him you had taken into custody.'

'As I said earlier, when Kurup sir pleaded ...'

'But it was a clear case of dereliction of duty.'

'No other go ...'

'What if I say to the honourable court that you too have the moral responsibility for that?'

'... the circumstances were such. May mercy be shown ...'

What was Pappayi trying to indicate through a stale news? Sivan felt the spearhead of a mysterious threat pointing towards him.

Sivan reviewed the happenings of the day since morning. The letters and the notes were secretly handed over to Ayyakkuru. What could he have done with it? Maybe he had handed it over to Moosa. And Moosa? Sivan recalled the conversation with Moosa on the night he arrived in the island. Was it possible that the country craft, which was the only link of that islet with the outside world, was functioning as a prison? There was something else too; what was the reason for Pappayi to leave for Pullani the same day? If that line of thought is stretched, the needle of suspicion turns to Ayyakkuru. This island is neither a transit camp nor a shelter. It is a trap, pure and true. And escape from here is impossible.

The more he thought about it, his mind became unbearably heavier. He did not read the full Kangazha report. There was no need. He had already read it several times. A group of violent people slit the throat of Komappa Menon, the mentally deranged head of Meledathu house. All of them were wearing masks. The women of the house were huddled into one room and locked up after forcibly seizing their ornaments. The women later on revealed that those ornaments were all fake. Biased news, biased conclusions. Komappa Menon was only a representative, a prototype. He was old and crumbling. The feudal era, still indulging in the aesthetics of decaying poetry was only making a tool of him. In reality he was a victim of his own circumstances. An individual who would have faded out by natural death in a short period of time, even if not annihilated. And so much was being written and publicised about whatever was left of his hallucinatory life. At the same time, no one was concerned about the people dying on the streets like flies.

Sivan stepped out of the room. He did not know what to do. He was losing all hope. He climbed down the staircase, careful not to make any sound. Everyone seemed to be asleep. Branches of trees were heaving mildly in the cool breeze. Sivan walked over the logs to the riverside. It was pitch-dark. No stars in the sky. Even the fireflies had disappeared. Sivan recalled the night of his arrival on the island. The echo of Achu's hoots from the other side of the river was still ringing in his ears. The journey in the country craft across the dark river was extraordinary. A decayed, stinking corpse had floated close to the craft. After a gap of many days, a decapitated human head too flashed across his mind.

Memories are prisons. They too create an island. They haunt one with spying eyes. No one can escape them. He saw a small light at some distance. Sivan walked up to that light. As he neared, he could hear conversations in a low tone. He thought the voices were familiar. Who are they, awake even at this hour of the night? It reminded him of the nights before Kangazha. Is there a conspiracy brewing against me in this island? As he neared the light, he felt some movement ahead of him. A black figure, fairly large. He stopped and that figure too stopped. Sivan was suddenly afraid.

'Who is there?' Sivan called out. There was no reply. He moved forward and that figure too moved forward. Sivan wondered whether it was all his imagination. Or was someone really chasing him? He stopped again and this time he had a glimpse of the figure in front. It was the old monkey of Thechappan that had been following him like a shadow. He felt loathing and fear all at once.

'Who is there?' He heard the question from the other side. It was Thechappan.

'It's me, Thechappan,' Sivan said. The single lamp in front was swinging. Its flame swayed in the light breeze. Thechappan lifted the lamp and looked at him. Sivan could see Thechappan's face lighting up with amazement.

'Eh, it's you sir! Had you told me, I'd have come and brought you here, sir.' There was excitement in Thechappan's voice.

'Oh, that wasn't necessary, Thechappan. I got time now, so I came,' Sivan lied.

'At last you have come! How many times have I invited you!' There was a tinge of complaint in Mary's voice from behind Thechappan.

'Sir is busy, woman. He is not like us. I knew that he'd come one day when he found time,' Thechappan attempted flattery.

'We had come out to walk the monkey, sir. It is a routine every night.'

The monkey was stinking. Flies must be swarming on its wounds. But Sivan did not reveal the disgust he was feeling.

'Hey, Ayyappa, it is our *vakil* sir. Did you frighten him?' Thechappan beckoned him. The monkey moved slowly as if lifting a heavy weight. It was quite aged.

'Oh, what is this? You still standing there? Please come in sir,' Thechappan invited him.

Thechappan's house had bamboo pillars and palm-leaves roof. Thanks to the huge trees around, it was as if the house was enveloped in darkness more deep and dense than the night. In the dim light of the room, Thechappan, his wife and their old monkey, all looked like strange creatures. Sivan sat on a bench. That was the only seat available there. And it was not really a bench. Just a plank of timber placed horizontally on two wooden stumps. A cloth tied across divided the room into two. On the whole, slightly bigger than the huts of labourers.

Thechappan and his wife were still standing nearby, staring at him.

'Very limited facilities, sir,' Thechappan was clearly embarrassed. 'Pappichayan had given me permission to construct another house last summer. But when I had made all the arrangements, he said wait, we can do it later, as if he had an inner call.'

'Oh, it would've been the handiwork of that dwarf,' Mary said. 'He just cannot bear the thought of anyone improving their lot.'

'We were one of the first to settle in this island , sir. What is the use? Just look at our plight.'

'How long have you been here?'

'Many years sir! A lot many ! What is the point in narrating all that! Our lot is worse than that of those labourers. A wretched hut just like theirs and as for food, someone else's leftovers,' Thechappan said.

'Why don't you go back?' Sivan asked, but then thought of it: What is the way out?

Sivan noticed Mary and Thechappan suddenly becoming silent. So he did not probe further.

'Why are you so gloomy? What happened sir?' Thechappan asked.

'Nothing. Today I was alone. And there was heavy work,' Sivan said.

'Why are you standing and staring, you woman? Get something to eat.' Thechappan signalled with his eyes.

To eat anything in this stinking environment! Sivan felt the onrush of nausea.

Thechappan sat near Sivan as Mary went inside. Sivan felt that he wanted to tell him something. The monkey came and sat at his feet.

'Shall we have a drink, sir?' Thechappan asked with hesitation.

'I don't drink,' Sivan replied.

'Sir this is good stuff. I myself distilled it from cashew apple. No adulteration at all! Just treat it as a medicine. It will cool you.' Thechappan insisted.

Clatter of vessels and water being poured from the kitchen.

'Sir, please don't think that I'm speaking ill of someone. But that happens to be the truth. That pygmy will sink this island. His mind is evil, sir.'

Thechappan was—as always—talking about Ayyakkuru.

'How long has he been here?'

'He has not come from anywhere sir. That is the fun of it. He has been here from before the beginning. Achachan picked him up from that slum. Achachan had a monkey like this one here. The dwarf was brought for taking care of the monkey. I tried to tell Achachan, A dwarf, no? How can one trust him? At first he had to put up with lot of abuses. But then Achachan took pity on him. After all a dumb creature, he'd say. Thus he was employed as a watcher, and you know what happened in the end?'

'Will you stop this? Talking all sorts of …' Mary shouted from inside the kitchen.

'He is crooked, sir. Don't be fooled by his dumbness.' Thechappan spat into the frontyard. Obviously, he was upset at the loss of privileges they had been enjoying in the mansion.

'You know, he practises black magic using the horns of bison. Sir, please take care,' Thechappan warned.

'The pygmy walks with a dead snake round his neck. It could spring alive any time,' he continued.

'Now, come on … don't you frighten him with all those tales,' Mary scolded Thechappan. 'You don't bother about it sir. Those tribals are innocent. They are being forced to do all sorts of things. But it will not affect those who are good.'

'No, you can't take it for granted ...' Thechappan stopped.

Then he went out and returned with a bottle. The monkey which had gone out with him, had not come back.

He poured out a clear liquid into a glass and added water from a cup.

'Take it sir! It's not liquor, problem only if it's liquor, no? I tell you, please treat it as a medicine.'

Sivan hesitated. Intoxication leads only to momentary solutions. In fact, alcohol camouflages the woes of the society. One should not surrender to it.

But all that is of the past. His own comrades had betrayed the revolution. They had driven the turbulent youth into darkness. Who is betraying whom?

Thechappan went on insisting. And why be bothered about all these in this prison? Sivan took the glass and finished it in one gulp. It was as if he was swallowing fire. Deep inside, he heard the reverberation of flowing blood. The filth around suddenly became tolerable. The stench faded away.

'Nothing to lick upon?' Thechappan asked Mary. She brought a plate of steaming meat curry.

Sivan picked up a piece. It was quite spicy. Sivan felt gradual changes in his body. The shaky bench was not shaking anymore. Or is it that he had levitated from the bench?

'How is the curry? Is it tasty?' Mary asked with anxiety. Sivan nodded.

'Mary's father used to be a curry seller in a toddy shop.' Thechappan downed his glass with awkward gestures. He covered his eyes with his left palm while drinking. It was as if he was engaging in a wicked procedure. When the glass was empty, he wiped his lips and continued. 'The daughter took over when he became too feeble to carry on. Her recipes were hotter than that of her pa's.

'He was her father, all right. But, let me say that, he was horrible. Just horrible! Still, to tell the truth, he was a good *maker*! Be it the daughter or be it the curry, it was such a *superb recipe*! Perfect!' Thechappan lowered his voice feigning he did not want his wife to hear, 'Sir, have one more.'

Sivan did not say no. Thechappan poured another round.

'There was a strong desire to go back, for quite some time after coming here, sir. But when you start thinking of life outside, you drop the idea. And then gradually, just didn't want to leave this place.'

Mary was listening to their conversation hiding behind a pillar.

'There's a whole world outside, Thechappan. Life is not just what we see here.' Sivan looked at him with unfocussed eyes.

'Our world is what we create, sir. What if we assume this island is the world? It's all a mind game. That's it! Look at ants. How small is their world! In a way, we too are ants. If we assume that the winding river and the dark forest are the boundaries of this world, then will there be any urge to go out?'

What Thechappan says is also correct, from one perspective. The world does not have any complexities when in the island. Outside, problems and crises lie in wait. Ghosts of those who failed peep from the pages of old newspapers. Alcohol was apparently liberating Sivan from the prison of his mind.

'Okay, let that pass. So, what were we discussing? Yes, this girl's curry preparations! In those days I was with the electricity people, you know, those cutting the tree branches that touch the supply line. And then there were two advantages in going to Mary's toddy shop. You got hot curry with toddy and then there was this girl Mary, all hot.' Thechappan's face lit up with desire.

'Oh, this shameless man! He has started. This man here has only one obsession.' Mary again disappeared behind the pillar. Sivan noticed, yes it's true. Mary must have been a stunning beauty in her heyday. Those who touched her would burn. There were quite a few shades of her past glory visible even now.

After some time, Sivan felt that the world around him had gone on a spin. The wind blowing through the thick foliages of the big trees in the island hissed and whistled. The burning sensation on the tongue induced by the hot meat curry had gone mild. What was Thechappan rambling about?

Thechappan was refilling the glasses regularly. Mary ensured that the meat plate was full.

'Will you keep a secret, if I tell you one?' Thechappan got up and shook Sivan awake.

'Karadi Papa was a good man, sir. He was kind. A great man indeed. He had come to the island long ago. And he stayed back to improve the living conditions of the tribals.'

'Kind man, eh? Then why does he not help you repair this house? He has a timber business, no?'

'But Achachan has left, no? They finished him off, no …' Thechappan was on the verge of tears.

'Achachan is there in the big house, no? Why don't you go and ask him for help?'

'Who? O, you are speaking about Pappichayan? Karadi Papa is a different person no?'

Sivan was suddenly alert. He recalled the crumbling flag and the daily routine jottings in the notebook he found in Pappichayan's badly lit room.

'You thought he is Karadi Papa! Phoo! He was brought here as a helper. He was involved in a bad scuffle and it was thought that he'd improve living here.'

Sivan poured himself a drink.

'Whereas Achachan was a great person!' Thechappan said again. 'But what to do? Gone, no?'

'Where to?' Sivan asked.

Thechappan threw up his arms skywards.

'They got him stung by a snake when he was sleeping. This guy is wicked. Posing to be Karadi Papa! You know who brought the snake in?'

'Who?'

'That Shorty, Ayyakkuru. Who else? It's old story, sir. It's been quite some time.'

'Then why didn't you speak out?' Sivan asked.

'How can one? One has to go on living, no?' He sipped from the glass hiding his face with one hand.

'You are our only hope, sir.' Thechappan who was almost sobbing, folded his palms in supplication.

'Eh, what are you doing Thechappan?' Sivan stopped Thechappan from prostrating before him.

'*Eda* Ayyappa, *Eda*!' Thechappan called out to his monkey. The monkey slowly walked into the hut. '*Eda* Ayyappa, this is our beloved sir ...' Thechappan said. After some hesitation, the monkey stood on his hind legs and folded his palms in Namaste.

'He is an obedient monkey, sir. Actually he was the monkey of the mansion. There were many animals in the mansion. Ayyakkuru was brought there to take care of those animals. What happened? That beggar kicked them out when Achachan departed.'

'God is there for the orphaned,' Mary raised her hands and said as if chanting a prayer. Was there a hint of sobbing?

'Sir, please listen. Ayyappan is the name of this monkey. Later on Pappichayan gave the name to that Shorty. Since he was so small, he became "Ayyakkuru."' Thechappan spat into the darkness.

'So, what was the original name of the pygmy?' Sivan asked. Immediately he regretted using the word. Thechappan seemed to be delighted hearing the word pygmy. He poured some more liquor and gulped.

'Who knows sir? These paniyas, do they have names? And even if they have, has God given him the ability to utter it? If he was given that capability, won't he have taken it out on God himself?'

It was quite late. Sivan imagined that he was trapped in a huge island surrounded by the sea of darkness. Is it that there is no freedom for me from here? Or as Thechappan said is this incarceration the real liberation? Was the world excluding me? Or is it me who is locking myself in, and pushing the world out?

'Sir, can you tell me what meat you had now?' Thechappan asked, swaying on the bench.

'O, what's the big deal? Whatever it is, should be tasty, that's all no?' Mary barged in as if blocking him from answering Thechappan's question.

'Let him know, Mary. We are not thieves nor do we practise deceit. It is *udumb*, monitor lizard. I caught it in the trap I laid. It's a good breed. Grips on to the walls so firm … Won't relax, once it gets a hold.' His tongue was wobbling.

'Actually it's python you should eat. It's like a fabulous fish curry. It may not sound great, but it is a great bite. That's the meat. But it is not available now. Those paniyas won't leave any alive. They don't spare even the small snakes.'

Eating lizards and snakes! Sivan felt he'd vomit. Getting up, he was unsteady on his feet.

'Now, what were we saying? Yes, what meat did we eat now? I told you no? Monitor lizard. Won't loosen its grip once it takes hold. It just clings on to the wall or the rock. *Udumb* is really a darling!'

Saying this Thechappan fell from the bench, on to the floor. His hands were up in the air as if trying to cling on to something.

Sivan bent down to raise him up. But Mary stopped him. '*Ayyo*, don't bother sir, he will sleep there. These are routine happenings.'

Ayyappan the monkey sat near the head of Thechappan and looked at him, and then scratched his head as if it had remembered something. Sivan noticed a collar like cloth around his neck.

As Sivan was walking to the door, Mary said, 'Do you want to go now, at this hour, sir? If you can adjust, you can sleep in whatever space is available here and leave early morning.'

Sivan looked out into the night. He saw loneliness intently staring at him like a silent animal. When standing close, Mary had the smell of roasted jungle meat.

He retched and felt that he'd fall down. She held him close to her.

A gunshot boomed somewhere in the mountain valleys in the distance. The monkey started moaning softly as if it was the one shot at. Sivan found that wailing sound more disturbing than the sound of the gunshot. He clung to the body of Mary like an iguana.

It was quite late by the time Sivan returned to the mansion. All the lights were out. To his partially inebriated mind, the mansion looked like a house of ghosts. Sivan climbed the staircase with unsteady feet. He stumbled even though the stairs were quite familiar.

The door of his room was not closed. He then remembered the words of Thechappan. He visualised the arrival of Karadi Papa to the island and his attempts to get involved in the lives of the local people. Thechappan says he was murdered treacherously. What were the reasons for that? Whose instrument was Pappayi?

He was overwhelmed by a desire to read the diary of the true revolutionary. Sivan raised the flame of the lantern. He took out the notebook which he had hidden from everyone.

That was the day when the crows made a loud cacophony. They cawed in unison perching on the young coconut tree near the well. Cawing of crows heralds the coming of guests. But who was there to visit me, Sakunthala thought.

It was a Friday. Sakunthala watched Sasi going down the steps of the front courtyard on his way to school with his books and lunch box. She knew that he'd be late today also. His classmates had left quite some time back. He was not ready when they had called him. That had now become a pattern. One day when she had been to the school, the class teacher had levelled number of complaints against him: late coming, always lost in thought and not paying attention in the class, hardly eating anything and emptying the lunchbox … that teacher may have been a newcomer. Sakunthala did not answer. She was also reluctant to broach the subject to Sasi on returning home. She knew that all these were the traits of Sreenivasan. Absentmindedness was a part of his character.

When Sasi went to school that day, she thought of Sreenivasan. Would things have been different had Sreenivasan been there? Lack of money was an issue even when he was around. That still persisted. Household expenses were now being met by the income from the small farmland. The crops had become quite lean during the time when there was no one to take care of the farm. She was after the case till about a few years ago and could hardly pay attention to anything else.

Sasi's textbooks were soiled. The cover pages of most of them had fallen off by the time of the first terminal examination. Sakunthala had purchased those books at half price from a boy who had been promoted to the next class. She had noticed the sad condition of the books when he had sat down for studying the previous evening. He had packed them together with a thick black rubber band in the morning. That was how Sasi was. Comes home, spreads the books, sits down to learn. Still he did not score well in the exams. Would even fail in some. And he was not willing to attend tuition classes. Sakunthala on her part did not insist. He would step out in the morning with the aluminium lunch box and the bundle of books. Studies did not seem to affect him in any way.

Justifying the cawing of the crows, she had a guest that day. Sakunthala could see him from the distance walking towards the house through the red sand path.

'Amma, someone is coming,' she said loudly.

'Who is it? Is it Sreeni? He has been gone since long!' her mother asked. Sakunthala did not answer. Amma had been living in an unreal world. She was talking about Sreenivasan's arrival all the time. Sakunthala used to be perturbed listening to it in the beginning. But she had got over it gradually as it became a habit. Habits do not distress anyone. She stood on the veranda looking at the approaching figure that was becoming clearer.

That was Samuel Ambukkan, a law student. On first glance he reminded one of a failed Christ. His facial features resembled the portrait of Christ on the calendars, lying on the ground under the weight of the cross. Though still a student, he was above forty. Long hair, unkempt beard. A long robe reaching the knees. The sleeves covered his palms. He also had a slight limp. And while walking he swayed like a softwood tree caught in the wind. Sakunthala noticed that he was barefoot. As he came nearer, she could feel a light radiating from his eyes. There were long, deep furrows on his forehead. The cloth bag on his shoulder sagged under the weight of heavy books. Maybe because of that, he looked tired.

Climbing the steps, he smiled at her like a friend of many years.

'Sakunthala, no?' he asked and then introduced himself. Learning law. Had passed the examinations for qualifying as a lawyer four years ago, but did not practise in any court. Instead he was doing a research into some important cases. His studies were mostly about people who had been victims of torture.

'Some years ago I too was in the lock-up and the sub jail for a month. Police had nabbed me, they said, on some suspicions. So I know what it is to be in there. I argued my case. That's why I decided to study law,' Samuel said. 'During my research I came across Sreenivasan's case. That case has many peculiarities. Rare cases, they call. It is one such rare case. But I've to get some clarity on certain aspects of the case. That's why I'm here.'

He refused tea. Had given up tea and coffee. 'I'm not a slave of any stimulants or intoxicants other than the quest for justice. In fact what could be more intoxicating than seeking justice?'

The monologue also contained some pointers to his past. He had been in a seminary for some time. But then came to loggerheads with the restrictive framework of religion. It was a world of compromises. Unquestioned obedience was the standard there. He quarrelled with the representatives of god. Justice was impossible behind those iron curtains. Ambukkan did not complete his studies at the seminary.

'Jesus too came out of the seminary with me,' Samuel smiled like Christ.

He had founded an organisation called 'Eternal Justice' and was working for it at present.

Sakunthala was thinking why such an individual should come and meet her.

'There are still many unanswered questions in Sreenivasan's case. I'm about to file a special petition regarding them. It is almost ready. Sister, if you are willing, you can join me. It will give me a moral support.' Samuel extricated his cane-thin hands from the sleeves of his robe and asked. Sakunthala did not know what to say. She had thought it impossible to get involved in the witness boxes of the courts anymore. Someone would invariably be there right in front of all such assemblies expelling her from those precincts.

'There is no need for that,' Sakunthala said. 'Nothing is going to work.'

'On the contrary, it is a case in which there are several possibilities even now. Especially, if we focus on certain important points.'

Samuel was looking at Sakunthala with great expectations. It was as if this was a case concerning a person very close to him and all that was required was a formal consent to carry on.

'What are you suggesting will happen?'

'Justice.' Samuel's eyes sparkled. 'This case has left behind many mysteries. The court has ordered a reinvestigation only to locate Sreenivasan. Maybe the court could not have ordered for anything else in the light of the evidence and arguments placed before it. However, there are many more things beyond this to be brought to light. Who is behind the disappearance of your husband? Is he staying away by choice? If so, whom is he afraid off? Or if he has been killed as is generally apprehended who are those responsible? Hounding them out and punishing them is the most simple and straightforward justice in this case.'

Sakunthala, however, did not give him a favourable reply. The very thought of the longwinded trial which had gone on for months, put her off. The troubled days of the trial was also the time when she was forced to disbelieve her own eyes and ears. Many of those who had promised to help withdrew from the scene most unexpectedly. Some were seen mouthing blatant lies without batting an eyelid. Others maintained a grim silence. Beyond all these, the nascent knowledge, that Sreenivasan had been hiding several things from her, stung her painfully. Sreenivasan had obviously felt that his wife was incapable of keeping his secrets. And she was now trying hard to free herself from the memories of her expeditions and investigations.

That day the law student, Samuel Ambukkan returned without securing an encouraging response from her. Before leaving he dipped his hand into the shoulder bag and presented her a fistful of chocolates.

'Why so many chocolates?' Sakunthala asked.

'Have it. Or give them to some children,' he said. 'At least this, in a world bereft of sweetness.'

Sakunthala took just one and returned the rest.

'I can't. I'm a diabetic,' he declined.

Before bidding farewell with folded hands, he took a piece of paper and jotted down his name and address.

'Sister, please think about it once more. I can understand your hesitation. But is it not a question of justice? Is it proper to evade it? I'm anyway going to make an attempt. I just cannot consider it to be a purely personal matter of yours. In the real sense, Sreenivasan is only a representative. So please think of it in the larger perspective. If you are in need of anything please contact me. The office of Eternal Justice is near the court. I'll be there most of the time,' he smiled.

Sakunthala watched him disappear into the distance, walking through the red sand path. Then she went through the address—which she felt to be rather strange—he had jotted down on the piece of paper.

Samuel Ambukkan,

Law Student

Office of the Eternal Justice

Dharma Path, (the Road to Justice)

Near the Court

Even though Ambukkan was sent away without any commitment on her part, Sakunthala was curious to know the direction in which he intended to proceed further with Sreenivasan's case. Was he going to produce new witnesses? Would there be new evidence? Difficult to believe that something which was beyond the reach of a proven legal luminary like Aravindaksha Menon, could be done by a novice. Not only that, there were traces of insanity in his behaviour. The long robe, hair, beard and the dirty shoulder bag … all of it was quite strange. At the same time, she did not feel like writing him off totally. Samuel's sparkling eyes and his unusually thin frame remained in her mind. The desire to meet him intensified everyday.

Two weeks after Samuel Ambukkan's visit, she left for the town in search of him. Sakunthala was getting out of her house after so many months. She noticed that everyone at the bus stop was staring at her.

Some out of sympathy, some accusingly and some others merely out of curiosity. Sreenivasan's disappearance and his case had created quite a stir in the media. Almost everyone in the village and the nearby areas knew her. Earlier she was known as the daughter of KP, the advocate's clerk and social worker. Now her 'status' had changed to that of the wife of the missing or killed poet Sreenivasan.

It was not easy to get to Samuel Ambukkan's office. No one had any idea of the 'Dharma Path' he had jotted down on the scrap of paper. Sakunthala tried several routes just on instinct. But all of them led her back to the narrow roads in front of the court. The shopkeepers of the locality too had never heard of the road.

'Dharma Path?' they asked. 'What the hell is it? There is certainly no such road in this area.'

'You've got it wrong, sister. May be the mad guy wrote it down to fool you. Tell me, did he fork any money out of you?'

Sakunthala was soon wary of making enquiries using his name. Maybe there were people who recognised her. She was also haunted by the pointless fear that she would once again be identified with the case. After futile attempts for almost two hours, she returned to the bus stop in front of the court, for getting back home.

Then, surprising her no end, she saw the figure which resembled the Crucified, ambling along the other side of the road. The heavy shoulder bag stuffed with law books was missing this time around. That was the only difference. He was limping and swaying with bent head and without paying any attention to what went on around him. She was so elated seeing him. Her mood was like that of one meeting someone who was very dear, after a long time. He had not seen her. She stared at him for sometime, crossed the road and stood in front of him blocking his way.

Samuel Ambukkan looked at her bewildered. He didn't seem to recognise her at first. But then the ice of amnesia melted and the sparkle returned to his sunken eyes. The cane-like hands peeped out of the long sleeves of the robe. He folded his palms in greeting.

'Actually this street does not have any such name,' Samuel said by way of explanation. 'People would know only if you mention the name of the Englishman who was a judge. Even though the British left India long ago we have not left them. That's the problem. It's my intention to get this name changed gradually. So I've made a beginning by using a nonexistent name for the street.'

'But that makes it difficult to locate the place,' Sakunthala said.

'Only in the beginning. Then it will become familiar to everyone. As more and more people come and enquire more and more people will know. Changes will take place. This is a mind boggling establishment. Changes can be brought about only slowly and gradually. It is not possible at one stroke. People like your husband had the holy intention of changing the set up. But they were all in a hurry. That backfired.'

The law student's office was on the first floor of an old building. On the ground floor there was a shop selling court fee stamps and stamped papers. In one corner of the shop two girls were incessantly typing on their machines with full attention on the paper in front of them. It seemed the sound of letters flying on to paper would never cease. The girls were watching him going upstairs. But even when glancing at him, their fingers were moving rapidly nonstop. The thundershower of letters continued.

The stamp vendor rested his head on the table and yawned.

The door to Samuel's room was closed. A board was hung across the door along the bolt. On the board was written both in Malayalam and English: 'Welcome. Office of the Eternal Justice. The Law Student is **Out**. He will come back and attend to you soon. Please wait.'

He took out the board from the wall, reversed it and hung it back. Now it read: 'Office of the Eternal Justice. The Law Student is **In**. You are welcome.'

He opened the door and invited her in.

Apparently it was also the living quarters of the law student. Another kurta of his was hanging on the clothesline. Books and papers were strewn all around the room. Files were heaped on the table. A cloth curtain separated the living room. A dirty canvas chair was lying near the table. There were books on the chair too. The ceiling fan started whirling with the moaning sound of a man with a parched throat. A chubby cat peeped from the windowsill discomfited by the sound.

'Sister I knew that you would come.' The eternal student of law said. When she looked up as if asking why he had thought so, he continued with a faint smile: 'Because it is the concern for justice that leads us all. One individual alone cannot exclude herself from that.'

He stroked his long beard and spoke after a brief pause.

'I had thought of asking you this question when we met first. There was a short story writer with the name Chitrabhanu, Chitran Kuroor. Where is he now?'

Chitran? That name was there in the fringes of her memory, like a faded photograph. Picture of a terrified face. A startled face filled with terror and self-loathing. What is the relevance of his whereabouts now?

'No idea,' Sakunthala said. Was he not working for a big newspaper?

'We have to find him.' Samuel Ambukkan continued. 'Some links went missing from that point onwards. We can proceed further only after we reconnect.'

'Chitran was excluded from all police records. Knowingly or unknowingly you too perhaps did the same thing. He was not tried at all.' Samuel Ambukkan said.

The terror-struck countenance of Chitran once again flickered in her mind.

'He was really a vital cog linking everyone.' Samuel said.

'But he doesn't know anything beyond that perhaps.' Sakunthala recalled her meeting with Chitran. He was sitting in a dimly lit untidy room brooding over his bruised body. There were telltale signs of the use of brutal force on his forehead.

Samuel suggested that Chitran had reached an understanding with the police to keep them informed of all those who contacted him, there and then.

'That was the information I got. He may have deceived many people.'

'I don't know whether it was possible for Chitran to do that. Anyway, what's the point now in getting through to him?'

'Have you thought about it? The man who stayed in Sreenivasan's house; he is the one we should get to first.'

'But he's gone underground.'

'Who knows? Maybe we can fill up a few squares if he is found out. For example, where was he last? Was Sreenivasan with him ... etc.'

Ambukkan resumed after sometime. 'Let's accept the police version. They haven't seen Sreenivasan. But where is the other guy?'

'They had claimed that he had jumped out of the jeep?' Sakunthala repeated the story fully aware that it was a hoax.

'Ok, but where to? Not into a void surely? He has to be found, no?'

What were the chances of finding him? The Kangazha case had been crawling like a paralytic. If proven guilty, harsh sentence awaited most of them. In such circumstances, would anyone with a modicum of intelligence come out in the open and accept the punishment?

'But some effort should be made. The effort to locate him.' Samuel said.

'Even if we are able to discover him, will he come out? Will he be ready to support us?'

'I'm not sure whether you know this. The Kangazha trial is practically at a standstill. The killed man's family does not have the resources to pursue the case. Now the prosecution has also lost interest in it.'

'So?'

'The accused may be acquitted. The police have not been able to come up with clinching evidence. So when he comes out, the truth of the matter can be accessed. We can at least expose the falsehoods circulated by the police. That will be a good start.'

'But, he has to come out no?'

'Yes, and someone will have to go to him for that,' Samuel said amidst a bout of coughing.

'But do you know where he is?' Sakunthala said thoughtfully.

'No, but I think it will be possible.'

'How?'

'That's where Chitran comes in. Maybe he knows. If not, he can give us a few contacts. We are going to complete the crossword puzzle by adding the missing alphabets. That's why I asked you about Chitran.'

'Is it that difficult? He is in that newspaper, no?'

The law student sighed and said, 'I did enquire there. He left that job sometime ago. They do not know where he is.'

'I had been to his house once,' Sakunthala recalled.

'He is not there now.' Samuel thought for a while. 'Was it a rented house? May be the next tenants can give us some information.'

'No chance. He was not the kind to mingle with people.' Sakunthala said.

'If we are able to locate him somehow or the other, my guess is that he'll open out at least to you.'

Sakunthala tried to draw his portrait in her mind. Pictures become faded. Time, like darkness, wipes out colours.

A siren screamed from far away. It was one o'clock. Sakunthala got up.

Samuel Ambukkan took out a fistful of sweets from his bag and gave it to her.

'Have them. Or give it to the children.'

Sakunthala accepted the sweets.

As she slowly came down the feeble steps of the staircase, the stamp vendor winked at her and said as if to no one in particular, 'Oh! Here goes the new victim of our eternal justice!'

The typist girls stopped working for the first time and laughed aloud.

Thechappan's hut had to be rebuilt before the windy season began. The wind goes mad on reaching the island. Laying the roof with coconut leaves will be a cumbersome task. The branches of trees may fall on the walls. The wind might even carry off the roof. Pappayi gave his consent with reluctance when Sivan brought up the subject.

'*Vakil* sir, you do not know these people well,' he was quite opposed to the idea initially.

'Animals! No gratitude. He and his woman have time only for complaints. I've asked him to leave if he is not happy here. But what to do if he doesn't want to?'

'May be he doesn't have any other livelihood ...'

'No, not because of that. If he goes, he will end up behind bars. It is that fear that keeps him here. Nothing else! There's a lot to say if one were to speak out. It took him just one kick to finish off his woman's father. She too was an accomplice. He knows that his tricks won't work with me.'

Sivan was taken aback. So that was the secret behind Thechappan and his wife not leaving the island. Is it a fact that this island is the last refuge of criminals?

'But then, we can choose not to dwell on such matters. Who will have any standing left if we start digging up old stories?' Sivan felt that the last sentence was a sly dig at him.

'Can one eat what she cooks? But I thought never mind. And a stinking monkey to top it all! I had tried to get rid of it long ago. But she is even letting it onto her bed! Yes, equals always gel. I've asked a couple of people to get me a good cook. If I get one, I can stop their visits to the mansion. I don't mind even if the new woman is from an orphanage or a convent. At least there will be peace of mind.'

Pappayi spat into the distance with a gurgling sound.

'Okay. After all it is something you have recommended. I'll not reject it. You can do whatever is necessary. Put the expense in Achayan's account.'

Sivan recalled Thechappan's narration of Karadi Achayan and his death.

Pappayi helped as promised. He sent carpenters from the workshop to take measurements. Workers cut trees from the forest and made rafters and beams for the roof. Thechappan and Mary fetched strong bonding sand from the hills and mixed and kneaded it at the riverside. They then burnt it with small branches of trees and made bricks out of the sand.

It was a very crude construction. The walls seemed to stoop like the monkey. The edges of the bricks were uneven and were protruded here and there. One night it rained and the bricks in the kiln were not fully baked. In spite of all this, Thechappan and Mary were happy. Their longstanding dream was taking shape.

One evening Sivan saw a country craft crossing the river. It was fully laden with the tiles for Thechappan's house. The boatman hooted out loud after carefully stopping at the landing place. There were silver streaks on the boatman's head. Sunken eyes. Sivan glanced at him with keen attention. The memory of a distant night brimmed within him.

It was Moosa.

Sivan did not feel like meeting Moosa and renewing their acquaintance. The exit routes from the island no longer held any interest for him.

Pappayi was walking up and down the long corridors of the mansion in woollen overalls. He was talking nonstop. It was about the impending auction of timber. Now the old enemies had gone, but the next generation had come up as fresh opponents. Money was not an issue for them and they would fling it out in heaps as the heat of the auction got to them.

Pappayi never left his bed so early in the morning. Sivan knew something important was on the cards when the summons came.

Dewdrops were falling from the leaves of the plants due to the mild morning sun. The light rhythmic sound it made was the background tune of the island.

'You must conduct the auction this year,' he said pausing in his stroll.

'Me?' Sivan looked at him in surprise.

'A new person handling it will be more advantageous. They go wild when they see me.'

Pappayi thought for a minute and continued, 'They have grabbed some areas in the last auction. We have got to do something up there. But that can be managed only by the paniyas.'

'What is it?' Sivan could not get it.

'Those who are in possession of the forest tract should not cut the trees, that's all.'

'But they got it in auction, no?'

'What of it? You know, there are ever so many gods in the forest. We will keep the paniya gods on our side. We will ask them to ensure that the axe does not fall on the paniya gods. Then what will those kids do? Tell me.' Even while aiming to get rid of the paniyas, Pappayi was trying to exploit their faith for his benefit. Sivan paused to think it over. Was this right?

Who decides what is right and what is wrong? The island is just a copy of the external world. He recalled the words of Thechappan.

It was not a busy day. Sivan remained in his room for most of the day. His interest in the diary jottings of the revolutionary had also subsided. Maybe his life too was over. He was fully conscious of his destination till the very last of the notes. However he was handicapped by the absence of communication from the external world. My life too is so similar, Sivan thought. No messages from the outside world. Maybe the likeness ends there. Sivan had ceased to think of escape routes.

The river and the ferry landing were visible through the window. There was no one there; neither paniyas nor their women. But for the heaving branches of old trees, the island seemed to have frozen still.

It was noon. Mary would have brought lunch. Very spicy food. Sivan felt an urge to go to Thechappan's house. Thechappan had been inviting him often. Sivan would go there whenever he found time. He was attaining freedom through the ecstasy of booze served to him by Thechappan. Thechappan distilled everything; cashew fruits, paddy, gooseberry … then he buried it underground to enhance the potency of the liquor. It has the might of tradition. Maybe because of that potency it could easily flatten the past and also the reminiscences.

Thechappan was there at his new house. The house built up with half baked bricks was large. Rafters and beams had been set up. Laying of tiles was left. New tiles had been brought and stacked up. Flooring was not yet over. Only a coating of cowdung had been given. Walls were up and the rooms were separated. The walls were to be whitewashed. A chimney was to be erected in the kitchen. Thechappan and Mary hoped to get all these done. Sivan had promised to take it up with Pappayi.

'You will do what is necessary, no? That's enough. I am not worried anymore. To be truthful, who else is here to speak on our behalf? It is the lord who has brought you here.' Thechappan went into raptures as the drink started taking effect. At times Mary too used to drink. Her drinking was in secret, standing at one end of the room. On such days Mary would burn like smouldering lime. She would hoot, slicing the stillness of the night. Thechappan, sleeping outside, would bare his teeth and sleep talk to his monkey in the darkness. Those nights were spicy and pungent.

'What happened sir? You did not go to the forest today?' Thechappan asked as he sat mending a small fishing net.

'There was no work today, Thechappan. Pappichayan told me that there is a shortage of workers for loading timber on the other side.'

'That's true. These days there's no one for jobs involving physical labour. Bad times indeed.' Thechappan kept aside the net he was knitting and turned to Sivan. 'Did you have your lunch, sir?' he asked. 'If not, you can have it here, warm from the hearth.'

Sivan nodded. The aroma of cooking wafted in from the kitchen. He no longer had any inhibitions about having his food there. Smells did not bother him anymore.

'Mary, sir has come. Hurry up,' Thechappan called out loud.

'No hurry Thechappan, it's not yet time.'

'O, that's true. Er ... I forgot to ask. Shall we have a drop?'

'At this time of the day?' Sivan asked for appearances sake.

'What's wrong with it? Today is a holiday, no? Have a couple of drinks and you can sleep soundly.' Thechappan went in, returned and poured crystal-clear arrack into glasses.

'No pickles?' He shouted again.

'Coming. I'll bring it just now. Or you come and take it. It's there in the plate. If I leave the kitchen, the curry will be burnt.'

Thechappan asked after sometime, 'Have you tasted the fish from this river, sir?'

Sivan said that he did not know. He had never asked whether the fish served to him were from this river.

'Look at the hand-net I knitted.' Thechappan showed him the blue net he had completed. 'You wait here. I'll go catch a couple of fish. We'll have meals with fried fish.'

'Should we? It will take time, no?'

'What do you mean? Just spread the net and fish will float in. Have one more drink sir. I'll be back in a jiffy.'

Thechappan ambled to the river with the net. Sivan poured himself another round.

The vigour of liquor increases at noon. After two drinks Sivan felt like a race horse. He stood up. No one seemed to be around. Sivan thought that catching fish was only a ruse. Thechappan was creating opportunities; striving to achieve more and more. Is Thechappan a good man? But who is really a good man?

Are there categories like the good and the bad in this world?

In which case there is not much of a difference between him and Thechappan, Sivan thought with a jolt. Thechappan is living in this island to escape from punishment and so was he. It is precisely to evade the law that he had been sent there by a group of people. But didn't he have greater motives?

The island had flattened the past. Its closed borders had gradually effaced the destinations. The paniyas were the only past of this island. Only thing is that they did not seem to be aware of it. They existed like the shadows of a long dead people.

Mary's body was ember hot. Her touch was scalding.

'*Ayyo*, what if someone comes?' Mary pretended to free herself from his grasp feigning reluctance.

'Damn it!' Sivan was reckless; the arrack was working.

Her body, with the smell of onions and curry leaves, was to him a marquee of tastes. Sivan, like a child seeking to unravel mysteries, leisurely sauntered through its canopies. They were lying on the bare floor. He saw dry cowdung sticking on to her body. And the sky, through the roof without tiles.

Sivan stopped hearing a sound.

'Is it Ichayan? No, it cannot be.' Mary frantically tried to get up.

'Thechappan will not come.' Sivan said. 'It is not yet time for the fish to get trapped in his net.' He turned around to take a look without getting up. The sound was heard again.

It was Ayyappan, the monkey. He was on the doorsteps munching something ...

'Who is it?' Mary asked in a low tone.

'It's the monkey,' Sivan returned to her.

'Ayyappa, go out,' Mary ordered the monkey somewhat loudly. But it continued eating as if it had not heard anything.

He kissed her sweat-drenched neck. The heat of fire had not yet left her body. Sivan thought she was burning like a hearth in which dry wood was stuffed.

'He is watching,' Sivan said softly.

She turned around. Ayyappan, the monkey, was gaping at them intently. She waved her hands at the monkey and shouted, 'Go, go.'

The monkey took a step towards him and growled in an unusual manner. Sivan rolled away.

'Chee! What's this Ayyappa? Get out!' Mary shouted at him menacingly. Wrapping her clothes around her, she approached him. But he leisurely watched her and went out without any hurry, taking a calm look around.

'Just look at the longing of the old monkey?' Mary laughed softly. Sivan had moved away.

She held him close and asked, 'Sir, are you cross with me?'

'Nothing like that.' But his passion had died out.

'Cowdung on your body? You can change it, if only you are keen.'

'Me?' Sivan did not understand.

'Who else? The floor has to be cemented, or tiles must be laid. Pappichayan will agree if you recommend.'

'I'll try.'

His reply pleased her. Mary kissed, wrapping him in her arms. Her arms possessed extra strength. He felt his body crushed as she pressed against him.

The scent of onion and curry leaves rushed back into him. Sivan was once again engrossed in her hot body. Like a wet piece of wood he was smouldering inside her.

Again another sound. A banging on the door.

'There is someone outside,' Mary said disentangling herself.

'May be the monkey,' Sivan said.

'No, it's someone else.'

'Thechappan back with the fish.'

'No. He will not bang the door; will not try to enter without announcing himself.'

Mary rolled away from him. He felt cold.

No more. He got up. One hindrance after another.

'You must come at night, sir. This will not work out now.'

Sivan did not say anything. He got dressed, combed his dishevelled hair.

He did not stay back, despite Mary's insistence to have lunch. He came out of the house. Thechappan had not returned with fish from the river. The monkey was sitting on a piece of wood. It ignored Sivan. Then who was it that banged on the door? Could it be one of the paniyas? No, none of them seemed to be around.

Suddenly Sivan knew who it was. Ayyakkuru was leaning against an areca nut tree. Sivan was terribly upset. For whom is this pygmy spying? Anyway, he did not run away as usual.

Sivan fixed his gaze on him in question.

Ayyakkuru drew a circle in the air lifting up both hands. Then he mimed the drawing of a moustache on his face. And walked ahead hurriedly. Sivan understood. Pappayi calling, is what he wanted to convey.

Sivan followed in silence. Rage towards Ayyakkuru was bubbling inside him.

After some distance, Sivan looked up and found that Ayyakkuru had vanished. Where did he slip away to?

Walking in the sun, Sivan recalled the sharp stare of the monkey. Where the paths crossed to the mansion, a flock of soiled-white goats blocked his way. They were bleating loudly in what he felt to be a strange sound. There was a group of paniya kids just behind the flock tending the goats. Even though mere kids, an unusual kind of gravity was evident on their visages. As if the racial symbol of paniyas, silence was stamped on their lips.

Sivan had the uneasy feeling that he had seen those goat-rearing kids somewhere before. Where was it?

In his first days on the island, a flock of goats had blocked the jeep of Pappayi. That day his jeep was driven straight into the flock and had smashed and scattered them. The scantily clad paniyas who were with the goats moved to the side with bent heads. Next generation of the goat-rearing paniyas. The same complexion, profile and stoic silence. Absolutely no change. Time stagnates in the island like water in a sewage canal.

Sivan brandished his arms threateningly at the goats. He watched with delight the flock scattering away. He then kicked away those animals which still stubbornly remained where they were. The goats bleated loudly. The paniyas kept to the side with faces averted. Sivan marched ahead with utter disregard to everything else through the path which he had cleared of all impediments.

'Hey, where were you sir? I've been waiting for you since long.' A smiling Pappayi was right there in the frontyard of the mansion. Was there a hint of something out of the ordinary in his tone, Sivan wondered.

He looked as if he had just emerged from the water. There were tiny drops of water on his body.

'I had a bath in the river. It has been quite a while since I went swimming. And then I saw Thechappan with his net. I asked him to get me some fish.'

'Did you get some?' Sivan asked.

'O, yes. Two big *valas.* Though utterly useless in everything else, Thechappan is an expert in fishing! It should be cleaned and grilled on embers. And then the taste is something out of this world!'

Under the neem tree Thechappan was squatting on the ground blowing on the embers in the makeshift hearth. He was roasting fish for Pappayi, bending as low as the earth.

They sat on the floor of the kitchen and ate.

'Taste it. Thechappa, give one piece to sir.' Pappayi said while separating the bones of the fish roasted on embers.

Thechappan sneaked a glance at Sivan from the kitchen courtyard. Sivan saw a smile taking shape on his face.

'I had been thinking of discussing something with you since long,' Sivan said.

Pappayi stopped eating and looked at him.

'What's the need of a preamble? *Vakil* sir can tell me anything at anytime.'

'I know that. But I didn't want to upset you.'

Pappayi put a big ball of rice into his wide mouth. He then started masticating it like a robot.

'It's about Ayyakkuru.' Sivan looked around and confirmed that Ayyakkuru was not there in the vicinity. 'Why do we feed and take care of him without getting any work done from him?'

Pappayi stopped chewing and looked at Sivan intently.

'A dumb creature, no?' He said after couple of minutes.

'He must be made to do some kind of work. Or he will waste his time just lazing around. Already ...' Sivan stopped deliberately.

A pair of eyes were staring at him from inside. He knew without looking that it was Thechappan.

'What happened?' Pappayi asked.

'No, it's alright.' Sivan indicated that he was no more interested in pursuing the subject.

'No, it is not like that. You must tell me whatever it is. Even if he cannot talk, we cannot tolerate insolence.'

'Nothing much. I don't have anything to hide. But why is he following me and spying on me all the time?'

'What is he investigating?' Pappayi seemed to be getting irritated.

'He enters my room and goes through my things. He follows me wherever I go. What is he, the police? Maybe it doesn't add up to anything. I did not say all this to prompt you to do anything. But do keep an eye on him.'

'I'll split that pig's head if I find him now!' Pappayi screamed. His eyes were bulging. Droplets splattered from his nose and mouth. His face turned crimson and the hair on his ears stood up and danced.

The sound of someone running down the staircase could be heard.

Thechappan was waiting. He placed one more piece of roasted fish on the plantain leaf of Pappayi.

'Don't take it too seriously. I just said it for records sake.' Sivan tried to calm him.

'Let the dwarf go to the forest and handle the logs. That will put an end to his impudence. When one monkey grew too old, I started taking care of another; that is all it has been to me,' Pappayi said.

Though he had promised, Sivan did not go to Thechappan's house that night. He was ruminating over the incidents of the afternoon. Coming across Ayyakkuru outside Thechappan's house, complaining to Pappayi about him … He now felt he should not have spoken about it to Pappayi, even though all that he had said were facts. What would Pappayi think of him now? Was that half witted paniya his enemy? He did not say anything about Sivan's going to Thechappan's house. He came there because Pappayi sent him. How could one say that he was following Sivan? What if it was just his impression that he was being tailed? Or couldn't they have been accidental? He had obeyed whatever Sivan had told him to after coming to the island. Even if it did not produce any result, it was he who handed over the notes for *Liberation Path* to Moosa.

Or is it that he did not hand it over at all?

Sivan stood there looking out into the night. The wind had stopped. The trees were standing still like frozen snow sculptures. A star was visible in the distant sky towards the river. He listened with keen attention. Did he hear a hoot? Moosa's boat on voyage even in the night? But it turned out to be the notes of a song. There used to be music and dance in the paniya colony once in a while. Nocturnal songs that shattered the shell of silence. The song and dance lasted through the night. Sivan had not seen them speaking to anyone during daytime. None of them had a permanent employment. Occasionally they would remove and take away the skin of certain trees in the forest. It was they who gathered the seeds from the reeds and collected mushrooms, come rains. Sometimes they were seen fishing with crude traps improvised from bamboo or trying to catch birds by applying birdlime on tree branches. Their children were always herding goats. Maybe the goats too belonged to Pappayi. They had not protested when his jeep had bumped them off the road. It was the same now also. The children too were so impassive.

It struck him suddenly. Those children bore resemblance to Pappayi. His eyes and forehead were replicated on their baby faces. That was why he had the feeling that he had seen them earlier. He was there in the soil and blood of the island. His presence was there in the breeze and the trees.

Maybe once this island belonged to them. They may have been terrified by the gun in his hands. Even otherwise, how could the dwarfish paniyas fight a strong and powerful man?

Sivan then realised that Ayyakkuru was also a paniya. His thick lips, depressed nose, broad ears and even his complexion indicated that. Had he been separated from his clan? Or was it that Pappayi had groomed him up to spy on his own community? The thought of agents and renegades refused to fade out. His past went through his mind like a grey picture. That world was so distant now. Its place was in some other universe.

That night Sivan was very late going to bed. The paniya songs were still there in the background even as he slept.

He woke up early next morning. Morning light was just spreading. Everything was still. The grass, trees and flowers remained motionless. The island existed like a wind-swept place. In the dim morning light the strange-shaped trees appeared to be in prayer.

He saw the earth gradually brightening and the dewdrops on the leaves of the trees falling off.

A group of small birds appeared in the sky. They were flying in the direction of light. The star that had risen in the night was still there with a fading glow.

He heard the sound of hooting from afar. He looked in the direction of the river through the window. A boat was approaching in the distance. It was like a dot. Someone was sitting in the front. Moosa was tall in the aft with the long barge pole.

Now the boat was nearer and he could see more clearly. Yes, it was a woman in the front. Who is the new guest of the island? That too a woman! Could this morning scenery be a part of the dream? Sivan pinched himself. No, it's not a dream. The boat is certainly approaching through the river. Moosa and a woman ... Was she also seeking refuge from the giant shackles of law, like Thechappan and himself?

Sivan got out of the house. The wooden staircase creaked. Ayyakkuru was at his usual place at the bottom of the stairs. O, what an omen!

He heard a growl. Did someone call in a soft voice from behind?

'Chee, you cur!' Yes, someone called.

Sivan turned around. Ayyakkuru!

After looking around, Ayyakkuru said, 'Who was it that followed you?'

Sivan looked at him closely. He was not wrong. The dumb was speaking. A miracle?

He was reminded of an old poem. A time when the blind would see, the dumb would talk and the words of the other would be music to the ears. In which issue of *Liberation Path* had it appeared?

The depressed nose and broad ears of Ayyakkuru began to tremble. The lump on his bull neck swelled. The wart on the upper lip throbbed.

Sivan tried to retort.

But Ayyakkuru raised his hand stopping him.

Then Sivan saw with a shock. A snake entwined around his hand. Whether it was alive or dead was not clear.

Instinctively, Sivan stepped backwards.

Suddenly the snake raised its hood and hissed with a terrible sound.

Sivan tried to hold on to the railings of the staircase. Words eluded him.

Is immobility the mark of a corpse? If so all of us are corpses. However, what right we have to continue as corpses when the whole earth is tottering?

From the short story 'The Corpse'
by Chitran Kuroor

Once again the same town, same street, small, look-alike houses in neat rows. Sakunthala was recalling the day she had met Chitran, while on her way, after a gap of many years, in search of the house he used to live. When she stepped in the morning into the mild rain, she found the town and streets quite familiar. The rain was the only difference, she felt.

The house he had been living in had not changed much. Maybe the walls were more soiled. The rain-drenched casuarinas had folded their palms. The door was closed. Sound of children playing could be heard from somewhere inside. Sakunthala pressed the calling bell and waited.

No one appeared. She pressed the switch once again. After waiting for few minutes, she knocked on the door. At first tentatively, then firmly. Footsteps were heard. An old man peeped out of the door he half-opened. His look was loaded with suspicion.

Sakunthala knew that Chitran was not living there anymore. But maybe the present occupants knew his whereabouts. At least roughly where he could be found. Maybe they redirect letters. Samuel Ambukkan had indicated as much. But Ambukkan had failed to find out anything. Not even his present residence.

Go after Chitrabhanu once again. Sakunthala had not taken that suggestion seriously. Later when she was alone she felt this was perhaps the last thread. Possibility of Chitran knowing the person who had been living in her house. And what if he was aware of more details? The chances of such possibilities made her restless. A faint glimmer of hope in the darkness.

But Samuel Ambukkan had not harboured any such optimism. She was aware of that too. For him all investigations began with the premise that Sreenivasan did not exist anymore. Ambukkan started from the nonexistence of a man called Sreenivasan with flesh and marrow, who used to think and write poems. How did his nonexistence happen? What sort of system wiped him off? How do such things happen in a civil society?

What remedies are available against such misdeeds in a system of justice that evolved centuries ago? For him Sreenivasan was a mere case study. Not so for Sakunthala. She still believed that he could yet transform into a body of flesh and blood. She had expectations that he would turn up one day. Even when a sob erupted that all these efforts were fruitless, the feeling that just like the man who was provided asylum by Sreenivasan, he too was still alive somewhere, inspired her to recommence her investigations.

The old man asked from the half open door, 'Have you been knocking for quite some time? I didn't hear. I've a hearing problem. And then those mischievous brats are making such a ruckus. Okay, what do you want?'

'I'm here to find out if you have any information about someone who used to live here,' Sakunthala said.

'Oh, it is about that journalist, no?' He asked with the air of dealing with something absolutely trivial. 'I've never seen him. He left long ago.'

'Any idea where he went to?'

'I don't know. Many people have come here enquiring about him. He should've left his address with me, if he was so popular. No decency!' And as if dismissing her, 'Ask someone else.'

Sakunthala did not get upset when he shut the door on her. So many doors had slammed on her in the recent past. The closed doors no more bothered her.

She was about to turn and walk away, when the door opened again.

'Wait, don't go away girl. Few months ago a young man came here asking about our friend. He was talking about a story written by this guy. It seems this story is special! Who knows? He gave me his address and requested to write to him if any information about our friend was obtained. Maybe that will be of use to you.'

Sakunthala accepted it. Many addresses, many men. The vanishing of one leads others to numerous trails and addresses. Some of the trails become dead ends, while some others lead to yet new ones.

'You keep it. I don't need it,' the old man said closing the door. 'From the urgency shown by that young man, it seemed he'd find out the writer the very next day. Who knows, perhaps he has succeeded!'

That address was of Nilesh, a student. He was doing research in the university on Comparative Literature. Sakunthala had no difficulty finding him.

'Teacher, you came in search of the corpse no?' Nilesh queried while waiting for tea at the canteen.

Sakunthala was upset. What on earth is this boy talking about? She looked at him intently, trying to conceal her emotions.

He appeared to be a fidgety individual. Stubble many days old. Throughout their talk, he was picking up and putting back the glass of water, without taking a sip from it.

'The story, "The Corpse" was an event.' The student closed his eyes as if in meditation. Oh, it's only a story! Sakunthala was relieved, partly.

'You came in search of that story, no?'

'No, not at all.' Sakunthala answered him leisurely. 'I haven't read that story.'

'No?' Nilesh looked at her with startled eyes. 'You are here to know about Chitran, but you have not read his story! How is this possible? What else is there apart from the story, to relate to him?'

Surely, there could be other connections to reach out to a man? Approaches beyond stories, and perhaps more truthful? Sakunthala thought.

But Nilesh did not seem to be convinced.

'Teacher, you must read it, if you haven't so far.'

It was for the first time someone was calling her a teacher. She was bewildered.

'It's an unusual story,' Nilesh continued.

'The publication of "The Corpse" will overhaul the short story segment in our literature. In content and form its structure itself is novel. With broken sentences, ... Do you know teacher, I could not sleep for many nights after reading that story. Have you ever had such an experience reading any other story?'

Not by reading stories, but by living through stories I've been sleepless, thought Sakunthala. But she did not mention it to Nilesh.

'Please try to remember. That is the power fiction wields.' Nilesh seemed to be persuading her.

'Can't remember Nilesh.' Sakunthala looked into his eyes and said, 'I'm not one who is well read as you seem to take me for. I may not even understand the story, even if I read it.'

Tea was served. Nilesh promptly started drinking the tea without waiting for her to join in.

'It was from the residence of a relative of mine that I got that magazine. *Liberation Path*. There was only one copy. This story was printed as its centrespread. No photos or illustrations. But that would suffice. The sheer power ...'

'From whose house did you get it?' Suddenly Sakunthala was eager.

'My uncle. Narayanan. Narayanan Nambisan is the full name. He used to be a *vaidyar*. Do you know him?'

She shook her head. She started drinking the tea.

'This guy did not write again. That's the pity of it. Had he continued writing …' Nilesh was excited.

'Had he continued writing …' Sakunthala raised her face.

'Our story would have been different.' He was throbbing with emotion, she thought.

'What I want to know …' Sakunthala did not complete as she felt that he was not paying attention.

Nilesh too became silent and seemed to calm down.

'Oh, I forgot. Teacher, why are you after Chitran?'

'Just to meet him. He is an old friend of my husband.'

'Where is your husband?'

Sakunthala did not reply. That's what she too wanted to know. It was this very same question that had been bothering her.

'Does he write,' Nilesh asked.

'Who? My husband? No.' That's what Sakunthala felt like saying. If she were to tell the truth, Nilesh might recognise him. The poem which appeared in the next issue of *Liberation Path*. With the by-line Buddha or something like that. No, that is of another poet, whom she doesn't even know. Why get into all those things once again?

'I also looked for him. It was for clearing certain doubts. Finally I secured his address. But that is far from here. I'm yet to meet him.'

'Can you give me his address?' Sakunthala asked, concealing her eagerness.

'Certainly. But there is no guarantee that he is there at that address.'

'Why?'

'I had sent a letter few months ago. There was no reply. Maybe it did not reach him. But if the address was incorrect, the letter should have been returned to me, no?'

'I don't know. But where else can it go?'

'Exactly. He may not be the type to reply. A writer, no? And to top it, someone who has turned silent! Anyway, I'll be going. I was busy with something else here. I've sent the story to a friend of mine. For translating it into English. I'll go find him after I get the translation.'

Sakunthala noted down the address. When she was leaving Nilesh said, 'If you see him, please tell him that it is a crime to keep silent. In that same story he has severely condemned the tendency to go silent. Another thing, tell him there are many more stories to be completed after "The Corpse".'

Can all stories be completed? Sakunthala was thinking sitting in the bus on her way back. So much more of life remains, as a novel or story that cannot be written to completion.

Sakunthala again set off three days later to the address provided by Nilesh. It was an arid village on the border. Four hours journey with a stopover.

It was noon when she reached the place. The bus stopped in the hot sun near the parched farmlands. She was the only one to get down there. Vast, desolate farmlands all around. All lying fallow. Dried up wild grass with the stamp of the preceding rainless months. She even had the feeling that the bus abandoned her in the wilderness and hurried away. A bullock cart passed by. The cart driver had no idea of the address and directed her to the village. It is not very far to the village, he said. The bus does not touch the village.

It was a cluster of small houses. Girls dressed in faded clothes were going about with milk cans. Hay was stacked near the houses. No greenery anywhere. The sun was scorching.

Her search ended in a lean and thin man sitting cross-legged in the veranda of a small house at the very end of a dusty street.

Chitrabhanu must have been taken aback seeing her after this long an interval. There was a distressed look on his face. She noticed her name shaping up on his lips as soon as he saw her: Sa ... kun ... tha ... la ...

'How are you Sakunthala?' he asked. He rubbed his palms together and tried to warm up his face. He was quite emaciated. Long hair and overgrown beard. Sakunthala entered the house without waiting for an invitation.

It was a small house with one room, a hall and a kitchen. There was a small cot in the hall, just sufficient for one man to sleep. Sakunthala found more order in this house than the one in which he was living in Avalam.

'How did you get here?' Chitran enquired.

'I asked people.' She noticed that there was no one else in the house. Sakunthala had never seen any of his family members.

'Who are you looking for? I'm alone.' Chitran smiled.

'What about your family?'

'There is no one now.' He was quite indifferent about it. She did not pursue it any further.

'You are the first of my old acquaintances to come here.' Chitran said. 'I've not given this address to anyone. But there maybe a few who may know that I could be here.'

'Yes. You have fans and they have found it out.'

'Fans? It is an insult I deserve. Loathing is what I should get.' Chitran continued with calmness. 'I'm the one who absconded, no?'

'But they still read your story.'

'A pity.' Sakunthala was aware that it was with pain that he uttered that word.

'Sorry, I forgot to ask you. Have you had anything to eat?'

No. she had not eaten anything since daybreak. She had started very early in the morning from home.

'Usually I don't eat lunch. But you must be hungry. What is the way out?' He thought for some time and then asked, 'Shall I give you some *payasam*?'

Sakunthala found it strange. One who skips lunch, having *payasam*?

'O, you must be wondering how this *payasam* has appeared here! Not just today, everyday, the only food item you'll get here is *payasam*. It's the leftover of the *prasadam*, the offering to god.'

She scrutinised him thoroughly. Was he under some delusion? Chitran talking about puja and offerings! Those words had no place in his vocabulary.

Chitran smiled. 'This is my job now. The traditional vocation. I've given up everything and have joined a small temple here as the priest.'

It was only then that she noticed a picture of Vishnu on the wall.

'I'm treating it as my karma.' Chitran spoke softly. 'Despite trying desperately I'm unable to conform to my faith. I've often felt that all my problems would be resolved if I could believe steadfastly. But that is not something new.' He transferred some quantity of *payasam* to a plantain leaf cup and offered it to her.

'There are no spoons or plates. Use your fingers.' The *payasam* prepared with jaggery was too sweet.

'It had always been like this. While writing stories or preparing bulletins for the party or participating in party activities, I had this very same uncertainty. A scepticism that doesn't allow me to stick to anything for long. It was there, from my boyhood days. Some of my friends used to tell me that all these vacillations are due to my atheism. And now performing puja for the god! Not with full conviction. One should believe in something, no? But doubts trail me. That is the nature of certain people. Always wavering. Like a wobbling canoe.'

Sakunthala stopped him when he began to serve her more *payasam*.

'You did not tell me the purpose of your visit,' Chitran asked her. 'I had heard of Sreenivasan's case.'

And then Sakunthala talked. Chitran listened to her silently and did not react or ask anything in between.

'What's the point in searching for him?' Finally Chitran asked. Sakunthala remained silent as she did not know what to say.

Neither of them spoke for quite a while. It was scorching hot. Everything was at a standstill. Not a leaf stirred. She was sweating profusely.

'It was I who sent him to your house after speaking to Sreenivasan,' Chitran broke the silence.

'I know that. You have told me earlier.'

'There are certain things I've not told you. That day when we met I was tormented by a sense of guilt and the feeling of having sinned. What to do? That was what I finally became in the end.'

A breeze wafted in, totally unexpected. Strands of hair fluttered around her face. That breeze too was hot.

'It will rain today,' Chitran said looking skywards.

Must leave before it starts to rain. Sakunthala was thinking about the next bus.

'I did not complete, did I? I had mentioned that I had him sheltered there. But I did not mention that it was I who informed the police about all this.'

Stunned, Sakunthala felt a strong adhesive had glued her to her seat. Her gaze fixed on his face, she remained in total shock.

Chitran covered his face with hands and said, 'I was trying to forget everything. But it is alright. I got an opportunity to confess. Please pardon me. I had no other alternative then.'

Evening. They waited near the desolate fields for the bus to make the return trip to town. She saw the dry slough of a snake amongst the burnt wild grass.

It was then that he talked about her request.

'I'll try to find out if it'll be useful to you,' he told Sakunthala. 'I know many former comrades who used to arrange shelters. Most of them have left the party since. I too don't maintain any contact with them. Even then I am hopeful of getting a trace. However, it would be too facile to assume that he would have any information about Sreeni. Because Sreeni was only an ordinary fellow traveller."

'Will you speak the truth if I ask you a question?' She asked him. 'Do you think that my husband is still alive?'

He was caught off guard. After a pause, he said that he had no answer to that question.

'I heard he was missing. That's all. I really don't know what happened to him. Sometimes … maybe …' Chitran bent his head not knowing how to complete the sentence.

In the distance, from beyond the parched fallow farmlands, Sakunthala saw the dot-like form of her bus approaching.

JUST AS THE TREES GROW

The hiss of the venomous words emitted by the deaf-mute pursued Sivan's thoughts.

All the men in the island are like Ayyakkuru. All of them lead double lives.

Which of those lives is the real one? The one that is being enacted in the island presently? Or is it the past? Past! All of its frills and pigments have withered away.

Looking down through the window he was surprised seeing a woman's dress on the clothesline. Who is using a woman's dress in the mansion? Suddenly the image of the woman he saw in the boat rushed to his mind. He came down the stairs. An unusual anxiety gripped him.

Water drops were trickling down from a garment hung on the branches of the neem tree. It was a light blue sari. He seemed to experience the presence of a woman. He went down the steps and found a woman combing her hair standing beyond the bushes as if in a movie camera frame. Wet strands of her hair were fluttering in the morning breeze. He stood there staring at her intently.

The woman turned around after braiding her hair. Now Sivan could see her clearly.

He could not believe his eyes.

It was Remani.

Though he had been with her only for one day, he recognised her at first sight. She had certainly changed. The sparkle of youth had faded from her face and she was less robust than before. Had a hair or two turned grey? She was wearing a rough and faded blue sari. Exactly the same as the one hung on the neem tree for drying. Her sad blue eyes, he could read the shadows of that one-off night in them.

'Remani,' Sivan softly called her. She turned to him. He could see the inkling of an old memory taking shape in her eyes.

He smiled at her. He felt that she was a visitor from his last birth.

She stood there looking at him for quite some time.

'Okay, so it was at your bidding that I was brought here?' Remani remarked.

Sivan was baffled. Why had she been brought to the island? He did not speak.

'Why did you take all this trouble?' The derision and insult in her tone was upsetting.

Soft words seemed to have abandoned her. There was an unusual hardening in her look as well as words. The passing years may have transmuted her life into an arid land.

'Maybe this is in exchange for saving you? Tell me, were you really saved?' Remani's words were sharp.

After a moment's silence, she fixed her eyes upon him and continued, 'No one escapes to anywhere is the lesson I've learnt. From one prison to another, that's all.'

'I really do not know how you reached here,' Sivan said.

'That's not true.'

'It's the truth. Simply because you had faded away from my memory,' he continued, 'However, it is good that you've come here.'

'What is in store for me here for it to be good?' Remani seemed to be laughing at herself.

'Unlike out there, you'll have full freedom here.' Sivan's words lacked conviction.

'In course of time any hell becomes tolerable. It was like that when I was living with Lasar,' Remani said.

Sivan looked at her in silence.

'Since when have you become a lawyer?' Remani enquired. 'When I was told, I had no idea that it would be you. In those days you were a playwright.'

'Those were the underground days,' Sivan reminded her.

'Even now, isn't it? But from whom are you hiding? From the police, or from your own comrades? Or is it from your past life?'

'You have obviously heard all the stories, no?' He was quite calm.

'Oh, so they were all mere stories?' Sivan recognised the tone of mockery in Remani's words. He would've loved to believe that they were only stories.

'But it was not so for many,' Remani continued. 'Many were caught. Some were killed. And a few went missing.'

'I do not know any of that. No one maintained any contact with this island.'

'There were not many left behind to maintain contact.'

His solitary flights and escapes gyrated in Sivan's mind as if glimpses from dim lights. The expeditions not only from one place to another, but from time too.

'But I was not responsible for any of them.' Sivan asserted.

'Maybe not. But they nabbed each and everyone who sheltered you.'

It was as if he was suddenly rising in the darkness of the hideout. Like the sun suddenly coming out during the dark rainy season. That light brightened up the shelters.

'I don't know anything. All communications from outside had ceased.'

Neither of them spoke for a while.

'And then? Are not people rising up in protest?' Sivan revived the memories of the past and asked.

'People? They do not have the time. They are busy standing in queue for rice and kerosene. Just as before. They were never aware that whatever you did was for their sake.' Remani laughed.

'Maybe what Lasar plotted was right.' Remani continued. 'If he had handed you over to the police, many lives would have been saved.'

Sivan did not look at her.

'Sometimes I get the feeling that what uncouth men do is right. Lasar was an ordinary man.'

'Where is he now?' Sivan tried to change the subject.

'Nowhere.' Remani said.

'What happened to him?'

'Happened? He was killed. I killed him.'

Sivan stared at her. He felt that his vision was getting dimmer in the unusual glow of her eyes.

'You?' he could not believe it. 'How could you?'

'Why, what is so special about me?'

'Why did you do it?' Sivan thought of Lasar and asked.

'Because I liked him.' Remani laughed. 'Sometimes I feel that I killed him out of love.'

'He used to exploit you in every possible way, no?' Sivan remembered Lasar taking photos of her for the new edition of the porno title.

'So? So does it mean that I should hate him all the time? I liked him, to tell the truth.'

Sivan looked at her in silence.

'My child was a true copy of him,' she whispered.

She recalled those days. The honey scent of a childhood. Lasar like a tired god. The toddler followed him. He learnt to walk holding on to Lasar's finger. He too walked with the same gait with which Lasar walked. The baby frolicked on his tired body. Boxed him with his baby fists. He called him dad. Lasar was a good father.

For the first time, Sivan saw tears welling up in her eyes. The weak figure of Lasar emerged in his mind. This woman here, is uttering good words about a man who deserved to be slighted by all, a man who made a living out of printing and selling nude pictures of women! Despite her body too being used, as a commodity for making money and despite having had to live under the constant threat of his iron fist. Sivan was astounded. A woman to love even a man like him!

'He printed and sold your pictures, no?'

'Yes. But that was his profession.'

'Do you mean to say that you had no objection to it?'

'What was the point in having objections? And he did it only with my consent.'

Sivan did not respond to that.

'There was no other go …' Remani did not complete.

Sivan looked at her intently.

'It was all inevitable. The same would have occurred had it been someone else.'

'Are you saying that there was no other way out, other than obscenity?'

'Human body is obscene only for the likes of you. It was never so for Lasar.'

Sivan became silent once again.

She looked at his face intently and asked in a subdued voice, 'Have you ever coddled a baby?'

'Whose baby are you talking about?'

'Anybody's?'

Sivan did not answer. The world of babies was different. He had no inkling of it.

'If you haven't, then you are not aware of many things.'

For her the baby was everything. When she caressed his baby pink arms for the first time, all the sorrows of life had faded away from her. She was a dried up, parched tree. But it rained incessantly, when he touched her nipples with his tiny nails. Leaves blossomed on the shrivelling branches. She had lived for him ever after. She woke up to his crying and slept humming lullabies for him. He was the hour and minute hand of her time. On those nights when he was afflicted by fever and went into delirium she too burnt from fever and could not close her eyes.

'Okay. But where is your child?' Sivan was getting restless. When he saw Remani he had thought that here is a woman who has had a degrading past and I will offer her an altogether new life. And now she was full of good words for that despicable life. Suddenly he was filled with a smouldering rage and jealousy.

'He died.' She did not look at him as she spoke those two words. But he was only relieved to hear that, Sivan thought with self contempt.

'It was a few days ago. The fever did not subside. He had always been a weak child. Would get tired easily. Incessant fever. His struggle for breath terrified me. It was only for his sake that I did not surrender to the police.'

Even though he wanted to know the details of Lasar's killing, Sivan was afraid to ask her directly to her face.

'Is the police after you?'

'That is immaterial. Now I don't bother about such things. What's the big deal in being imprisoned? It doesn't matter which prison I'm in,' she said.

Sivan shared his breakfast with her. Remani did not eat much. Sivan kept the empty plates outside the room. Ayyakkuru was waiting there. As he was leaving with the plates, Sivan told him, 'Tell Thechappan that there will be one more person for lunch.' Ayyakkuru nodded without any emotion on his face. Was it not the same fellow who shouted at him, Sivan wondered. Just a few hours after, he is here back as a dumb guy.

Remani's disposition changed within a week. She became more attuned to the surroundings. She was much more pleasant now. One evening, as Sivan returned from work, Remani was waiting for him with tea. He was glad that she was smiling and was more intimate with him while talking. His own life was changing. The weight of loneliness seemed to be on the wane.

He took her to the riverbank during his free time. Her sandals had been lost in the swamp—on the day she arrived at the island, she had told Sivan. He recalled that his sandals too had been lost in the swamp on his landing at the island. He searched the riverside for her sandals, but in vain.

'Leave it. Moreover, this soil is very fertile, no? Maybe it will sprout,' she joked.

'If whatever is lost starts sprouting, there won't be any space left here in the island.' Sivan laughed.

The current was very weak. The landing at the opposite shore and the two sentinel-like coconut trees with burnt heads were dimly visible. The headless tress had become leaning towers. The sky held by them was also slanting now. Down, on the other side, paniya huts. Beyond those huts, at the next bend, the river disappeared.

'Have you gone beyond that point?' she asked.

'We'll go one day.' He assured her. Not only there. She will be taken to the forest where huge trees line up. Bullocks with big humps on their necks lying under the shadows of trees chewing the cud and reliving their memories and then in the evening loads of wood being carried with the same bullocks tied to the carts. Beyond that the river could be seen resting as a huge pool in the check dam constructed by the paniyas. The wind generated waves crashing on to the walls of the check dam was a real sight. Only life could transform a prison into a garden. A nascent life. Remani's arrival brought this idea into Sivan's mind. A budding life with all the stains of time wiped clean. A new path of liberation.

Remani was in a very cheerful mood on the night they went to the riverside. Sivan felt that she had overcome all the sorrows of the past. The breeze that wafted in was very cool. He lay on his side in the warmth of her body.

'Did you see the last issue of that porn magazine?' Remani laughed as she asked.

'How could I? What was special about it?'

'That was full of my pictures.'

'Lasar might have threatened you, no?'

'No. I volunteered.'

Sivan stared at her, but did not say anything.

'It was for money,' she said. 'It was at my bidding that he brought out that book. I even wrote a few stories for that. My father's playwriting tradition!'

Sivan could not appreciate it. How could Remani ask *Kambanam* Lasar to print her nude pictures? Had she gone mad?

'All of it was for me only. It was just before my dad died. Our house was going to be attached by the authorities for non-payment of loan dues. By the time we were to vacate the house, dad's condition had worsened. Whenever he regained consciousness for short periods, he would scream not to take him away. I too wanted him to live in that house till his death. Many well known people had been our guests in that house, once upon a time. When he came to visit dad, Lasar told me that he would sort out the problem of attachment of the house. But he did not have the necessary funds for that. When he was lamenting about it, sitting in the press, I was the one who suggested that he raise the money by doing what he knew best.'

'So, did you get the required amount?'

'That was what went wrong. Just as *Kambanam* came out of the press, someone informed the police. Only a few copies had been sold. The police confiscated the rest. Thus that project too failed.'

They not only confiscated the last issue of *Kambanam*, they took away the publisher also. Maybe because he had tried to be helpful to the police in the past they did not beat him up. But he was remanded for six months. Remani was in no position to try for his bail, with the little baby to be looked after. No one came to her help.

Except one, a policeman.

Chandran, was his name. He was one of the policemen who had made the raid to seize *Kambanam*. He started frequenting the house even after Lasar was remanded. Chandran would tell Remani that he was trying to get Lasar out. And that he had engaged an advocate for this. He claimed that he could not directly intervene, as he was part of the police squad that had arrested Lasar. Chandran occasionally gave her money. There was no other means to meet household expenses. Since a policeman was a regular at her house, others stopped troubling her. After sometime, Chandran started to stay overnight. He had convinced Remani that it was impossible for Lasar to obtain bail.

However, Lasar was out on bail one day.

'Bitch, you sleep with the one who put me behind bars?' Lasar yelled. He resumed bashing her from that night. He would clutch on to her hair and bang her head on to the wall and kick her abdomen. She would be locked out of the house, not even permitting her to breastfeed the baby. Chandran never turned up on those days. He was terrified of Lasar.

'When I could not bear it anymore, I went to meet Chandran. He seemed to be upset that I had come to meet him. What if anyone saw, he was asking repeatedly.'

'What if anyone saw, I retorted. Haven't you slept with me?'

'Remani, please cool down, I'm thinking of a way out, he said.'

'What do you have in mind?'

'Why not trap him again?'

'And then?'

'Then we will get time. We can go somewhere else and set up home.'

'Like in the movies,' I said.

'It was not a workable plan. It was not easy for an ordinary policeman like Chandran to lock up a person. Lasar came to know of it. He was enraged and he took it out on me. He was drunk and kicked me. The baby was crying. But that did not stop him. He was in a frenzy. And I was burning with vengeance.'

It was Chandran who advised her to poison the arrack Lasar brought home. Chandran bought the poison for her.

'He sheltered me for a few days at various places. My baby became sick and treating and nursing him became a big problem. And I began to feel that I was becoming a liability for him. That was the way he was behaving with me. At times I felt that men are the most cowardly beings. I was laid up for quite some time after the baby died. By that time the police had traced me out. When it was certain that I would be nabbed, you know, what he asked me for? I should swear that I'll never reveal that he was the one who bought the poison.'

'Then?'

'I spat on his face. I also asked him not to come to me offering any help thereafter.'

After a few moments of silence Remani said, 'I was in a convent for some time. Look at this, this blue sari, it is too faded, no? This was the uniform there. I was brought here to work as a domestic help. That was what I was told at the convent.'

Sivan did not ask who brought her to the island. Such questions were unwarranted in the island. And who brought me here, anyway? He thought.

'But if had known that you were here …' Remani stopped.

'What if you had known …'

'I'd never have come here. Not because I had known you. I did not want to see anyone who knew the old Remani. The old Remani is like the photos Lasar clicked, a mere body with a veiled or erased face.'

Sivan looked at her. He did not notice her body at all. He felt that the presence of a being with the aroma of the soul, was transforming him into a new man.

'Each passing moment we are new beings,' Sivan said. He kissed her forehead, like a saint. Her forehead was warm. He felt his lips scald.

Raising his hands Ayyakkuru drew in the air the picture of a country craft. Then pointed in the direction of the river. It was to convey that a boat was waiting at the riverbank. The shell of a language which had shed all its words. The communication of the netherworld that translates mysteries. Having spent many lonely summers in the island, Sivan could comprehend all of it by now.

Sivan walked behind Ayyakkuru. Sunlight lay weak and pale over the treetops. The gloomy sky of evening. Here and there clouds with crimson edges. Group of birds below, like the shadows of the clouds.

A tired looking Thechappan was working on the land near the path they were passing through. He stood aside not looking at Sivan. Maybe because Sivan did not keep up his word to help with the completion and beautification of his house. There were stories that the roof had been blown away by the heavy wind. Sivan had not bothered. He had not been to Thechappan's house for a long time. After Remani's arrival, food was prepared at the mansion and Thechappan or Mary rarely came there. It had been days since he had seen either of them.

From a distance, Sivan saw a boat coming to a stop at the landing. The boat was bobbing up and down in the soft waves. Moosa, the boatman, was talking to someone who was squatting on the sandbank. He must be the new guest. Running away from what crime and afraid of what punishment? As he drew nearer, he could make out that the visitor was an elderly person.

The water level was low. It had been months since it rained. Hordes of dry leaves were flowing downstream. Even though it was evening, the heat was overpowering.

As they reached the river, Moosa raised his hand and waved at Ayyakkuru. Perhaps Moosa had not recognised him, Sivan thought.

The new entrant stood up. He was quite tall. The distance between years flashed through Sivan's mind. Those eyes had lost their old sparkle. Still it was not possible to evade that tough scrutiny. Its brightness seemed to light up a fading summer evening of yesteryears. That evening when he arrived at Pullani. The memory of walking to the riverbank like the shadow of the man in front, under the black clouds. The two coconut trees with burnt heads like two pillars of the sky.

Time has debilitated the body, Sivan observed. Wrinkles all over the face. The wound on the forehead above the left eye which was bulging red like a reptile had healed.

It was Achu. The comrade who led him from the junction at Pullani to the island. He had aged. Even the eyelashes were greying. Sivan could read the shadow-like lines of changing times on Achu's face. That day's bus journey and the hurried scamper to the river filled Sivan's mind. He was running like a machine. The loud hoot of Achu to summon Moosa echoed in his ears. Achu had lunged as if to kiss and ended up whispering 'Lal Salaam' in his ears. When he had uttered the code word, Achu had only nodded his head instead of coming up with the appropriate reply. That had also aroused suspicion about him. Today, after a very long interval, Sivan stood there unable to explain where to the absence of a code word had led him.

'Greetings, comrade!' Achu said with his clenched fist raised high.

Sivan looked at Achu carefully. Yes, he had grown weak. His words were wavering as if swayed by the wind. Syllables could no more stand firm as a few teeth were missing from the front row. The rest had yellowed, struck by the lightning of time.

Sivan saw it with a shock. His left palm has been severed. Torn flesh like a tattered map. What had happened to him?

'Do you remember me?' Achu asked.

'Achu.' But he did not return the raised-fist greetings.

'Yes, comrade Achu,' Achu repeated. Sivan smiled as if he had recalled something from memory.

Silence smouldered between them like a burning body.

'It has been a very long time,' Achu walked up to him.

Moosa turned the boat in the opposite direction, ready to leave at short notice. Ayyakkuru sat near him. They were talking in sign language, Sivan noted.

'It's really surprising. I'm here for the first time.' Achu looked at him with friendliness and continued, 'It has also been long, since we met. But comrade, you did not utter any code word this time.'

'The time for code words is over.' Sivan replied with total detachment.

The sun had set. A little bit of light lingered over the river as if in memory of the sunlight.

'That's right. We had parted promising to meet very soon,' Achu said.

'Only that it took years for that, no?' Sivan asked derisively.

'You did not respond to my messages,' Achu said.

'Messages? I never received any message,' Sivan looked at him.

'But why send messages? You could've come directly, had you wanted.' Sivan suspected that the sense of loss of the last so many years had caught up with him. He cursed himself.

'Yes. But it was not my fault. My assignment was only to reach you to this place. All other decisions were to be taken by the organisation. I was only a messenger. And unfortunately, no replies were received for any of my communications.'

What communications was Achu referring to? Who came as a messenger?

Achu continued, 'There were no messages from you either. The river divided the two sides.'

'I had sent my notes to you.'

'No, I did not receive any.' Achu hesitated for a moment. 'Maybe I might not have accepted them, even if they happened to reach me. We went different ways. Do you know? Our organisation split within days. Both factions expelled the other from the organisation. I was in the faction which opposed you. And because of that you were no longer my responsibility.'

'If so what has happened now? You have come in search of me. Have you changed sides?'

'I no more think in terms of factions or groups,' Achu mumbled in a low voice.

Sivan smiled, recalling something from old memories. But he did not reply. Achu seemed to be troubled by Sivan's silence.

'It's not as you think comrade. There are not many organisations for one to take sides. Only individuals. At the most a few small groups. No one has kept count of the number of splits we've undergone in these years.'

Achu tried to explain. Huge masses thinning out and confining to small spaces as individuals. It was like the multiplication of cells. People removed each other and formed groups. The groups too splintered later on.

'But where are they?'

'They are present anywhere,' There was a tone of guilt in his voice. Then he corrected himself. 'They are everywhere, comrade.'

'Omnipresent like God, isn't it, Achu?' Sivan laughed. But Achu did not seem to hear.

'There were contradictions in our thoughts. A time would come when the voices of men would harmonise and become enjoyable like music, was what was said.' There was a tinge of sadness in Achu's remark.

Sivan recalled. That old romantic poem. It was quoted in one of the issues of *Liberation Path*.

'And now even setting the eye on each other evokes hatred,' Achu said as if cursing. 'Everyone behaves as if they are in enemy camps. Conversations are in demonic voices. Where did we go wrong? Where and why did we part ways?' Achu asked in a broken voice. He may not have expected an answer.

'We had not gone wrong anywhere. We hadn't strayed from the course too,' Sivan corrected him. 'Perhaps we were all going through the correct and specific paths of history.'

'I don't understand you, comrade,' Sivan felt that Achu was gasping through words.

'That's easy, Achu. There's nothing in it to understand as such.' Sivan watched the craft bobbing up and down.

'You are a thinking person. Was it in the practice that we committed errors?'

'Never. We were quite correct in the practice. On the contrary, it was the theory that failed us. Human beings were always like this, friend!'

Achu could not understand what Sivan was trying to communicate.

Sivan continued, 'Showering love on each other and raining music and all else were mere romantic illusions of poets. I had always held that imagination is madness. Who was there to heed? Words sweetened by poets, that was our ideological base. But practice went its own way. In fact practice was perfect. That and that alone was the truth.'

'My instinct tells me that all these are reactionary thoughts. Maybe it is the drawback of my knowledge and education. But I don't understand how a comrade like you is harbouring such ideas.'

Achu tried to raise the stump of his left hand. The sleeve of his long dress was hanging out with nothing.

'Comrade, you are not saying anything.' Sivan felt there was a tinge of pain in his voice.

'It was trees that taught me all this,' Sivan said disregarding the pain in his tone.

'Trees?' Achu looked at him with astonishment.

'Yes, the trees of this forest. Teak, rosewood, mahogany, ballnut tree, flame of the forest, *anhili*, *arjun*, *babul* ... the trees that grew up without our planting them. Trees that took roots and grew up in sun and rain. Have you ever looked at them carefully? They don't wait for anything or anybody. They compete with each other for survival. They fight for water. They leap for light.'

Sivan looked at Achu who was waiting for his words and continued, 'They don't yield to anyone. Heights, their only destination. The struggle of life. But they are not ready to sacrifice anything for that. Therefore the practice of those who fight and kill and eliminate each other for the sake of growth is certainly the right one. *That this cannot be explained could be the shortcoming of the doctrine.*'

'You are trying to establish that man is nothing but a mere animal.'

'Law of nature! That's all. What is the point in pretending otherwise?'

'Okay. I'm not arguing comrade. Each argument leads to yet other arguments. They spread like vines.' Achu's frustration was quite obvious.

'There's no point worrying about it, my friend. All trees will fall, was the next lesson taught by the forest.'

Dusk was falling. The blood red tinge vanished from the clouds in the sky. Birds vanished. A star had appeared on the horizon. The burnt trunks of the headless coconut trees on the other side of the river were bent like question marks. The boat, the boatman slouched in it and the dwarf talking to him in sign language appeared like a pale picture on a canvas. A paniya's shrill hoot reverberated. But it was not responded.

'It's getting late. There are people in the mansion waiting for me,' Sivan showed signs of being in a hurry. 'Achu, you've not told me why you have come in search of me.'

'Are you aware of the proceedings in the Kangazha case?' Achu asked.

'O, Kangazha! What about it?'

'The verdict was out last month.'

Sivan did not ask for the details. The dark night in Kangazha, the stuffed heads of animals, the bison horns on the wall ... and the severed head of a man. A silenced Kathakali song on its lips. To which life did all that belong?

'The prosecution had not taken the case very seriously. But, yet the verdict was against us. Sekharan was declared to be the prime culprit. Life term for him. Two years each for three. The others were acquitted,' Achu said.

'What was in it for me?' Sivan asked without any apparent emotion.

'Your verdict has not been pronounced. There was no proof as to whether you were alive.'

'I too was not sure.' Sivan laughed.

'But ultimately no one may actually have to be in the prison. The sentenced period has been covered as undertrials. Sekharan is the only one in prison now. He will go on appeal.'

'Ridiculous!' It seemed as if Sivan was regaining his old self.

Achu stared at Sivan. He seemed to be baffled by Sivan's reaction.

'Does Sekharan trust this government?' Sivan asked.

'I do not know. Comrade, why do you ask?'

'He will not have any trust. Not only him, but anyone who yearns for revolution. And to go for mercy to the judiciary, which is nothing more than the tool that protects the interests of the establishment!'

Even in the dark light of the river bank, Sivan could see the facial muscles of Achu tautening. A point of dispute was sprouting in him.

'You can voice such an opinion. You were underground. You were out of the larger society.' Achu composed himself to the extent possible and said.

'Sent out, Achu, you should say, sent out. I was plucked out from the open. You were also one among those who schemed for it. I waited for months and months, preparing new notes and fresh explanations. Thinking about and formulating new methods. You will get enough to laugh about if you can recall my past.'

Maybe Achu made an attempt to do so. Then he nodded with detachment. It was not clear whether he was in agreement or in denial.

'My focus was on the new *Liberation Path*,' Sivan said.

'*Liberation Path* never saw the light of the day ever after.'

'It was neither wanted nor essential. No Achu?'

'Yes. Even the name was not right,' Achu said head downcast. 'Each one sought out their own liberation path. Some in alcohol, some in wealth, some in sex or in other pleasures. Many returned to the same organisations they had deserted early on. They wanted that scorching past. They took over its flesh and blood. And then they tried to exhibit them as skeletons in glass cases.'

Sivan tried to summon up those faces. Dark clouds extinguished the light over the river.

'Some committed suicide,' Achu tried to fill up the blanks.

'I guessed as much. It must be them, those men who wrote romantic poems. They in fact had no other alternative,' Sivan said.

'Sivan, you were always averse to poetry and poets.'

'That's only because they are always in opposition to life. Okay, tell me, are the days of those poems over? Where's he now? O, what's his name? It was in his house that I had lived last.'

Not just lived there, it was he who bestowed on me the rest of my life. Even the dress I was wearing when I came to this island belonged to him. And how many others like him!

'Poet Sreenivasan.' Achu mentioned that name in a very low tone. Just as he uttered it, a star had risen in the sky.

'Yes, that's him. What is he writing now?'

Achu did not answer. He was thinking of Sakunthala.

It was an evening months ago that Sakunthala had come in search of him. He was engrossed in his work. Though his left palm had been severed off, he continued with his job of repairing watches. In his shop as small as a box, he sat amidst his tools and solutions. His shop was in a small shopping complex attached to the bus stand. Buses from different directions would come and leave. His concentration was broken at times by the loud horns of the buses. Emaciated old clocks stared at him in silence from the walls of the room. He was the representative as well as the keeper of stupefied time. He tried his utmost to bring them up to date with the new time. Failure was the result more often than not.

'There's someone waiting for you,' the shopkeeper next to his, called out. He saw a woman standing beyond the glass cage.

He raised his head and looked at her. Looking through the lens fitted on his eye, her face had assumed gigantic proportions. The lens could not contain her face.

'I'm Achu.' He confirmed and asked her what she wanted.

'It's regarding a matter …' she started softly.

'I cannot take up any new work. Already I'm behind schedule.'

'I'm not here for any such things. I'd like to talk to you.'

He removed the lens from his eyes and looked at her. Have I seen this woman before, he wondered. Yes, in couple of photos, in certain news reports.

He fixed the minute handle of the watch he was repairing and got out of the shop. The lights were being switched on as the evening was darkening.

'... wife of poet Sreenivasan.' She introduced herself.

'I know. But I have never seen him.'

She told him that she had not come in search of Sreenivasan and that searches to that effect were practically over. Now she was after the comrade who was provided shelter by Sreenivasan.

'He is not there in my party anymore. He too was sacked from the party along with those who tried to implement incorrect policies.'

'Do you know where he is now?'

'Who told you about me?' Achu countered. He had not been in contact with anyone for quite some time and was living a totally isolated life.

Sakunthala thought: is Chitrabhanu known to Achu? She did not answer him.

'Didn't you hear me? Who gave you information about this watch repairer?'

'Perhaps you know him. Sreenivasan had a friend called Chitrabhanu.'

Chitrabhanu. The name did not ring a bell.

Chitran had given her Achu's address. He had to spend quite a lot of time and energy to ferret it out from his old acquaintances. And he had written to Sakunthala that Achu was last in charge of that mysterious comrade.

'I took him to a shelter,' Achu said. 'I do not know anything after that.'

'He has to be found out.' The firmness in her tone surprised him.

'It's not easy,' Achu said. 'He was expelled from the party immediately after that. I too did not try to contact him as it was against party discipline.'

'You have to make enquiries,' Sakunthala said. 'Wherever he is. Perhaps …'

'Please carry on.' Achu was humbled by the steadfastness in her eyes.

'Perhaps he may know where Sreeni is. Or that he is no …'

'I don't think so, comrade,' Achu said. 'He was alone when I led him to the shelter.'

'Perhaps he can tell us what happened before that?' Sakunthala looked at Achu expectantly.

'Do you think that will be of any use now?'

'Not for any use. But for confirmation. The investigations about a missing person never end. Unless some certainties are obtained.'

Achu stared at her hard for a moment.

Expectations are what scare her now. At least those lights must be put out ...

She stared at his severed palm. It looked like the needle of a huge clock that had gone still.

'Oh it's nothing,' Achu hesitated and changed the position of his arm. 'It has been like that since some time.'

Sakunthala just stood there trying to read the changing expressions on his face.

'It was a country bomb planted by a group of angry young men. On a crowded evening in the weekly market. I rushed to the spot when

I got wind of it. But it was too late by the time I tried to disconnect the wires.'

Yet another memorial-like human body. She recalled her first meeting with Chitrabhanu. He too had talked about body.

A few erratic clocks chimed from Achu's workshop.

Memories rushed into Sakunthala's mind like a typhoon. She tried in vain to cover her face with the tip of her saree. Even after so many years, tears were welling up in her eyes ... He averted his glance not to embarrass her further. Frequency of arrivals and departures had come down in the bus stand. Small clusters of people stood around the street vendors. Tired voices. Men hurrying into departing buses.

Sakunthala went away. Achu did not commence any sort of search even after days. In his cage-like room he continued his struggle against time that had come to a halt.

At last, one day he heard an old clock on the wall reverberating with rage after a very long time. Achu thought it was the vibrations of the blood that had again started to flow in its dead veins.

He had stepped out from that hospital of time into the street. A dimly lit evening, a landing on the river and the boatman rushed into his mind suddenly.

Achu recalled all that now, sitting over the river bank's darkness. 'After years, I've come to you for removing the darkness from at least a few spaces. How much do you know?'

'I do not know the whereabouts of Sreenivasan. I've never seen him after that day. The only thing I know is that he too was a fool like every other poet.' The scorn in his tone was palpable.

Achu heard Sivan's words. It had grown darker and his face was not clearly visible.

'He could've escaped that day, had he wanted to. All that he had to do was to give me up and help the policeman. It was a ludicrous moment when the romantic in him became too active and overshadowed all else.'

'So, can it be taken for certain that he was taken into custody by the police?'

'Sure. Because he was the one who saved me from their clutches. What do they do then? It's all simple logic, no Achu? Not only that, in those times—and perhaps even in these times—there are no romantics in the police force.'

'Comrade, are you sure that they took him away?'

'As big a truth as this darkness.' Sivan looked into the pitch dark that had mercilessly enveloped them by now.

Achu got into the boat. There was sound of moving water.

'What shall I tell Sakunthala finally?' Achu shouted from the boat.

'Ask her to forget everything and move forward. Because what she has been trying is to seek an answer for the past. She will never get it. And also ask her to make a bonfire of that fool's poems if she has preserved them.' It was as if Sivan was addressing the darkness. His voice was unusually intense.

Achu was panting like a wounded animal.

'Okay, Achu, you have lost your palm. What happened? Which tower did you try to bomb?' Sivan asked Achu calling him back.

'That's a secret,' Achu ignored the derision in Sivan's question.

'On the contrary, it is now an open thing, friend. It was the palm that was the secret. A palm that could be closed, folded in. Fingers that point like weapons. All of that has been severed off. It is all now in the open.'

Achu instinctively felt like moving the fingers of the missing palm and fold his fist at least in imagination.

Returning from the river along with Ayyakkuru, Sivan's mind was as calm as the river. Meeting Achu had not affected him in any way.

After walking some distance, Ayyakkuru who was ahead, turned around. He was visible as a shadow.

'Corpse.' He was talking once again.

Corpse? Sivan recalled a story of that name.

He just ….

'Dead: corpse,' Ayyakkuru repeated. Is there a tone of ridicule?

'A corpse?' Sivan asked with absolute disinterest.

The shape of a still animal was partly visible in the path ahead. Deer, fox or wolf? Stench of decay. It was not there on his way to the river bank.

Sivan did not hesitate. He pushed it away from the path with his foot.

For the first time, he put his hand across Ayyakkuru's shoulders and walked alongside with friendly feelings. Touching the neck where snakes had curled up, Sivan thought that an invisible accord was being formulated between them.

That night Sivan rummaged around the room and came up with an old note book. Someone who was reading it had kept a bookmark half way through. A daily journal of an old revolutionary. Who was the one reading it?

He felt disdain for himself. But he was afraid that *those words, so alien from the times, would one day point their finger at him.*

Should be cut off. Like the palm of Achu. No one from the past should raise a finger against me.

Sivan shredded the pages of the note book as if he was shredding the letters and threw it away through the window.

When he turned around he saw Remani standing there looking at him with rapt attention. She had no questions for him.

It was an extended summer. Springs dried up, the flora on the hilltops shrivelled. Rocks were scalding hot. Wild beasts groaned with parched throats in the smouldering nights. The fire spitting wind from across the rocks whooshed through the skeletons of dead animals with a hissing sound. The animals which came to the weak flow of the river for quenching their thirst were caught in the traps set by the paniyas. They were tempted both by the water and the thirst for freedom as they moaned nonstop through the night in the trap.

In the evening Sivan would go to the river along with Remani. The water level was very low. Plants on the moistureless land were withering. The skins moulted by the snakes were lying around like memories. Snakes come following the scent of the sand hills, Sivan was telling Remani. She did not seem to have heard him. It had been like that many a times lately. She would be floating in her dream world.

'I saw Achachan swimming.' One day Remani told him.

'Pappayi?' Sivan asked.

'Yes. He doesn't at all look old when swimming. Paddling with extended arms ... it is a sight, really.' It was a warm morning. Sivan was shaving in front of the mirror fixed on the wall. She had just come in from the river bank. She used to go early to the river for washing clothes.

'Anyone can swim in the river these days.' Sivan said holding the razor still for a while.

'If so why haven't I seen you go for a swim?' Sivan did not sense the innocence behind that question.

'You just don't understand. Water level is very low. All sorts of dirt is flowing out. Decayed leaves, plants, shit, even decayed carcasses. A putrid stench is ever present. Better than taking a bath in that water, is not to have a bath at all.' Sivan smiled.

'Maybe the water level is low, but the water is as pure as tears. Very cool too. What a relief it is to immerse in that water.' Remani said.

'Did you try swimming in the river?' Sivan did not like her talk.

'I can't swim. I don't know how to swim. Otherwise I would've tried it at least once.'

'Those who do not know swimming, should not enter the river. They will be carried away by the stream. Death by drowning is not a very pleasant thing.'

'What kind of death will be pleasant?' she smiled.

Sivan disliked any arguments. He kept quiet and resumed shaving. There was a lapse of concentration and blood sprouted as the blade swished through angularly.

'I'll try. I've been told that one can learn to swim by tying the plantain stems together,' Remani said.

'Who told you?' he turned to look at her. She saw the cut on his cheek.

'Blood.' Remani went out into the yard for fetching few herbal leaves for applying on the wound.

Sivan thought about Remani. Is not Pappayi occupying most of the words Remani speaks, of late? What is it that Remani finds so interesting in him? Perhaps it's that journal. It may be the fascination for the revolutionary. A well of derision rose up inside Sivan, breaching the walls.

But he was also occasionally pained by the excursions of her mind.

However, he reconciled that it was quite natural on her part. She had always been like that. Not only had she shared the bed of *Kambanam* Lasar, but had also made him print pictures of that. When he was jailed she lived with one of the policemen who had taken him into custody. Then she left him. Lasar was poisoned. Does she have a fetish for old men? Vengeance raged inside him. The feminine mind is a difficult terrain. Its methods are inscrutable.

On another occasion, Remani said, 'Yesterday I had a dream; of my dead baby. He was playing with his tiny feet. Was suckling at my breast with his tender mouth. Was touching me tenderly with his tiny fingers. Kissing me. Babbling meaningless words. He was laughing throughout. I thought that he was really with me. Like seeing him. You know, he was very naughty. It was then that you shook me awake. And everything was lost. The baby and all his pranks. Everything. Why did you wake me up?'

'You were kicking and beating the bed with your hands. And also crying out loud.' Sivan said.

'We were playing. My baby and me. You came between us, eh?'

Sivan did not respond. She was sliding through the slippery slopes of memory. The pace was too fast for anyone to catch up.

'I want a baby like him,' Remani continued. 'A mischievous baby just like him.'

'How could there be a baby like him?' Sivan was disgusted. 'All of that is merely your dream.'

'Why is it that a baby is not being born to us?'

'Or, maybe new babies will no more be born in this island.' Although he had made that comment just on the spur of the moment, he felt that there was some kind of truth in what he said. He had never seen a baby in the island. Thechappan and his wife did not have any children. The children of paniyas were all grown up and were almost the same size as their parents. Even the goat-tending kids had the aged face cut of Karadi Achachan. The inhabitants of this island were all old. Even the monkeys.

'Do you have to blame the island for this?' Remani retorted angrily. Sivan felt that it was a barb aimed at him. It was true. She had a baby even from a grey haired old drunkard like *Kambanam* Lasar. So she was a fruit yielding tree.

'You had said that *Kambanam* Lasar had tormented you severely?' Sivan asked.

'Yes. But still he had love for me.'

'Perhaps ...' He stopped deliberately.

'Perhaps ...'

'Perhaps when he kicked you ...'

'... why do you hesitate?'

'Maybe you got hurt, I'm afraid.'

Remani looked at him with disbelief. He watched with satisfaction, the seeds of doubt growing inside her.

One day Sivan took Remani to the hills. She was in a great mood. Everything was new for her. Huge trees, their roots severed from base, falling with sad shrieks and groans, logs being cut by handsaws and loaded into bullock carts ...The carts were lined up and the bullocks harnessed to them waited for their turn, basking in the sunlight peeping between the trees. The trees on their part displayed their dry bodies and stood nonchalantly with their branches reaching out to the sky.

'All those trees, they were all planted by Karadi Achachan?' In the night, Remani asked Sivan.

'He only fells them. All those are wild trees that have grown by themselves.' Sivan was busy noting down the day's expenses and payments.

'Still, what all hardships he undergoes just to live here, that too all alone. Sometimes I feel sorry for him.'

Sivan closed his account book and extended it to her.

'Why give this to me?' Remani asked.

'Go through it, if you know arithmetic. The account book of Karadi Achachan!' Sivan was almost shouting. 'His life comprises these falsified accounts.'

'In whose accounts are there no falsehoods?'

Sivan was wondering if there were any barbs in her remark.

Remani looked into the darkness that was taking shape betwixt them. When he lay down by her side, she pulled the blanket around her and turned to the other side. Another desolate island separated them.

Next night, Sivan went to Thechappan's house. He had not been there even once after Remani's arrival. Remani was euphoria all this while. It had lasted for quite some time. His life developed a regularity, going to work and attending to domestic rituals. It was springtime when the tree of life blossomed and flowered. He had forgotten the way to Thechappan's house. He had also forgotten the blazing liquid he used to serve. The taste and distaste of the wild meat cooked with spices in earthen pots too had faded from his palate. And beyond, the hot body of hers, redolent of onion and coriander was wiped out from his memory.

Now it was all coming back. The potency of the exhilaration provided by Remani had whittled down. Disagreements erupted between them and they became clashes to be won. She also could have undergone similar sensations. Does she have a fascination for a stronger physique, even if aged? Loathing for Remani was smouldering in his mind, like wet lime shells. Even the act of sex tasted of that loathing. The nights were now for defeating her and making her submit.

The lantern hung in front of Thechappan's house could be seen from afar. It was giving out only a dim light as the glass had not been cleaned. Outside the house a new veranda had been constructed. There was a slouching figure on the veranda. Thechappan? Sivan looked carefully. It's not Thechappan. He was taller. Sivan could see more clearly after two more steps. It was Ayyappan, the monkey.

Yes, he had forgotten Ayyappan too along with Thechappan and Mary. Ayyappan did not show any signs of unfamiliarity. It did not move away from the veranda. It was engaged in removing lice and other insects from its aging body.

Neither Thechappan nor his wife were there in the courtyard. He peeped in through the half closed door. Perhaps they were in the kitchen. But the aroma of food was missing. Sivan thought of going in. After some hesitation, he knocked and called out, 'Thechappa, Thechappa.'

There was no sound from the inside. The silence was prolonged. He was about to knock again when there was a small sound and Mary came out with a smoky lamp in hand.

'Have been knocking for quite some time now,' Sivan said without concealing his displeasure.

She kept the lamp on the floor and looked at him. 'I was taking bath and did not hear you.'

Mary's face was devoid of emotions. Sivan was bewildered that she was not at all excited at his arriving after a long time.

He had been standing there for a considerable time, but she had not welcomed him to the house nor offered a seat.

'Where is Thechappan?' Sivan asked. 'He does not come to the mansion these days?'

'Nobody needs us these days. Then what is the point in coming there bowing and scraping?' Mary did not make any attempt to conceal her indifference.

She had a special scent of herbal leaves used for bathing. He could see drops of water trickling from her hair.

He sat on the bench that was there on the veranda.

'Are you not getting any jungle meat these days?' Sivan asked.

'Oh, you now have a fabulous chef, no? You will not have any appetite for a poor man's food.'

'What do you mean Mary? Everything comes only second to your cooking. That spicy taste still lingers on my tongue.' Sivan was quite passionate.

She did not answer. Raising the wick of the lamp she gazed into the darkness outside.

'Don't you have any hooch?' He enquired.

'Oh, no! Everything is in short supply.'

'Where's Thechappan?'

'One has to eat something or the other for survival, no? He has gone to see if anything can be managed.' Her indifference continued. He was convinced that she was ignoring him deliberately. He stood up.

'I've recommended to Achayan that the flooring should be completed early. Being an indoor job it can be got done during the rains,' Sivan told her.

Mary did not evince any interest.

Sivan deliberately touched her as he was leaving. That she didn't flinch or withdraw her hand was a consolation.

'I had hoped to have a session with you,' Sivan said in a low voice.

'O, I'm in no mood for anything. Not well. And fairer women are there, no? Just stick to them.'

Sivan made an effort to cover up his embarrassment. He turned around, only to find Thechappan standing there squarely looking at him. He was sporting a stony expression and was holding a couple of fish on a rod he was carrying.

'I was looking for you.' Sivan did not sound quite confident. 'You've fish with you. Tell me, do you have the drink?'

'No sir, this time the summer is too damned severe. Could not get sufficient cashew fruits. How can one distil without enough of them in stock? But sir, why are you here at this untimely hour?'

Untimely? What is that? Sivan had never felt that in the island. There was a bad taste in that question.

Thechappan did not try to stop him when Sivan said he was leaving.

Sivan had hardly taken two steps when Ayyappan the monkey sprang towards him and scratched just below his elbow. Sivan was shocked and terrified. The monkey did not make any signs of moving out of his way. What was surprising was that neither Thechappan nor Mary asked the monkey to leave him alone.

Sivan waited for some more time. Ayyappan did not move. Sivan summoned his courage and broke a twig from a nearby plant and threatened the monkey. But it further infuriated the monkey and it jumped at Sivan and mauled him again.

Sivan gave him a blow with the stick.

Thechappan's voice could be heard from behind, 'It's a dumb creature, no, sir? If you consider the life-span of their species, it will be as old as your grandfather. Don't hurt him. Hurting him is as good as insulting your elders.'

'Come here, Ayyappan,' Mary called him. Ayyappan turned away. Sivan walked ahead without looking behind.

The scratch wound at the elbow was painful. But it was the mind that was really burning. Blood trickling from the wound?

Remani was not there when he reached his room. It was quite late by now. Where was she?

Not feeling sleepy, Sivan set about entering the day's accounts. By now he had become a master in accounting. An expert even of the falsified accounts. Karadi Achachan's real profit was concealed in the deliberately fudged figures. Profit is supposed to be the surplus value of toil. His profit was the surplus value of what kind of toil? Where was he going to take all this wealth?

He was not in a mood to work. Still he continued with the accounting. Were the figures right?

Sivan turned around as he heard footfalls. It was Remani. She was smiling nonchalantly despite being so late.

'I had been to serve dinner for Achachan. He was late coming home.' She said.

Sivan was angry. Achachan and his dinner! But he kept quiet.

'He had gone out. He came back with a pair of earrings for me.' She unwrapped a small packet and displayed two tiny earrings. He glanced at it casually. A pair of gold earrings with small hooks and drops.

'He did not buy them. It seems someone gave it to him.'

Sivan just nodded.

'Have you given me a present till date?' Remani complained.

'Buying presents is not my kind of love,' Sivan said trying to suppress the anger he felt.

'O, love!' She playfully repeated his words.

He continued with his work. But he was unable to concentrate. She removed the stone studs from her ears and put on the golden ones. Taking a small hand mirror, she examined her face and the new ornament from various angles.

'Forget your accounts for a minute. Please take a look at this.'

'Mmm. Nice,' he said without bothering to look at her.

'Do you have eyes on your back as well?'

'What exactly do you want now?' he turned around and stared at her with intense anger. 'Can't you see that I'm working?'

'I wanted to tell you something special,' Remani laughed.

Her face was shining due to the effect of the new pair of earrings. She imitated his fuming face and asked,

'Tell me, where were you till now? Coming home late in the night and then getting busy with accounts?' her words had a mocking tone.

He got up from the chair. The trees were swaying in the wind like ghosts.

Remani approached him and embraced him from behind. She pressed him to her body with affection. Then she freed him and giggled. Sivan could not comprehend.

'Any idea what you smell of now?' Remani continued to giggle. He widened his nostrils, but could not get any smell.

Remani again laughed with delight and said, 'That's nice. Only the lice and bugs are lacking. Man, you smell of that monkey. Did you cuddle that Ayyappan monkey?'

Sivan could not hold back any longer. He slapped her. And then on the other cheek too. It was quite unexpected and she fell on to the ground. He pulled her up. His rage did not subside and he bashed her head on the wall clutching her hair. She was crying loudly. Sivan closed her mouth with one hand and pulled at her earring. She tried to free herself from his clutches and was howling. It reverberated through the mansion.

'I will go away,' she stopped crying and shouted loudly.

'To jail?' Sivan was contemptuous and mocking.

'Does not matter whichever hell it is. It'd be better than living with you.'

'Go and get damned.' Sivan screamed.

'Not that easily. I'll leave only after making sure that you too are done for.' There was fire in her eyes as she spoke.

Sivan again raised his hand.

'Don't you dare touch me,' Remani was trembling.

There were footsteps on the staircase.

Sivan exited from the room and walked through the corridor. There was someone standing near the stairs.

'Who is that?' Sivan shouted. There was no response. He took two more steps.

It was Ayyakkuru. He was standing with head bent, very respectfully.

Must have heard the sounds. Or was he sent by Pappayi?

'What's it? Why did you come Ayyakkuru?' Sivan asked very casually, as if nothing had happened.

Ayyakkuru raised his hands in the air and signalled that he had not come there for anything in particular.

'That's it. Nothing has happened.' Sivan told him with affection. Ayyakkuru glanced at him mysteriously and slowly nodded his head.

As Sivan traced his way back, he could hear the stairs rumble. It resounded like the heartbeat of a huge animal waiting for its prey.

Next morning, the hubbub of people talking could be heard from the frontyard of the mansion. The early morning sun peeped in through the window, warm even at daybreak. The breeze had left the trees. Sivan experienced an unmanageable heaviness weighing down his head. He got up pushing away the accounts books.

The void left by Remani on the bed did not evoke any emotion in him.

Through the window he could see four of them underneath the old neem tree. Thechappan, Mary, Ayyakkuru. Pappayi was facing them. It was very unusual to find them together. Obviously something that linked them had happened. Sivan stood there looking at them. Then he went back to the normalcy of the accounts.

The staircase was making a noise again. Someone was coming. Perhaps Ayyakkuru. Let him come. Sivan did not stir. He sat there as if totally engrossed in figures.

It was Ayyakkuru. This time he did not draw pictures in the air. Nor raised his hands. Just stood there as if he had forgotten the sign language. Silence continued to reign between them.

Then Ayyakkuru left and started climbing down the staircase. Sivan followed him after a while.

They were still there, in the grey shade of the neem tree. Mary and Thechappan stared at him as if he was a total stranger. Sivan also noticed Ayyappan the monkey—who now had a string round his neck—vengefully looking at him. At first glance itself he observed that a branch of the neem tree had broken off. Perhaps that was the only live branch in that old tree.

Sivan saw the huddled up figure under the broken branch. Nascent leaves of the neem tree lay around it as if forming an outline. It seemed as if they were all waiting for him. They made way. But Sivan did not hurry.

Thechappan removed the sheet that was covering the head of the prone figure.

It was Remani.

The light blue sari in which she had arrived at the island had fallen off from her body. A white cloth was almost covering her upper body. She was lying face down. The threads of the same sari which had broken off due to weight were like blue veins on her neck. There were thick blue patches on the neck where the sari had tightened and blood had clotted. Strands of hair bereft of oil were spread over those patches.

Thechappan bent down and turned the body on to its back. Remani's face had stretched to one side. The mouth was open. Her tongue had become blue. The blue tinge had spread to the face. The colour recurred around the navel.

Sivan did not bend down. He peered at the body standing there. The earrings which she got as present the previous day were there at their appointed place. The ear lobe which had become red when he had pulled at the earrings was just as red as it was the night before.

'It was Ayyappan who saw it first.' Thechappan pointed to his monkey and said as if it was a great thing. 'He was making "mm" sound throughout the night. Very restless. And he was missing in the morning.'

Sivan wondered for whom he was doing all this detailing. Thechappan was not looking at Sivan as he spoke. Not only him, Thechappan was not looking at anyone in particular. He was chanting words in a very low tone as if it was a vengeful mantra. Pappayi coughed. Thechappan became silent and glanced at him in trepidation.

'Ayyappan usually comes to the kitchen side in the morning for his meal. When he was not seen, we searched for him all over the island. I had scolded him in the night. Ayyappan is very sensitive. I was worried whether he had fled to the forest and was praying to my maker to keep him safe. For us he is like our eyes, so dear. We were really scared. What would we answer if Achachan were to ask us what happened to the monkey I gave you for taking care? It was then that we sighted him under this tree.' Mary concluded her long explanation. Sivan thought her words lacked conviction. Not only that, it was as if the missing of Ayyappan and the subsequent finding of him was the event of the day. That a corpse was lying right in front did not seem to have had any effect on her.

Sivan looked at Pappayi. He was silent. His face was pale. His eyes had shrunk like that of a terrified man. It was strange. Sivan had never seen Pappayi with so worn-out a face and so weary a body. A mysterious pleasure bubbled inside him seeing Pappayi in that state.

'Achachan is all steel, real steel!' that was what was always said of him. Whose were those reassuring words he had heard at the end of his previous life, when he had commenced his journey to the island?

'She had fallen off from the branch. Ayyappan saw it first. Animals know everything, Achacha,' Mary said.

'And the old sari. It was not strong enough for one to hang,' Sivan mumbled feeling a dry branch of the tree with his hand.

'This is the second death in the island, as far as my memory goes,' Thechappan recalled.

'A paniya boy had died, of snakebite. Subsequent to that it was made a practice to sprinkle the solution of garlic juice and asafoetida. All snakes disappeared into the forest.'

'No, the snakes are still here. I do see them now and then.' Mary spoke to herself, sneaking a glance at Ayyakkuru.

'An old woman had died of some sickness, isn't it Achacha?' Thechappan was all decorum and humility. Pappayi didn't deem it necessary to reply.

'Yes. But the death did not take place on the island proper,' Thechappan himself clarified. 'She died on the way to the *vaidyar*. That too after reaching the other shore. She was breathing very heavily. But she was still conscious. Are we out of the island she asked. In that case, please give me some water, she said. She was given the water from the river in cupped palms. She died almost immediately. The body was brought back and cremated here.'

'O, my lord!' Mary raised her hands and praised the lord.

'Sir, do you know of any relative of hers?' Pappayi turned to Sivan.

Sivan contemplated for a while. Remani's father had died. The child too had gone. *Kambanam* Lasar was shown his last by Remani herself. No, she didn't seem to have any relatives left at least as far his knowledge went.

Thechappan ventured to say something, when Pappayi stopped him raising his hand.

'Hey, Thechappan, you get along with your woman. Go and cook something for breakfast. I'm hungry.' Pappayi had something to tell him, Sivan reckoned.

Thechappan and his wife seemed to be relieved to be allowed to leave.

'Take the monkey too. He had walked out on me once. I don't want him to stick around.'

Thechappan tugged on the rope on Ayyappan's neck and led him away. The wounds on Sivan's body made by the monkey began to burn.

When they left, Pappayi ambled to the front of the house. The sun was hot. Sivan sweated profusely.

'What exactly happened?' Pappayi asked in a tired voice.

'You mean ...' Sivan was cool.

'No, but what happened? For her to hang? That too at a time when she was happy ... something wrong with her mind?'

'Who can say for sure that she hung herself?' Sivan asked. Pappayi did not answer.

When Mary brought breakfast, the scenes of the previous day at their house crowded into his mind. The wound inflicted by that damned monkey had become a scar. He was also scared whether the monkey had rabies. Maybe no such issues, since it was a domesticated monkey. Sivan did not even glance at Mary while eating. He concentrated on the plate in front of him. When he looked up, for a change he found that Pappayi was barely eating anything. He was deeply immersed in thought. No one spoke.

The sun was very warm now. The shade over the corpse had disappeared. Pappayi asked Ayyakkuru to come closer.

'You shift it to that side, but don't drag it. And you should be there in the vicinity. Neither fox nor wolf should come prowling.'

Sivan had his eyes fixed on him throughout.

'How long can you let it lie there like that?' Sivan asked.

'I'm worried about the police coming in search. Is it not better to send Balan with his cart to the police?'

'You mean, involve them in this? Is it necessary?'

'Not necessary?' Pappayi looked at him with interest. 'Not that I'm interested. But what if someone rakes up things? Police will make a visit in all such cases, that is the norm, no?'

'Does everyone here live according to all those norms?' Sivan asked softly.

'Are you suggesting a burial?' Pappayi asked after maintaining silence for a few minutes.

'That has to be done anyway.'

'Let the sun go down. We'll get a pit ready.'

'It should be quite deep. Wild beasts should not start burrowing.' Sivan said.

'There are blotched marks on various parts on her body. No clues at all to what happened,' Pappayi remarked in a subdued voice, looking at Sivan.

'Yes. I also noticed,' Sivan said. 'She is dead. That's the only thing that is clear as of now.'

'Alas! The taste of her cooking is still lingering on my tongue,' Pappayi despaired.

'Tastes can wait.' Sivan was restless. 'Anymore delay and the corpse will start stinking.'

'What if the paniyas come? That's what I'm worried of.'

'Could very well have been dumped into the river had it been a pig or a fox, isn't it?' Sivan asked derisively.

Pappayi looked at him uncomprehendingly.

They were silent for a while.

'We can think of cremation. Anyway there is no shortage of trees for wood.' Sivan broke the silence with a new idea.

'That can be done. But the stench of burning corpse is very strong. The paniyas will easily recognise it.'

'In that case, we will dig a grave at the riverside. Thechappan and his wife will do it. We will bury it there.' Sivan suggested.

'We will bury her. But not at the riverbank. It's all swamps there. Water will seep in. There's also the risk of jackals digging up.'

'Thechappan was just mentioning that this island is not a place to die.'

'That's true. Neither birth nor death suits this place. See, in a way, a half-birth-cum-death too has happened,' Pappayi said.

'Birth?' Sivan looked at him with bewilderment. 'It is Remani's death that has happened.'

'I mean, it would have. She was pregnant no?'

Shocked, Sivan stood stiff like the idol of a jungle god.

He recalled Remani telling she had something special to communicate to him.

For lunch, there was a special dish of the river fish caught by Thechappan. It was prepared with sour raw mangoes and had ample gravy. Mary had prepared lunch at the mansion after a very long time. But the curry with grated coconut did not taste good. Papads roasted on embers and the pickle that was usually served with arrack was also there. Sivan ate mechanically, uncaring for the tastes. It was as if he was trying to stuff out memories with food. Yet Remani's weeping resounded in his ears.

No decision was reached on the burial of the body. Sivan lay down on the bed unable to withstand the heat of the noon. The cot, the bed, the bed sheets and the pillows … all were emitting heat as if from a funeral pyre. His body was sweating like melting iron. The sky was like a hearth with cinders. The sun and the innumerable invisible stars were boiling in it.

He ran his fingers on that side of the bed where Remani used to sleep. Her warmth, sweat and smell were still lingering there. As also the memories of his nail marks on her body and the suppressed sounds of afternoon sex. He thought of olden days. That day in Lasar's press, when she had narrated her story. How she had rolled him up in the mat and saved him from the police. Her playful conversations on arrival in the island. Sivan got up from the bed when he became apprehensive that her memories were about to hunt him down. Her body was still lying in the uneven shade provided by the few leaves left on the neem tree. Ayyakkuru, partly drenched in sunlight, was sitting guard.

What had really happened? Sivan tried to recall. At what time did Remani leave the bed? How come I did not notice it even though I was lying sleepless for hours? Sivan could not conceive her to be that weak-willed as to commit suicide. In fact, she was throwing a challenge at him even the previous night. That she had taken a firm decision to return and continue living, was taken for granted by him. Remani who was craving for a baby, could she commit suicide after learning that a tender life had started taking shape in her? If so what happened? What are those marks on her body? Who is that unseen enemy? Or is it a friend? Just like everything else in this island; there are only questions. This place is a big swamp where answers cannot grow. All the big questions surrounding her death will get extinguished here.

Not only that, but who is the one responsible for the life that had sprouted? He writhed in the reminiscences of the delirious sexual bouts of the summer nights. But had she not already been fascinated by the physical strength of Pappayi? Is it not possible that she had been to him seeking the euphoria of that vigour? He gave her presents and gold. She liked to be with him. Jealousy was smouldering in him.

That was perhaps the logical line of thought. In which case the baby was not his, he sighed with relief. But he was immediately rocked by another thought. Thoughts always take one to the contraries. Remani had revealed to him her desire for a baby and they had got into arguments over it. He had confronted her citing the beating and kicks inflicted on her by Lasar. And she had lost out. But now her garden had flowered. Little blue flowers were raising their heads above water. Who was it that had really lost? That he was as arid as a desert was unbearable for him, far more than the death of Remani.

Sivan came down from his room even as the golden hues of twilight enveloped her lifeless body. Pappayi was scribbling and doing some calculations on a piece of paper. He just waved to Sivan and did not speak. But Sivan knew that he was actually not doing any calculations, but attempting to overcome his loneliness through digits. Labouring to shroud the tragedy with numbers. Sivan felt that he would remain there for ever like a monolith.

Sivan walked to the backyard of the mansion. The weed-green stamp affixed on the axed trees were falling off. Plants withered under the hot sun. The soil was totally bereft of moisture. His steps were firmer now.

After a round of the mansion Sivan stopped near Pappayi. It seemed the number games were not able to mitigate the loneliness of Pappayi.

'The sun has gone down. It cannot be delayed any further.' Sivan sort of woke him up.

'It is quite difficult to dig a pit. But I've found out an easy way out.' Pappayi raised his face to look at Sivan.

Sivan stared at him.

'Let it get dark. The well is the way.' Pappayi said.

Sivan thought about the suggestion. There was no water in the well, but it was quite deep. Depth would resolve all issues. No question of jackals or other animals digging it up. Even the decaying smell may not come out. Some sand could be strewn over, to ensure that.

The well was very deep and its sides had started to fall off. The day he arrived at the island, he could have been a casualty in that well. It was Ayyakkuru who had saved him from death. Thereafter Sivan had given the well the go by. Once or twice, he had peered into it. Roots of trees had penetrated the side walls. Broken bottles and abandoned metallic objects were strewn on the dry bed of the well. It was as if rainwater was reluctant to seep in. It was quite a safe space for a corpse. There was not even an iota of life in there.

Dusk was falling. Pappayi stepped out of the mansion with lanterns in each hand. Sivan accompanied him. Ayyakkuru lifted her, wrapping the body in the blue sari. Sivan held her legs. She was very heavy and he could feel the taut skin of her legs.

Her body was like a snake that hisses when touched, he recalled. How many nights he had slumbered like a spent force, bitten by that! And now it had become lifeless and senseless like moulding hump of earth. Sivan found it difficult to keep pace with Ayyakkuru. Even the light from lanterns did not seem to be an impediment for the reign of darkness.

As they reached the well, the sari with which she was draped fluttered in the breeze. Ayyakkuru suddenly changed direction and Sivan was apprehensive that the body was slipping out of his grasp.

Pappayi extended the lantern into the well. Light did not go down the well and remained confined to the broken side walls. Leaving the body on the ground, Sivan approached the well and hooted into the well as if to assess the depth of the well. It must have been years since he had hooted that loud, Sivan thought. The hooting sound went deep down into the well, but there was no echo in reply from the depth.

Ayyakkuru tightened the shroud and turned about, to look at Pappayi. The two lanterns were swinging slowly. The light was swaying like a swing. Ayyakkuru raised the body all by himself. Then he flung it into the well. And then there was the thud from deep down.

'Fallen,' Pappayi mumbled raising the lanterns. The light from the lanterns could not erase the shadows of grief in his words. The earth swayed like a dark cradle. The laments of thirsty beasts resonated like a poignant lullaby.

Sivan hooted loudly into the well as if to check once again.

From the depths of the well, his hoots rebounded as the wailing of Remani.

True, he said. It is easy to live like this. But can't help feeling that it is better to die.

He was dead the next moment. Only a spasm of breath remained in the throat.

(The last section of the story 'The Corpse' by Chitran Kuroor)

Chitrabhanu received a reply from Sakunthala, a week after he had mailed her the address of Achu.

It was written in an ordinary Inland letter. Since Sakunthala's name was there on the back of the Inland, he presumed that it was an intimation of thanks. Or is it that she has accessed some new information about Sreenivasan? But it would not have been possible for her to seek out Achu and depute him to go after Sivan in so short a space. Even if she managed to do all that, what benefit was she going to derive out of it. He could not comprehend.

But Chitrabhanu was shocked when he cut open the Inland. Old memories crushed him as if hit by an earthquake.

It was blank.

Not a single alphabet was written on the blue sheet of paper. He stared at it for quite some time. He felt as if someone who belonged to his past was talking silently to him after a long time. In a gentle, at the same time, menacing tone. So the 'Sakunthala' on the back cover was a ruse. The silence on that page was a strange language familiar only to

Chitran. However, the dreadful silence in it was terrifying him. Bestiality far more abnormal and dangerous than written words staggered him.

Reverberating silences, lacunae …

Memories came rushing back. The days when he was working in the newspaper. The night which woke up to the morning of his first and last story, 'The Corpse.' And the following nights, when he made corrections. Correcting stories is like nursing a wound that refuses to heal. There is a kind of burning pleasure in that act. He would sit down to write after returning to his room by midnight, after work. He had no specific idea as to what he was trying to achieve. Those were days when the nature of work in the office was becoming too much for him to bear and which was also making a different person out of him.

His job was scrutinising each and every item of news that was received at the desk and editing them, keeping within the strict controls that were in vogue those days. He lived like a machine that took care of the news that *should not* appear in the newspaper rather than ones that should appear. The truth leaked out through the sieves of his filter. What was left were the half truths and untruths that he allowed to remain.

Through the news items he did not select for publishing, he came to know of the disappearance from civil life of those with whom he had worked during his college days, belonging to different political groups, fellow travellers and even poets. Some were taken into custody, some left the country and some others simply became silent. It was all colours and dances that were carried in the news and the dailies became festival supplements. Silence and nothingness were the sediments in the filter. It was this dual life that led him to the writing table.

He started writing as if inflicting a punishment on himself. The same story in many forms, revised and corrected and re-revised over and over again.

An unidentified dead body found in an isolated corner of the city was the beginning. The news and the photograph came to Chitrabhanu. He filtered it through his sieve and did not feel that it deserved to be blacked out. Moreover there were very few sensational stories that day.

He sent it to the press by evening. The body lying on its side could have been that of a middle-aged man. He promptly forgot about it and passed on to the rest of the items with his microscope and filter.

It was then that the editor called him over the phone. 'Chitran, please come over immediately. There is something urgent.'

A tall fat man was sitting at the editor's table. Closely cropped hair, thick moustaches. He just looked at Chitran without any attempt to smile. Chitran took him to be a policeman even though he was not in uniform.

'I asked you here for a particular reason.' The editor straightaway came to the point, without any preface. 'I want to know whether a story has gone to the press.'

'Which one sir?'

'It seems the dead body of an unidentified man was lying on the road. Someone had taken a photograph of the corpse, this gentleman says. Did it reach you?'

'Yes, a middle-aged man, no? I just sent it to the press.'

'You must get it back. There are some issues involved.'

'Not issues, errors.' The visitor corrected.

'Yes. It is erroneous news,' the editor agreed.

'What happened sir? Has the person been recognised?' Chitran asked casually. 'In that case printing the name will set it right, no?'

'That news and photo must not see the light of the day.' The stranger demanded in a commanding tone.

'The country is passing through difficult times. At this juncture we must not provide a stick to the enemies of the state. Not that anything has gone wrong. But there is a general tendency to interpret everything in a perverse manner. Ours is an organisation with a great tradition. We should not be party to disruptive practices.'

Chitran could not understand how publishing the news of an unknown man's dead body would be disruptive practice or why it would go against the glorious traditions. But he did not retort.

'So get it back right now,' the editor's tone was milder.

Tea from the canteen. The stranger stared at Chitran sipping the tea. Chitran felt that the visitor was scrutinising him like a prey. He became restless.

'I'll go and get it right now. But what do we fill that space with? It's already late.'

'Yes. That's what I just mentioned to him. He has made a good suggestion.' The editor continued, 'It seems many groups of vagrants pitch up tents and spend the nights in the vacant space behind our press. There are many burglaries happening in the neighbourhood. You prepare a letter of complaint as if from a citizen. Sir here has brought a photograph of that vacant ground. And tomorrow the police can take action based on this letter and photo. The government will earn some goodwill too.'

As he was accepting the black and white photograph, the editor prompted him to hurry. 'Both have to be done at the earliest. Go to the press, take back the news and the photo. Replace it with this and the note you write.'

Chitran nodded and was leaving when the stranger asked him, 'What is your name?'

'Chitrabhanu. He is a new man here. He is the one who screens the news and he does it neatly,' The editor replied.

The stranger just nodded.

Something was troubling Chitran as he went to the press, collected the news and photograph and substituted it with the note and photo of the vacant ground. It kept on disturbing him like undigested food particles. Even though logic was asking him why he was upset over such a trifle, peace eluded him. He capped his pen and left it in the table drawer. He picked up a few magazines from the table and was leaving for home. Already he was late.

The phone rang. Who was calling him at this hour of the night he wondered as he picked up the phone. A rough voice asked, 'Chitrabhanu?'

He mumbled yes wondering where he had heard that voice earlier.

'I was there earlier in the night. In your editor's room, to talk about that news.'

Chitran now knew who it was. The police officer. But why was he calling now?

'Nothing important. Just to confirm. Our news and photo has gone to the press, no?'

'Yes.'

'I'll send a man in the morning. Give him the picture and the film of the dead body.'

'Okay. But I'm not on duty in the morning. I'll keep them in an envelope and leave it in the editor's room. Ask your man to collect it from there.'

'It's all right. And don't forget to flash the picture and a report on tomorrow's action. You remember, no, the vagrants' issue? The SP has an interest in it.'

He agreed to that too and kept the receiver back on the cradle. Chitran felt that he had been molested.

He could not sleep that night. Restless, he marched back and forth in his room throughout the night with all kinds of thoughts. He felt that he had committed a huge mistake. This was followed by instinctive attempts to justify his action. All part of the profession. Perhaps he may not have selected the death of that unknown man for publishing on another day. Particularly if it was a day with more news. Or had the editor given a hint. How many incidents sink in the ocean of news without getting any preference! How many become sediments in the censor's filter! This too is just similar. Even when he construed it in this manner, a feeling that this was not right remained in his subconscious. He had omitted many news items earlier too. But there was no open compulsion. Here, in this instance, was he not striking it off at the insistence of an outsider? Moreover, did he not substitute it with another report because of that menacing glance? It was like whoring.

Finally, in order to pacify his mind, he transferred those thoughts on to paper. He might not have dreamt even for a moment that this would become a story that totally reconstructed even the form and structure of short stories. At that time he did not know that he was writing a story nor did he ever think that he was capable of writing a story. He went on writing whatever came to his mind through the night. In broken sentences, in broken words, the language had the basic cadence of mantras being chanted. By the time he had jotted down the often conflicting thoughts, the six o'clock siren of the nearby factory wailed. On the top of the sheets that piled up before him, he inscribed the words 'The Corpse.' What he had in mind at that time was not the unidentified corpse, but he himself who had watched all this without even a prick of conscience and thus became a corpse. That was the significance he had attributed to the heading. But this was not deciphered by anyone; not even those readers who were overawed by it in later years.

Chitran poured water in a big glass and drank it in a gulp.

Then he lay down on the bed and slept like a child, peacefully.

It was the students who assured him that what he had written was a story and that it should be published as it is. Commencing the publication of *Liberation Path* was imminent then. Chitran could not believe it. He was only a silent listener of that group. His wide reading and his writing abilities had caught their attention. He thought by working with them he would be atoning for the despicable work he was doing at the newspaper. A mute confession.

Chitrabhanu, however, did not give up his job at the newspaper. His colleagues or his superiors did not have any suspicion about his activities. Later on when police came asking questions about his connection with the *Liberation Path* many in the office thought it to be a joke.

'Chitran? Our priest? What story does he have? Comes to the office, gets immersed in his work, doesn't even talk to anyone and leaves for home.' His colleagues shared this opinion.

A personality that could never quarrel with the establishment, that was Chitran's peculiarity.

In an unknown place, in a dark room, writhing from the pain of continuous torture, Chitran was still distressed by the conflicts of his own mind. When the conflict in thoughts was making him as free as the sky his body was curling up like a centipede. He went through the hellish ordeal not knowing what was right and what was wrong. The police ploughed through his body as if it was a paddy field after harvest. A pestle like rod was rolled over his limbs. Sticks were pierced through his genitals and he was forced to drink his urine. He would be kicked and tortured back to unconsciousness as and when he regained consciousness. For three days he was left without food in his piss and shit. He mumbled words that century old men would mouth as they approached death.

There was a change to all that on the fourth day. He was taken for a bath in the morning. He writhed as water fell on the wounds. The body was presenting before him its manifestation inch by inch. His clothes were returned to him. He was served breakfast. Though extremely hungry, it was not easy for him to swallow the food. Once in a while he looked up from his plate and gazed at the policemen around him. They turned away from him.

A police officer was waiting for him in the office of the camp. A short and fat man with dark complexion. His eyes were hidden behind dark glasses.

'So you are Chitrabhanu? Sit down please,' he said. Chitran hesitated. But the officer persuaded him to take a seat. His bottom was burning as he sat on the rough bench.

'Did they hurt you badly?' he asked gently. 'Sometimes they beat you up without any limit. That is still the standard policy in the police department. But it is different in other countries. Chitran may be aware of that. You are one of those who read a lot, no? But what can be done! Those things do not work here.'

Chitran did not know how to react. He felt that he was coming across a human being after days. Devils were dealing with him till then. The pain from his wounds lessened. His mind attained composure.

'I'm seeking your pardon on their behalf. Please don't curse them. I've heard that a Brahmin's curse really hurts. What they have done here is to torture everyone indiscriminately. But there is no point in blaming the policemen. They are not familiar with the new methods. And there will also be the frustration of working day and night without rest. Very busy time, no?' Sincerity was throbbing in the words of the officer. He lit a cigarette and asked Chitran whether he smoked.

'I too used to read a lot. While in college, I have written a few stories too. Maybe because of that I felt a kind of respect for you. I read your story, "The Corpse." Fantastic! I'm not lying, it was really a strange experience.'

He cited certain passages from the story and argued that they demolish and reconstruct certain old edifices of literature. It was not a story to be confined to the pages of a magazine like *Liberation Path*.

'I've asked them to set you free. So you can go. But I'll call you after a few days. You should come then. Not like now, we can discuss literature. Let your body recover.'

As he was getting into the jeep the officer shook his hand and said, 'Please don't bear a grudge. My sincere apologies for all that happened here.'

The officer kept his word. Chitran was summoned. The venue was not the Chaloorkunnu police camp this time. The officer was waiting for him in the drawing room of the government rest house in Avalam.

The officer was all eloquence about his heavy official responsibilities. Violence and anarchy was ruling over the land. Many among the intelligent youth were going astray. What kind of world are we going to leave for posterity?

This is where the responsibility of writers like you increases. I need your support and help.

'What can I do sir?' Chitran asked in a voice laced with helplessness.

'Quite a lot. You can do a lot, Chitrabhanu. We are not fully aware of the inherent power in us.'

Still Chitran did not understand. He was merely a journalist. That too under so many controls. A high ranking police officer was seeking help from such an ordinary person. He felt himself growing smaller.

But it was as if he was hit by a bolt of lightning when he heard the demand made by the police officer. His body froze.

The officer wanted Chitran to provide the police with all the details of all the comrades and sympathisers he knew. He maintained silence.

'I know that it will be difficult for Chitrabhanu to give me an immediate answer. But if you think deep, you will understand that it is only a service to the nation and to tomorrow's society. Isn't it the same that you do by writing stories?'

For the first time Chitran felt that there was a hint of ridicule in his words.

'Have your wounds healed?' he asked as if changing the subject. 'They tortured you very badly, no? Less said the better. In fact, many of them were not in favour of letting you go. They wanted you back. But I assured them that Chitrabhanu is not someone they mistake him to be. He is large hearted; he is also an artist. And beyond all that he is a Brahmin. Maybe there were a few aberrations. But that happens. So you must help me, at least for proving my words true. Please treat it as a request from an elder brother.'

Taking a blank sheet of paper from the file on the table, he asked, 'What do you think? Do you know what is there on this?'

'Nothing is written ...' Chitran was hesitant.

'Nothing?' the officer smiled.

'Nothing sir.' But Chitran was not very confident now. Has my eyesight faded due to the torture?

'On the contrary, blank pages speak a lot more. They can speak volumes,' he said keeping the paper in the file. The smile had vanished from his face.

The agreement of blank paper commenced from that day.

It was to avoid suspicion. If Chitran wanted to convey information, he had to send a letter to the police officer. Nothing need be written in the letter. Not even the 'From' address. On receipt of the letter, either the officer or his representative would meet him. Nobody else would know. On the other hand if the officer had some urgent work with him, he would send a similar dumb message. That would be the secret signal instructing Chitran to go and meet him. The police would stand guard if needed. Nothing to fear. No question of anyone smelling anything. No records would be left behind.

The fate of so many was decided by the blank sheets exchanged between them. Many lives got messed up in the rumble of nothingness. This continued for quite some time. And then time, at some point in its whirlpool, ditched those paper boats of empty deceit.

Chitran gave up the garb of a journalist. He left for the border village without informing anyone. He did not take with him even the books which were his friends till then.

He became a priest hoping to get at least a strong foundation for his life full of misgivings. Just a Brahmin. The second birth of the twice born. His life thereafter was simple and uncomplicated.

And today the message which reached him by mail, purpotedly from Sakunthala, reminded him of all this in a strange language. It told him without any mercy that he is but a filthy leftover of those ghastly times. Chitran slumped on the bed wearily. Outside, the mid-noon sun continued its demonic dance.

Tense, but silent months—like the days of a dumb being—passed away. Nothing was heard from the outside world. Then on a dry afternoon, the postman once again appeared with a letter. It was sent by Samuel Ambukkan, the law student from the strange address of the Office of Eternal Justice.

In the letter he had mentioned about the meeting Sakunthala had with Chitran. After thanking Chitran for being a kind host and for the promise of assistance, he continued,

'Respected friend, as you know Eternal Justice is a concept. A great hope. That even a weak individual should get justice in every sense of the word is its ultimate aim. Now, here is the case of poor Sreenivasan who has vanished. The police had earlier admitted to his wife that they had taken him into custody. Subsequently they claimed that yes, we had taken him into custody, but he had run away. And when the case reached the trial court, they made a U-turn and submitted that he had not been taken into custody, ever. But the fact remains that he is missing. Where is he? Is he alive? All these questions are to be answered. It is a human rights issue, for society, above all for his family. Many such incidents happen in the world. The laments of those who have no one to depend on fade out dashing against the fortresses of injustice. This humble worker of Eternal Justice understands that you are one of the very few persons who had close contact with Sreenivasan. It was Sakunthala who gave me your address. We anticipate that you were aware of the happenings of the days immediately prior to Sreenivasan's disappearance. Those testimonies have to become public. Sakunthala knows certain other relevant things. She too was a witness to certain incidents. However the law may have certain limitations in accepting her testimony. So we want you to take up this responsibility and speak out to the people about those things of which you were an eyewitness. This letter is written requesting you to fix a convenient date for this. Along with this our people are also in the search of a former leader who is still living underground for unknown reasons. We are hopeful that we will be in a position to bring that person from hiding and to reveal the things he knows to the civil society without further delay. We are grateful to you for the help you provided us to facilitate this.

(Expect to get financial contributions from you for the activities of Eternal Justice. In order to ensure the participation of common people, we have fixed a ceiling of Rs 50 per contribution; please note.)

In anticipation of your reply

For Eternal Justice,

Yours truly,

Law student Samuel Ambukkan BA BL.

Chitran sat on the letter thinking of a reply. Three days went by. Should he go and meet him? Finally he decided to ignore the blank letter. A decision was taken to meet Samuel. That was the best way to make amends, Chitran felt. He sent a letter saying that he'd be at their office on Monday the 23rd.

He slept as peacefully as he had on the night of completing 'The Corpse.'

On the sixth day of writing that letter, the postman came again with a bigger envelope. There was no sender's address on it.

On opening it, he found that it was a bigger void that had come for him.

He was terrified by the boom of that silence. He fell shattered into its depths. He then knew the old wounds on his body were budding and the flowers of pain blooming.

Two days later the news that Chitrabhanu aka Chitran Kuroor had committed suicide was published in the obituary column in the newspaper he was formerly working for. The photo alongside was very old and it differed substantially from his present appearance. Sakunthala stared at the photo. The image of Chitran waiting along with her, near the desolate fields on a warm evening, for the bus going to the city crowded her mind.

Chitrabhanu had taken his life in a bizarre manner. He chopped different metals into small pieces and glued them together with a very strong gum. Then he went on to swallow them along with sleeping pills. He wanted a steady base for ending his unsteady life. So he was constructing a strong foundation with metals and gum to ensure it.

Two days after his death, a letter was received at the office of the Eternal Justice addressed to Samuel Ambukkan. The from address was that of Chitran Kuroor. Samuel was full of anguish-filled excitement to read the last words of someone who had just died.

On opening the letter, Samuel Ambukkan found that the sea-blue sheet was blank.

It was beyond his comprehension.

Remani's lifeless body dumped into the abandoned well had somehow liberated his life, Sivan felt. As if a weight was lifted off his chest. The mysteries behind the death had made him more powerful in the island.

The proof was the change in the approach of the people in the island towards him. Ayyakkuru no more came to him with his sign language to convey the commands of Pappayi. The disturbing footfalls in the nights had ceased. He maintained a respectable distance with humility when they came across each other or waited for orders. As for Thechappan, the arrogance and contempt which was in open display of late had vanished. He stooped low every time and reminded Sivan of a tail wagging mongrel. He now brought extra strong arrack in sealed bottles to the mansion. Sivan could now drink in his room along with the wild meat roasted and wrapped in a plantain leaf by Mary.

'Thechappan, you don't have to take the trouble of coming here every evening. You work hard during the day and must be tired. Send Mary now onwards,' Sivan told him.

'Will she return alone? It will be late.'

'Who said she has to return? She will sleep here. You anyway have that monkey for company. What is his name?' Sivan asked disdainfully.

'Ayyappan.' Thechappan stooped some more.

'Yes. And you should take care. That monkey can get rabies. Man will also go mad if bitten by a mad monkey. Need I tell you that you will have to walk on all fours if you get mad monkey bite?'

'I'll take care, sir,' Thechappan nodded.

'You should be very careful. I'm telling you all this for your own good,' Sivan said in a serious tone. Thechappan broke the wax seal and poured the liquor into a glass.

Changes were visible in Pappayi too. His sun was setting. Remani's death had impacted him badly. Or was it the death of the embryo that had sprouted within her? He was silent these days. His cheeks had sunk with the teeth falling off. He spoke very little during the trips to the hills. Instead it was Sivan who was more eloquent about the trees and the business and the forthcoming auctions. More and more young rivals were showing up. How long could one withstand the pressure of competition from them was crucial.

Pappayi would not speak a word. Perhaps he was thinking of his past.

The jeep sped ahead crushing the dry wild grass. Fagged out sheep lay down on the side of the jeep track. The shepherds were nowhere to be seen.

Mary started visiting him at night. On the first night when she came to his room in the mansion, Sivan confronted her with a vengeance. He had not forgotten the way she had treated him the last time he had been to her home. He glared at her run-down body with scorn. You are only a quarry, he said to himself. I'll play with you, fix you under my legs, hurt you. Your freedom is where my hands let you. You don't exist beyond that. He slapped her in an alcoholic fit. He bit all over her body. When she tried to break free he tightened his grip. She was choking for breath. When she thrashed about for breath, his ascent of ecstasy began. The knots were tightening. Finally she writhed and moaned out of unbearable pain. He came.

The mansion was shuddering under the impact of her wild cries. But there were no probing footsteps.

One day it was Pappayi who woke him up in the morning. Summer was still reigning. He had gone to bed late and was still sleeping. Even the mornings were extremely hot in the height of summer. Sivan could see the cloudless grey sky through the window. The trees had shed their leaves and so the island was well lit as if it was a wide open space. The river and the landing were clearly visible. He noticed Moosa's boat at the landing.

Sivan opened the door to find Pappayi. What could be the matter so early, he wondered.

'Someone is waiting for you,' Pappayi informed him.

'Who is it?'

'You know him. Achu from Pullani. He is there at the landing with Moosa.'

'O, Achu. He has come again?' Sivan was quite firm. 'Doesn't matter. Let's go to the hills earlier than usual.'

Pappayi asked, 'What should I tell Achu?'

'Tell him that I will not come. Why should we lie to Achu?'

When Pappayi left, Sivan went to the other window and gazed out. The green foliage of the island had dried up. Even the grass was dry. The island was waiting with the terrifying calmness of a fireworks production centre which would explode if a spark fell.

Sivan heard the sound of someone clearing his throat. It was Achu. He had come to the mansion. Sivan felt that Achu had become an old man within the last few days. His hair had fallen and what was left had turned grey like the summer. The eyelashes too had fallen off.

His eyes which were trained in rectifying the needles of time had sunk further. The tall body had become lean. His face was ashen white with all the blood drained off. The scar on his forehead had become alive again, Sivan noticed. Exhaustion and confusion were stamped on his face. Sivan passed on to him the pitcher containing water. Sivan saw his shattered palm as he accepted the pitcher. It seemed as if the fingers were trying to move what was no more there. Raising the pitcher Achu slowly drank the cool water. It was as if he had come with a thirst severe enough to drain an ocean. Sivan stood there staring at the bobbing throat as water coursed through it.

'Chitran died,' Achu said, putting the pitcher down. 'Suicide.'

Chitran? That name was familiar. But where had he met him?

'Comrade, don't you remember Chitrabhanu? Chitran Kuroor.'

Yes, the writer. His story was published in *Liberation Path.*

'Yes, I remember. The journalist.' Sivan could recall his face. He also recalled the story that was published as the centrespread of *Liberation Path* without any illustrations or other embellishments. But what was the name of the story? How did he die?

'It was suicide. He swallowed a strange concoction of metal bits, gum and sleeping pills.'

'The end of another romantic fool,' Sivan laughed. 'He copied his foolishness in death too.'

Achu did not respond. He just stood there staring through the bars of the window. Achu saw an old neem tree and its broken branch. A torn piece of cloth, blue in colour was lying under the tree.

'Ok, but comrade Achu, you took the trouble to come all the way here just to tell me this?' Sivan asked with sympathy.

'That was certainly one reason. But that was not all …' Achu broke off in the middle. And then he looked at Sivan with total detachment. Yet Sivan understood that an ocean of emotions was churning inside. He was hesitating. It must be something important. Or he would not have come to the island. He had not set foot on the island even when he had first brought Sivan to the island years ago. Then he came to the island after years to speak about Sreenivasan. That evening he had disappeared into the darkness. Sivan had never expected another visit from him. And today he had put in an appearance right at the balcony of the mansion.

'I had decided last time not to come back again to meet you comrade.'

'Then why did you change your mind?' Sivan asked. 'Chitran's death? So many like him keep on dying!'

'His death was different.'

'Are you speaking about the method of his death? He was a man with imagination, no? Must have decided to be different in death too.'

'Not that, comrade. I'm no one to analyse the method or about being different. With Chitran's death a link in the chain has been lost. It was Chitran who sent you to Sreenivasan's house.'

'So? Do you really carry the notion that Sreenivasan would have come back had Chitran lived for a long time?'

'Sreenivasan may not come back. But there are people around who want to have a final confirmation that he is never going to be back.'

'Why should there be certainties even about the non appearance of a person? Achu, didn't I tell you last time? That he has not come back is the proof. What else? I don't understand. Achu, you are talking like those poets.'

'Death is far more simple, comrade. Here it's the opposite, no? They can carry on their lives without an individual only when that person's unambiguous end is confirmed. There are people left in this world requiring such a confirmation. That's really necessary. Or it could lead to hallucinations; a beckoning from behind, a knock on the door late night, or his scent and presence in the room. It's an agony worse than death. If that comeback is not going to happen, at least they should get the proof for that. That much of justice is a minimum requirement, no?'

'Strange? You too are becoming a poet!' Sivan was very calm. 'Who can provide proof for a non-existing Sreenivasan's not returning?'

'Maybe you could. Maybe your words could.'

'I? What can I do?'

'Your present life is a gift from Sreenivasan. Don't forget that. The continuity you got from him. Your life in this island is the cumulative interest for many such endurances. Instead of him, it could have been you ...'

'I don't bother about possibilities these days, Achu. What's the point in analysing the past in this manner? Even otherwise I never had a past.'

'You are trying to evade. Was not Kangazha your past? Journeys in search of shelters, organisational activities, writing, the issues of *Liberation Path*, are you trying to forget all these?'

'It was you who taught me to forget. Perhaps today I'm even indebted to you. If *Liberation Path* had come out again, if your comrades had discussed the articles in it, my past would have been boiling over even now. But its momentum was lost at some point. It is like a clock that does not tick anymore. It stares at me with lifeless eyes from the dirty wall of the past. Still it may show the right time once in a while. That is the advantage of the clocks that have stopped for ever. I've learnt to ignore them out of practice.'

The clock that doesn't tick. The familiar simile distressed Achu. He gazed listlessly into the sun's glare. A crow flew in and perched on a branch of the neem tree.

'Shall we take a walk to the river?' Achu asked. 'The heat is unbearable.'

Sivan hesitated at first, but then started walking along with Achu.

'Comrade, you should come out of hiding,' Achu said to Sivan, sounding helpless.

'To the former activities? For rehabilitating a magazine that has ceased to be? What do you mean, Achu?'

'The problems are all alive, comrade, as they always were. Hunger, exploitation, torture, pestilence, power … each one of them. Perhaps with more intensity.'

Sivan smiled. Then he looked into the distance. The sun was a burning fire at the river landing. The boat was moored there, alone, like an orphan. Moosa may have taken refuge in the shade. Neither of them spoke for a while. Silence was pulsating like the heart of a wounded water mammal.

'Comrade, you did not respond,' Achu reminded Sivan.

'What is the point in returning? You said that all the problems are alive. The problems of today's world may not be those that can be solved by those of an earlier age. It is simple logic. Achu may be reducing the world into a mere clock that can be set right and ticking with old tools. Or because you celebrate the past. You are inviting me too for ... for the sake of the past, no?'

'The past is not fabricated stories comrade, but history. Narrating it will only brighten the vision of the new generations, isn't it?'

'Yes, the brightness of Hell! I don't have any urge to be the preacher of its gospel.'

'What's wrong in speaking about the paths trodden?' Achu asked after a while.

'You are justifying it. Yes. You are unable to see because of all those blind stories circulating.'

'At least a few mysteries will be solved if you come out, comrade,' Achu tried to persuade him.

'I'm not frightened any more of mysteries. Nor of darkness. It is the teaching of the island. Achu, you cannot have forgotten the night you brought me here.'

Achu became silent in the old memory. It seemed as if he was losing the links to memories just like the palm that had been severed.

'What are the developments in the Kangazha verdict?' Sivan was very calm. Achu suspected that he was trying to wriggle out of the subject of discussion.

'Sekharan has gone on appeal. Other comrades have come out.'

'What are they doing?' Sivan enquired.

'They are not active.'

'Humbug. It is only a matter of time before they start talking. They will speak like god's witnesses.' Sivan continued. 'Achu, you told me that my verdict is yet to come?'

Achu nodded. 'They are just completing the enquiry of your role in the action.'

'Perhaps they will sentence me to death?'

'No chance of that. The prosecution does not have clear evidence. Moreover, nobody is pressurising them to get on with the case,' Achu tried to console.

'You had killed me much before that, eh?'

They had reached the landing. Moosa was not to be seen. Sivan made a hooting sound.

'So what's the decision?' Achu asked. 'I'm asking you for the last time, comrade. You can do a lot. Will you come or not?'

'Never. I'll never come. Achu need not take the trouble anymore.'

The subterranean arrogance in his tone annoyed Achu. The blood of the old revolutionary rushed into his pale body.

'Comrade, Kangazha may not have taught you any lessons. But that was not a vain struggle. It still has messages for the new generations. And my understanding is that a traitor is more despicable than a class enemy.'

'You must have learnt this from the books, no? Paper cows do not eat grass, you know? ...'

'Sometimes they will come out. Not just grass, they will gobble flesh and blood too. *Time will proclaim to them that the season to revolt against the class enemies is round the corner.*'

'Is it a threat?' Sivan laughed.

'You can treat it whichever way you like. However, spilled blood cannot get back into the veins.'

Achu raised his left hand into the sky with vengeance. His hand with the crippled palm reminded one of the coconut trees with burnt heads.

Achu stood facing the boat. He did not look at Sivan.

Moosa stepped into the boat and helped Achu to board.

Sivan waved to Moosa.

As the boat started moving, Sivan turned around to find Ayyakkuru as if waiting for him.

'Ayyakkuru, it is blazing hot. Water in the river is decreasing. Fish are dying. The river might dry up if further delayed.' Ayyakkuru just stood there unsure of what was to be done.

'Don't just stand there. Go! If the river dries, that boat will run into a sandbank. Go!' he shook Ayyakkuru by his shoulder.

Ayyakkuru did not leave. Instead he hooted loudly keeping his hands close to his mouth. It was like the cry of a writhing wild animal. Silence spread through the island as the terrifying cry faded.

After a while the return hoot was heard. Then one more and then another. Hoots followed one after the other enveloping the island like mushrooms.

As the hoots went up the hills, the check dams constructed by the paniyas burst. Water gushed down the river filling both the banks. Wild beasts lost their foothold in the deluge. Trees were uprooted. The water had a delirious red hue.

For the first time in years, Moosa's calculations failed him. They were at the midpoint of the river. Moosa could not withstand the roaring waters from the hills. His barge pole could not get a hold in the soil beneath the surging water. Water lashed at the boat with its huge wings. The boat turned upside down. Moosa was seen trying to swim across the current.

'Our boat sank,' Sivan told Pappayi. He was watching the river banks fill with water.

The olden days filled his mind like the river. Moosa and his father Ibrayi rowed rafts through the river.

'Where is Moosa?' Pappayi was anxious. His voice was trembling.

'I saw Moosa swimming away,' Sivan said softly. 'He must have reached the opposite shore by now.'

'What about Achu?' Pappayi stared at Sivan.

'What can he do with just one hand? Poor man! That comrade never even knew how to swim,' Sivan said gazing at the river.

There was a long queue in front of the doctor's consulting room. Patients and those who accompanied them. Sakunthala had come on receiving an intimation from the doctor and she could walk in without waiting for her turn in the queue, she thought. Dasan, her aunt's son who had accompanied her to the hospital thought likewise. However, she decided to wait.

When she finally entered the doctor's cabin, he asked her, 'I was expecting you since morning. Why did you wait in the queue?'

'I thought I shouldn't trouble you,' she said.

'You see, I thought I could confirm it through you, it's just a notion,' the doctor said. 'I'm familiar with the case through the media and that was the reason I called you here.'

'You had mentioned that in your letter.'

'This guy has been here for quite some time. But I could not find much of a resemblance with the photograph I managed to get. But the photo was old and changes do take place. And this fellow here, he goes on changing his name every time you ask him. So ...'

'In that case, why this doubt?' Dasan enquired. He was not hopeful even when they set out for the hospital. But he didn't want to upset her.

'He recites poems,' the doctor said.

'Just because he recites poems ...' Dasan was sceptical.

'No, it is not poems by others. Those are all written by him. And they are good poems. I can't say why, but I was reminded of Sreenivasan.

He used to write poems, no? Besides that, police torture often results in mental disturbances …'

As they walked through the corridors, they could see the cells in which patients were locked up. Some of them were out in the veranda. Some of them stood up as they saw the doctor. Some ignored them totally, while some others tried to run away.

The patient who reportedly recited poems was sleeping. Greying strands of hair. Broad forehead. Skinny body. He was wearing glasses even when sleeping. On his feet was a pair of worn out slippers. With closed fists placed across his chest, he was sleeping like a child. He was not wearing a shirt. Bones were sticking out from his thin body. Sakunthala required only a glance to confirm that it was not Sreenivasan.

'Shall I wake him up?' Dasan asked.

'No.'

'If you talk to him … or if you listen to one of his poems …' the doctor was still optimistic.

'No sir, no need of that.'

Someone was moaning from the other ward.

They were silent as they marched back through the corridor. Sakunthala was only relieved that Sreenivasan was not found in that hospital.

I came here only to confirm that the patient the doctor cited was not Sreenivasan, she thought.

There wasn't any information about Samuel Ambukkan or his Eternal Justice, after Sreenivasan's case was abandoned midway through. He had become news by contesting an election and securing lesser votes than even the total invalid votes. Gradually everything was over. Sakunthala also forgot to revive the case, lost as she was in the rut of routine life.

One day she received a letter from the office of advocate Aravindaksha Menon.

She found the letter on the veranda when she returned with her mother from a visit to the doctor. It was after a long time that she was receiving such a letter. Sakunthala guessed that it contained the details regarding the appeal to be filed. She was pained that she had no curiosity whatsoever to find out the contents of that letter. Perhaps time had made her weary. Everything seemed to be a search from one emptiness to another.

Sakunthala took her mother to her bed, gave her medicines and then cut open the envelope. Nothing in detail. Only that he wanted to meet her in person. Usually it was the clerk who penned the communications. But this time it was the lawyer himself.

The verdict of the lower court was not favourable. But what are the implications even if the court's decision was favourable?

Arguments, counter arguments, legal points, logical reasoning, dispute, questions … And what conclusion have all these reached? That Sreenivasan will never come back? Who will decide so? Can the court decide that, even if the case is won?

Didn't the court too indicate the hope that Sreenivasan will be back one day?

Is it possible that he is alive in a mental hospital writing and reciting poems? How long can one proceed on such seemingly absurd propositions?

The old days of intense arguments crowded into Sakunthala's mind as she walked to Aravindaksha Menon's house. That was the road she had trudged innumerable times over the years. Yet she thought she had lost her way.

It was blistering hot. She felt that she was walking through the hot wind blowing in from a desert.

There was no one in the front room of Aravindaksha Menon's house, maybe because it was a holiday. The front gate had been changed. During her previous visits the lawyer's pet dog would bark nonstop and announce her arrival loudly. As she became a regular, the dog did not bother her anymore. That dog was not to be seen now. Its kennel was vacant.

The car in the porch had not changed. But its colour had faded. The lawn in the frontyard was a new one. A low brick wall had been raised enclosing the lawn. Red roses in flowerpots were arranged near the wall. A praying mayfly perched on one rose stem. She pressed the calling bell and waited.

'I received the letter you sent me, sir,' she told him as she entered.

'O, Sakunthala? Good that you came today. We can talk in peace. Come, sit down.'

More of Menon's hair had greyed. He was using a thicker lens now.

'It's okay sir, I'll stand.'

'I asked you to come to discuss something important,' said the advocate. 'That had to be done face to face, so I didn't make a mention of it in the letter.'

Sakunthala listened in silence.

'You are aware that I was genuinely interested in your case. That you are the daughter of KP was also one of the reasons. KP was not just the clerk of my father, he was like an elder brother to me. In fact I learnt the procedures of the court from your father. What you learn from college is not what you practise. That was why I took up your case without a second thought.'

Sakunthala did not speak. She was apprehensive that the shadow of comrade Sankaran Adiyodi's words had been cast over the advocate's talk. But, no, it cannot be so. Aravindaksha Menon had never been like that. He had not taken even a rupee as fees from her till date. Menon had come forward to plead for her on his own when many others whom she approached had backed out.

'There was nothing much I could do for the case. Hardly anything was in our favour. All we had was the deposition of Bhaskara Kurup. They demolished it using falsehood. Everyone knew it was all lies. But what the judiciary want is evidence, not the truth or dharma.'

'And yes, some time ago that man, what's his name ... Yes Ambukkan, Samuel Ambukkan came here, copied all relevant documents and studied the case. He had also told me that he had met you. Even though a crackpot, I felt he was knowledgeable to a certain extent. He tried in his own way. Anything positive from his labours?'

'I have not heard anything about it since then.'

'What could materialise, eh?' the lawyer became silent lost in thought.

Sakunthala too was lost in thought. She had been in search of Sreenivasan for long and had been trying to get justice done in the case of his mysterious disappearance. Many individuals had come to her assistance at various stages of her mission. But all of them had ditched her at crucial junctures. And as time passed by, his disappearance ceased to be a matter of concern for anyone. Even close relatives had started asking her whether it was not better to think that he was gone. Okay, but who could guarantee that he was no more? In a remote corner of the mind, hope still remained alive like a little flame that refuses to snuff out. Suppose what the police claimed was correct? That Sreenivasan had not been taken into custody? Suppose he was also hiding in some remote and inaccessible place like the absconding accused of the Kangazha case?

If so … if so … by that time all her doubts fade away and his figure surfaces in her mind. The figure of Sreenivasan in a rag and with marks of beating all over his body. It was him. It was him definitely. It was that vision that overturned her life. If she had not gone there, if she had not seen that figure for fleeting seconds, she could have lived with more hopes. She would have had more affinity towards life.

Even then, for how long would it have lasted? Life during the last few years had made her older. Silver streaks had already started appearing on her head.

'They had bought that old man,' Aravindaksha Menon was speaking about Anthony, the duck man. 'I had also heard that he had died. Were you aware of it?'

'Yes.' she recalled the face of old Anthony who used to visit them early in the morning to borrow beedis from Sreenivasan.

'Sakunthala, you should not take it to heart. We don't have much hope in appeal too. We should not nourish high expectations. Things have changed to that extent.'

What the advocate was saying was something that could have been guessed by anyone. The case had been dragging on for years. And that was a lost case. What was success in a case like this? It was not going to bring back anyone. Life was not going to be retrieved. Still, were there not some smouldering embers, yet ?

Sreenivasan gets involved in disruptive activities, or quarrels with her and abandons her. Will her loss be the victory of such arguments? Sreenivasan had made a bonfire of his poems. Which fire had he thrown his life into? The rebirth of which poem did he subsequently secure? She had the hallucination that she was hearing his voice. The self mocking laughter of his. She was stunned.

'They are aware that all of their arguments are falsehoods. Yet they are not sure, on certain aspects.'

Sakunthala looked at him expectantly.

'Some of them had approached me.' His words brought her back to reality.

'No, I've not agreed to anything. Your decision is what matters in all such things.'

Sakunthala tried to guess what the lawyer was trying to impress upon her.

'I happened to meet a person who was close to Kumaran Nair last month. A retired Dy SP. He belongs to my father's family. He was the right hand of Kumaran Nair while in service. Kumaran Nair has high hopes that Sreenivasan will be back. He should be located somehow or the other is what Kumaran Nair told this friend.'

'It is a lie, sir …'

'Possible. Police excesses are obviously there. But such things happen not necessarily with the knowledge of the minister. And why should he lie about it now to this ex-police friend? Also, the reappearance of Sreenivasan will be a boost to Kumaran Nair politically, no?'

But from which great void was Sreenivasan going to emerge?

'You know, what I'm trying to say is, how can we say for sure that this young man did not escape from police custody? He was taken away is all that even Bhaskara Kurup asserts?'

'Then why doesn't he surface?'

'Yes, that's true. Especially in the changed political circumstances. He could have at least written a letter if he was far away. It is not as if I did not consider that aspect.'

Menon continued after a brief silence.

'Perhaps he has lost his mental balance? Such are the stories of torture coming to light. Last week I made an attempt in several mental hospitals. Among them, I heard about a hospital in the south, where there's this guy with a craze for poetry.'

She remembered the face of a man sleeping like an innocent child with hands crossed on his chest.

She did not however, mention anything about her visit to that asylum.

'No, it's not him. I made enquiries. This fellow is much older. But we can widen our enquiries to include such possibilities. Not openly. That would harm the case. In any case, at least some of them have the feeling that a wrong has been done. But they will not confess it because they are afraid that any such revelations will affect their position in the case. If they lose, they will lose their jobs and imprisonment too cannot be ruled out.'

'The guilty deserve it no?'

'That's true. What you say is absolutely correct. But ...'

'But?'

'None of that will get him back to us, no? Then why ...'

He took a swig from the water jug on the table.

'Suppose we win the case. The verdict is going to be for some compensation. If we lose, and that is what is on the cards, we don't get anything. You are not very old and you have a kid. How's his health these days?'

'He was quite all right till recently. Just last week he fell down and hurt his forehead. And then he had a bout of fits ... with spasms and frothing. Like in the early days ... I've mentioned this to you, no?'

'You took him to a doctor?'

'It's not an ailment that will go away that easily. Perhaps if I can take him to more sophisticated hospitals ...'

'That will be very expensive no?'

Sakunthala became silent.

'Exactly what I'm trying to tell you. The better part of your life is yet to be. We are not going to get anywhere if we go on with this case and its legalities. I'm not making this statement in the capacity of a lawyer, but take it from me: such is the fate of all cases of similar nature.'

Sakunthala fixed her eyes on him. She had never seen him with such low levels of self confidence.

'Now, you should not get me wrong. It is not as if we are giving it up for lost. But certain approaches are being made to us. This was what I ... that is ...'

'That is ...?'

'If they offer us a sum of money, wisdom will be in accepting it, no?'

Everything around her suddenly went into a spin. Advocate Aravindaksha Menon, his table, the hefty books on the wall shelf, the idol of Sreekrishna, the stack of files ... Sakunthala sat down.

'Please have some water.' Aravindaksha Menon tried to pacify her. 'Nothing need be done in a hurry. Take your own time to decide.'

'It will be the sales proceeds of a man, sir.' Sakunthala took a sip of water and was strangely relaxed. 'Perhaps blood money. If I accept it the smell of it will stick to my hands all through my life.'

'Sakunthala, as I told you, there is no hurry. Life is to be carried forward not on sentiments but on wisdom. Let me tell you again, no hurry.'

'No, sir. There is nothing for me to deliberate in this.'

'Please don't take me amiss, my girl. I've only your wellbeing in my mind.'

'I'm aware of that sir. But this ... this will not work. Never mind if we lose the case. But I cannot agree to this.'

Sakunthala was very calm when she said this.

She came down the steps and walked to the bus stop. The stupendous calmness that had enveloped her did not leave her in the jostling crowd of the bus or when answering the probing questions of her mother on reaching home.

Sasi was sleeping. The wound on his forehead was healing. Poor boy, he doesn't go out to play on his own. He had grown up. She knew that his peers were shunning him perhaps afraid of the sickness he had. By and by, he was withdrawing into his own world. Last week he fell down when he was getting out of the house hearing the sound of children playing. Blood poured out from the wound on the head. She had panicked when the bleeding did not stop. He was feverish for the next two days.

Sasi had become more tight-lipped after the fall. Sakunthala caressed his hair. He resembled Sreenivasan. The broad forehead, thick lips and narrow eyes reminded her of Sreenivasan. Will he be carrying any memories of his father other than that of a man in a black and white photograph sitting with his mother?

All of a sudden, she remembered that advocate Aravindaksha Menon was making enquiries in mental asylums.

That man sleeping peacefully? Or the stereotyped image of a man with long beard and tangled hair loudly reciting poems? She closed her eyes with her palms to shut out the images.

When she was certain that no one else could see her, she cried in a low muted voice nobody could hear.

The crazy winds of the turbulent months visited the island and left it desolate. Trees were uprooted by the whirlwinds that swirled up from the navels of the distant oceans. At the riverbank, dry leaves and sand danced in ghostly unison. The river, the shore and the landing vanished from sight.

They did not go to the mountains during those months. The sound of huge trees falling reverberated occasionally. The wind returned to the ocean and the dance of dust stopped. The river and the landing and the shore were visible again. Evenings regained their saffron charm. The wheezing of the wind, resembling the last gasps of a dying man, ended at last.

But Sivan woke up one morning hearing an unusual rumbling. Something akin to the buzz or drone of a giant mountain wasp. What was it? Where was it coming from? Not the echo of the wind; not a leaf stirred. Not an animal because the growl was continuous, not even stopping for breath. Not rains as the sun was up in full fury. Such a sound had never been heard in the island. It was getting louder by the minute. Sivan was full of apprehensions.

'An unusual sound,' Pappayi craned his neck upwards and shouted.

Sivan knew what Pappayi was referring to, but pretended as if nothing unusual was happening.

Pappayi's health had gone down considerably. The windy months had shaken him up. And above all an unknown fear had its tentacles around him like poison. What was it? Whom was he terrified of? This island, the paniyas, the old trees, the labourers, the bullocks, Moosa the boatman, Ayyakkuru, Thechappan and his wife were all his obedient servants waiting for his commands. Sivan had never heard anyone raising his voice against Pappayi. Who then was he afraid of? Sivan sensed the needle of suspicion turning towards him. Yes, it was him that Pappayi was afraid of. Some innate sense had filled him with apprehensions about me. Sivan was secretly delighted about it.

Some more time elapsed. The decibel level had changed. It had become louder.

'It's a boat. A motor boat is approaching the landing,' Thechappan announced.

Sivan looked through the trap door. Yes, a boat was approaching from a distance. The buzz was the droning of the boat's engine. The water level in the river was quite low. The river had been laid bare by the seamless summer. The boat was cutting across the weak current. There were a few men in the boat, but their visages were not clear. Who were these new visitors to the island?

'Who are they?' Sivan called out.

'No idea. It's for the first time that a motor boat is arriving here,' said Pappayi.

'Okay, let's go to the landing and find out,' Sivan suggested.

He came down and Pappayi accompanied him.

'Moosa has not been seen for quite some time,' Sivan observed.

'He has not been seen since the boat was sunk,' Pappayi mumbled.

'The usual practice was for him to bring outsiders to the island,' Sivan reminded.

Pappayi was about to comment on it perhaps, but then a terrible barking erupted shattering the boundaries of the island.

Dogs! After many years and for the first time since arriving in the island, Sivan was hearing dogs bark. His blood seemed to freeze. The barking was from the boat, which had stopped at the landing. Two huge dogs were about to leap out on to the land and were barking fiercely. It was as if they were declaring a war on the island.

'Ayyo! They are dogs!' exclaimed Pappayi. Sivan noticed that Pappayi was confused even as he himself was struggling to gather his wits about him.

The dogs leapt out onto the land. But because of the tight leash on their necks, they could not go ahead. Still they strained on their leashes to the maximum and barked as if wreaking vengeance. The seams of the island trembled in the violence of that sound.

At the same time they heard an animal moaning from fear for life. Sivan tried to guess where that death-cry like prolonged lament was emanating from. The paniyas hooting? Or was it from across the river? Again the same cry that now seemed to be of a wounded animal. Suddenly Sivan got it. It was Ayyappan the monkey. It must have caught on to the scent of the dogs. Animals can feel the presence of enemies instinctively.

These dogs could be the adversaries of the island.

Three men stepped out of the boat, controlling the dogs. They were clad in thick black clothes. The two with the leashes had a cane each in the other hand. The fat man who marched behind the two was wearing a hat. He had been the one manning the boat. He secured the boat to a tree with a long rope and tried its strength and tautness tugging it.

All the while the dogs were barking incessantly. Their handlers seemed to be baffled at this.

One of them probed the earth near the place where the dogs were barking with his cane and came out with a faded rubber slipper.

Sivan recognised it. It was Remani's. Once her slippers had been stuck in the swamp and could not be retrieved. She had then joked that it would sprout one day. The dogs had retrieved it now.

The one who got the slipper, raised his cane and displayed it to the fat man. He merely nodded. The dogs circled the slipper twice and then suddenly stopped barking. A tremendous peace descended there for a while.

The dogs resumed their work. After going about the landing and the surrounding swamp, they started running on the path that led to the mansion. Their keepers struggled to keep pace with them.

'What was it that they unearthed?' whispered Pappayi.

'A slipper. Remani's.'

'Have they come in search of her?'

'The dogs might have caught on to her scent.'

'But how did they come to know of her death? That too after so much time has elapsed?'

'Who knows? It's also possible that they are not aware that she has died,' Sivan spoke in very low voice, only for their ears.

'But I don't get it. Who are they? What are they here for?'

'I've no clue. But are there not so many things to be investigated in the island? And ever so many things to be unearthed! The old flag, the diary in the leather bag and why even the revolution!'

Pappayi fell silent at Sivan's unexpected outburst.

'Maybe all this has nothing to do with her, no?' Pappayi asked, more to console himself.

'It's more likely to be her,' Sivan looked at him straight. 'Didn't you see the slipper surfacing?'

'But after all this time?'

'Time has a tendency to trace the scent of certain things. It does not require any specific reason.'

Pappayi slowed down. It was as if he was seeking few certainties.

'Oh, those horrible dogs! To unearth her slipper!' Sivan sensed that Pappayi was once again stumbling on the slopes of terror. And Sivan was delighted at every fall of Pappayi. Sivan was sure that those dogs would smell out her death. But will not that be the end of all? The chain that had extended to the island from the mainland terminates in her.

The pitiable lament of Ayyappan, the monkey, again broke the silence of the island. When that stopped, the barking resumed. Sivan thought that maybe they had reached the mansion.

The dogs were panting with their tongues hanging out, standing in front of the mansion. Both of them stared at the mansion from the frontyard. The dogs had very little hair on their back, Sivan noticed. Taller than the normal species. Arched like a bow. The tail was nothing more than a stump, as if the rest was cut off. Eyes were narrow slits and the ears too long and large. All the proportions were distorted. The protruding tongue was blood red. The duo did not seem to care for the surroundings or those around them.

Thechappan and his wife were watching the canine visitors on the sly, from the cover of the mansion's walls.

The monkey was not to be seen anywhere. Perhaps it had fled from there out of fear. And where was Ayyakkuru? Had he also vanished from the scene out of fear for the dogs?

The fatty, who brought up the rear, took out a pocket diary and started noting in it. He was also drawing some figures, placing the small notebook on his knees. Could've been the map of the mansion and its surroundings.

'The dogs are not barking now, sir,' said the one with the leash.

'That they are not barking is exactly the problem. You take them for a walk around the place,' he advised continuing with his writing.

'Around this house?'

'First the frontyard, then the sides and the backyard afterwards. Every inch has to be covered,' he stopped writing.

'Where is the handkerchief?' asked the one with the leash.

The fat man took out a packet from his pocket and opened it carefully. In it there was a faded and soiled handkerchief. He held it to the nose of the dogs one after the other. The dogs crouching on their hind legs calmly inhaled the scent of the kerchief. It was blue in colour. It was the same colour as the sari Remani was wearing the day she arrived at the island. It was the same sari she was wearing the day she died. This rag looked like it was a piece cut out of one such sari.

After the kerchief the dogs smelled the slipper. Everything had a certain order. The dogs which were calm till then started panting with their tongues out.

'The dogs are ready sir,' the keepers announced.

'Okay. Start,' he said returning the small diary to his pocket. The dogs leapt and ran helter-skelter in the frontyard. Unable to cope with their ferocious hurry, one of the handlers fell down.

'Should hold the leash firmly,' advised the fat one. Within a short while the canine-duo covered every inch of the frontyard. It was the keepers who were panting now. Sweat was pouring down their forehead and shoulders.

All of a sudden, one of the sniffing dogs turned around and started barking at the neem tree. The remnants of the blue sari could be seen on one of its branches.

'Get that piece of cloth,' ordered the fat one. He shifted his position to the shade of a tree.

'It seems a case of suicide,' one of the keepers commented.

'You cannot easily arrive at such a conclusion,' said the fat man, scornfully, lighting a large cigar. 'There should be evidence and it should fit in with the contexts.'

'The edges of this cloth ...'

'Are frayed, is all that can be said now,' the fat man said calmly gazing at the smoke rings from his cigar.

One of the two handlers collected the fragments of the cloth from the broken branch and kept it along with the handkerchief. It was surprising that neither of them was showing over enthusiasm or over excitement. They went about like researchers engaged in experiments, concentrating only on their work. They ignored all those who were around anxiously watching them. In spite of this, Sivan guessed that they would recover everything and would perhaps connect the threads from Lasar's murder to Remani's suicide. Who would be the next to be linked to that thread? To which pole would it be fastened ultimately? The arrow that originated from the murder of Lasar, which target would it pierce?

Pappayi was exhausted. The blistering sun and an unknown fear seemed to have extinguished his light.

One phase of the investigation ended with the finding of the remnants of the blue sari. Now on to other evidence. From one to another. Every investigation has its own pathways. Time recaptures and recreates lives from the sweat and smell left behind by man in the pathways of life. That is how history is created and documented.

The dogs were being taken to the back of the mansion. Thechappan and Mary slipped away from their hideout and migrated to the front. Mary's dress was soaked with sweat. Age had caught up with her. Her former glory in bed was on the descent. She had slept with him the previous night. He recalled her eyes wandering and her attention wavering during sex. Her body was no more eager to engage his in combat. The cry of the starving flesh thrashing about for more was not heard anymore. It was like sleeping with a corpse. He had felt slighted and was vengeful. Sivan ignored Mary.

Barking could now be heard from behind the mansion. The dogs must have reached the well. They will run around it. Her body would have decayed and turned to earth by now. The skeleton would be there. Bones and teeth and hair would remain. And from the well, where would the barking stretch to?

The monkey's lamentation was heard again. It had been silent for quite long. 'Achacha, our monkey …' Thechappan looked at Pappayi.

'What about it?'

'It may die out of fright, I …' Mary started crying.

'Where is the monkey?' Sivan asked.

'On the rooftop,' said Thechappan. 'Right since the morning when he heard those animals bark he has been squatting on the tiles.'

'Let the dogs leave. We'll get the old man down,' mocked Sivan.

The dogs were circling the well. They would stop, smell, dig the sand. This was repeated several times. Then both of them together started digging a particular spot with their hind legs. One of them came up with something between its teeth.

Something familiar …

Sivan was thunderstruck. Yes that was it, the knife that he lost the day he arrived at the island. Its gleam was gone. The handle was soiled. The rusted time had blunted its sharpness.

An old printing press and a drunk printer wallowing in his own vomit flashed across. A buried past. In which life had all that happened?

THE DOG DAYS

One of the dog handlers pressed the knife's crumbling wooden handle and rubbed its blade. Once upon a time it would've sprung to life like a live animal. But it was still now.

Sivan stared at the dogs with trepidation. Their next move could be towards me he feared. Any moment they could spring at him. The knots were tightening. Those mad dogs would smell out the past. To what extent could they go in the past? Surely, the evidence of scents is against me. Where did things go wrong? He sat down on the floor to cover up the trembling of his body.

Perhaps all of this is the vengeance of Achu. His curse. Achu had nourished the dreams of another world till the last breath of his life. Those dreams were throttled by the powerful flood waters that burst the check dams. Those eyes that nursed time and were forever young closed for ever. Multitudes of mysteries and secrets around messages and signals got dissolved in the waters as turbid as time.

Achu was not merely an individual. He was a society, a people that marched ahead unmindful of the injuries inflicted on self. Even when in pain, they dressed the wounds of others. What was the hunger that led them forward? Which was that unseen power that had united them?

I could have accompanied him when he beckoned, Sivan thought. The masses would have received the revelations about hundreds of Sreenivasans with deafening cheers. Now he would be taken away from the island not for his ideals or for revolution, but for murder and lust. He felt insulted and humiliated.

'Let's take it as a piece of evidence, no sir?' the one who was examining the knife called out to the fat man. He handed it over to the fat one after cleaning the soil and dirt once again.

The fat one verified it from different angles. He slammed it into the soil and tested its strength and its sharpness on a dried twig.

'O, this, a piece of evidence! Good enough to cut shit!' he handed it back with absolute scorn.

'But the dogs barked,' the first one said taking back the knife.

'All barking does not carry the same meaning.'

'Then what do we do with this?'

'Throw it away. Or it will lead us to wrong conclusions,' the fat one was supremely disinterested.

Sivan sharpened his ears for the sound of the knife falling into the well. But that was not heard. However, the dogs resumed their barking.

'They are again barking,' the one who threw away the knife said, unsure of himself.

'There could be different reasons for that,' answered the fat man scribbling in his diary.

The fat one had a look around and then asked Thechappan to come closer. It was for the first time that they were talking to a person from the island. Thechappan went to him, shivering all over.

'You are shivering!' the fat one said.

Words got choked in Thechappan's throat.

He touched Thechappan's body and commented, 'You don't have a fever, but you are shivering. Take care.'

Thechappan's shivering increased.

'Okay, go, get a ladder. You have to go, down this well,' he said with a hard stare at Thechappan. He went to the other side of the mansion, relieved to be away from the eyes of the fat one. But where was he to find a ladder long enough to get to the bottom of the well?

The fat one examined the remnants of the sari through a lens. 'The edge of the cloth has been stretched and the threads are torn. There has been use of force.'

'So, death is confirmed?' One of the handlers raised a doubt.

'Not exactly. But all evidence are pointing towards murder.'

'There could be stretch marks even if it was a suicide.'

'But, what does this blood stain indicate?' the fat one pointed to the fragment under the lens.

'Are you saying that a suicide does not leave blood stains?'

'That's the primary conclusion. Till we get other hard core evidence, that will be the premise on which we will be proceeding ahead.'

'Murder is the conclusion, isn't it sir? But on what basis?' the first one said, attempting to raise a dispute.

'That is to be found out. And it is for that I'm taking care of you four dogs,' the fat one continued derisively. 'You must try. Proof will emerge if you make earnest attempts. Because no criminal can obliterate all traces. That's the general experience. He leaves enough pointers for those who come after. He will be kind enough to that extent.'

Instead of a ladder, it was a long bamboo pole that Thechappan brought to the well. One had to climb down stepping on the branch notches that were there on the pole at regular intervals.

One of the two handlers held the leashes of both the dogs, while the other slowly went down the well using the bamboo pole. Sivan saw him gradually disappear into the netherworld. What would be the next move? Sometime during his past, he had flitted like a shadow steeped in fear, from one place to another. Many nights, different shelters, different people. He recalled all that. Everything seemed to be just as it were. The fear was there even now, in blue. Reasons had changed. Perhaps even life had changed. But still the shackles of law follow me like an unseen presence, he thought.

Law? Which law has its writ over this island?

The one who had gone down the well, climbed back to the top. There were a few strands of hair in his hands. Since he was holding his hand up above his head, that was what was first visible. Gradually his head, body … he jumped up and off the bamboo pole out of and the well as he reached the top.

The fat one examined the strands of hair under his lens. Then he rolled it and kept it along with the handkerchief. The one who went into the well was now trying to get the bamboo pole out of the well. Thechappan helped him. Silence reigned as no one spoke.

The dogs started barking the very next moment. With protruding tongues they were jumping up like wolves that had come across ghosts. The handler with the leashes was unable to cope up with their frenzy. He was going round in the air spinning like a top. A shadow was seen flitting around the young plantains in the direction in which the dogs were raring to rush.

'Someone is running away,' the one who had gone down the well shouted.

'Who is it?' the fat one asked without raising his head.

'Someone!' the barking of the dogs was now reaching a crescendo. The fat man looked up.

'Running away? Don't let him go. Get him!' He was suddenly excited. The one who had gone down into the well ran after the fleeting shadow. The terrible dogs and their handler raced after him. Crackling of the thick layer of dead leaves intermingled with the ferocious barking of the dogs. Someone had fallen down. Yes, those two men and the two dogs on the shadowy figure who was fleeing. He had been nabbed. The barking had stopped. Will those brutes tear him to pieces?

It was Ayyakkuru.

He was led to the well by the dogs and their handlers. There were scratches on his face. Blood was oozing from the scratches. His face was expressionless. His fists were closed tight.

'Okay,' the fat one examined the stain on the kerchief and ordered, 'bring him here!'

They pushed Ayyakkuru towards him.

'Why did you run?'

Ayyakkuru did not reply.

'Didn't you hear me? Rascal dwarf! Why did you run?'

Ayyakkuru stood motionless, head bent.

The fat man slapped Ayyakkuru on his cheek. It was a vigorous blow. Ayyakkuru lost his balance and fell down.

'Get up,' he shrieked. As soon as Ayyakkuru got up, the fat one slapped him on the other cheek. There was sand all over his body. He looked at Pappayi piteously.

'There's something in his hand,' Sivan shouted. The fat one glared at Sivan, but did not utter a word.

One of them forcibly opened Ayyakkuru's fist. There were bloodstains on his palm. He was beaten again.

When Ayyakkuru shook his hand, a crushed baby snake fell down. The one who was standing beside Ayyakkuru withdrew a step instinctively.

Ayyakkuru was pushed to the shade and the two handlers sat on the ground. They seemed to be very exhausted. The fat one was scribbling furiously in his handbook standing in front of Ayyakkuru.

'Get his measurements. And also identification marks that are visible normally. No need to delay anymore. We are leaving,' he said stopping his notes.

'What about interrogating the others, sir?' one of them asked.

'What for?' he fanned himself with his hat and asked. 'Do you think that the dogs lie?'

'Not that the dogs are lying … But they can also commit mistakes. Maybe they barked only because he happened to run.'

'Or, the dwarf would not have run, had not the dogs barked, eh? But nobody else took to heels when they barked, no?'

'That could be because …'

'This is exactly what is wrong. You don't observe keenly and do not bother to understand correctly.'

The fat one again started fanning himself and murmured, 'We should've got that snake alive.'

'Sir, did you say something?' one of the two who was sitting on the floor enquired.

The fat one shook his head and continued to fan himself.

And no one spoke thereafter.

'Will they take him?' Pappayi asked Sivan in a whisper.

'Let them take him,' Sivan was quite casual about it. 'It is better that way. He is a deaf mute no? He will not speak. What is it that they can prove?'

'Do you think the paniyas will keep quiet if they take him? He's their blood after all.'

'What can they do?'

'You don't seem to know anything about them. They have the potential to sink this entire island.'

'Let them. Or you think that all this will remain as it is till *pralaya*, the deluge?'

Sivan went on to make some calculations on his fingers. The past of the giant trees, the present, the dimensions of a lifetime; when he turned around to look at the island like the Chitragupta of the forest, he saw a hot dusty wind swirling up the dried leaves.

His mind bubbled over with joy like a sparkling glass of champagne.

The one who had gone down the well took the measurement of Ayyakkuru's body with a tape. The fat man recorded it in his little notebook. He then donned his hat and enquired,

'Does anyone have anything else to present?'

Ayyakkuru looked at Pappayi with pleading eyes.

Pappayi looked down. The cries of goats could be heard in the distance. The sounds of the goatherds, the paniyas, was drowned in it.

'Let the law take its own course,' Sivan was emphatic. 'Or do you have any other concerns?'

The fat man looked deep and hard into his eyes. Then he took a long rope and tied Ayyakkuru's hands.

'That was well said. The law will find its own course,' the fat man said with absolute composure.

Sivan could see blood trickling down from the eyes of Ayyakkuru.

The boat lurched to one side when Ayyakkuru was pulled in. But then it regained stability. The dogs boarded the boat after him. They sat on the floor of the boat facing the island. They had stopped barking. Silence reigned but for the panting of the dogs. The fat man took off his hat and held it in his hand. He totally ignored the island and those who were present.

'Rain clouds,' the fat man said to the other two putting on his hat again. The dogs too looked up at the sky along with them. But they averted their face because of the strong light.

By now the boat was at quite a distance from the island. The sound of the boat had gradually faded. But beyond the sounds, it remained a distant speck visible afar.

Attempts were on to get the monkey down from the roof. Thechappan was cajoling it. But the animal didn't seem to hear him.

'Leave him alone, Thechappan. He'll be alright once he gets over the fright,' Pappayi called out.

'I don't think it will come down that easily, Achachan. Something has happened to him,' Thechappan said with grief.

'He was frightened by the barking of the dogs, don't worry,' Pappayi tried to console him. 'He is old now, no? May not be able to withstand all that sound.' He walked back to the mansion.

'That's true. However, he has to be brought down. You bring that bamboo pole, man! Mary asked Thechappan.

Thechappan fetched the pole and leaned it against the wall. Mary held it firm as Thechappan slowly climbed up the pole. On reaching the top he sat on the tiles.

'Son, dear one, come here,' he beckoned. The monkey did not move.

'Come here, baby!' Thechappan pleaded. But the monkey sat there immobile. Thechappan got up, extended his hand and carefully walked two steps towards Ayyappan.

Suddenly the animal sprang up and scratched Thechappan's face with its sharp nails. Like a beaten snake, Thechappan turned and leaped on to the bamboo pole. The pole swayed with his weight, but as Mary had a firm grip on it the pole did not slide down. Thechappan climbed down swiftly.

Blood was oozing from the scratches on his face.

'Ayyo, what scratches he has made! My lord, what do I do now? It is too frightened,' Mary touched the wounds on his face.

'That animal is not in fright, it has gone mad,' saying this Sivan walked towards the mansion with a determined look on his face.

Mary led Thechappan to the backyard. She applied a paste of onion and turmeric on his wounds and started reciting a prayer to ward off rabies. The hood of sunlight rose and swayed like a snake.

A gunshot was heard from the frontyard. A moment later there was the thud of something heavy falling from the roof. Thechappan and Mary scrambled with trepidation to the frontyard only to find Ayyappan lying on the ground bleeding. The monkey was not breathing anymore. They could see the shadow of some primitive fear still lurking in its bulging eyes. Thechappan started sobbing.

'There is no point in crying Thechappan. What is to be done with animals that go mad?' Sivan was all kindness as he spoke to Thechappan.

Thechappan tried hard to control his tears. The turmeric paste on his face was soaked in his tears.

'My aim did not fail, though it was my first shot ever. But the recoil hit my shoulder,' Sivan rubbed his shoulder.

Thechappan and Mary, unable to restrain their tears, stood there helplessly staring at him.

'Thechappan, you go to the forest and tell the paniyas that Ayyakkuru has been eliminated by Achachan,' ordered Sivan after a while.

'Won't they ask where the dwarf has gone, sir?' Mary asked wiping her nose. 'After all, he was their blood.'

'You just tell them that the boatmen took him out of the island,' said Sivan slowly folding his fingers.

'What will they do with him, sir?' Thechappan asked.

'Kill him,' Sivan said. 'Go and tell them. Quick.'

Sivan caressed with tenderness the double barrelled gun he had lifted from Karadi Achachan's room as he watched Thechappan trudge past, huddled up like a monkey.

By afternoon there were terrifying hoots. When the roars and shouts reached the ears breaching the crumbling doors of slumber, Sivan got up. He suspected that someone was banging great drums in his head. In a little while he understood that it was real. It must be them, the paniyas, he thought. Thechappan has informed them that Pappayi has got rid of Ayyakkuru. My aim doesn't fail, Sivan told himself, with a smile.

Outside, the paniyas buzzed like bees with sharp bamboo spears and granite stone pieces. Their hoots which could breach even check dams, reverberated across the walls of the mansion along with the bleating of the sheep. When he could not withstand its roar any further, Sivan slowly got out.

When he climbed down the stairs one by one at a leisurely pace, he saw Pappayi restlessly walking around. He was like a huge beetle in a glass jar. He seemed to lose direction in the dim light. Any time he could dash himself on the staircase or on the dirty walls.

'Are you not hearing the turmoil outside, sir? The paniyas are out' ... Pappayi's voice seemed to be trembling. 'They will demolish the mansion. Something must be done immediately.'

'I cannot. My shoulder bone is paining like anything,' Sivan said dispassionately. 'There 's nothing to be done even as it is.'

The windows were being smashed. The rusty hinges creaked like the sinning souls thrown into hell. The sound of a heavy door collapsing with a huge thud. Sheep and men were talking in the same language. Stones rained on the tiles. Wind hissed.

'Where is the gun?' Pappayi was grunting like a bear. In the confusion, he banged his forehead on the wall.

'No point in searching for it,' said Sivan. 'The bullets are over.'

One more door collapsed outside.

Sivan started climbing the steps to the top floor very slowly.

Despite a second attempt, Sasi could not pass the English paper in the pre-degree examination. He had passed all other subjects at the first attempt, but had scored very few marks in English. Sakunthala then sent him for tuition in the town. It was an old institute where Sreenivasan used to teach college students. The principal was astonished when she took him to the institute. 'How is it son, that you can't manage English of all the subjects? Your father was excellent in handling English classes. There were students who would attend only Sreeni's classes. I'd even formed a batch of such students for Sundays.' The regards he had for Sreeni's classes was evident from his words.

'He has been weak in English since childhood, master,' said Sakunthala. 'He could not continue his studies for two years after passing his matriculation. He was sick. Certain things just elude his mind how much ever he learns. English is tough. He manages even maths. But he is a total failure in English. And I don't have the ability to teach him.'

'That doesn't matter. We can somehow manage the minimum required marks. But you should not be indifferent,' he told Sasi.

'That will not happen, master. It is not as if he is not keen to learn. He doesn't loiter around or get into the wrong kind of friendships. He'll be with his books, most of the time. But the very mention of examination makes him nervous. He forgets everything,' Sakunthala explained. She had thought of telling him about the bouts of fits he used to have, but decided against it since she did not want to broach the subject in front of Sasi.

'Okay, tell me, has he inherited the sickness of Sreeni?' the principal was smiling when he asked this question. Sakunthala thought he was referring to the hysteria her son used to be affected by. She was at a loss as to what to say.

'I mean the fad for poetry! I was of the opinion that he was not doing justice to his talents. However, I've never seen anyone reciting poems with such involvement. Once Sreeni recited a poem by Kunjiraman Nair in the meeting of Navasahithi. Just six lines. Oh, what an applause he got! Don't forget, the poet himself was on the stage. And later when it was his turn to recite, the poet handed over the paper on which he had scribbled his latest poem to Sreeni, 'I can only pen these. But it will be recited beautifully by this young talent here.' And then he sat cross-legged in the front row! This incident is mentioned in '... *Foot Prints*, no?'

She was not aware of it. But this was a story often narrated by Sreenivasan with pride, Sakunthala recalled.

'Son, don't you have your father's interest in poetry,' the principal again asked. Sasi was careful not to look at his mother's face.

'Yes, it is bound to be there,' the principal insisted. 'What is it that you write?'

Sasi did not answer. Sakunthala remembered Sreenivasan's attempt to make a bonfire of his poems on a remote morning in the distant past. His images in her memory were quite faded by now.

'Please pay special attention to him, master. He is all I have,' her eyes were brimming with tears. She averted her face so that he didn't notice.

When she asked about the fees, the principal stopped her. 'Fees? What fees? You can't teach this boy here paying fees. You know, Sreenivasan was my close friend. When this college was going through a bad patch, he had taken classes without taking even a rupee as salary. If I take money from his son, even his soul will not pardon me.'

Even his soul ... the principal noticed blood draining from her face.

'Sorry ... it was unintentional,' the principal apologised.

'Doesn't matter, master. What else is left?'

Sasi was regular in attending classes and meticulous in learning. The teachers paid special attention to him. He got more than pass marks in the model exams. He was also able to revise the lessons in time before the exam.

But it was his ailment that undid things this time. Sakunthala had noticed that he was becoming restless from the morning before the exam. She would peep into his room and find him reading. But was there not something unusual? He was sweating. His face was flushed. She was afraid that the sickness which had stayed away from him for quite some time was trying to stage a comeback. She did not ask him anything, not wanting to upset him.

But it happened in the evening.

Sakunthala came running hearing the sound of something falling from his room. The stool on which he was sitting lay upturned on the floor. Sasi too was on the floor thrashing his limbs. Froth oozed out of his mouth. The book he was reading had been flung to a corner.

'Sasikkutta, O my dear ...' she called out. He was groaning and mumbling something that was unintelligible.

Unlike the last time he had such an attack years ago, Sakunthala was not able to control his convulsions or lift him. He had grown up and had become heavier. She came out and shouted for her cousin living next door. 'Dasa, come quickly, Sasi has collapsed, hurry Dasa!'

Dasan and his mother came running. Sasi's convulsions ceased after some time. He calmly looked at those around him. Her aunt wiped clean the froth from his mouth.

That night Sasi told his mother, 'I'm not appearing for the exam, Amma. I'm not well.' He was lying on his bed. Sakunthala had a good look at him from the other end of the cot. How much he resembled Sreeni! The same forehead, long nose and lean face. Black tinge on the upper lip. Weary eyes. She was full of compassion.

'No need, if you don't feel like it,' Sakunthala caressed his hair. 'You can appear for the exam next time.'

Sasi seemed to be contemplating. She had been noticing that he had not been very communicative these days. What was he thinking about? Sreenivasan? Does he remember him? Sasi was a small boy when Sreenivasan went missing.

'Will you be upset if I tell you something?' Sasi looked at her face.

'What is it?' She was anxious.

'I'm not writing that exam anymore. I'll never get it right.' Sasi's eyes were brimming. She was upset.

She did not respond. She could not say no to him. He was a boy without any desires or demands. A tender 'touch-me-not.' Sometimes she wondered how he would carry on in this world. Even Sreenivasan had not been such a simpleton.

Later that year, Dasan took him to a friend's tailoring shop with the idea of making Sasi join there as an apprentice. It was a unit with a good reputation and many of those who had learnt tailoring from there had set up shops in various parts of the town. Sasi would have to show some patience and stick on there.

'After all it is a skill, no, sister? Let him be there for some time. Bhaskaran *Chettan* is quite strict. Of course, Sasi is not an idler. There will always be work and he cannot afford to be indifferent.' Dasan went on to describe the advantages of being in that tailoring shop. 'A mopla from Ponnani is opening a textile shop right in front of the tailoring shop. Clothes from even Dubai will be available there. So there won't be any dearth of work.'

For the first few days Sasi accompanied Dasan to the town. He started going alone as he became familiar with the route and the bus. Sakunthala became worried if he was unduly late in returning home once in a while.

Sasi seemed to like the job. The owner was quite friendly towards him. Moreover everyone extended to him the consideration of being the son of Sreenivasan. Slowly he graduated from stitching buttons to cutting the dress material and stitching sides. Sakunthala got him an old sewing machine from a relative as Sasi grew in confidence. On a holiday, he stitched a blouse for Sakunthala. There were some defects in his maiden attempt. It turned out to be too over-sized, when she wore it.

'What is this? Did he take your measurement twice?' teased her aunt.

'It does not matter. It is his first attempt, no? He will be disappointed if I don't wear it.'

Sasi too was aware that she had put it on to avoid hurting him.

The year sped past at a breakneck speed. How crowded is life! Time was running away.

The north-east monsoon was very lean that year. The town had gone dry by January. It was very warm.

The elections to the assembly was in January. Kumaran Nair was one of the candidates from that constituency. The tailoring shop had got bulk orders for flags and banners to be used in his campaign. Work that did not require much expertise.

'Those of you who feel like, can take these home and work on it there,' the owner told the apprentices. 'You can take whatever payment that comes in. I don't want any share. I accepted the work only because he is a politician.'

'I can't, Bhaskaran *Chettan*, this flag is going to be hoisted against our party,' Lalappan refused the offer.

'You and your party! Out, you oaf! Okay, Sasi, you take all these with you,' said Bhaskaran.

'Sasi? Should you make him do that work, Bhaskaran *Chettan*?' Lalappan raised a doubt.

'What's wrong with that?'

'Everything. Who is the candidate here? Kumaran Nair. Who is Sasi? Bhaskaran *Chettan*, it is a pity that you don't have an iota of historical awareness.'

'*Eda*, you and your lot can babble like this and wag your tail for your partymen. But this poor boy has no one else other than himself. Let him make his life secure. Where were your party comrades all this while? Will the party come to his aid if he and his mother starve?'

Sakunthala did not say anything against it since it was Sasi who had brought the stuff. In fact she even helped him in cutting and stitching the flags and buntings of Kumaran Nair's party.

'Will Kumaran Nair win, my dear?' She enquired, while packing the flags and other paraphernalia.

'I don't know. But his campaign is going very strong. Take a look around and you will find only his banners and only his name on the walls.' He did not understand why she asked that question. He had never seen her taking any interest in politics.

'Amma had sent a letter to him, long ago ...' Sakunthala did not continue. It was not a letter, it was more of a memorandum. One of the many written regarding Sreenivasan. Kumaran Nair did not reply. Ever.

'Really? He'll be the next Chief Minister. It is the talk of the town.' Sasi laughed.

Sakunthala did not respond.

One evening Sasi was late getting out of the shop. Two young men, whom he had not seen earlier, were waiting for him as he got down from the bus and took the narrow path to his house.

'Comrade, one minute,' one of them stopped him.

'We are workers of the Popular Front. We come from Avalam. I'm George and he is Pushpangadan.' He must have been around twenty-five. Sunken eyes and broad forehead. Dressed in a loose shirt.

'We are starting a new unit at Muttuthara. We are here as part of its campaign. We have arranged for a meeting in the godown behind the cracker shop of Chettiar, tomorrow night. Comrade Sasi must participate in it,' George said.

'Is it an election meeting?' Sasi asked.

'Election! There are more important matters than that. Comrade must have heard about people's trial and struggles. Elections just happen to come in between. They are not of much significance. But we will discuss election too.'

'Everyone is now aware that election is a bourgeois strategy,' Pushpangadan tried to explain. He had a shaggy beard. He looked older than George.

'Of course, we know that there is no need to explain these things to a person like you. Who doesn't know the place of comrade Sreenivasan in the history of the movement?' said George.

'What is it in your hand?' Pushpangadan asked looking at the big bag carried by Sasi.

'Few flags and banners. Election purpose. Taking it home for stitching the edges,' said Sasi.

'Comrade, you should have a more serious approach to such matters,' George said.

'Even if we discard it, history has a tendency to follow us, do not forget,' Pushpangadan suddenly became serious.

'Anyway, don't forget tomorrow's meeting. Behind Chettiar's shop, after nine.' As Sasi resumed his walk home, George shouted from behind, 'We will be expecting you.'

Sasi forgot about the meeting the next day. Nor did he make any mention of the encounter to his mother.

Kumaran Nair won the election with a solid majority. Certain political setbacks in the earlier years had made him a more determined man. He had had to face opposition from his own partymen on the disappearance of writers like Sreenivasan and a few other extremists. Though the court had exonerated him, the last few years were for him an unwanted sabbatical from active politics. But now he had won the elections with an unprecedented majority and was back in the arena with increased vigour. He enjoyed the support of a majority of the newly elected legislators. No one could keep him away from the coveted post. Kumaran Nair was sworn in as the Chief Minister.

Kumaran Nair was known for his protective attitude towards those who supported him. He would go to any extent to safeguard their interests. He raked up from the dustbin all those who had been dumped for past misdeeds. They were appointed in crucial posts as his minions. No distinctions were made between menials or top bureaucrats.

Circle Inspector Pankajakshan was one of those who was rescued from obscurity in this operation. It was salvation for him after years of anonymity in training camps and isolated stations in remote villages. Increments of salary that were barred, promotions that were denied tumbled down into his lap in a frenzy. He had become extremely influential now. Those who were his immediate bosses in the past had reached the top echelons of the state police. He was posted at Avalam on promotion to the rank of Circle Inspector.

Lalappan, his colleague in the tailoring shop told Sasi, 'It was this guy Pankajakshan who had taken away your father, you know?'

He had heard of it. But that was all, mere hearsay.

'And you are sitting idle? Such fellows should not be allowed to set foot in this vicinity.'

Lalappan was an ardent partyman. He attended meetings and participated in processions bunking from the shop. It had been almost six years that he had been doing apprenticeship and he could not even fix a button.

'Pankajakshan was a master of *rolling*. Do you know that? He must have *rolled* your father too. Bloody rascal.'

Sasi did not respond. He had only vague memories of his father. He used to feel that the father he had in his memory was not the one he saw in the photographs on the wall. Father for him was so distant from his life, cut off from the present times. He was merely an idea.

The day the textile shop opened in the building opposite to them, a police jeep stopped in front of it. Everyone peeped out.

'It's Pankajakshan getting into the showroom. Come, take a look,' Lalappan told Sasi. Sasi raised his face, but did not get up from his seat. Lalappan slipped out keeping aside the shirt he was working on.

'Pankajakshan has swollen like a pig. See, now he can't do without the dresses from the Dubai shop. He is selecting clothes there. Only people's trial will work. He should be trapped in the middle of the road. But our party does not have the spirit for that.'

'You finish the work on that dress, Lalappan. It has been one month you've been working on it. There's no dearth of words, but absolutely no deeds from you,' Bhaskaran shouted at him.

'What impact has been there in the last six months after the new government came into power, you tell me Bhaskaran *Chettan*,' Lalappan tried to change the subject.

'What have you achieved in the last *six years* you've been learning tailoring?' Bhaskaran taunted.

'You are cracking jokes when we are discussing serious issues!'

Sasi did not mention anything to his mother about Circle Inspector Pankajakshan's visit to the textile show room.

But it was predominant in his mind. A man who had taken away his father or even killed him, sauntering about in front of him. Shopkeepers, drivers and all others in the marketplace treating him with veneration. He had now become a powerful police officer. There was much less crime committed in the town now. Buses kept to their scheduled time. Drunkards turned into dutiful citizens. There was no gambling in public places. Once in a while he parked his jeep in the centre of the town. People passing by glanced at him with great respect. Sasi had seen even Bhaskaran *Chettan* stealing a glance at him with mild trepidation.

One evening Sasi happened to see Pankajakshan. He was standing besides two constables who were questioning a person for some traffic violation. Lalappan was there with Sasi at that time.

'Take a look if you want. That is CI Pankajakshan,' said Lalappan.

Somewhat bulky. But not the least like the swollen pig Lalappan was referring to. Balding. Curly moustache.

'Couple of blows, if I get him cornered. That is my longing.'

'What good will come out of it, Lalappan *Chettan*?'

'What? Okay, what good, you are asking? *Eda*, do you know how many comrades he *rolled*? How many made to drink urine? He is the monster who cannibalised your father. How can he be left alone? I'll tear up his intestines.'

Those words of Lalappan affected Sasi deeply. They got embedded in his subconscious mind.

After many days, Pushpangadan and George were waiting for him at the same old shop as Sasi was returning home at night. There was one more person with them this time; Ramachandran, a teacher at a tutorial college and also a distant relative of Sasi.

'Comrade, you did not turn up for the meeting. It's okay. Now we have a good unit at Muttuthara. Young comrades like you should cooperate with it,' said George.

'It's due to lack of time,' Sasi said in a low tone.

'You have got to find out time for certain things, comrade,' Pushpangadan counselled.

'Okay, we waited for you here to tell you something. It's a secret. Ramachandran master is the unit secretary. It is the decision of the unit to involve you in this matter.'

Sasi waited for the secret.

'You know Pankajakshan. We are going to try him,' George said in hushed tones. 'Not in the bourgeois courts. Even children know he will escape unscathed from there. This will be in the midst of people, in the peoples' court. It will happen shortly. It is the desire of the organisation that you should also be there comrade. This is a kind of justice in itself.'

'Maybe, this is one of the ways in which history confirms that justice is meted out,' said Pushpangadan solemnly.

'We'll keep you informed. In the meanwhile, do maintain contact with comrade Ramachandran. Please go through the books that he'll give you.'

Ramachandran subsequently visited Sasi's house twice, but he was not in. Sasi on his part did not make any attempt to meet comrade Ramachandran.

Monsoon time. As schools reopened after summer vacation in June, there was heavy rush in the tailoring shop. There was work on holidays too. Sasi could now manage most of the tasks assigned to him on his own. Bhaskaran had developed confidence in him. Most days it was Sasi who opened the shop in the morning and shut it down in the evening. He'd reach the shop very early and would leave in the evening only by the last bus.

It was a Saturday. He would not be free to work the next day due to a family engagement and so wanted to finish off as much as possible. Bhaskaran had left by half past eight. Sasi was alone in the shop.

A police jeep came and halted in front of the shop. Two policemen came out and commenced checking the passing vehicles for drunken driving, driving without a driving licence, etc. Sasi could see Pankajakshan sitting in the jeep. He hadn't got down from the jeep. The two policemen would skim the waters and fetch the fish to the chief. He only had to consume them.

Suddenly the words of Lalappan rushed into his mind. The words of George and Pushpangadan too. An old wound was suddenly burning and bleeding. Sasi remained there vacantly looking at the police inspector without doing any work. He remembered the fading photograph of his father hanging on the wall of his home. He remembered his mother who lived all alone like an island of memories. He tried to get immersed in his work. But he was unable to concentrate. The needle of the machine was slipping from the cloth he was stitching and was pricking his fingers.

It was drizzling. But he felt his body heating up. He was also sweating. Sasi saw the lights fading and the rain becoming heavy. However, he was blind to all but the one in the jeep. Sasi's eyes were glued on to that massive body with the balding head.

Sasi clutched a pair of scissors used for cutting dress materials. He got up slowly from his seat prompted by an unknown inner power. He got out, shutting the door of the shop. Rain soaked streets. Most of the shops had shut down. There were a few people in the textile showroom. Light trickled down from the streetlights. The rain became heavier.

A beggar trudged along soaked to the skin. A lame dog accompanied him. The streets were more or less deserted. The two policemen were interrogating a pavement shopkeeper. Not bothered by any of this, the Circle Inspector was noting down something in his handbook.

Sasi stared at him. Lalappan's words reverberated in his mind like a thunderbolt.

... the monster who cannibalised your father!

Sasi walked quite slowly. He was quite near now. Ten steps more, maximum. He clutched firmly on to the scissors.

But suddenly the grip seemed to loosen. Flow of blood increased. His body started trembling uncontrollably. Like the returning of a long lost friend, those shivers, convulsions, bulging of the eyes. The scissors slid down from his grip.

Sasi fell headlong on to the ground. The thunderous rain soaked him.

Those who were around lifted him and laid him down on the veranda of the showroom.

'He is the boy from the tailoring shop. Seems to have an attack of fits,' an employee from the textile shop informed the policemen.

'Can you sit up? Can you see us?' the policemen asked. No one had noticed the scissors that had slipped out of his hand.

Sasi sat up. The one who was standing right in front was Pankajakshan, CI Pankajakshan.

'What is your name?' he asked. Sasi mentioned his name. He felt tired.

'Where is your house?'

'Muttuthara.'

'The last bus in that direction has already left,' one of the policemen said.

'Some other vehicles headed in that direction will come,' the other policeman said. Sasi wanted to tell them that he did not want any help; but he seemed to have lost his voice.

'Do you recognise him, sir?' asked the employee of the showroom keen to please the officer. 'He is the son of that guy ...'

'Which guy?'

'The one who went missing long ago. Sreenivasan ...'

Pankajakshan was apparently taken aback. No one spoke.

'Mohan, stop any vehicle going that side and send him home,' Pankajakshan seemed to be thinking even as he spoke. He concluded his checking of vehicles and got back into the jeep.

Sakunthala was waiting at the gate. Her life had been one of incessant waiting. She would become fearful every night Sasi came late. She could never sleep till he came home.

Sasi had stopped the rickshaw quite some distance from his home. He did not want to upset his mother. The rain had not ceased but had decreased in intensity.

'Son, you are soaked,' said Sakunthala.

'Forgot to take the umbrella, Amma,' Sasi avoided looking at her. 'Thought of it only after getting out of the shop.'

Sakunthala held him close and dried his wet hair with the tip of her sari. She was afraid that he would contract fever. She recalled the rainy night when she had taken him to the hospital in the town, his body scalding hot with fever. The lonely life of theirs lit up like a fading picture. The torrential rain of memories poured down.

'When we went to the tuition master sometime ago, the master asked no, whether I write poems like *Achan*?' Sasi asked Sakunthala. She had forgotten that incident. Poetry was not in her mind at all.

'I had not said anything then.'

'Why didn't you?' she asked combing his wet hair affectionately.

'I had started writing a poem, Amma.'

'Oh, and then?'

'Then ... I've not been able to complete it even now.'

It surprised Sakunthala that there was the secret screen of an unfinished poem between them for almost two years. Didn't his father too have a secret poetic life? Poetic creations concealing even one's name?

'What is the name of your poem?' Some sort of fear seemed to envelop her.

'Eyes …' Sasi said, as if chanting a mantra. 'But that is not certain. At times I change it to Eyes of Epilepsy. Then again merely Eyes … O, even the heading has not been finalised.'

My child, you getting confused not able to finalise the title of a poem …

She looked at him, from the opposite bank, not of poetry but of an undetermined life. Even when standing so close, she felt he was so distant, for the first time.

The rain had ceased.

Another rain started pouring down from her eyes.

EPILOGUE; ALATA CHAKRA

It was late when they reached the boat landing at the river. Darkness had become an all encompassing canopy. The sky over the river was clouded. There was no one around. A bird which was concealed from sight hooted in a strange note breaching the prevailing silence. Silence reigned again.

Even though the sky was overcast throughout the day, rain had kept away. The heat seemed to settle on the earth like a spider. It had to rain; it was so warm. Serpent like lightning flashes streaked through the dark sky. The clouds which rubbed each other imitated the growling animals.

They were three. Two young men and the old man, 'J,' their guide. One of the young men was about thirty-five, not very tall and slightly stocky. He was sporting a thick pair of glasses and had a skimpy beard. The other guy was younger, perhaps a student. Lean, dark and tall. Sunken eyes and broad forehead. Both of them had started from Avalam town early in the morning. Exhaustion was writ large on their faces. Reaching Pullani circling the Kolli mountains had taken its own time.

It was at Pullani junction, the comrade with the code name J was waiting for them. Both of them were worried that he may have gone, fed up waiting.

At Irutti on the top of the hills, the bus they were in had broken down. It was only about one in the afternoon then. Engine trouble. The

---

Note: Alata Chakra, (the circle or ring of fire), is an illusory circle created by rapidly waving around a flaming wooden torch in a circular motion. According to Indian Philosophy, this metaphor denotes the unrealistic and ephemeral nature of Life.

mechanic had to come from Avalam and it would take time. The crew of the bus excused themselves, refunding the fare for the remaining part of the journey. It would be four in the evening when the next bus reached there. What was to be done? It was prudent to stay at Irutti rather than arrive at Pullani after dark. Fortunately they got a jeep that had landed up there, having lost its way. It was going to Pullani with diesel cans. The cans were stacked on the backseat and so the passengers had to stand. There were thirteen of them instead of the normal seven. The cans fell down on the passengers at hairpin bends, turnings and steep ascents.

'There is a rumour that Chettiar's shop was raided,' the younger one whispered into the ear of his friend. 'I heard them talking about it in the bus.'

'I had expected it,' the elder one responded.

'His son was arrested. The shop was sealed.'

'The documents should not have been left there.'

'Will they have noticed it?'

The elder one tried to catch a glimpse of the outside world through the jam-packed human bodies. It was not possible to see even the sky. The revolting smell of sweat and body odour overpowered the interior of the jeep.

'Please give me some space,' the younger one tried to elbow the guy whose bottom was crushing him.

'O, you are inconvenienced? Get into a cab if you are so particular about others touching your body, you snob!' The one who was jostled, rebuked the young comrade.

When he tried to counter, his friend stopped him, 'Don't. It's a risk. People will notice. It seems lookout notices have been pasted throughout the length and breadth of the road. Someone might recognise us.'

He was speaking in whispers, just loud enough for the other person to hear.

Everyone got down at Pullani junction. Two porters who were hanging around the junction started unloading the diesel cans. The jeep driver collected his fare from the passengers.

The junction had its fair share of hustle and bustle. The vegetable and fruit vendors were whiling away their time bandying words. 'Arrack,' loudly announced a banner stuck to an old tiled building with its wooden shutters only half open. There were a few gathered in front of the arrack shop and a drunken man was pissing on the lamp post.

Away from the dim light of the street lamp, they waited under the cover of darkness.

'What will we do if J doesn't turn up?' the younger one asked.

'J will come.' The elder one was quite sure. He lit a *beedi*.

'How can you be so certain? What if he was there and left not finding us?'

'No, J will come,' said his friend, sounding more like he was reassuring himself.

'Do you know him personally comrade?' the youngster asked.

The other guy shook his head.

'Then how will we recognise him? Do we have any code to exchange?' The tall guy was restless.

'That's what I too am worried about. There was a code word. But I don't remember it.'

The young fellow was visibly angry. But he controlled himself.

'Don't know why, but I seem to forget things these days,' the first one said, more to himself. 'Maybe the days of code words are over.' Both of them became silent.

About twenty minutes elapsed. The frustration and fears of an apparently futile wait seized them.

'I'm J,' they heard a voice from behind. They turned around to see a very old man intently looking at them. His hair grey, there was an immeasurable depth of exhaustion visible in his eyes. He was wearing a loose and soiled kurta its sleeves almost covering his fingertips. The scar of an old wound stretched like a centipede above his left eye on his wrinkled forehead.

The two friends breathed a sigh of relief. The comrades had assured them that J would take care of the rest of the things. But how did this man who was seeing them for the first time recognise them so easily? No code words were exchanged.

'There's no point in it,' J smiled, alleviating the doubts in their mind, exposing his toothless gums like a grandpa. 'Forgot, isn't it? Doesn't matter. What is the point in remembering all those anymore? Your photos are there in all the lookout posters. What is strange is that no one recognised you till now. Forget it. There is no time to dilly dally. Let's go. It'll become difficult if we delay further,' he continued.

That was almost an order. The two of them followed him like domesticated animals.

They went along the deserted tarred road beyond the junction. No one spoke as they trudged through the dark occasionally brightened by the headlights of passing trucks.

'Actually, whose blunder was it?' J suddenly asked, stopping for a while at the beginning of a steep turn.

'Huh?' The elder one looked at him as if waking up from a reverie. The tarred road was ending at that point.

'You didn't hear me?' J asked again taking out a long-stemmed torch from his pocket and flashing it. He stepped off from the road to a dirt track at a much lower level.

'What did comrade say? Blunder? I don't understand,' the elder one exclaimed.

'Where did things go wrong?'

'That officer was a class enemy. The decision against him was taken quite some time back.'

'Then?'

'We could not get him.'

'So?'

'It was the driver who was hit,' the young man's tone was emotionless.

J did not slacken his pace.

'We had no previous experience. Since we hurried, the bomb did not go in the right direction,' the young man tried to explain.

A heavily laden lorry crossed them very slowly, its headlights emitting a strong beam.

'Any information?' the younger one asked.

'What?'

'The driver. Did he die?' There was anxiety in the young man's voice.

'I don't know. But it should not have happened,' said J.

'It cannot as such be dubbed as a "blunder." Our struggle is against the tools of the state …'

J stopped him from talking anymore by waving the torch at him. Silence took over once again. The three walked like shadows in the narrow light provided by the torch.

'Now, even if it was indeed a blunder, don't such shortcomings occur when working for a larger cause?' the elder one didn't seem to be quite sure.

The one who brought up the rear slipped and fell down. He got up dusting himself.

'You should be careful about the path. It's unfamiliar, no?' J continued helping him by flashing the torch. 'See, the paths are important too.'

The young man had hurt his knee. He was limping.

'Unfortunately most of them fell down on the path,' J said as if reminding them.

'Was it the fault of the objective?' the taller man asked.

'Not necessarily. The objectives quite often were precise. All those who had thought about justice had clear vision. They rushed to the light like fireflies. Men with hearts! They were the ones who fell on the way. And finally there was no one left to reach the destination.'

Their steps slowed down further. The path leading up to the river was very narrow. It was almost like a tunnel with wild plants and overgrown shrubs. The rough edges of the leaves brushed against their body as they walked. Then the path widened. A faint light, though gloomy, spread across the sky. J switched off the torch. Silver flashes of lightning were visible in the distant horizon.

The sound of river flowing. They had reached the landing.

'The river has to be crossed,' J said.

'How?' the tall youth asked. 'There are no ferries. Do we swim across?'

'It is a broad river, child. You can't cross it swimming. You will sink halfway through,' J said. 'There's a ferry on the other side. It will come if you call. There's an uncertainty only because it's quite late.'

They could see something big jutting out of the river near the landing. Like the tail of Satan.

'It's a boat which was drowned in a deluge long ago,' J explained. 'It got struck in the sandbank.'

'One of you hoot loudly. I'm old and don't have the lungs for hooting,' J told them.

The two young men hooted loud, fingers held close to the mouth. But they stopped as soon as they had begun as if afraid of their own sound.

'Is the shelter safe, comrade?' the elder one asked.

'What a question!' J said without any emotion in his voice. 'Reaching there is the only problem. Once you reach there Karadi Achachan will take care. Not even a fly from the outer world can enter the place. It's that safe.'

They hooted once again.

'He is the comrade of the Kangazha action. The entire police was in his pursuit at that time. But couldn't trace him. So don't bother about the safety of the shelter.'

They saw a dim light at the opposite bank swaying as if in a cradle.

'Yes, the ferry is coming.'

After some time, the light obtained a direction. It was certainly coming across. They prepared to hoot again.

'Don't hoot anymore,' J stopped them. 'You be here. The ferry will be here now. I'm leaving.'

'Please wait till the ferry arrives, comrade.'

'No, I'm already late. I've a lot of work to finish.'

'What do you do comrade?' the younger one asked.

'Repair. You can also call it doctoring,' J smiled. 'Only that it is time I treat. To be precise, *Kalakalpa*.'

He did not elaborate any further. Nor did the two demand it.

'Even then, without comrade … we alone …'

'It'd have been better if you could leave us there and then return …'

'I told you no, nothing to be afraid of. The ferryman will take you there if you tell him that you are friends of Karadi Achachan.'

J slowly walked away leaving them there. He was bisecting the darkness in frequent intervals flashing his torch. The two visitors watched him leave. They felt that he was journeying to the estuary of night like an old ... ship.

After reaching some distance he turned around and greeted them for the last time, raising his left hand.

His palm had been cut off. An unknown fear enveloped them like darkness as they watched the huge void where fingers should have been there.

AFTERWORD

There are many mysteries in this novel. Some of them get resolved in the end and some remain as they are. It is only fair for a book, which has no claims to be a whodunit, to stay tight-lipped on a few of its secrets, perhaps because they are beyond the author too.

But there is a claim: that it is a political work, though the characters do not live strictly according to the political colour and calendar of a period. Emergency, the darkest phase in post-independence India is roughly the time frame of the story. Characters may resemble people from that age. A few seem familiar, the majority do not. But they can belong to any place, any era. The power, its games and its victims are a recurring theme in many a novel; perhaps it is the most common theme in contemporary literature.

I do not know why my friend P.N. Venugopal started translating this work into English. It still is an unresolved mystery for me. He started off while it was being serialised in *Mathrubhumi Weekly*, the most prominent literary magazine in Malayalam. Therefore my first thanks go to him, for without his labour and patience this book would not have been possible in English.

My friend Ramdas Mulloth had been instrumental in sending the manuscript to the publisher. He thus acted as a one-man literary agency; my warm regards to him for his help, encouraging words and the wonderful evenings we spent together.

Thanks to Kamalram Sajiv, the Editor-in-charge of *Mathrubhumi Weekly*, who had published the novel serially.

Thanks also to Narendran for penning the poem for Sreenivasan, the missing poet in the novel.

Mathrubhumi Books, publishers in Malayalam; and my readers of the original. Dear friends, I really value your words of support.

Mr Bikash De Niyogi (Publisher and Managing Director) and Mrs Tultul Niyogi (Co-Publisher) Niyogi Books, who on a fine morning rang me up to say yes to our request. My gratitude to them and to Team Niyogi including Lakshmi Nair for bringing out the book in English.

I don't know how I should thank Gita Rajan, our meticulous Editor, who has been so considerate most of the time, but persistent on a few other occasions. Hers was a mission to make the project as immaculate as possible. Hats off to her passionate interventions and priceless contributions.

Finally to the time that was; to the people who lost the battle and those who somehow survived.

My apologies, if my writing has not done them justice.

Warmly,
E Santhosh Kumar